Karin Slaughter grew up in a small south Georgia town and has been writing short stories and novels since she was a child. She is also the author of the national bestsellers *Blindsighted*, *Kisscut*, and *A Faint Cold Fear*, and contributed to and edited *Like a Charm*, a collaboration of British and America crime fiction writers. *Faithless*, the fifth novel in the Grant County series, will be published in hardback in 2005. She is currently working on *Triptych*, a standalone novel set in the same world as the Grant County series.

Praise for Karin Slaughter

'*Indelible* is a salutary reminder that Slaughter is one of the most riveting writers in the field today'
Sunday Express

'Don't read this alone. Don't read this after dark. But do read it'
Mirror

'*Kisscut* is a great read. Karin Slaughter deserves all the praise she gets for her razor-sharp plotting and forensic detail. But for me the hook is in her characters and relationships. They are right on the money. This is crime fiction at its finest'
MICHAEL CONNELLY

'... her brilliantly chilling prose ...'

'It's not easy to transcend a model like Patricia Cornwell, but Slaughter does so in a thriller whose breakneck plotting and not-for-the-squeamish forensics provide grim manifestations of a deeper evil her mystery trumpets without ever quite containing'
Kirkus Reviews

'A tension-filled narrative with plenty of plot twists . . . This is just the ticket for readers who like their crime fiction on the dark side' *Booklist*

'Wildly readable . . . [Slaughter] has been compared to Thomas Harris and Patricia Cornwell, and for once the hype is justified . . . deftly crafted, damnably suspenseful and, in the end, deadly serious. Slaughter's plotting is brilliant, her suspense relentless'
Washington Post

'An extraordinary debut . . . Slaughter has created a ferociously taut and terrifying story which is, at the same time, compassionate and real. I defy anyone to read it in more than three sittings'
DENISE MINA

'Wildly readable . . . *Blindsighted* hits the bull's eye'
New York Post

'It is difficult to believe this is a first novel, such is its grasp of pace and character'
MIKE RIPLEY, *Birmingham Post*

'A shockingly good novel . . . Slaughter may very well be the next Thomas Harris' LAURA LIPPMAN

'Readers seeking a . . . cutting-edge thriller need look no further'
The Good Book Guide

'Taut, mean, nasty and bloody well written. She conveys a sense of time and place with clarity and definite menace – the finely tuned juxtaposition of sleepy Southern town and urgent, gut-wrenching terror' STELLA DUFFY

'Taut and tight and tinged with terror'
Houston Chronicle

'If you're looking for an unflinching suspense thriller with an emphasis on character, this is the one'
GEORGE P. PELECANOS

'A story that roars its way through the final pages, Slaughter's thriller is scary, shocking and perfectly suspenseful. Already earning comparisons to Patricia Cornwell, Slaughter's *Blindsighted* is a first novel that doesn't read like one' *BookPage.com*

'A very promising debut by a very talented writer'
Deadly Pleasures

'This is storytelling at its finest, written in perfect pitch. A scary, sure-fire winner'
JOHN WESTERMANN

'A page turner . . . has more twists than a Slinky Factory' *People*

'A debut novel that blows your socks off. Karin Slaughter has immediately jumped to the front of the line of first-rate thriller writers . . .'
Rocky Mountain News

Also by Karin Slaughter

Blindsighted
Kisscut
A Faint Cold Fear
Faithless

Like a Charm (Ed.)

INDELIBLE

Karin Slaughter

arrow books

Published by Arrow Books in 2005

1 3 5 7 9 10 8 6 4 2

Copyright © 2004 by Karin Slaughter

Karin Slaughter has asserted her right under the Copyright, Designs
and Patents Act, 1988 to be identified as the author of this work

First published in the United Kingdom in 2004 by Century

Arrow Books
The Random House Group Limited
20 Vauxhall Bridge Road, London SW1V 2SA

Random House Australia (Pty) Limited
20 Alfred Street, Milsons Point, Sydney,
New South Wales 2061, Australia

Random House New Zealand Limited
18 Poland Road, Glenfield,
Auckland 10, New Zealand

Random House (Pty) Limited
Endulini, 5a Jubilee Road, Parktown 2193, South Africa

The Random House Group Limited Reg. No. 954009

A CIP catalogue record for this book is available
from the British Library

Papers used by Random House
are natural, recyclable products made from wood grown in
sustainable forests. The manufacturing processes conform to
the environmental regulations of the country of origin

ISBN 0 09 946224 9

Typeset by SX Composing DTP, Rayleigh, Essex
Printed and bound in Great Britain by
Bookmarque Ltd, Croydon, Surrey

For D.A.
river deep, mountain high

ONE

'Well, look what the cat dragged in,' Marla Simms bellowed, giving Sara a pointed look over her silver-rimmed bifocals. The secretary for the police station held a magazine in her arthritic hands, but she set it aside, indicating she had plenty of time to talk.

Sara forced some cheer into her voice, though she had purposefully timed her visit for Marla's coffee break. 'Hey, Marla. How're you doing?'

The old woman stared for a beat, a tinge of disapproval putting a crease in her naturally down-turned lips. Sara forced herself not to squirm. Marla had taught the children's Sunday school class at the Primitive Baptist from the day they opened the front doors, and she could still put the fear of God into anyone in town who'd been born after 1952.

She kept her eyes locked on Sara. 'Haven't seen you around here in a while.'

'Hm,' Sara offered, glancing over Marla's shoulder, trying to see into Jeffrey's office. His door was open but he was not behind his desk. The squad room was empty, which meant he was probably in the back. Sara knew she should just walk behind the counter and find him herself – she had done it hundreds of times before – but survivor's instinct kept her from crossing that bridge without first paying the troll.

1

Marla sat back in her chair, her arms folded. 'Nice day out,' she said, her tone still casual.

Sara glanced out the door at Main Street, where heat made the asphalt look wavy. The air this morning was humid enough to open every pore on her body. 'Sure is.'

'And don't you look pretty this morning,' Marla continued, indicating the linen dress Sara had chosen after going through nearly every item of clothing in her closet. 'What's the occasion?'

'Nothing special,' Sara lied. Before she knew what she was doing, she started to fidget with her brief-case, shifting from one foot to the other like she was four instead of nearly forty.

A glimmer of victory flashed in the older woman's eyes. She drew out the silence a bit more before asking, 'How's your mama and them?'

'Good,' Sara answered, trying not to sound too circumspect. She wasn't naive enough to believe that her private life was no one else's business – in a county as small as Grant, Sara could barely sneeze without the phone ringing from up the street with a helpful 'Bless you' – but she would be damned if she'd make it easy for them to gather their information.

'And your sister?'

Sara was about to respond when Brad Stephens saved her by tripping through the front door. The young patrolman caught himself before he fell flat on his face, but the momentum popped his hat off his head and onto the floor at Sara's feet. His gun belt and nightstick flopped under his arms like extra appendages. Behind him, a gaggle of prepubescent children squawked with laughter at his less-than-graceful entrance.

'Oh,' Brad said, looking at Sara, then back to the kids, then at Sara again. He picked up his hat, brushing it off with more care than was warranted. She imagined he could not decide which was more embarrassing: eight 10-year-olds laughing at his clumsiness or his former pediatrician fighting an obvious smile of amusement.

Apparently, the latter was worse. He turned back to the group, his voice deeper than usual as if to assert some authority. 'This, of course, is the station house, where we do business. Police business. Uh, and we're in the lobby now.' Brad glanced at Sara. To call the area where they stood a lobby was a bit of a stretch. The room was barely ten feet by eight, with a cement block wall opposite the glass door at the entrance. A row of photographs showing various squads in the Grant County police force lined the wall to Sara's right, a large portrait in the center showing Mac Anders, the only police officer in the history of the force who had been killed in the line of duty.

Across from the portrait gallery, Marla stood sentry behind a tall beige laminate counter that separated visitors from the squad room. She was not a naturally short woman, but age had made her so by crooking her body into a nearly perfect question mark. Her glasses were usually halfway down the bridge of her nose, and Sara, who wore glasses to read, was always tempted to push them back up. Not that Sara would ever do such a thing. For all Marla knew about everybody and their neighbor – and their dog – in town, not much was known about her. She was a widow with no children. Her husband had died in the Second World War. She had always lived on Hemlock, which was two streets over from Sara's parents. She knitted and she taught Sunday school and worked full-time at the station answering phones and trying to make sense of the mountains of paperwork. These facts hardly offered great insight into Marla Simms. Still, Sara always thought there had to be more to the life of a woman who had lived some eighty-odd years, even if she'd lived all of them in the same house where she had been born.

Brad continued his tour of the station, pointing to the large, open room behind Marla. 'Back there's where the detectives and patrol officers like myself conduct their business . . . calls and whatnot. Talking to witnesses, writing reports, typing stuff into the computer, and, uh . . .' His voice trailed off as he finally noticed he was losing his audience. Most of the children could barely see over the counter. Even if they could, thirty empty desks spread out in rows of five with various sizes of filing cabinets between them were hardly attention grabbing. Sara imagined the kids were wishing they had stayed in school today.

Brad tried, 'In a few minutes, I'll show y'all the jail where we arrest people. Well, not arrest them,' he gave Sara a nervous glance, lest she point out his mistake. 'I mean, this is where we take them after we arrest them. Not here, but back in the jail.'

Silence fell like a hammer, only to be interrupted by an infectious giggle that started in the back of the group. Sara, who knew most of the children from her practice at the children's clinic, hushed a few with a sharp look. Marla took care of the rest, her swivel chair groaning with relief as she raised herself above the counter. The giggling shut off like a faucet.

Maggie Burgess, a child whose parents gave more credence to her opinion than any child of that age

4

ought to be given, dared to say, 'Hey, Dr. Linton,' in a grating, singsong voice.

Sara gave a curt nod. 'Maggie.'

'Uh,' Brad began, a deep blush still souring his milk-white complexion. Sara was keenly aware of his gaze lingering a little too long on her bare legs. 'Ya'll . . . uh . . . y'all know Dr. Linton.'

Maggie rolled her eyes. 'Well, *yeah*,' she said, her sarcastic tone reviving a few giggles.

Brad pushed on. 'Dr. Linton is also the medical examiner in town, in addition to being a pediatrician.' He spoke in an instructional tone, though surely the children already knew this. It was a subject of great humor on the bathroom walls at the elementary school. 'I imagine she's here on county business. Dr. Linton?'

'Yes,' Sara answered, trying to sound like Brad's peer rather than someone who could remember him bursting into tears at the mere mention of a shot. 'I'm here to talk to the Chief of Police about a case we're working on.'

Maggie opened her mouth again, probably to repeat something horrible she had heard her mother say about Sara and Jeffrey's relationship, but Marla's chair squeaked and the child remained silent. Sara vowed she would go to church next Sunday just to thank the woman.

Marla's voice was only slightly less condescending than Maggie's when she told Sara, 'I'll go check-see if Chief Tolliver is available.'

'Thank you,' Sara answered, promptly changing her mind about church.

'Well, uh . . .' Brad began, brushing off his hat again. 'Why don't we go on back now?' He opened one of the swinging doors in the counter to allow the children through, telling Sara, 'Ma'am,' giving her a polite nod before following them.

Sara walked over to the photographs on the wall, looking at all the familiar faces. Except for her time at college and working at Grady Hospital in Atlanta, Sara had always lived in Grant County. Most of the men on the wall had played poker with her father at one time or another. The rest of them had been deacons at the church when Sara was a child or had policed football games back when she was a teenager and was desperately infatuated with Steve Mann, the captain of the Chess Club. Before Sara moved away to Atlanta, Mac Anders had caught Sara and Steve making out behind the House of Chilidogs. A few weeks later, his squad car rolled six times during a high-speed chase and Mac was dead.

Sara shuddered, a superstitious fear creeping along her skin like the legs of a spider. She moved on to the next picture, which showed the force when Jeffrey first took over the job as police chief. He had just come from Birmingham and everyone had been skeptical about the outsider, especially when he hired Lena Adams, Grant County's first female cop. Sara studied Lena in the group photograph. Her chin was tilted up in defiance and there was a glint of challenge in her eye. There were more than a dozen women patrolling now, but Lena would always be the first. The pressure must have been enormous, though Sara had never thought of Lena as a role model. As a matter of fact, there were several things about the other woman's personality that Sara found abhorrent.

'He said come on back.' Marla stood at the swinging doors. 'It's sad, isn't it?' she asked, indicating the picture of Mac Anders.

'I was at school when it happened.'

'I won't even tell you what they did to that animal that chased him off the road.' There was a note of approval in Marla's voice. Sara knew the suspect had been beaten so severely he'd lost an eye. Ben Walker, the police chief at the time, was a very different cop from Jeffrey.

Marla held open the doors for her. 'He's back in interrogation doing some paperwork.'

'Thank you,' Sara said, taking one more look at Mac before walking through.

The station house had been built in the mid-1930s when the cities of Heartsdale, Madison, and Avondale had consolidated their police and fire service into the county. The building had been a feed store co-op, but the city bought it cheap when the last of the local farms went bust. All the character had been drained from the building during the reno-vation, and not much had been done to help the decor in the decades that followed. The squad room was nothing more than a long rectangle, with Jeffrey's office on one side and the bathroom on the other. Dark fake paneling still reeked of nicotine from before the county's antismoking policy. The drop ceiling looked dingy no matter how many times the inserts were replaced. The tile floor was made of asbestos and Sara always held her breath when she walked over the cracked portion by the bathroom. Even without the tile, she would have held her breath near the bathroom. Nowhere was it more evident that the Grant County police force was still pre-dominantly male than in the squad room's unisex bathroom.

She muscled open the heavy fire door that separated the squad room from the rest of the building. A newer section had been built onto the back of the station fifteen years ago when the mayor had realized they could make some money holding prisoners for nearby overburdened counties. A thirty-cell jail block, a conference room, and the interrogation room had seemed luxurious at the time, but age had done its work and despite a recent fresh coat of paint, the newer areas looked just as worn-down as the old ones.

Sara's heels clicked across the floor as she walked down the long hallway, then stopped outside the interrogation room to straighten her dress and buy herself some time. She had not been this nervous around her ex-husband in a long while, and she hoped it did not show as she entered the room.

Jeffrey sat at a long table, stacks of papers spread over the surface as he took notes on a legal pad. His coat was off, his sleeves rolled up. He did not glance up when she came in, but he must have been watching, because when Sara started to close the door, he said, 'Don't.'

She put her briefcase on the table and waited for him to look up. He didn't, and she was torn between throwing her briefcase at his head and throwing herself at his feet. While these two conflicting emotions had been par for the course throughout the nearly fifteen years they had known each other, it was usually Jeffrey prostrating himself in front of Sara, not the other way around. After four years of divorce, they had finally fallen back into a relationship. Three months ago, he had asked her to marry him again, and his ego could not abide her rejection, no matter how many times she explained her reasons. They had not seen each other outside of work since, and Sara was running out of ideas.

Withholding an exasperated sigh, she said, 'Jeffrey?'

'Just leave the report there,' he said, nodding toward an empty corner on the table as he underlined something on the legal pad.

'I thought you might want to go over it.'

'Was there anything unusual?' he asked, picking up another stack of papers, still not looking at her.

'I found a map in her lower bowel that leads to buried treasure.'

He did not take the bait. 'Did you put that in the report?'

'Of course not,' she teased. 'I'm not splitting that kind of money with the county.'

Jeffrey gave her a sharp look that said he didn't appreciate her humor. 'That's not very respectful to the deceased.'

Sara felt a flash of shame but she tried not to show it.

'What's the verdict?'

'Natural causes,' Sara told him. 'The blood and urine came back clean. There were no remarkable findings during the physical exam. She was ninety-eight years old. She died peacefully in her sleep.'

'Good.'

Sara watched him write, waiting for him to realize she was not going to leave. He had a beautiful, flowing script, the kind you would never expect from an ex-jock and especially from a cop. Part of her had fallen in love with him the first time she had seen his handwriting.

She shifted from one foot to the other, waiting.

'Sit down,' he finally relented, holding out his hand for the report. Sara did as she was told, giving him the slim file.

He scanned her notes. 'Pretty straightforward.'

'I've already talked to her kids,' Sara told him, though 'kids' hardly seemed appropriate considering that the woman's youngest child was nearly thirty years older than Sara. 'They know they were grasping at straws.'

'Good,' he repeated, signing off on the last page. He tossed it onto the corner of the table and capped his pen. 'Is that all?'

'Mama says hey.'

He seemed reluctant when he asked, 'How's Tess?'

Sara shrugged, because she wasn't exactly sure how to answer. Her relationship with her sister seemed to be deteriorating as rapidly as her one with Jeffrey. Instead, she asked, 'How long are you going to keep this up?'

He purposefully misunderstood her, indicating the paperwork as he spoke. 'I've got to have it all done before we go to trial next month.'

'That's not what I was talking about and you know it.'

'I don't think you have a right to use that tone with me.' He sat back in the chair. She could see that he was tired, and his usual easy smile was nowhere to be seen.

She asked, 'Are you sleeping okay?'

'Big case,' he said, and she wondered if that was really what was keeping him up at night. 'What do you want?'

'Can't we just talk?'

'About what?' He rocked his chair back. When she did not answer, he prompted, 'Well?'

'I just want to –'

'What?' he interrupted, his jaw set. 'We've talked

this through a hundred times. There's not a whole lot more to say.'

'I want to see you.'

'I told you I'm buried in this case.'

'So, when it's over . . . ?'

'Sara.'

'Jeffrey,' she countered. 'If you don't want to see me, just say it. Don't use a case as an excuse. We've both been buried deeper than this before and still managed to spend time with each other. As I recall, it's what makes this crap' – she indicated the mounds of paperwork – 'bearable.'

He dropped his chair with a thud. 'I don't see the point.'

She gave humor another stab. 'Well, the sex, for one.'

'I can get that anywhere.'

Sara raised an eyebrow, but suppressed the obvious comment. The fact that Jeffrey could and sometimes did get sex anywhere was the reason she had divorced him in the first place.

He picked up his pen to resume writing, but Sara snatched it from his hand. She tried to keep the desperation out of her voice as she asked, 'Why do we have to get married again for this to work?'

He looked off to the side, clearly annoyed.

She reminded him, 'We were married before and it practically ruined us.'

'Yeah,' he said. 'I remember.'

She played her trump card. 'You could rent out your house to someone from the college.'

He paused a second before asking, 'Why would I do that?'

'So you could move in with me.'

'And live in sin?'

She laughed. 'Since when did you become religious?'

'Since your father put the fear of God into me,' he shot back, his tone completely devoid of humor. 'I want a wife, Sara, not a fuckbuddy.'

She felt the cut of his words. 'Is that what you think I am?'

'I don't know,' he told her, his tone something of an apology. 'I'm tired of being tied to that string you just yank when you feel lonely.'

She opened her mouth but could not speak.

He shook his head, apologizing. 'I didn't mean that.'

'You think I'm here making a fool of myself because I'm lonely?'

'I don't know anything right now, except that I've got a lot of work to do.' He held out his hand. 'Can I have my pen back?'

She gripped it tightly. 'I want to be with you.'

'You're with me now,' he said, reaching over to retrieve his pen.

She put her other hand around his, holding him there. 'I miss you,' she said. 'I miss being with you.'

He gave a halfhearted shrug, but did not pull away.

She pressed her lips to his fingers, smelling ink and the oatmeal lotion he used when he thought no one was looking. 'I miss your hands.'

He kept staring.

She brushed his thumb with her lips. 'Don't you miss me?'

He tilted his head to the side, giving another indefinite shrug.

'I want to *be* with you. I want to . . .' She looked over her shoulder again, making certain no one was there. She lowered her voice to barely more than a whisper and offered to do something with him that any self-respecting prostitute would charge double for.

Jeffrey's lips parted, shock registering in his eyes. His hand tightened around hers. 'You stopped doing that when we got married.'

'Well . . .' She smiled. 'We're not married anymore, are we?'

He seemed to be thinking it over when a loud knock came at the open door. It might as well have been a gunshot from Jeffrey's reaction. He jerked his hand back and stood up.

Frank Wallace, Jeffrey's second in command, said, 'Sorry.'

Jeffrey let his irritation show, though Sara could not guess if it was for her or Frank's benefit. 'What is it?'

Frank glanced at the phone on the wall and stated the obvious. 'Your extension's off the hook.'

Jeffrey waited.

'Marla told me to tell you there's some kid in the lobby asking for you.' He took out his handkerchief and wiped his forehead. 'Hey, Sara.'

She started to return the greeting but stopped at the sight of him. He looked dead on his feet. 'Are you all right?'

Frank put his hand to his stomach, a sour look on his face. 'Bad Chinese.'

She stood, putting her hand to his cheek. His skin was clammy. 'You're probably dehydrated,' she told him, putting her fingers to his wrist to check his pulse. 'Are you getting enough fluids?'

He shrugged.

She stared at the second hand on her watch. 'Throwing up? Diarrhea?'

He shifted uncomfortably over her last question. 'I'm okay,' he said, but he obviously wasn't. 'You look real nice today.'

'I'm glad somebody noticed,' Sara said, giving Jeffrey a sideways glance.

Jeffrey tapped his fingers on the table, still annoyed. 'Go on home, Frank. You look like shit.'

Frank's relief was obvious.

Sara added, 'If this isn't better tomorrow, call me.'

He nodded again, telling Jeffrey, 'Don't forget about the kid in the lobby.'

'Who is it?'

'Something Smith. I didn't catch . . .' He put a hand to his stomach and made a sick sound. He turned to leave, managing a garbled 'Sorry.'

Jeffrey waited until Frank was out of earshot to say, 'I have to do everything around here.'

'He's obviously not well.'

'It's Lena's first day back,' Jeffrey said, referring to Frank's ex-partner. 'She's supposed to be in at ten.'

'And?'

'You run into Matt yet? He tried to call in sick, too, but I told him to get his sorry ass in here.'

'You think two senior detectives gave themselves food poisoning so they wouldn't have to see Lena?'

Jeffrey walked over to the phone and put the receiver back in the cradle. 'I've been here over fifteen years and never seen Matt Hogan eat Chinese.'

He had a point, but Sara wanted to give both men the benefit of the doubt. No matter what he said about her, Frank obviously cared for Lena. They had worked together for nearly a decade. Sara knew from personal experience that you could not spend that kind of time with someone and just walk away.

Jeffrey pressed the speaker button, then dialed in an extension. 'Marla?'

There was a series of clicking noises as she picked up the receiver. 'Yessir?'

'Has Matt shown up yet?'

'Not yet. I'm a little worried what with him being sick and all.'

'Tell him I'm looking for him as soon as he walks in the door,' Jeffrey ordered. 'Is there someone waiting for me?'

She lowered her voice. 'Yes. He's kind of impatient.'

'I'll be there in a second.' He turned the speaker off, mumbling, 'I don't have time for this.'

'Jeff –'

'I need to see who this is,' he said, walking out of the room.

Sara followed him down the hallway, practically running to keep up. 'If I break my ankle in these heels . . .'

He glanced down at her shoes. 'Did you think you could just waltz in here whoring yourself out and I'd beg you to come back?'

Embarrassment ignited her temper. 'Why is it you call it whoring myself out when I *want* to do it, but when I don't want to and I do anyway, all of a sudden it's sexy?'

He stopped at the fire door, resting his hand on the long handle. 'That's not fair.'

'You think so, too, Dr. Freud?'

'I'm not playing around here, Sara.'

'Do you think I am?'

'I don't know what you're doing,' he said, and there was a hardness around his eyes that sent a cold chill through her. 'I can't keep living like this.'

She put her hand on his arm, saying, 'Wait.' When he stopped, she forced herself to say, 'I love you.'

He gave her a flippant 'Thanks.'

'Please,' she whispered. 'We don't need a piece of paper to tell us how we feel.'

'The thing you keep missing,' he told her, yanking open the door, 'is that I do.'

She started to follow him into the squad room, but pride kept her feet rooted to the floor. A handful of patrolmen and detectives were starting their shifts, sitting at their desks as they wrote up reports or made calls. She could see Brad and his group of kids congregating around the coffeemaker, where he was probably regaling them with the brand of filter they used or the number of scoops it took to make a pot.

There were two young men in the lobby, one of them leaning against the back wall, the other standing in front of Marla. Sara took the standing one to be Jeffrey's visitor. Smith was young, probably Brad's age, and dressed in a quilted black jacket that was zipped closed despite the late August heat. His head was shaved and from what she could make of his body under the heavy coat, he was fit and well muscled. He kept scanning the room, his eyes furiously darting around, never resting his gaze on one person for long. He added the front door to his rotation every second time, checking the street. There was definitely something military in his bearing, and for some reason, his general demeanor put Sara on edge.

She looked around the room, taking in what Smith was seeing. Jeffrey had stopped at one of the desks to help a patrolman. He slid his paddle holster to his back as he sat on the edge of the desk and typed something into the computer. Brad was still talking over by the coffeemaker, his hand resting on the top of the mace spray in his belt. She counted five more cops, all of them busy writing reports or entering information into their computers. A sense of danger coursed through Sara's body like a bolt of lightning. Everything in her line of vision became too sharply focused.

The front door made a sucking sound as it opened and Matt Hogan walked in. Marla said, 'There you are. We've been waiting for you.'

The young man put his hand inside his coat, and Sara screamed, 'Jeffrey!'

They all turned to look at her, but Sara was watching Smith. In one fluid motion he pulled out a sawed-off shotgun, pointed it at Matt's face, and squeezed both triggers.

Blood and brain sprayed onto the front door as if from a high-pressure hose. Matt fell back against the glass, the pane cracking straight up the center but not breaking, his face completely blown away. Children started to scream and Brad fell on them en masse, pushing them down to the ground. Gunfire went wild and one of the patrolmen collapsed in front of Sara, a large hole in his chest. His gun discharged on impact, skidding across the floor. Around her, glass flew as family photographs and personal items shot off desks. Computers popped, sending up the acrid smell of burning plastic. Papers floated through the air in a flurry, and the sound of weapons firing was so intense that Sara's ears felt as if they were bleeding.

'Get out!' Jeffrey screamed, just as Sara felt a sharp sting on her face. She put her hand to her cheek where a piece of shrapnel had grazed the flesh. She was kneeling on the floor but could not remember how she had gotten there. She darted behind a filing cabinet, her throat feeling as if she had swallowed acid.

'Go!' Jeffrey was crouched behind a desk, the muzzle of his gun a constant burst of white as he tried to give her cover. A large boom shook the front of the building, then another.

From behind the fire door, Frank screamed, 'This way!' pointing his gun around the jamb, shooting blindly toward the front lobby. A patrolman slammed open the door, exposing Frank as he ran to safety. On the other side of the room, a second cop was shot trying to reach the group of children, his face a mask of pain as he slumped against a filing cabinet. Smoke and the smell of gunpowder filled the air, and still more firepower came from the front lobby. Fear seized Sara as she recognized the snare-drum *tat-tat-tat* of an automatic weapon. The killers had come prepared for a shoot-out.

'Dr. Linton!' someone screamed. Seconds later, Sara felt a pair of small hands clinging to her neck. Maggie Burgess had managed to break loose, and instinctively, Sara wrapped her own body around the girl's. Jeffrey saw this, and he took out his ankle holster, giving Sara the signal to run as soon as he started firing. She slipped off her high heels, waiting for what seemed like hours until Jeffrey raised his head above the desk he was hiding behind and started shooting with both guns. Sara bolted toward the fire door and threw the child to Frank. Floor tiles splintered and exploded in front of her as bullets sprayed, and she backed up on her hands and feet until she was safely behind the filing cabinet again.

Sara's hands moved wildly as she checked to see if she had been shot. There was blood all over her, but she knew it was not her own. Frank cracked open the door again. Bullets popped off the heavy-gauge steel and he returned fire, sticking his hand around the edge and shooting.

'Get out!' Jeffrey repeated, preparing to give her cover, but Sara could see one of her kids from the clinic hiding behind a row of fallen chairs. Ron Carver looked as terrified as she felt, and Sara held up her hands to stop the child from running before a signal from Jeffrey. Without warning, the boy took off toward her, his chin tucked into his chest and his arms pumping as the air exploded around him. Jeffrey started rapid-firing to draw the shooter away, but a stray bullet zinged through the air, practically severing the child's foot. Ron barely broke stride, using the pulp that was left of his ankle to propel himself forward.

He collapsed into Sara's arms, and she could feel his heart fluttering in his chest like the wings of a small bird as she ripped off his cotton shirt. She tore the material length-wise and used the sleeve to wrap a tight tourniquet. She used the other half of the shirt to tie his foot on, hoping it could be saved.

'Don't make me go out there,' the child begged. 'Dr. Linton, please don't make me.'

Sara made her tone stern. 'Ronny, we have to go.'

'Please don't make me!' he wailed.

Jeffrey screamed, 'Sara!'

Sara scooped the boy close to her body and waited for Jeffrey's signal. It came, and she held Ron tight as she ran in a crouch toward the door.

Halfway there, the boy started to kick and scratch at her in wild panic, shrieking, 'No! Don't make me!' at the top of his lungs.

She clamped her hand over his mouth and forced

herself toward the door, barely registering the pain as his teeth cut into the flesh of her palm. Frank reached out, snatching Ron by his shirt and yanking him to safety. He tried to grab Sara, too, but she ran back to the filing cabinet, looking for more children. Another bullet whizzed past her, and without thinking, she went farther into the room.

She tried twice to see how many children were with Brad, but with the bullets and chaos all around her, she lost count each time. She searched frantically for Jeffrey. He was about fifteen feet away reloading his gun. Their eyes locked just before his shoulder jerked back, throwing him against the desks. A plant fell to the floor, the pot breaking into a thousand pieces. His body convulsed, his legs gave a violent twitch, and then he was still. With Jeffrey down, everything seemed to stop. Sara darted under the nearest desk, her ears ringing from the gunfire. The room went quiet but for Marla's screaming, her voice trilling up and down like a siren.

'Oh, God,' Sara whispered, looking frantically under the desk. Just over the front counter, she saw Smith standing with a gun in each hand, scanning the room for movement. The other young man was beside him, pointing an assault rifle toward the front door. Smith was wearing a Kevlar vest under the jacket, and she could see two more guns holstered to his chest. The shotgun lay on the counter. Both gunmen were out in the open, but no one fired on them. Sara tried to remember who else was in the room but again could not keep count.

Movement came to her far left. Another shot was fired and there was the ping of a ricochet followed by a low groan. A child's scream was stifled. Sara flattened herself to the floor, trying to see under the other desks. In the far corner, Brad had his arms spread open, keeping the kids down on the floor. They were huddled together, sobbing as one.

The officer who had fallen against the filing cabinets moaned, trying to raise his gun. Sara recognized the man as Barry Fordham, a patrol cop she had danced with at the last policeman's ball.

'Put it down!' Smith screamed. 'Put it down!'

Barry tried to raise his gun, but he couldn't control his wrist. His gun flopped wildly in the air. The man with the assault rifle turned slowly toward Barry and fired one shot into the cop's head with frightening precision. The back of Barry's skull banged into the metal cabinet and stuck there. When Sara looked at the second gunman, he had returned to guarding the front door as if nothing had happened.

'Who else?' Smith demanded. 'Identify yourself!'

Sara heard someone scramble behind her. She saw a blur of colors as one of the detectives ran into Jeffrey's office. A spray of bullets followed him. Seconds later, the window was broken out.

'Stay where you are!' Smith ordered. 'Everyone stay where you are!'

A child's scream came from Jeffrey's office, followed by more shattered glass. Remarkably, the window between the office and the squad room had not been broken. Smith broke it now with a single shot.

Sara cringed as the huge shards of glass splintered against the floor.

'Who else is here?' Smith demanded, and she heard the shotgun being cracked and loaded. 'Show your face or I'll kill this old lady, too!'

Marla's scream was cut off by a slap.

Sara finally found Jeffrey near the center of the

room. She could only see his right shoulder and arm. He was lying on his back. His body was motionless. Blood pooled around him and his hand held his gun at his side, the grip relaxed. He was five desks away on the diagonal, but she could still see the band of his Auburn class ring on his finger.

A hushed 'Sara' came from her right. Frank was crouched behind the steel fire door, his weapon drawn. He motioned for her to crawl back toward him, but Sara shook her head. His voice was an angry hiss as he repeated, 'Sara.'

She looked at Jeffrey again, willing him to move, to show some signs of life. The remaining children were still huddled with Brad, their sobs slowly stifled by fear. She could not leave any of them and she told this to Frank with another sharp shake of her head. She ignored his angry snort of breath.

'Who's left?' Smith demanded. 'Show yourself or I'm gonna shoot this old bitch!' Marla screamed, but Smith screamed louder. 'Who's fucking back there?'

Sara was about to respond when Brad said, 'Over here.'

Before she could let herself think, Sara ran in a crouch toward the closest desk, hoping Smith was looking at Brad. She held her breath, waiting to be shot.

'Where're those kids?' Smith demanded.

Brad's voice was amazingly calm. 'We're over here. Don't shoot. It's just me and three little girls left. We're not gonna do anything.'

'Stand up.'

'I can't, man. I gotta take care of these kids.'

Marla cried, 'Please don't –' and her words were cut off by another slap.

Sara closed her eyes for a second, thinking about

her family, about all that had been left unsaid between them. Then she pushed them out of her mind and instead thought about the children left in the room. She stared at the gun in Jeffrey's hand, pinning everything on the weapon. If she could get to Jeffrey's gun, maybe they would have a chance. Four more desks. Jeffrey was only four more desks away. She let herself look at him again. His body was still, his hand unmoving.

Smith was still focused on Brad. 'Where's your gun?'

'It's here,' Brad said, and Sara darted toward the next desk, overshooting it but managing to stop short behind a lateral filing cabinet. 'I gotta bunch of little girls here, man. I'm not going to draw on you. I haven't touched my gun.'

'Throw it over here.'

Sara held her breath and waited until she heard Brad's gun sliding across the floor before she ran to the next desk.

'Don't move!' Smith screamed as Sara skidded to a stop behind the desk. Her feet were sweating, and she saw her own bloody footprints tracing her route across the floor. She stumbled, but caught herself before she fell into the open.

Marla wailed, 'Please!'

There was the loud retort of flesh against flesh. Marla's chair gave a god-awful groan, as if it had snapped in two. Sara watched under the desk as Marla's body slammed into the ground. Saliva spurted from her mouth and her teeth slid across the tiles.

'I told you not to move!' Smith repeated, giving Marla's chair a vicious kick that sent it spinning into the wall.

Sara tried to control her breathing as she moved closer to Jeffrey. One desk stood between them, but it was turned the wrong way, blocking her path. She would be in Smith's line of fire if she ran. She was almost directly across from the children. They were three desks away. She could get the gun and . . . Sara felt her heart stop. What could she do with the gun? What could she accomplish that nearly ten cops could not?

Surprise, Sara thought. She had surprise. Smith and his accomplice did not know that she was in the room. She would surprise them.

'Where's your backup?' Smith demanded.

'I'm patrol. I don't carry a second –'

'Don't lie to me!' He fired in Brad's direction and instead of the screams Sara expected, there was silence. She looked back under the desks, trying to see if anyone had been shot. Three sets of glassy eyes stared back. Shock had taken over. The girls were too afraid to scream.

Silence filled the room like a poisonous gas. Sara counted to thirty-one before Smith asked, 'You still there, man?'

She put her hand to her chest, scared her heart was beating too loudly. From what she could see of Brad, he was not moving. Her mind flashed on an image of him sitting there, his arms still around the children, his head gone. She squeezed her eyes shut, trying to force the image from her brain.

She chanced another look at Smith, who was standing where Marla had greeted her less than ten minutes ago. He had a nine-millimeter in one hand and the shotgun in another. His jacket was open and Sara could see two empty holsters along with extra shells for the shotgun strapped to his chest. Another pistol was tucked into the front of his jeans and at his feet was a long black duffel bag that probably contained more ammunition. The second gunman was behind the counter, his weapon still pointing toward the front door. His body was tensed, his finger resting to the side of the trigger on his rifle. He was chewing gum, and Sara found his silent gum-chewing more unnerving than Smith's threats.

Smith repeated, 'You there, man?' He paused before trying again. 'You there?'

Finally, Brad said, 'I'm here.'

Sara let out a slow breath, relief weakening her muscles. She flattened herself to the floor, knowing the best way to get to Jeffrey would be to slide past a row of overturned filing cabinets. Slowly, she made her way along the cold tiles, reaching her hand out toward his. The tips of her fingers finally grazed the cuff of his jacket. She closed her eyes, inching closer.

The gun in his hand was spent, though Sara could have guessed as much if she had let herself think about it. Jeffrey had been reloading when he was shot, and the magazine had dropped to the floor, splitting on impact. Bullets were everywhere – useless, unused bullets. She shouldn't be surprised by that, just like she shouldn't be surprised to feel the coldness of his skin or, when her fingers finally rested upon his wrist, the absence of his pulse.

TWO

'Ethan,' Lena said, cradling the phone with her shoulder as she tied the laces on her new black high-top sneakers. 'I've got to go.'

'Why?'

'You *know* why,' she snapped. 'I can't be late for work my first day back.'

'I don't want you to do this.'

'Really? Because it wasn't clear the eighteen million other times you said it.'

'You know what?' he said, his tone still controlled because he was actually stupid enough to think he could talk her out of this. 'You can be such a bitch sometimes.'

'It took you long enough to figure that out.'

He embarked on one of his little tirades, but Lena only half listened as she stared at herself in the mirror on the back of the door. She looked good today. Her hair was tied up and the suit she had bought on sale last week was cut just right for her build. She slid back the jacket, resting her hand on her holstered police-issue nine. The metal felt reassuring under her hand.

'Are you listening to me?' Ethan demanded.

'No,' she said. 'I'm a cop, Ethan. A detective. It's who I am.'

'We both know who you are,' he told her, his tone sharper. 'And we both know what you're capable of.' He waited a beat, and she bit her tongue, forcing herself not to respond to the challenge.

He changed tactics. 'Does your boss know you're seeing me again?'

'It's not like we're sneaking around.'

He had heard the defensiveness in her tone, and pounced. 'That'd make things real good for you at work, don't you think? It'll take less than a week for it to get around that you're being nailed by an ex-con.'

She dropped her hand from the gun, swearing under her breath.

'What'd you say?' he demanded.

'I said it's already gotten around, you idiot. Everybody at the station already knows.'

'They don't know everything,' he reminded her in a low, threatening tone.

Lena glanced at the clock by her bed. She could not be late her first day back. Things were going to be tense enough without her breezing in five minutes behind. Frank would use it as another reason she was not ready to return to the force, and Matt, his cohort, would agree. Today would be a harder test for Lena than her first day in uniform. Just like then, everyone would be looking at her to fail. The difference was that now they would feel sorry for her if she fucked up, whereas before they would have cheered. If she was honest with herself, Lena would rather have their cheers than their pity. If this did not work out today, she did not know what she would do. Move, probably. Maybe they were hiring in Alaska.

She told Ethan, 'I'll probably have to work late tonight.'

'I don't mind,' he told her, relaxed by the implication that she would see him later. 'Why don't you come over?'

'Because your dorm smells like puke and piss.'

'I could come over there.'

'Yeah, that'd be great. With my dead sister's gay lover in the next room? No thanks.'

'Come on, baby. I want to see you.'

'I don't know how late I'll be,' she told him. 'I'll probably be tired.'

'Then we can just sleep,' he offered. 'I don't care. I want to see you.'

His voice was soothing now, but Lena knew if she kept resisting he would turn nasty. Ethan was only twenty-three, almost ten years younger than Lena, and he had yet to figure out that a night spent apart was not the end of their relationship. Though, sometimes, Lena wished it could be that easy to make the break from him. Maybe now that she had a job again, something more demanding to occupy her brain than the daytime TV schedule, she could finally get away.

'Lena?' Ethan said, as if a sixth sense told him she was thinking about leaving. 'I love you so much, baby.' His voice grew even softer. 'Come see me tonight. I'll make us dinner, maybe get some wine . . . ?'

'I missed my period last month.'

He sucked in air and her only regret was that she could not see his expression.

'That's not funny.'

'You think I'm joking?' she asked. 'I'm three weeks late.'

Finally, he came up with 'Stress can do that, right?'

'So can sperm.'

He was quiet, his breathing the only noise on the line.

She forced something that sounded like a laugh. 'Still love me, baby?'

His voice was tight and controlled. 'Don't be like that.'

'Lookit,' she said, wishing that she had never even mentioned it to him. 'Don't worry, okay? I'll take care of it.'

'What does that mean?'

'It means what it means, Ethan. If I'm . . .' She couldn't even say the word. 'If something's happened, I'll take care of it.'

'You can't –'

The phone beeped, and Lena had never been so thankful for call-waiting in her life. 'I've got to get this. I'll see you around.' She clicked the phone to the other call before Ethan could say anything else.

'Lee?' a raspy voice said. Lena suppressed a groan, thinking she would have been better off sticking with Ethan.

'Hey, Hank.'

'Happy birthday, girl!'

She smiled before she caught herself.

'Didja get my card?'

'Yeah,' she told her uncle. 'Thanks.'

'You get yourself something nice?'

'Yeah,' Lena repeated, tugging the jacket back into place. Hank's two hundred dollars could have been better spent on groceries or her car payment, but Lena had splurged for once. Today was an important day. She was a cop again.

Her cell phone rang, and she saw from the caller ID that it was Ethan, calling on his cell phone. He was still holding on call-waiting.

Hank said, 'You need to get that?'

'No,' she told him, turning off the phone mid-ring and tucking it into her jacket pocket. She opened the bedroom door and walked into the hallway as Hank started his usual birthday story about how the day Lena and her twin sister, Sibyl, came to live with him was the happiest day of his life. She stopped in the bathroom, checking herself in the mirror again. She had dark circles under her eyes, but the tinted foundation she'd used helped take care of the problem. Nothing could be done about the deep purple gash on her bottom lip where she had bitten down too hard and split it.

A picture of Sibyl was tucked into the frame of the mirror. It had been taken a month or so before she was killed, and though Lena wanted to remove the photograph, this wasn't her house. As she did almost every morning, Lena compared the picture of her twin to her own reflection in the mirror, not liking what she saw. When Sibyl died, they had appeared almost completely identical. Now Lena's cheeks were hollow and her dark hair wasn't as thick or shiny. She looked a hell of a lot older than thirty-three, but it was the hardness in her eyes more than anything else that gave her that appearance. Her skin didn't glow like it used to, but Lena was hoping to get that back. She was running every day and doing free weights at the gym with Ethan almost every night.

Call-waiting beeped again, and Lena gritted her teeth, wishing she hadn't said anything to Ethan about her period. She had never been regular, but neither had she ever been this late. Maybe it was because she was working out so much, training to get ready for the job again. The last six weeks had been like preparing for a marathon. And then, Ethan was right about stress. She was under a lot of stress lately. She had been under a lot of stress for the last two years.

Lena pressed her hand to her eyes. She wasn't going to think about it. Last year, a pretty good shrink had told her that sometimes denial could be a good thing. Today was definitely a good day to pull a Scarlett O'Hara. She would think about it tomorrow. Shit, maybe she wouldn't think about it until next week.

She interrupted Hank's story, which had left out some important details, like the fact that he'd been a speed freak and an alcoholic when social services had dropped Sibyl and Lena on his lap – and that was the happy part of the story. 'How'd this weekend go?'

'Better than I thought,' Hank said, sounding pleased. He had turned The Hut, his dilapidated bar on the outskirts of the shithole town where Lena had grown up, into a weekend karaoke bar. Considering Hank's regular clientele, this was somewhat of a gamble, but Hank's success proved Lena's long-held theory that a drunk redneck would do anything when the lights were turned down low.

'Baby,' Hank began, his tone turning serious. 'I know today's a big day and all. . . .'

'It's no big deal,' she said. 'Really.'

'You don't have to talk all tough with me,' he said, his temper flaring. Sometimes, he was so like her that Lena felt a flicker of shock when he spoke.

'Anyway,' Hank said, 'I just want you to know if you need anything –'

'I'm fine,' she interrupted, not wanting to have this conversation again.

'Just let me damn finish,' he snapped. 'I'm trying to say that if you need anything, I'm here. Not just money and all, but you know you've got that if you need it.'

'I'm fine,' she repeated, thinking hell would freeze over before she went to her uncle Hank for help with anything.

The phone beeped, and Lena ignored it again. She walked into the kitchen and would have turned back around if Nan hadn't grabbed her arm.

'Happy birthday!' Nan said, clapping her hands with sheer joy. She took a box of matches from her apron, and Lena watched as she lit the single candle on top of a white-frosted yellow cupcake. There was another cupcake on the counter with a similar candle, but Nan left that one alone.

Nan began to sing, 'Happy birthday to you,' and Lena told Hank, 'I've got to go.'

'Happy birthday!' he repeated, nearly in time with Nan.

Lena ended the call. The phone began ringing almost immediately, and she turned it on then quickly off again as Nan finished the song.

'Thanks.' Lena blew out the candle, hoping to God Nan didn't expect her to eat anything. Her stomach felt like she had swallowed a rock.

'Did you make a wish?'

'Yeah,' Lena said, thinking it best not to tell her what.

'I know you're too nervous to eat it,' Nan said, peeling the paper away from the little round cake. She smiled, taking a bite. Sometimes Nan was so damn intuitive it made Lena uncomfortable; it was like they were an old married couple.

Nan asked, 'Is there anything I can do?'

'No, thanks,' Lena said, pouring herself a cup of coffee. The coffeemaker was one of the few things

Lena kept in the shared parts of the house. Most of the time, she stayed confined to her room, reading or watching the small black-and-white television she had gotten free from the bank when she opened a new checking account.

Lena had moved in with Nan out of dire necessity, but no matter what Nan did to try to make her feel comfortable here, Lena had a strong sense of not belonging. Nan was the perfect roommate, if you could tolerate that kind of perfection, but Lena had finally gotten to the place where she wanted her own house with her own things. She wanted a mirror she could look at in the morning without having the last two years thrown back in her face. She wanted Ethan out of her life. She wanted the rock in her gut to go away. For the first time in her life, she wanted her period.

The phone rang again. Lena pressed the buttons in rapid succession, hanging up the call.

Nan took another bite of cupcake, watching Lena over the mound of frosting. She chewed slowly, then swallowed. 'It's such a shame you have to wear makeup now. You've got great skin.'

The phone rang again, and Lena clicked it off. 'Thanks.'

'You know,' Nan said, sitting down at the kitchen table, 'I don't mind if Ethan stays over sometimes.' She indicated the house with a wave of her hand. 'This is your place, too.'

Lena tried to return the smile. 'You have frosting on your lip.'

Nan patted her mouth with a napkin. She would never use the back of her hand or lick it away. Nan Thomas was the only person Lena had ever met who actually kept napkins in a dispenser on the table.

Lena was a neat person herself and God knows she liked to have things orderly, but it was disconcerting the way Nan couldn't just put something in its place. She had to have a crocheted cover for it, preferably with tassels or a teddy bear.

Nan finished the cupcake, using the napkin to clean crumbs off the table. She stared at Lena in the ensuing silence. The phone rang again.

'So,' Nan said. 'Big day today. First day back.'

Lena clicked the phone on, then off. 'Yep.'

'Think they'll have some sort of party?'

Lena snorted a laugh. Frank and Matt had both made it more than clear that Lena didn't belong back on the force. Most days, Lena wasn't sure she disagreed with them, but this morning when she had put on her holster and clipped her cuffs onto the back of her belt, Lena had felt like she was falling back into the natural pattern of her life.

The phone rang, and Lena thumbed the keys again. She looked at Nan to gauge her reaction, but Nan was busy folding the paper from her cupcake into a tiny, neat square, as if this was just an ordinary moment in her ordinary life. If Nan Thomas ever decided to be a cop, she'd have criminals lining up to confess. If she chose a life of crime, there was no way she would ever get caught.

'Anyway,' Nan resumed. 'You don't have to move out. I'm fine having you around.'

Lena looked at the lone cupcake on the counter. Nan had bought two: one for Lena and one for Sibyl.

'They had a two-for-one special at the bakery,' Nan said, but then amended, 'Actually, I'm lying. Sibyl loved cupcakes. It was the only sugar she would ever eat. I paid full price.'

'I guessed.'

'I'm sorry.'

'You don't have to apologize.'

'Oh, I know.' Nan walked over to the trash can, which was decorated with green and yellow bunny rabbits to match her apron. 'I did go to the bakery for you, though. I wanted to get you something to celebrate. Just because she's dead –'

'I know, Nan. Thanks. I really appreciate it.'

'I'm glad.'

'Good,' Lena said, making herself meet Nan's steady gaze. As much of a neat freak as the woman was, she never cleaned her glasses. Lena could see the fingerprints from six feet away. Still, behind the lenses, Nan's owl-like eyes were piercing, and Lena clamped her mouth shut, fighting the urge to confess.

Nan said, 'It's just hard without her. You know that. You know what it's like.'

Lena nodded, a lump rising in her throat. She tried to chase it down with a swallow of coffee, but ended up scorching the roof of her mouth instead.

'The thing is, it's nice having you here.'

'I appreciate you letting me stay this long.'

'Honestly, Lee, you can stay forever. I don't care.'

'Yeah,' Lena managed over her coffee. How would Nan feel about a kid? Lena gave a mental groan. Nan would probably love a kid, would probably crochet booties for it and dress it up in something stupid every Halloween. She would switch to part-time work at the library and help raise it, and they would be a happy little married couple until Lena was so old her teeth fell out and she needed a walker to get around.

As if to remind her of Ethan's part in this, the phone rang. Lena silenced it.

Nan continued, 'Sibyl would like you living here. She always wanted to protect you.'

Lena cleared her throat, feeling a sweat break out over her body. Had Nan guessed?

'Protect you from things maybe you think you can handle, only you can't.'

The phone rang. Lena turned it on and off without looking at the keypad.

'It's nice for me to have someone around who knew Sibyl,' Nan continued. 'Someone who loved her and –' she paused as the phone rang and Lena turned it off '– cared about her. Someone who knows how hard it is to have her gone.' She paused again, but this time not for the phone. 'You don't even look like her anymore.'

Lena looked down at her hands. 'I know.'

'She would have hated that, Lee. She would have hated that more than anything else.'

They both started to tear up for their own reasons, and when the phone rang for the hundredth time, Lena answered it just to break the spell.

'Lena,' Frank Wallace barked. 'Where the fuck have you been?'

She looked at the clock over the stove. She wasn't due at the station for another half hour.

Frank didn't wait for her response. 'We've got a hostage situation at the station. Get your ass down here right now.'

The phone slammed down in her ear.

Nan asked, 'What?'

'There's a hostage situation,' Lena said, putting the phone down on the table, fighting the urge to put her hand to her chest, where her heart was thumping so hard that she felt it in her neck. 'At the station.'

'Oh, God.' Nan gasped. 'I can't believe it. Was anyone hurt?'

'He didn't say.' Lena gulped down the rest of the

coffee, though her adrenaline did not need the boost. She looked on the counter for her keys, her nerves on edge.

Nan asked, 'Remember when that happened in Ludowici?'

'I'd rather not,' Lena said, feeling her heart stop. Six years ago in a nearby county, some prisoners had managed to grab one of the cops walking through the cells. They had pistol-whipped him with his own gun and used his keys to free themselves. The stand-off had lasted three days and fifteen prisoners had been wounded or killed. Four officers had died. In her mind, Lena ran through all the cops she knew at the station, wondering if any of them had been injured.

Lena checked her pockets, though she knew she hadn't seen her keys all morning.

The phone rang again.

Lena said, 'Where are my –'

Nan pointed to a duck-shaped hook by the back door. The phone rang a second time and she picked it up without answering. 'What should I tell him?'

Lena grabbed her keys off the duck's bill. She avoided Nan's gaze as she opened the door, saying, 'Tell him I left for work.'

Lena drove her Celica down Main Street, surprised to find the town deserted. Heartsdale wasn't exactly a thriving metropolis, but even on a Monday morning you would usually find a few people walking down the sidewalks or students tearing through on their bikes. There was a four-way stop at the mouth of the street, and Lena rolled through, looking around for signs of civilization. The hardware store's neon OPEN sign was darkened, and the dress shop had a piece of paper taped to the window with a hastily scribbled

37

CLOSED. Two Grant County cruisers blocked the road twenty feet ahead, and she pulled her car into one of the vacant spots in front of the diner. Lena got out, thinking it was like being in a ghost town. The air was still and quiet, almost expectant. She glanced past her reflection into the darkened diner as she walked by. Chairs had been upended onto tables and the dollar menu had fallen off its suction cup in the window. That was nothing new. The diner had been closed over a year now.

Up the road, she could see two unmarked cop cars in front of Burgess's Cleaners, directly across from the police station. More cop cars were in the children's clinic parking lot, and three cruisers were parked on a diagonal in front of the police station. The main entrance to the college was blocked off by a campus security Chevy, but the rent-a-cop who should have been with the car was nowhere to be seen.

Lena stood on the sidewalk, looking up the street, half expecting some tumbleweeds to roll by. The windows to the cleaners were tinted nearly black, and even at close range they were hard to see into. She imagined that was where Jeffrey had set up the command post. There was nothing but a long parking lot behind the jail, and the prisoners had probably already barricaded the doors. The cleaners was the only position that made sense.

She said, 'Hey,' to the Uniform standing by the cruisers. He was looking up the street, the wrong way for his post.

He turned, his hand on his gun. Tension radiated from him like a bad odor.

She held out her hands. 'I'm on the job. Chill out.'

His voice shook. 'You're Detective Adams?'

She did not recognize the man, but even if she had, Lena doubted she could say much to calm him. His face was ashen, and if he did manage to pull his gun, he'd probably shoot himself in the foot before he managed to aim it at anyone.

'What's going on?' she asked.

He clicked his shoulder mic on. 'Detective Adams is here.'

Frank's response came almost immediately. 'Send her around the back.'

'Go through the five-and-dime,' the Uniform said. 'The back door to the cleaners is open.'

'What's going on?'

He shook his head, and she could see his Adam's apple bob as he swallowed.

Lena did as she was told, walking through the front entrance of the Shop-o-rama. There was a cowbell over the door, and the loud banging set her teeth on edge. She reached up and stilled the bell before entering the empty store. A half-filled shopping basket sat in the middle of the center aisle as if a shopper had abandoned it in place. Someone had been putting up a neon green sign advertising a special on suntan lotion, but it had been left hanging by one corner from a thin wire. All the lights were on, the neon pharmacy sign brightly lit, but the place was deserted. Even the yellow-haired freak who was always at the desk in the back office was nowhere to be seen.

The doors to the stockroom made a sucking sound as she pushed them open. Rows of marked bins lined the walls from floor to ceiling: toothpaste, toilet tissue, magazines. Lena was surprised some enterprising kid from the college had not figured out the shops were wide open and unguarded. She had worked at Grant Tech for a few months and knew from experience that the bastards spent more time stealing from each other than they did actually studying.

The back door stood wide open, and Lena blinked at the unrelenting sunlight. Sweat dripped down the back of her neck, but she was not sure if that was from the heat or her own apprehension. Her shoes crunched the gravel as she walked toward the cleaners, where two uniformed cops stood guard. One of them was a shortish, attractive woman who would have probably had Lena's job if Lena had not come back. The other was a young man who looked more skittish than the guy by the cruisers.

Lena pulled out her badge and identified herself, though she knew the woman. 'Detective Adams.'

'Hemming,' the cop said, resting her hand on her gun belt. She stared openly at Lena, managing to convey her distaste despite the circumstances. She did not introduce her partner.

Lena asked, 'What's going on?'

Hemming jabbed her thumb toward the cleaners. 'They're in there.'

Inside, the cool air almost immediately dried the sweat on her neck. Lena pushed past the rows of laundry that were waiting to be picked up. The smell of chemicals was overwhelming, and she coughed as she passed the starching area. The industrial ironers were still turned on, heat coming off them like an open flame. Old man Burgess was nowhere to be found, and it seemed odd that he would just leave things like this. Lena turned off the dials on the ironers as she passed, watching a group of men fifteen feet away. She stopped at the last machine when she recognized the tan pants and dark blue shirts of the Georgia Bureau of Investigation. They had gotten here fast. Nick Shelton, Grant County's GBI field agent, was standing with his back to Lena, but she knew him from his cowboy boots and mullet haircut.

She scanned the room for other Grant County cops. Pat Morris, a detective who had been recently promoted from patrol, sat on top of a dorm-size refrigerator holding a bag of ice to his ear. His carrot red hair was plastered to his head. Thin red lines of blood cut across his face, and Molly, the nurse from the children's clinic, was poking at them with a cotton swab. Aside from a Uniform over by the folding table, Frank was the only other cop from the county.

'Lena,' Frank said, waving her over. Blood streaked down his shirt, but from what Lena could tell, it wasn't his. He looked sick as hell, and Lena didn't know how he was standing up on his own, let alone trying to run this thing with Nick.

On the table in front of them was a rough map of what had to be the station. Red and black X's riddled the areas by the coffee machine and the fire door, each of them with a set of initials to identify a person. She guessed the oblong rectangles and lopsided squares were desks and filing cabinets. If the map was accurate, the room had been pretty much torn apart.

'Jesus,' she said, wondering how the prisoners had managed to take the squad room.

Nick motioned her closer as he finished drawing a long rectangle for the filing cabinets under the window to Jeffrey's office. 'We were just about to start.' He indicated the map, asking Pat, 'This look right, buddy?'

Pat nodded.

'All right.' Nick dropped the marker on the table and indicated Frank should begin.

'The gunman was waiting here with his accomplice here.' Frank pointed to two spots in the front lobby. 'Around nine a.m., Matt came in. He was shot in the head at point-blank range.'

Lena put her hand on the table to steady herself. She looked across the street at the station. The front door was propped open a few inches, but she did not know with what.

Frank pointed to a desk by the fire door. 'Sara Linton was here.'

'Sara?' she asked, unable to follow. How had this happened? Who would want to shoot Matt Hogan? She had assumed the prisoners had rioted, not that someone from the outside had come in to kill in cold blood.

Frank continued, 'We got two kids out.' He pointed to other red X's near the door. 'Burrows, Robinson, and Morgan were taken down in the first minute.' He nodded at Pat. 'Morris managed to break the window in Jeffrey's office and drag out three more of the kids. Keith Anderson jumped over me through the fire door. He was shot in the back. He's in surgery right now.'

When she could speak, Lena asked, 'There were kids?'

Nick provided, 'Brad was giving them a tour of the station.'

Lena swallowed, trying to get enough spit in her mouth to talk. 'How many are left?'

'Three,' Nick said, indicating the three small black X's by a larger one. 'This is Brad Stephens.' He pointed to the others. 'Sara Linton, Marla Simms, Barry Fordham.' His finger rested on a black X by a filing cabinet that indicated Fordham. There was a question mark beside it. Lena knew Barry was a beat cop, eight years on the job, with a wife and kid at home.

Nick said, 'Barry was injured, we don't know how bad. There was another shot fired about fifteen minutes ago; we think it was from an assault rifle. Two more officers are unaccounted for. We don't think anyone else is in there.' He amended, 'Anyone else alive.'

Frank coughed into his handkerchief, his chest rattling like a chain. He wiped his mouth before he continued. 'Two cruisers came in right at the beginning of it.' He indicated the cars on the map. Lena saw them still parked outside along with a third that she recognized as Brad's pulled into his usual space. She had not noticed them in the street, but from this vantage point she could see four cops crouched behind the cruisers, their guns drawn on the building.

Frank continued, 'Old man Burgess came out with his shotgun.' He meant the old guy who owned the cleaners. Burgess had a difficult enough time hefting her laundry. She could not picture him with a shotgun. 'His granddaughter was over there,' Frank said. 'She was the first one Sara got out.' He paused, and Lena could see the pain it caused him to remember what happened. 'Burgess tried to shoot through the glass, but –'

'It's bulletproof,' Lena remembered.

'It held,' Frank told her. 'But a ricochet hit Steve Mann in the leg down by the hardware store. Everybody backed off after that.'

Nick said, 'Between Burgess and the patrols, they pretty much boxed the shooters inside.' He pointed

43

behind the front counter, where Marla always sat. 'From what we can tell, the second shooter is standing here behind the counter guarding the front door while the other one keeps the hostages in line.'

Lena looked back into the street. The windows to the station were tinted, but not as dark as the cleaners'. There were white blast marks and spiderwebs where the buckshot hadn't been able to break the glass. She guessed the splotches from the inside were Matt's blood. There was a darker, solid mass at the bottom; a headless image from the back. The door was being held partially open by the weight of Matt's body.

She made herself turn away, asking, 'Have you found their car?'

'We're checking right now,' Nick told her. 'They probably parked on campus and walked to the station.'

'Which would mean they've been here before,' Lena surmised. She asked Frank and Pat, 'Did y'all recognize either one of them?'

They both shook their heads.

She looked at the map again. 'Jesus.'

'The first guy has at least three weapons. He used the sawed-off on Matt, probably a Wingmaster.' Nick paused respectfully. 'The second shooter has the assault rifle.'

'It'll pierce the glass with the right cartridges,' Lena said, thinking the gunmen had done more than a casual reconnaissance of the station.

'Right,' Nick confirmed. 'He hasn't used it on anyone in the street.'

Frank added, 'Yet.'

'We're trying to establish contact, but they won't pick up the phone.' Nick indicated one of his guys standing with the phone to his ear. 'Meanwhile, we've got the negotiator on the way from Atlanta. Helicopter should have a team here in under an hour.'

Lena studied the street, wondering how the hell all of this had started. Heartsdale was supposed to be a small, sleepy town. People came here to get away from this kind of violence. Jeffrey had told her a long time ago that the reason he had moved here from Birmingham was because he couldn't take the big-city horrors anymore. From what Lena could see, it had followed him.

She felt a shudder, like somebody had walked over her grave. There was a red X in the center of the map with two initials beside it. Lena's eyes blurred and she could not read it. When she looked back up, everyone was staring at her. She shook her head, smiling like this was all a really bad joke. 'No,' she said, seeing the initials stamped on her retinas, reading them clearly now even though she was no longer looking at the map. 'No.'

Frank turned his back to her, coughing into his handkerchief.

Lena grabbed the black marker. 'You made a mistake,' she said, yanking off the top. 'He should be in black.' She started to draw over the red, but her hand was shaking too much.

Nick took the marker from her hand. 'He's dead, Lena.' He put his hand on her shoulder. 'Jeffrey's dead.'

THREE

Tessa flounced back on the bed, her feet flopping into the air. 'I can't believe you're going to Florida without me.'

Sara responded with an absent 'Hm' as she folded a T-shirt.

'When's the last time you went on a vacation?'

'Don't remember,' she said, but she did. The summer Sara graduated from high school, Eddie Linton had dragged his wife and two reluctant daughters on their last family vacation to Sea World. Sara had spent every summer since then either in classes or working in the hospital lab for credits so she could graduate early. Except for an occasional long weekend spent at her parents' house, she had not gone on an actual vacation in what seemed like forever.

'But this is a *real* vacation,' Tessa said. 'With a *man*.'

'Hm,' Sara repeated, folding a pair of shorts.

'I hear he's pretty hot.'

'Who said that?'

'Jill-June at the Shop-o-rama.'

'She's still working there?'

'She's the manager now.' Tessa snickered. 'She's dyed her hair this awful yellow.'

46

'On purpose?'

'Well, you wouldn't think so, but it's not like she doesn't have access to two damn aisles of hair-care products.'

Sara threw a pair of pants at her sister. 'Help me fold some of these.'

'I will if you tell me about Jeffrey.'

'What'd Jill-June say?'

'That he's sex on a stick.'

Sara smiled at the understatement.

'And that he's dated every woman in town worth dating.' Tessa paused, mid-fold. 'There's an obvious joke in there, but I'm gonna let it go because you're my sister.'

'Such a price to pay.' Sara threw a sock back into the laundry basket, recalling from the last time she'd washed clothes that it didn't have a mate. She tried to change the subject, asking, 'Why is it that you never lose the socks you want to lose?'

'Is he good in bed?'

'Tess!'

'Do you want your underwear folded or not?'

Sara smoothed out a shirt, not answering.

'Y'all've been seeing each other for two months.'

'Three.'

Tessa tried again. 'You have to be sleeping with him or he wouldn't have invited you to the beach.'

Sara shrugged off a response. The truth was that she had slept with Jeffrey on their first date. They hadn't even made it out of her kitchen. Sara had been so ashamed the next morning that she sneaked out of her own house before the sun came up. If not for a robbery-homicide that forced them to work together three days later, she probably would never have spoken to Jeffrey Tolliver again.

47

Tessa turned serious. 'Was he your first time since . . . ?'

Sara gave her sister a sharp look, making it clear that topic was off-limits. 'Tell me what else Jill-June said.'

'Uh . . .' Tessa dragged it out, giving a sly smile. 'That's he's got a great body.'

'He's a runner.'

'Mmm,' Tessa approved. 'That he's tall.'

'He's three inches taller than me.'

'Look at that grin,' Tessa laughed. 'All right, all right, you don't have to give me the speech about how horrible it was being six feet tall in the third grade.'

'Five eleven.' Sara threw a dishrag at her sister's head. 'And it was ninth grade.'

Tessa folded the rag, sighing. 'He has dreamy blue eyes.'

'Yes.'

'He's incredibly charming and has very nice manners.'

'Both true.'

'Extremely good sense of humor.'

'Also true.'

'He always pays with correct change.'

Sara laughed as she pushed more clothes toward her sister. 'Talk and fold.'

Tessa picked the lint off a pair of black slacks. 'She says he used to be a football player.'

'Really?' Sara asked, because Jeffrey had never told her this. As a matter of fact, he had told her very little about himself. His general dislike of talking about the past was one of the things she enjoyed about him.

'I hope he's worth it,' Tessa said. 'Is Daddy talking to you yet?'

48

'Nope,' she answered, trying to sound as if she did not care. Though her parents had never met Jeffrey, like everyone else in town they had already formed their own opinions.

Tessa pressed on. 'Tell me some more. What do you know about him that Jill-June doesn't?'

'Not much,' Sara admitted.

'Come on.' Tessa obviously thought she was teasing. 'Just tell me what he's like.'

From the hallway, Cathy Linton said, 'Too old for her, for a start.'

Tessa rolled her eyes as their mother walked into the room.

Sara said, 'You'd never guess this was my house.'

'You don't want people walking in, don't leave your front door unlocked.' Cathy kissed Sara's cheek as she handed her a green Tupperware bowl and a grease-stained paper bag. 'I brought this over for your drive down.'

'Biscuits!' Tessa reached for the bag but Sara slapped her away.

'Your father made cornbread, but he wouldn't let me bring it.' Cathy gave her a pointed look. 'Said he didn't slave over a hot stove just to feed your fancy man.'

Her words hung in the air like a black cloud, and even Tessa knew better than to laugh. Sara picked up a pair of jeans to fold.

'Give me those.' Cathy snatched the jeans away from her. 'Like this,' she said, tucking the cuffs under her chin and magically working the jeans into a perfect square, all in under two seconds. She surveyed the mountain of laundry on Sara's bed. 'Did you just wash this today?'

'I haven't had –'

'There's no excuse for not doing laundry when you live alone.'

'I have two jobs.'

'Well, I had two children and a plumber and I managed to get things done.'

Sara looked to Tessa for help, but her sister was matching up a pair of socks with the kind of focus that could split an atom.

Cathy continued, 'You just put your dirty clothes right in the washer, then every other day or so you run a load, and you don't ever have to deal with this again.' She snapped open one of the shirts Sara had already folded. Her mouth turned down in disapproval. 'Why didn't you use a fabric softener? I left you that coupon on the counter last week.'

Sara gave up, kneeling down on the floor in front of a stack of books, trying to figure out which ones to take to the beach.

'From what I've heard,' Tessa volunteered helpfully, 'you won't have much time for reading.'

Sara was hoping the same thing, but she didn't want it announced in front of her mother.

'A man like that . . .' Cathy said. She took her time before adding, 'Sara, I know you don't want to hear this, but you are in *way* over your head.'

Sara turned around. 'Thanks for the vote of confidence, Mother.'

Cathy's frown deepened. 'Are you planning on wearing a bra with that shirt? I can see both your –'

'All right.' Sara untucked her shirt as she stood.

Her mother added, 'And those shorts don't fit. Have you lost weight?'

Sara looked at herself in the mirror. She had spent nearly an hour choosing an outfit that looked both flattering and like she had not spent an hour picking it out. 'They're supposed to be baggy,' she said, tugging at the seat. 'It's the style.'

'Oh, Lord's sake, Sara. Have you seen your ass lately? I sure haven't.' Tessa cackled, and Cathy moderated her tone if not her words. 'Honey, there's just your shoulder blades and the backs of your calves. "Baggy" wasn't meant for women like you.'

Sara took a deep breath, bracing herself against the dresser. 'Excuse me,' she said as politely as possible, and went into the bathroom, taking great pains not to slam the door behind her. She closed the toilet lid and sat down, dropping her head into her hands. She could hear her mother outside complaining about static cling, and asking again why she bothered to leave coupons if Sara wasn't going to use them.

Sara slid back her hands to cover her ears, and her mother's complaining subsided to a tolerable hum, slightly less annoying than a hot needle in her ear. From the moment Sara had started dating Jeffrey, Cathy had been riding her about one thing or another. There was nothing Sara could do right, from her posture at the dinner table to the way she parked her car in the driveway. Part of Sara wanted to confront Cathy on her hypercriticism, but another part – the more compassionate part – understood that this was the way her mother coped with her fears.

Sara looked at her watch, praying that Jeffrey would show up on time and take her away from all of this. He was seldom late, which was one of the many things she liked about him. For all of Cathy's talk about what a cad Jeffrey Tolliver was, he carried a handkerchief in his back pocket and always opened the door for her. When Sara got up from the table at a restaurant, he stood, too. He helped her with her coat and carried her briefcase when they walked down the street. As if all of this was not enough, he was so good in bed that their first time together she had nearly cracked her back molars clamping her teeth together so that she would not scream his name.

'Sara?' Cathy knocked on the door, her voice filled with concern. 'Are you okay, honey?'

Sara flushed the toilet and ran water in the sink. She opened the door to find her sister and mother both staring at her with the same worried expression.

Cathy held up a red blouse. 'I don't think this is a good color for you.'

'Thanks.' Sara took the shirt and tossed it into the laundry basket. She knelt back down by the books, wondering if she should take the literary authors to impress Jeffrey or the more commercial ones that she knew she would enjoy.

'I don't even know why you're going to the beach,' Cathy said. 'All you've ever done is burn. Do you have enough sunscreen?'

Without turning around, Sara held up the neon green bottle of Tropical Sunblock.

'You know how easily you freckle. And your legs are so white. I don't know that I'd wear shorts with legs like that.'

Tessa chuckled. 'What was that girl's name in *Gidget* who wore the big hat on the beach?'

Sara gave her sister a 'you're not helping' look. Tessa pointed to the bag of biscuits, then to her mouth, indicating her silence could be bought.

'Larue,' Sara told her, moving the bag farther away.

'Tessie,' Cathy said. 'Run fetch me the ironing board.' She asked Sara, 'You *do* have an iron?'

Sara felt the heat from her mother's stare. 'In the pantry.'

Cathy clicked her tongue as Tessa left. She asked Sara, 'When did you wash these?'

'Yesterday.'

'If you'd ironed them then –'

'Yes, and if I didn't wear clothes at all, I'd never have to worry about it.'

'That's the same thing you told me when you were six.'

Sara waited.

'If I'd left it up to you, you'd've gone to school naked.'

Sara absently thumbed through a book, not seeing the pages. Behind her, she could hear her mother snapping out shirts and refolding them.

Cathy said, 'If this was Tessa, I wouldn't be worried at all. As a matter of fact,' she gave a low laugh, smoothing out another shirt, 'I'd be worried about Jeffrey.'

Sara put a paperback with a bloody knife slash down the cover in the 'take' pile.

'Jeffrey Tolliver is the sort of man who has had a lot of experience. A lot more than you, and I see that smile on your lips, young lady. You'd best realize I'm not just talking about the stuff going on between the sheets.'

Sara picked up another paperback. 'I really don't want to have this conversation with my mother.'

'Your mother is probably the only woman on earth who will tell you this,' Cathy said. She sat on the bed and waited for Sara to turn around. 'Men like Jeffrey only want one thing.' Sara opened her mouth, but her mother wasn't finished. 'It's okay if you give them that thing as long as you get something back out of it.'

'Mother.'

'Some women can have sex without being in love.'

'I know that.'

'I'm serious, baby. Listen to me. You're not that kind of woman.' She tucked back Sara's hair. 'You're not the kind of girl who has flings. You've never been that kind of girl.'

'You don't know that.'

'You've only had two boyfriends your whole life. How many girlfriends has Jeffrey had? How many women has he slept with?'

'I would guess quite a few.'

'And you're just another one on his list. That's why your father is mad about –'

'Don't y'all think it would be nice to actually bother to meet him before you jump to all these conclusions?' Sara asked, too late remembering that Jeffrey was on his way here now. She chanced a look at her alarm clock. In about ten minutes, her mother would be able to see for herself that she was exactly right. If Jill-June Mallard could pick up on it, Cathy Linton would know it the moment Jeffrey entered the room.

Cathy persisted. 'You're just not a "fling" kind of girl, honey.'

'Maybe I am now. Maybe I became that sort of person in Atlanta.'

'Well.' Cathy picked up a pair of underwear to fold, her brows furrowed. 'These are too delicate for the machine,' she chastised. 'If you wash them by hand and dry them on the line, they won't get torn like this.'

Sara gave her a tight smile. 'They're not torn.'

Cathy raised an eyebrow, showing a spark of appreciation. Still, she asked, 'How many men have you been with?'

Sara looked at her watch, whispering, 'Please.'

Cathy ignored her. 'I know about Steve Mann. Good Lord, the whole town knew after Mac Anders caught you two behind the Chilidog.'

Sara stared at the floor, willing herself not to spontaneously combust from embarrassment.

Cathy continued. 'Mason James.'

'Mama.'

'That's two men.'

'You're forgetting the last one,' Sara reminded her, feeling a tinge of regret as she saw her mother's expression darken.

Cathy folded Sara's pajama bottoms. She asked very softly, 'Does Jeffrey know you were raped?'

Sara moderated her tone, trying to be gentle. 'It hasn't exactly come up in our conversations.'

'What did you tell him when he asked why you left Atlanta?'

'Nothing,' she said, leaving out the fact that Jeffrey had not pressed for details.

Cathy smoothed the pajamas. She turned around for something else to put to order, but she had already folded or refolded everything on the bed. 'You should never be ashamed about what happened to you, Sara.'

Sara shrugged noncommittally as she stood to get her suitcase. She wasn't ashamed, exactly, just sick to death of people treating her differently because of it – especially her mother. Sara could take the concerned looks and the awkward pauses from the handful of people who knew why she had really moved back to Grant County, but her strained relationship with her mother was almost too much to bear.

Sara opened the case and started to pack. 'I'll tell him when it's time. If it's ever time.' She shrugged again. 'Maybe it'll never be time.'

'You can't expect to have a solid relationship if it's founded on secrets.'

'It's not a secret,' she countered. 'It's just private. It's something that happened to me, and I'm tired of . . .' She did not finish the sentence, because talking about the rape with her mother was not a conversation she was ready to have. 'Can you hand me that cotton top?'

Cathy gave the shirt a look of disapproval before handing it over. 'I've seen too many women fight to get to where you are and give it all up in a minute for some man that ends up leaving them in a couple of years anyway.'

'I'm not going to give up my career for Jeffrey.' She gave a rueful laugh. 'And it's not like I can get pregnant and stay home raising babies.'

Cathy absorbed the remark with little more than a frown. 'It's not that, Sara.'

'Then what is it, Mama? What is it you're so worried about? What could any man possibly do to me that's worse than what's already happened?'

Cathy looked down at her hands. She never cried, but she could go silent in a way that broke Sara's heart.

Sara sat on the bed beside her mother. 'I'm sorry,' she said, thinking that she had never been so sick of having to apologize to people in her life. She felt such guilt for bringing this on her otherwise perfect family that sometimes Sara felt like it would be better for her to just go away and leave them to heal on their own.

Cathy said, 'I don't want you to give up your *self*.'

Sara held her breath. Her mother had never come this close to voicing her true fears. Sara knew better than anyone how easy it would be to just give in. After the rape, all Sara had been able to do was lie in bed and cry. She had not wanted to be a doctor, a sister, or even a daughter. Two months passed, and Cathy had pleaded and cajoled, then physically pushed Sara out of bed. As she had done a hundred times when Sara was a child, Cathy had driven her to the children's clinic, where this time Dr. Barney had made things better by giving Sara a job. A year later, Sara had taken a second job as county coroner in order to buy out Dr. Barney's practice. For the last two and a half years, she had struggled to rebuild her life in Grant, and Cathy was terrified Sara would lose all of that for Jeffrey.

Sara stood up and walked to her dresser. 'Mama . . .'

'I worry about you.'

'I'm better now,' Sara said, though she did not think she would ever be fully whole again. There would always be the before and after, no matter how many years distanced her from what had happened. 'I don't need you to look after me, or try to toughen me up. I'm stronger now. I'm ready for this.'

Cathy threw her hands up. 'He's just having fun. That's all this is to him – fun.'

Sara opened several drawers, looking for her swimsuit. She said, 'Maybe that's all it is for me, too. Maybe I'm just having a good time.'

'I wish I could believe you.'

'I wish you could, too,' Sara told her. 'Because it's true.'

'I don't know, baby. You have such a gentle heart.'

'It's not that gentle anymore.'

'What happened to you in Atlanta doesn't change who you are.'

Sara shrugged, tucking her swimsuit into the case. It was how other people had changed that made what happened even more horrible. Sara was angry as hell that she had been raped, and livid that the animal who had attacked her could, and probably would, get out of jail in a few years with good behavior. She was pissed off that her whole life had been turned upside down, that she'd had to resign her internship at Grady Hospital, the job she had worked toward her entire life, because everyone in the ER treated her like broken china. The attending who had worked on Sara could no longer look her in the eye, and her fellow students wouldn't joke with her for fear of saying the wrong thing. Even the nurses treated her with kid gloves, as if being raped made Sara some sort of martyr.

Cathy said, 'Is that all I get? That look from you that says you don't want to talk about it?'

'I *don't* want to talk about it,' Sara told her, exasperated. 'I don't want to talk about anything serious. I'm tired of being serious.' She tugged at the zipper on the suitcase. 'I'm tired of being the smartest girl in the class. I'm tired of being too tall for the cute boys. I'm tired of dating men who are worried about my feelings and wanna take it slow and be gentle and *process* what we're doing and *plan* our future together and treat me like I'm some delicate flower and –'

'Mason James is a very sweet boy.'

'That's the point, Mama. He's a boy. I'm sick of boys. I'm sick of people walking on eggshells around me, trying to protect my feelings. I want somebody to shake things up. I want to have fun.' Without thinking, she said, 'I want to fuck around.'

Cathy gasped – not because she had never heard the word before, but because she had never heard it from Sara. Sara could think of only a few occasions when she had used the expletive, but never in front of her mother.

All Cathy said was, 'Language, please.'

'You don't mind when Tessa says it.'

Cathy wrinkled her nose at the logic. 'Tessa says it like she means it, not like she's trying to shock her mother.'

'I say it all the time,' Sara lied.

'Do your cheeks always get that red when you do?'

Sara felt her cheeks go redder.

'From here,' Cathy coached, pressing her hand below her diaphragm. She gestured broadly with her other hand, singing an operatic 'Fuck.'

'Mother!'

'If you're going to say it, say it with gusto.'

'I don't need you to tell me how to say it,' Sara snapped, and when Cathy laughed in her face, she added a mumbled 'Or how to do it.'

Cathy laughed harder. 'I suppose you know all about it now?'

Sara jerked the suitcase off her bed. 'Let's just say some of that expertise rubbed off.'

'Oh-ho-ho,' Cathy chuckled appreciatively.

Sara tucked her hands into her hips. 'We do it all the time.'

'Is that a fact?'

'Night and day.'

'And day?' Cathy laughed again, sitting back on the bed. 'Scandalous!'

'It's not like I'm seeing him for the scintillating conversation,' Sara bragged. 'I don't even know if he went to college.'

From the doorway, Tessa said, 'Sara?'

'As a matter of fact,' Sara continued, wanting more than anything to take the smug look off her mother's face, 'I'm fairly certain he's not even that smart.'

Cathy smiled like she knew better. 'That so?'

Tessa tried again. 'Sara?'

'Yes, that's so, and you know what? I don't even care. He's probably stupid as a box of hair and I don't give a rat's ass. It's not like I'm dating him for his mind.'

Tessa said, 'For chrissake, Sara. Just shut up and turn around.'

She did as she was told, regret taking hold like a fever.

Jeffrey was leaning against the door, his arms crossed over his chest. There was a half-smile on his lips that did not quite reach his eyes as he nodded toward her suitcase. 'Ready to go?'

A gentle mist of rain met them as they drove out of Grant County, and Sara watched the wipers sluice water off the windshield at steady intervals, trying to think of something to say. With each pass, she told herself she was going to break the silence, but the next thing she knew, the wipers were swiping across the glass again and nothing had been said. She stared out the side window, counting cows, then goats, then billboards. The closer they got to Macon, the higher the number got, so that by the time they took the bypass, Sara had reached triple digits.

Jeffrey shifted gears, passing an eighteen-wheeler.

He had not spoken since they left Grant, and he chose to break the ice with 'Car handles well.'

'Yes,' Sara agreed, so glad he was talking to her that she could have cried. Thank God they had taken her car instead of his truck or there was no telling how long the silence would have lasted. To keep the conversation going, she said, 'German engineering.'

'I guess it's true what they say about doctors driving BMWs.'

'My dad bought it for me when I got into medical school.'

'Nice dad,' he said, pausing before he added, 'Your mom seems nice, too.'

Sara cleared her throat, unable to recall any of the apologies she had been rehearsing in her mind for the last hour. 'I would have preferred for you to meet her under different circumstances.'

'I never expected to meet her at all.'

'Oh, right,' she said, flustered. 'I didn't mean –'

'I'm glad we got to meet.'

Sara nodded, thinking that the fewer times she opened her mouth, the less likely she was to put her foot in it.

'Your sister's cute.'

'Yes,' she agreed, knowing a lesser person would hate her sister by now. Sara had been hearing the same thing all her life. Tessa was the cute one, the funny one, the cheerleader, the one everyone wanted to be friends with. Sara was the tall one. On a good day, she was the tall redheaded one.

Before Sara could phrase something more elegant, she blurted out, 'I'm so sorry about what I said.'

'That's okay,' he told her, but she could tell from his tone that it was not. Why he had still wanted her to go to Florida with him was anyone's guess. If Sara had any self-respect, she would have let him leave without her. The forced smile he had kept on his face as he loaded her bags into the trunk could have cut glass.

'I was just trying to . . .' She shook her head. 'I don't know what I was trying to do. Make an idiot of myself?'

'You did a good job.'

'It's part of my personality to want to excel in everything I do.'

He did not smile.

She tried again. 'I don't think you're stupid.'

'As a box of hair.'

'What?'

'You said "stupid as a box of hair."'

'Oh. Well.' She laughed once, like a seal's bark. 'That doesn't even make sense.'

'But it's good to know you don't really think that.' He glanced behind him and passed a church van. Sara stared at his hand on the shift, watching the tendons work as he passed the cars. His fingers gripped the shaft, his thumb tapping lightly on the knob.

'By the way,' he told her. 'I *did* go to college.'

'Really?' she asked, unable to check her surprised tone. She made it worse by saying, 'Well, good. Good for you.'

Jeffrey gave her a sharp glance.

'I mean, that's good as in . . . well . . . because it's . . .' She laughed at her own ineptitude, putting her hand over her mouth as she mumbled, 'Oh, God, Sara, shut up. Shut up.'

She thought he smiled, but wasn't certain. She dared to ask, 'Exactly how much did you hear?'

'Something about me rubbing off on you?'

She tried, 'I meant it in the good way.'

'Uh-huh,' he said. 'Just FYI, I've heard you say that word before.' This time, he showed his teeth when he smiled. 'Well, not say it. More like scream it.'

Sara bit the tip of her tongue, watching the passing scenery.

He said, 'It's good your mama worries about you.'

'Sometimes.'

'Y'all are pretty close, right?'

'I suppose,' Sara answered, knowing there was more to it than that.

He asked, 'Did you tell her I passed the test?'

'Of course not,' Sara answered, surprised he had even asked. 'That's private.'

He nodded his approval, keeping his eyes on the road.

Their second date had ended with a kiss at the door and Sara asking Jeffrey to get tested for HIV. Granted, the request was a little late in coming – their frenzied first time hadn't exactly stopped for a frank discussion about the prevention of sexually transmitted diseases – but Sara had picked up on Jeffrey's reputation well before the news had hit the Shop-o-rama. For his part, Jeffrey had seemed only slightly insulted when she asked him for a blood sample.

She said, 'I saw so many cases at Grady. So many women my age who never thought it could happen to them.'

'You don't have to explain it to me.'

'Hare's lover died of AIDS last year.'

His foot slipped off the gas pedal. 'Your cousin's gay?'

'Of course.'

'You're kidding?' he asked, giving her an uneasy look.

'He wasn't born with that falsetto.'

'I thought he was just joking around.'

'He was,' Sara said. 'Is. I mean, he just does that to annoy me. Everyone. He likes to annoy people.'

'He played football in high school.'

'Only straight people can play football?'

'Well . . . no,' he said, but he did not seem certain.

They both stared at the road again. Sara could think of nothing to say. She knew hardly anything about the man beside her. In the three months they had dated, she had heard nothing about Jeffrey's family or his past. She knew he had been born in Alabama, but he was vague with the details. When they weren't in bed, Jeffrey mostly talked about cases he had worked in Birmingham or things that were happening in Grant. Now that she thought about it, when they were together it was Sara who did most of the talking. He seldom volunteered any personal information about himself, and if she pushed him too far with questions, his response was to either shut down completely or run his hand up and down her thigh until she forgot what she was saying.

She chanced a look at him. His dark hair was getting long in the back, which was a little dangerous considering the Grant County school system routinely sent boys home from class if their hair touched the back of their collars. As usual, his face was clean-shaven and smooth. He was wearing a pair of worn jeans and a black Harley Davidson T-shirt. His tennis shoes looked high-tech, with extra padding in the sole and black waffle treads for running. The muscles in his legs were well defined under the denim, and though his shirt was not tight enough to show the firm abs underneath, Sara was more than familiar with them.

Sara stared down at her legs, wishing she had worn something different. She had changed into an ocean blue wraparound skirt, but her white calves were the color of fat on uncooked bacon against the dark floor mat. Despite the air conditioning, she was sweating under the cotton shirt she wore, and if Sara could have waved a magic wand to stop time, she would have stripped off her constricting bra and thrown it out the window.

'So,' Jeffrey said.

'So,' she returned, trying to think of something to restart the conversation. All she could come up with was, 'You're a universal donor.'

'Huh?'

'A universal donor,' she repeated. 'You can donate blood to anyone.' Grasping another straw, she added, 'Of course, you can't accept from anyone. You can only accept from other O negatives.'

He gave her a strange look. 'I'll keep that in mind.'

'Your blood has antigens that –'

'I'll donate some as soon as we get back.'

The conversation was lagging again, and she asked, 'Do you want some chicken?'

'Is that what I keep smelling?'

Sara leaned over the backseat and rummaged around for the plastic bowl her mother had packed. 'I think there's some biscuits if Tess didn't steal them.'

'That'd be nice,' he said, tickling the back of her thigh. 'Too bad we don't have some tea.'

She tried to ignore his hand. 'We could stop for some.'

'Maybe.'

He pinched her leg and she slapped at his hand, saying, 'Hey.'

He laughed good-naturedly at the rebuke. 'Do you mind if we take a detour?'

'Sure,' she said, finding the Tupperware under a pillow. She dropped back into the seat as he passed a Winnebago. 'Where to?'

'Sylacauga.'

Sara stopped in the middle of removing the plastic lid. 'Sill-a-what?'

'Sylacauga,' he repeated. 'My hometown.'

FOUR

10:15 A.M.

'Matt?' Someone said, more like a stutter. 'M-a-a-a-a-att.'

His ears held on to the echo, stretching the 'a' even more.

'M-a-a-a-a-a-a-att.'

He tried to move but his muscles would not respond. Inexplicably, his fingers ached. They were cold. Everything was cold.

'Matt,' Sara said, her voice suddenly sharp as a tack. 'Matt, wake up.' She put her hands on either side of his face. 'Matt.'

He forced open his eyes, his vision blurring, then doubling. He saw two Saras looming over him. Two Marlas. Two kids he had never met before in his life. They were all huge, like giant versions of themselves. The ceiling tiles above their heads were even larger, like flying saucers with mammoth fluorescent lights.

He tried to sit up.

'Matt, no,' Sara stopped him. 'Don't.'

He put his hand to his head, feeling like his brain was in a vise. His right shoulder burned as if someone was grinding a hot poker into the flesh. His moved his left hand to touch it, but Sara stopped him.

'Matt,' she said. 'Don't.'

He felt around his mouth with his tongue, trying

to find the blood he could taste in the back of his throat.

She pushed back his hair and he saw a glint of gold on her finger. She was wearing his Auburn football ring. Why was she wearing his ring?

'Matt?'

He blinked, hearing a distant ringing in his ears. Jeffrey squeezed his eyes shut, trying to orient himself. The ringing came from the phone on Marla's desk. The blood he tasted was from a cut somewhere on his head.

'Matt?' Sara repeated. 'Can you hear me?'

He said, 'Why are you –'

She put a bottle of water to his lips. 'Drink this. You need water.'

Jeffrey drank, feeling the cool liquid opening up his parched throat. Water pooled down his neck as Sara tilted the bottle too far to keep up with his swallowing.

'Okay,' he said, pushing away her hand.

He squeezed his eyes shut again, trying to clear them. When he opened them, the two Marlas melded into one. Her cheeks were sunken, her eye bruised and bleeding. There was actually a pair of kids, but their expressions were identical. A third was leaning against Sara, the young girl's breathing more like gasps as she tried to control her fear.

Jeffrey turned back to Sara. He had never seen her so frightened. She met his gaze pupil to pupil, staring a hole into him like she was trying to force a thought into his brain. Slowly, he nodded his understanding. He was supposed to be Matt.

She still asked, 'Okay?'

'Yeah.' He looked around, trying to figure out what was going on. They were on the floor in the back of the squad room, the area cleared out around them. Brad was stacking filing cabinets in front of the fire door. Jeffrey's office window and door were similarly barricaded. Bodies were scattered around with the debris. Burrows, Robinson, Morgan. Morgan had five kids at home. Burrows was an avid animal lover fostering a pair of rescued greyhounds. Robinson . . . Robinson was new. Jeffrey could not even remember the man's first name, though he had hired him less than a week ago.

Jeffrey's vision blurred and he closed his eyes as the vertigo brought on a wave of nausea.

'Breathe,' Sara coaxed, smoothing back his hair. His head was in her lap and, judging by the blood on her skirt, had been for a while. He tried to move, but found that his feet were tied together with his own belt.

Suddenly, a man stood over them, pointing a shotgun at Marla while keeping a military-issue Sig Sauer trained on Brad. He had two more guns holstered to his chest along with a full complement of ammunition.

Smith. Jeffrey remembered he had given his name as Smith. He remembered it all now: Sara screaming his name, Matt's head exploding against the front door, the ensuing gun battle, the deaths. Sam. The new patrolman's first name was Sam.

The killer gave Jeffrey a cold look of appraisal. 'Sit up.'

Sara said, 'He needs to go to the hospital.' She did not wait for a response. 'The children are in shock. They all need to go to the hospital.'

Smith cocked his head like he had heard something. He turned toward the lobby, where another man rested an assault rifle on the front counter, pointing it toward the front entrance. He was similarly dressed with a dark coat and Kevlar vest. A black ball cap was pulled low on his head, casting his face in shadow. The man did not look Smith's way, but he gave a curt nod.

Sara took advantage of the brief exchange, whispering something to Jeffrey that sounded like 'Stall it.'

Smith turned back to Jeffrey. 'Sit up.' He kicked Jeffrey's feet, and the movement jarred his shoulder enough to make him yell from the pain.

'He needs to go to the hospital,' Sara repeated.

'Hey,' Brad said, like a child trying to get between his arguing parents. 'I need a hand over here with this one.'

Smith pointed the shotgun in Sara's face. 'Help him.'

Sara stayed where she was. 'Matt needs medical attention,' she said, keeping her hand on Jeffrey's good shoulder. Her words came out in a rushed panic. 'The pulse in his arm is thready. The bullet probably nicked the artery. He lost consciousness for God knows how long. His head wound needs to be assessed.'

'You don't seem too worried about me,' Smith said, indicating a piece of white cloth tied tightly around his left arm. A circle of dark blood spotted the center.

'You both seem capable of taking care of yourselves,' she told him, then looked past his shoulder to his partner in the front lobby.

'Damn right,' Smith said, bouncing on the balls of his feet. Jeffrey tried to get a good look at the second man's face, but the overhead light was so bright that he could not keep his eyes open.

Brad stumbled and dropped a filing cabinet. With lightning speed, Smith and the second gunman turned around, both ready to shoot.

Brad held up his hands. 'Sorry,' he said. 'I just –'

The second shooter turned back to the front door as Smith walked over to Brad. Sara kept her eyes on the second man as she slipped her hand under Jeffrey's back. Wallet. She had said 'Wallet.'

He raised himself up to help her, biting through the pain in his shoulder, and she took out his wallet just as Smith swung around on them. He stared, his eyes darting to each person in the group, some sort of sixth sense igniting his suspicion. The children were so frightened that they were hardly moving, and Marla seemed to be in her own world as she stared blindly at the floor.

Brad said, 'Maybe you can –'

Smith held out his hand, cutting him off. The room was silent, but the gunman could obviously hear something they could not. Or maybe, Jeffrey reasoned, he was just a paranoid fuck hopped up on cocaine or meth. Why the hell would someone do something like this? What could they possibly gain?

Smith walked backward, both guns trained on Brad. He stopped in front of the bathroom door, looking at his partner and getting a quick nod in return. The two men worked together like a precision instrument. Even without the military gear, it was obvious that they had either trained or been in combat together.

The bathroom door opened soundlessly as Smith went in, gun raised. Jeffrey counted off the seconds, staring at the door as it slowly closed. Suddenly, they heard a woman's scream and a single gunshot. Less than minute later, Smith came out of the bathroom holding up a police-issue gun belt like it was a trophy.

Smith told his partner. 'She was hiding under the sink.'

The second man shrugged, like it was none of his concern, and Jeffrey felt his heart sink at the thought of another one of his officers shot dead by these animals. She must have been hiding under the sink cabinet all this time, hoping to God they would not find her.

Smith threw the gun belt toward the lobby before going back to Jeffrey. 'Sit up,' he said, and when Jeffrey did not move fast enough, he grabbed him up by his collar.

Jeffrey felt his stomach pitch as his brain tried to adjust to the sudden change. Sara sat up too, putting her hand on the back of his neck, coaching, 'Breathe through it. Don't get sick.'

He tried to do as he was told, but the grits he'd had for breakfast would not obey. They came up in a hot rush of bile.

'Jesus fuck,' Smith stepped back quickly to avoid the splatter. 'What'd you have for breakfast, man?'

Jeffrey gave him another clue, throwing up the rest of the grits. He felt Sara's hand at the back of his neck, the metal of his Auburn class ring pressing into his skin. Why had she taken his ring?

Smith said, 'Give me your wallet.'

Jeffrey wiped his mouth with the back of his hand. 'It's in my coat,' he said, saying a small prayer of thanks that he had been too pissed at Sara in the interrogation room to stop and put his jacket back on.

'Where is it?' Smith challenged. 'Where's your coat?'

Jeffrey inhaled deeply, trying to quell the squall building in his stomach.

Smith kicked Jeffrey's feet. 'Where's your coat?' he repeated.

'In my car.'

Smith grabbed Jeffrey's collar and jerked him up to standing. Jeffrey screamed from the pain, fireworks detonating behind his eyelids. He pressed his face to the wall as he tried not to slide back to the floor. The muscles in his shoulder were throbbing with every beat of his heart, and his knees were so weak they started to buckle.

'You're okay,' Sara told him, gripping him under his arm. Her strength was surprising, and he loved her more in that moment than he had in his entire life. 'Keep breathing,' she told him, rubbing his back in a soothing, circular motion. 'You're okay.'

'Move.' Smith pushed her away. He tucked the shotgun into his belt and gave Jeffrey an expert pat-down. The man knew the correct way to frisk a suspect, and he did not go lightly near Jeffrey's shoulder.

'All right.' Smith backed up and Jeffrey struggled to face him, leaning against the wall so he would not collapse. The phone started ringing again, the metallic clang grating on every nerve in his body.

'Y'okay, Matt?' Smith hit the *t*'s hard, like he was testing them. Jeffrey did not know if it was paranoia or panic, but he got the feeling Smith knew exactly who he was looking at, and that it was not Matt Hogan.

'He's not,' Sara said. 'The bullet's probably pressed against the artery. If you keep pushing him, it might dislodge. He could bleed to death.'

'My heart's breaking,' Smith said, glancing over at Brad to check his work.

The phone continued to ring in the background, and Sara said, 'Why don't you pick that up and tell them you're sending out the children?'

Smith cocked his head to the side as if he was considering her suggestion. 'Why don't you wrap your lips around my dick and suck it?'

Sara ignored the remark, telling him, 'You need to show them good faith by letting the children go.'

'I don't *need* to do anything.'

Brad added, 'She's right. You're not a baby killer.'

'No,' Smith said, taking the shotgun out of his belt and pointing it at Brad's chest. 'I'm just a cop killer.'

He let this sink in, the phone's insistent ringing punctuating the tension.

Sara told him, 'The sooner you make your demands, the sooner we can all get out of here.'

'Maybe I don't want to get out of here, Dr. Linton.'

Jeffrey clenched his jaw, thinking there was something too familiar about the way the man had said Sara's name.

Smith noticed his reaction. 'You don't like that, boy?' he asked, standing a few inches from Jeffrey's face. 'Dr. Linton and me, we go way back. Don't we, Sara?'

Sara stared at the young man, looking unsure of herself. 'How long has it been?'

Smith gave her a crooked smile. 'A while, don't you think?'

Sara tried to hide her uncertainty, but to Jeffrey it was clear as day that she had no idea who the boy was. 'You tell me.'

They held each other's gaze, tension held between

them like a tight wire. Smith gave a suggestive flick with his tongue and Sara looked away. Had Jeffrey been able, he would have jumped the man and beaten him dead.

Again, Smith picked up on this. He asked Jeffrey, 'Are you gonna be a problem for me, Matt?'

Jeffrey stood as straight as he could with his ankles belted together. He shot the other man a look of pure hatred. Smith returned it in kind.

Brad spoke up, breaking the tension. 'Keep me,' he volunteered.

Smith kept his face turned toward Jeffrey, though his gaze slid slowly toward Brad.

Brad said, 'Let them go and keep me.'

Smith laughed at the suggestion, and in the lobby his partner joined in.

'Then keep me,' Sara said, and they both stopped laughing.

Jeffrey told her, 'No.'

She ignored him, addressing Smith. 'You've already killed Jeffrey.' Her voice caught on his name, but she said the rest clearly enough. 'You don't want Brad or Matt. You certainly don't want an old woman and three 10-year-olds. Let them go. Let them all go and keep me.'

FIVE

The drive to Sylacauga turned out to be a longer detour than Jeffrey had promised. He said they would stay the night at his mother's, but at the rate they were going, Sara thought it would be more like morning. Closer to Talladega, the highway started to back up with traffic for the race at the NASCAR super speedway, but Jeffrey took this more like a challenge than an obstacle. After weaving in and out of cars, trucks, and RVs at such a close distance that Sara put on her seatbelt, Jeffrey finally exited. She was relieved until she realized that the last vehicle to use the road was probably a horse and buggy.

The deeper they drove into Alabama, the more relaxed Jeffrey seemed, and the long stretches of silence became companionable instead of unbearable. He found a good Southern-rock station and they listened to the likes of Lynyrd Skynyrd and The Allman Brothers as they drove through backwoods country. Along the way, he pointed out different attractions, such as three recently closed cotton mills and a tire factory that had been shut down after an industrial accident. The Helen Keller Center for the Blind was an impressive set of buildings, but hardly much to look at going ninety miles per hour.

Jeffrey patted her knee as they passed yet another

country jail. He smiled and said, 'Almost there,' but there was an odd expression on his face, like he regretted asking her to come.

They took a last-minute turn onto another ill-used roadway, and Sara was contemplating how to ask him if he was lost when a large sign loomed in the distance. She read aloud, 'Welcome to Sylacauga, birthplace of Jim Nabors.'

'We're a proud people,' Jeffrey told her, down-shifting as the road curved. 'Ah,' he said fondly. 'There's a point of local interest.' He indicated a run-down-looking country store. 'Yonders Blossom.'

The sign was faded, but Sara could still read that it was, in fact, called Yonders Blossom. Various items one would expect to find in front of a country store were strategically placed around the yard, from a radiator with a fern growing out of it to a couple of rubber tires that had been painted white and turned into flower planters. To the side of the building was a large Coca-Cola freezer.

Jeffrey told her, 'I lost my virginity behind the cooler there.'

'Is that so?'

'Yep,' he said, a crooked grin on his face. 'The day of my twelfth birthday.'

Sara tried to hide her shock. 'How old was she?'

He gave a self-satisfied chuckle. 'Not too old to be taken over her mama's knee when Blossom got thirsty and happened upon us.'

'You seem to have that effect on mothers.'

He laughed again, putting his hand on her leg. 'Not all of them, honey.'

'Honey?' she repeated, thinking from his tone that he might as well have called her his favorite side of beef.

He laughed at her reaction, though she had never been more serious. 'You're not going to turn into a feminist on me?'

She looked at his hand on her leg, sending a clear message that it should be removed now. 'Right before your very eyes.'

He squeezed her leg in response, flashing that same grin that had probably gotten him out of trouble a thousand times before. Sara was not so much angry as feeling he had paid her back for calling him stupid in front of her mother. Against her better judgment, she let it slide.

They drove slowly through downtown, which was similar to Heartsdale's but half the size. He showed her other 'points of interest' from his childhood along the way. Sara got the distinct impression from his lopsided smiles that there were different girls attached to each of these spots, but she decided she would rather not know the details.

'There's where I went to high school.' He pointed to a long, flat building with several trailers outside. 'Ah, Mrs. Kelley.'

'Another one of your conquests?'

He gave a low growl. 'I wish. Good God, she's probably eighty now, but back then . . .'

'I get the picture.'

'You jealous?'

'Of an eighty-year-old?'

'Here we go,' he said, taking a left. They were on Main Street, which again looked very much like Heartsdale's. He asked, 'Look familiar?'

'Your Piggly Wiggly's closer in town,' she said, watching a woman come out of the grocery store with three bags in her hands and a small child on either side. Sara stared at the children as they held on to their mother's dress, wondering what it would be like to have that kind of life. Sara had always thought that once she got her practice going, she would get married and have a few children of her own. An ectopic pregnancy subsequent to the rape had removed that possibility forever.

She felt a lump rise in her throat as she was reminded yet again of how much had been taken from her.

Jeffrey pointed to a large building on their right. 'There's the hospital,' he said. 'I was born there back when it was just two stories and a gravel parking lot.'

She stared at the building, trying to regain her composure.

He handed her his handkerchief. 'You okay?'

Sara took the cloth. She had been tearing up before, and for some reason his gesture made her want to really cry. Instead, she wiped her nose and said, 'Must be the pollen.'

'Here,' he said, leaning over to roll up the window. 'Damn dogwoods.'

She put her hand on the back of his neck, brushing her fingers through his hair. She was always surprised by how soft it was, almost like a child's.

He looked up at the road, then back to her. He gave her one of his half-smiles, saying, 'God, you're so beautiful.'

She blew her nose to defray the compliment.

He sat up, slowing the car more. 'You're beautiful,' he repeated, kissing her just below the ear. The car slowed more, and he kissed her again.

'You're going to block traffic,' she warned, but theirs was the only car on the road.

He kissed her again, this time on the lips. She was

torn between enjoying the sensation and the odd feeling that half the hospital was looking out the blinds at the spectacle they were making.

She gently pushed him away, saying, 'I don't want to end up being one of the "local points of interest" for the next girl you bring here.'

He asked, 'You think I bring other girls here?' and she could not tell if he was serious or not.

A car horn beeped behind them and he resumed the posted thirty-five-mile-an-hour speed limit. Sara knew better than to point out that this was the first time he had driven the speed limit since they had gotten into the car. Something had shifted, but she was not quite sure what. Before she could think of a way to frame the question, he turned onto a side street by the hospital and pulled into a driveway behind a dark blue pickup truck. A pink child's bike was propped against the front porch and a tire swing hung from the tall oak in the yard. She asked, 'This is your mother's house?'

'Last detour.' He gave her a smile that seemed forced. 'I'll be right back,' he said, and got out of the car before she could ask him who lived here.

Sara watched Jeffrey walk up to the front door and knock. He tucked his hands into his pockets and turned back around. She waved, but then realized he probably couldn't see her because of the glare. Jeffrey knocked again, but there was still no answer. He turned back toward the car, shielding the sun out of his eyes and holding up his finger to her, indicating he would just be another minute. She opened the car door to get out as he ran around the back of the house.

Sara surveyed the neighborhood as she waited for him. The street was fairly similar to those in

Avondale, which was not exactly the nicest part of Grant County. The houses looked to have been hastily built to accommodate the soldiers who returned from World War II, ready to start their families and put the war behind them. During the mid-1940s, the area must have been nice, but now it looked run-down. There were a couple of cars on blocks, and a fair number of the yards needed to be trimmed. The paint was peeling on most of the houses, and weeds grew out of the sidewalks. Some of the owners had not yet given up the fight, though, and their immaculate yards and vinyl-sided houses showed meticulous care. The one Jeffrey had parked in front of fell into this second category, with its carefully manicured lawn and well-raked gravel driveway.

Sara went up the drive, passing the truck. A large orange stripe went down the side, with the words 'Auburn Tigers' painted in blue. There was an orange flag with a blue paw print on it swaying by the front door. She noticed the mailbox was painted orange and blue, too. Apparently, someone in the house was a college football fan.

Without warning, a small dog ran up the sidewalk and jumped at her, putting his dirty paws on Sara's skirt. She told him, 'No,' to no avail, then finally knelt down to pet the overly excited animal so he would stop jumping.

The dog barked, and Sara tried not to gag at his breath. She stroked back the fur on its head, thinking she had never seen an uglier animal in her life. Half-way down his back, he had curly hair like a poodle, but the fur on his legs was wiry like a terrier's. The coloring was an ungodly mixture of black, gray, and tan. His eyes bugged out as if someone were squeezing his testicles, even though a quick check proved he didn't have any. The check also revealed he was a she.

Sara stood, trying to brush the paw prints off her skirt. Georgia clay didn't have a thing on Alabama dirt, and nothing short of a long soak would take the stains out.

'Zaftig!' a man called from the driveway, and Sara felt herself blush crimson until she realized the man was not talking to her.

He held a shopping bag in one hand and patted his leg with the other. 'Tig! Come're, girl.' The dog did not leave Sara's side, and the man laughed good-naturedly as he walked across the front yard. He stopped in front of Sara, giving a low whistle as he looked her up and down. 'Darlin', if you're one a them Jehovah's Witnesses, I'm ready to convert.'

The front door banged open, and a dark-haired woman around Sara's age walked outside. 'Don't listen to that fool,' she told Sara, giving her the once-over with considerably less appreciation than the man had showed. 'Sara, right?'

'Uh,' Sara stammered. 'Right.'

'I'm Darnell, but everybody calls me Nell. This'n's my husband, Jerry.'

'Call me Possum,' he said, tipping his orange and blue baseball cap.

Confused, Sara told them, 'Nice to meet you both.'

'Ma'am.' Possum tipped his hat again before heading into the house.

Nell let the dog in, but not Sara. 'So,' she said, leaning against the doorjamb. 'You're Jeffrey's new thing?'

Sara could not tell if she was joking, but she had

had enough of this sort of treatment in Grant. She crossed her arms, resigned. 'I suppose so.'

Nell twisted her lips to the side, still not finished. 'Are you a stewardess or a stripper?'

Sara barked a laugh, but stopped when Nell didn't join in. She squared her shoulders, choosing 'Stripper' because it sounded more exotic.

The woman narrowed her eyes. 'Jeffrey said you work with children.'

Sara tried to think of something witty, but could only come up with 'I use balloon animals in my act.'

'Right.' Nell finally stepped aside. 'They're all in the back.'

Sara walked into the living room of the modest home, which contained more Auburn paraphernalia than was probably legal. Pom-poms and pennant flags draped the fireplace, and a framed jersey with the number seventeen hung over the mantel. Under a glass dome on the coffee table was a small village that must have resembled the university campus. A rack held several college football magazines, and even the lampshade had an orange and blue AU logo painted on it.

Nell led her down a hall toward the back door, but Sara stopped in front of a framed magazine cover. Underneath the *SEC Monthly* banner was a picture of Jeffrey standing at the fifty-yard line. His hair was longer and his mustache dated the picture by about fifteen years. He was wearing a blue jersey and rested his sneaker on a football. The type at the bottom said, 'The Next Big Thing for the Tigers?'

Before she could stop herself, Sara asked, 'He played for Auburn?'

Darnell finally laughed. 'He got you into bed without showing you his Sugar Bowl ring?' she asked, managing to make Sara sound stupid and loose at the same time.

'Hey,' Jeffrey said, coming in a little too late for Sara's liking. He was holding a bottle of beer in his hand. 'I see y'all met.'

Nell said, 'You didn't tell me she was a stripper, Slick.'

'Only weekends,' he said, handing Nell the beer. 'Just until she gets on full-time with the airline.'

Sara tried to catch his eye to tell him she wanted to get the hell out of here, but either Jeffrey had not learned to read her signs in the last few months or he was fully aware of the treatment she was getting and did not mind a bit. His shit-eating grin told her the truth of the matter.

Jeffrey threw his arm around her, dragging her close and kissing her head. It felt more like he was telling her to be a good sport than anything else, and Sara pinched the fire out of the back of his arm to let him know she was not up for that kind of play.

He winced, rubbing his arm. 'Nell, can you give us a minute?'

Nell walked down the hall and went into what was probably the kitchen. Outside the open back door, Sara could see a pool in the yard with another couple sitting around in beach chairs. In the distance, a dog was barking. Possum stood behind a grill with a long fork in his hand, and he waved at them both through the screen door.

Sara said, 'This detour seems a little planned to me.'

'Sorry?'

She kept her voice low, mindful that Nell was probably listening. 'Is this part of the indoctrination for all your new things?'

'My what?'

She indicated the kitchen. 'That's what your friend called me.'

To his credit, he looked annoyed. 'She's just –'

'Thinking I'm one of your sluts?' Sara finished, her throat straining even as she whispered. 'Because that's what she pretty much said, that I'm one of your sluts.'

He tried his smile again. 'Sara, honey –'

'Don't you *dare* call me that, you asshole.'

'I didn't –'

She fought to keep her tone low. 'I don't know who the hell you think you are, dragging me all the way down here below the damn Gnat Line just to embarrass me, but I don't appreciate it and you've got about two seconds to say goodbye to these people, because I'm driving back to Grant right now and I don't give a damn whether you're in the car or not.'

About three seconds passed before he burst into laughter. 'My God,' he said. 'That's more than you've said to me the entire trip.'

Sara was so furious that she punched him in the shoulder as hard as she could.

'Ow,' he said, rubbing the spot.

'Mr. Big Football Player can't take a hit?' She punched him again. 'Why didn't you tell me you played football?'

'I thought everybody knew.'

'How would I know that?' she demanded. 'Rhonda at the bank?' He grabbed her hand before she could punch him again. 'That slut at the sign shop?' She tried to get her hand back but he held her too tightly.

'Honey –' He stopped himself with a grin that said he was humoring her. 'Sara.'

'You think I don't know you've screwed practically every woman in town?'

He took on a wounded look. 'They were just place-holders while I waited for you.'

'You are so full of shit.'

He stepped toward her, reaching out to put his hands on her waist. 'Do you kiss your mama with that mouth?'

She tried to push him away, but he backed her toward the wall. Sara felt the familiar weight of his body press into her, but all she could think about was the fact that his friends were right outside the door watching. She expected him to give her a passionate kiss or make some other show of his manly prowess, followed by a victory lap around the pool and a high-five from Possum, but all he did was kiss her forehead and say, 'I haven't been back here in six years.'

She stared at him, mostly because his face was less than two inches away from hers.

Suddenly, the door banged open, and one of the most gorgeous men Sara had seen outside of a fashion magazine sauntered into the house. He was as tall as Jeffrey but with broader shoulders and more swagger.

When he opened his mouth, he spoke with the sexiest Southern drawl Sara had ever heard. 'You too scared to introduce me to your new girl, Slick?'

'Course not,' Jeffrey said, slipping a proprietary arm around Sara's waist. 'Honey, this is Spot. He and Possum were my best friends growing up.'

'Still waiting on this one to finish,' the man said, feigning a punch at Jeffrey. 'And it's Robert now.'

Possum called from outside, 'One 'a y'all fetch me

them burgers from the fridge.'

Robert said, 'Slick, why don't you handle that?' then took Sara by the arm and led her down the hall before Jeffrey could stop them.

Robert opened the screen door for Sara, asking, 'How was your trip over?'

'Good,' she told him, though that was debatable. She cast about for something positive to say. 'My God, what a gorgeous yard.'

Possum beamed. 'Nell loves being outside.'

'It shows,' Sara said, meaning it. Lush flowers bloomed all over the place, spilling out of pots on the deck, climbing up the wooden fence. A huge magnolia tree shaded a hammock at the back of the yard, and several holly trees added contrast to the fence line. Except for the barking dogs next door, the yard was an oasis.

'Whoa,' Robert said, bumping into her as the dog shot past them.

'Tig!' Possum yelled halfheartedly as the dog dove into the pool. She swam a lap across, climbed out, then rolled around in the grass, kicking her legs in the air.

'Man,' Possum said. 'What I wouldn't do for that life.'

The woman sitting by the pool looked over her shoulder. 'She learned everything from Jeffrey.' She indicated the chair beside her. 'Come sit by me, Sara. I'm not as horrible as Nell.'

Sara gladly took the offer.

'Jessie,' the woman introduced herself. She indicated Robert with a lazy wave of her hand. 'That specimen's my husband.' She pronounced the word 'huzz-bun,' managing with her tone to make it sound slightly pornographic.

Sara offered, 'He seems nice.'

'They all do at first,' she said offhandedly. 'How long have you known Slick?'

'Not long,' Sara confessed, wondering if everyone here had a nickname. She was getting the distinct impression that Jessie was probably worse than Nell. She was just more polite about it. Judging by the woman's breath, a liberal dose of alcohol was responsible for her mellow tone.

'They're all a tight little group,' Jessie commented, leaning over to pick up a glass of wine. 'I'm new in town, which means I've only been here twenty years. I moved from LA during my freshman year.'

Sara guessed from her accent she meant Lower Alabama.

'Robert's a cop, just like Jeffrey. Isn't that nice? I call 'em Mutt and Jeff, only Jeffrey hates being called Jeff.' She took a healthy swallow of wine. 'Possum runs the store over by the Tasty Dog. You should meet his and Nell's children, especially the oldest. He's a beautiful little boy. Children are such a joy to have around. Isn't that right, Bob?'

'What's that, sugar?' Robert asked, though Sara was certain he had heard her.

Nell sat down beside Sara, handing her a bottle of beer. 'Peace offering,' she said.

Sara took it, though beer had always tasted like swill to her. She forced herself to make an effort, saying, 'You've got a beautiful yard.'

Nell inhaled deeply, then exhaled, 'The azaleas bloomed and went away quicker than spit. Neighbor's never home to take care of his dogs so they bark all day. I can't get rid of the fire ants by the hammock and Jared keeps coming in with poison ivy, but for the life of me, I can't figure out where he's getting it.' She paused for another breath. 'But thank you. I try.'

Sara turned to include Jessie in the conversation, but the other woman's eyes were closed.

'She's probably passed out.' Nell fanned herself with her hand. 'God, I was such a bitch to you.'

Sara did not argue.

'I'm not normally so testy. If Jessie was awake, she'd tell you otherwise, but you can't trust a woman who drinks a whole bottle of wine before four in the afternoon, and I'm not just talking on Sundays.' She swatted a fly. 'She tell you about being new here?'

Sara nodded, trying to keep up.

'You should be glad she passed out. Couple'a more minutes she'd be telling you how she always depends on the kindness of strangers.'

Sara took a sip of beer.

'Slick hasn't been back here in forever. Left town like he was running through hell with gasoline britches on.' She paused. 'I guess I was mad at him and took it out on you.' She put her hand on Sara's chair. 'What I'm saying is I'm sorry I showed my ass.'

'Thank you for apologizing.'

'I near about cracked up when you said that about the balloon animals.' She laughed. 'He told me you were a doctor, but I didn't believe him.'

'Pediatrician,' Sara confirmed.

Nell sat back in the chair. 'You have to be smart to get into medical school, right?'

'Pretty much.'

She nodded appreciatively. 'Then I'll assume you know what you're doing with Jeffrey.'

'Thank you,' Sara told her, and meant it. 'You're the first person I've met who's said that.'

Nell turned serious, looking at Sara with something like pity. 'Don't be surprised if I'm the last.'

SIX

During the five hours she spent at Nell's, Sara found out more about Jeffrey Tolliver than she had in three months of dating him. Jeffrey's mother was a confirmed alcoholic and his father was serving time in prison for something no one was very specific about. Jeffrey had dropped out of Auburn two classes away from graduating and joined the police force without telling anybody why. He was an excellent dancer and he hated lima beans. He was definitely not the marrying kind, but Sara did not need Nell to tell her this. Jeffrey radiated the words 'confirmed bachelor.'

Considering Nell had managed to mumble most of these details under her breath during a particularly competitive game of Trivial Pursuit, Sara was only privy to the headlines and none of the details behind them. It was pitch dark by the time they left the group, and as Sara and Jeffrey walked down the street toward his mother's house, she tried to think of a way to find out more.

She settled on 'So, what does your mother do?'

'Different things,' he said, not offering anything else.

'And your dad?'

He switched her suitcase to his other hand and

wrapped his arm around her. 'You seem like you had a good time tonight.'

'Nell's just full of insight.'

'She likes the sound of her own voice.' He slid his hand to her hip. 'I wouldn't believe everything she says.'

'Why is that?'

His hand slid lower as he nuzzled her neck. 'You smell good.'

She got the message, but did not exactly change the subject. 'Are you sure your mother won't mind us staying over?'

'I called her from Nell's a few hours ago,' Jeffrey said. 'You remember when Nell was telling you my life story?' He gave her a look that said he knew exactly what had been going on with Nell, though Sara had to assume Jeffrey would not have taken her to meet his friends without knowing exactly what would happen.

She decided to call him on it. 'This is a pretty cheap way for me to find out all about your life without you having to say a word.'

'I told you, I wouldn't believe everything Nell has to say.'

'She's known you since you were both six.'

'She's not exactly my biggest fan.'

Sara finally picked up on the tension between them. 'Don't tell me you dated her, too?'

He didn't answer, which she took for an affirmation. 'It's right here,' he said, indicating a house with a beat-up Chevy Impala parked in the driveway. Even though Jeffrey had called ahead, his mother hadn't bothered to leave on any lights for them. The house was completely dark.

Sara hesitated. 'Shouldn't we stay in a hotel?'

He laughed, helping her as her foot caught on some loose gravel. 'There aren't any hotels here except the one behind the bar that truck drivers rent by the hour.'

'Sounds romantic.'

'Maybe for some of them,' he suggested, leading her up the front steps. Even in the darkness, Sara could tell the house was one of the ones that had been allowed to fall into disrepair. Jeffrey warned her, 'Watch that board,' as he slid his hand along the top of the doorframe.

'She locks her door?'

'We were robbed when I was twelve,' he explained, jiggling the key in the lock. 'She's lived in fear ever since.' The door stuck at the bottom and he used his foot to push it open. 'Welcome.'

The smell of nicotine and alcohol was overwhelming, and Sara was glad the darkness hid her expression. The house was stifling and she could not imagine spending the night, let alone living here.

'It's okay,' he said, indicating she should go in.

She lowered her voice, 'Shouldn't we be quiet?'

'She can sleep through a hurricane,' Jeffrey said, closing the door behind him. He locked it with the key, then, judging from the sound, dropped the key into a glass bowl.

Sara felt his hand on her elbow. 'Back this way,' he said, walking close behind her. She took about four steps through the front room before she felt the dining room table in front of her. Three more steps and Sara was in a small hallway, where a nightlight revealed a bathroom in front of her and two closed doors on either side. He opened the door on the right and followed her through, closing the door again before he turned on the light.

'Oh,' Sara said, blinking at the small room. A twin bed with green sheets and no blanket was pushed into the corner under a window. Posters of half-naked women were taped around the walls, with Farrah Fawcett given a place of prominence over the bed. The closet door was the only departure from the decorating scheme: a poster showed a cherry red convertible Mustang with an exaggerated blonde leaning over the hood – probably because the weight of her enhanced breasts prevented her from standing up straight.

'Lovely,' Sara managed, wondering how bad the hotel was.

Jeffrey seemed embarrassed for the first time since she had met him. 'My mother hasn't changed things much since I left.'

'I can see that,' she said. Still, part of Sara was intrigued. As a teenager, her parents had made it clear that boys' rooms were off-limits and Sara had therefore missed the experience. While the Farrah Fawcett poster was predictable, there was something else to the room, some sort of essence. The smell of cigarette smoke and bourbon did not exist here. Testosterone and sweat had muscled it out.

Jeffrey put her suitcase flat on the floor and unzipped it for her. 'I know it's not what you're used to,' he said, still sounding embarrassed. She tried to catch his eye, but he was busy sorting through his duffel bag. She realized from his posture that he was ashamed of the house and what she must be thinking about him for growing up here. The room looked different in light of this, and Sara noticed how neatly everything had been arranged and the fact that the posters were hung equidistant, as if he had used a ruler. His house back in Grant County reflected this need for orderliness. Sara had only been there a few times, but from what she had seen, he kept everything exactly in its place.

'It's fine,' she assured him.

'Yeah,' he said, though not in agreement. He found his toothbrush. 'I'll be right back.'

Sara watched him leave, pulling the door shut quietly behind him. She took advantage of the situation and quickly changed into her pajamas, all the while keeping her eye on the door in case his mother walked in. Nell had not sounded exactly complimentary when she had talked about May Tolliver, and Sara did not want to meet the woman with her pants down.

Sara sat on the floor and went through her suitcase, looking for her hairbrush. She found it wrapped up in a pair of shorts and managed to remove her hair clip without tearing out too much of her curly, tangled hair. She looked around the room as she brushed her hair, taking in the posters and the various items Jeffrey had collected throughout his childhood. On the windowsill were several dried bones that had once been in a small animal. The bedside table, which looked homemade, had a small lamp and a green bowl with a handful of loose change. Track ribbons were scattered on a bulletin board, and a milk crate held cassette tapes with song titles typewritten neatly across the labels. Across from where she sat was a makeshift bookshelf of two-by-fours and bricks, stacked end to end with books. Where Sara had been expecting comic books and the occasional Hardy Boys, she found thick tomes with titles such as *Strategic Battles of the Civil War* and *The Socio-Political Ramifications of Reconstruction in the Rural South.*

She put down the brush and picked up the least intimidating-looking textbook. Flipping to the front, she found Jeffrey's name, followed by a date and course information. Thumbing through the pages, she saw where he had taken copious notes in the margins, underlining and highlighting passages that were of interest. Sara was slightly shocked to realize that she was completely unfamiliar with Jeffrey's handwriting. He had never left her notes or written lists in her presence. Contrary to her own cramped printing, he wrote in a beautiful, flowing script, the kind they no longer taught in school. His *w*'s were impeccable, transitioning neatly into adjoining vowels. The loops on his *g*'s were all the same identical pattern, as if he had used a stencil to make them. He even wrote in a straight line, not diagonally like most people did without a baseline to follow.

She traced her finger along his notations, feeling the indentation the pencil had made in the page. The words seemed almost engraved, as if he had gripped the pencil too tightly.

'What are you doing?'

Sara felt a flicker of guilt, as if she had been caught reading his diary instead of a textbook from long ago. 'The Civil War?'

He kneeled beside her, taking the book. 'I majored in American History.'

'You're just full of surprises, Slick.'

He winced at the name as he slid the book back into place, lining it up carefully so that it was flush with the others. A thin line of dust marked the exact spot. He pulled out a slim leather-bound volume. Gold letters stamped the cover, saying, simply, LETTERS.

'Soldiers wrote these to their sweethearts back

home,' Jeffrey said, thumbing through the fragile-looking book, turning to a page he must have known from heart. He cleared his throat and read, '"My darling. Night comes and I lay awake, wondering at the character of the man I have become. I look at the velvet sky and wonder if you look up on these same stars, and pray that your mind holds on to the image of the man I was to you. I pray that you still see me."'

Jeffrey stared at the words, a smile at his lips like he shared something secret with the book. He read the way he made love: deliberately, passionately, eloquently. Sara wanted him to continue, to lull her to sleep with the deep cadence of his voice, but he broke the spell with a heavy sigh.

'Anyway.' He tucked the book back into place, saying, 'I should have sold these back when the classes ended, but I didn't have the heart.'

She wanted to ask him to continue, but said, 'I kept some of mine, too.'

He sat down behind Sara, his legs on either side of her. 'I couldn't afford to.'

'I wasn't exactly rich,' she told him, feeling defensive. 'My father's a plumber.'

'Who owns half the town.'

Sara did not comment, hoping he would drop it. Eddie Linton had invested well in real estate down by the college, which Jeffrey had found out on a couple of landlord calls about soon-to-be-evicted noisy tenants. She supposed by Jeffrey's standards the Linton family was wealthy, but Sara and Tessa had grown up with the impression that they should never spend more money than what they had in their pockets – which was never much.

Jeffrey said, 'I guess Nell told you about my dad.'

'A little.'

His laugh had a harsh edge to it. 'Jimmy Tolliver was a small-time crook who thought he was walking into a big score. Two men were shot and killed robbing that bank, and now he's locked up with no chance of parole.' Jeffrey picked up the hairbrush. 'You talk to anybody in town, they'll tell you I'm just as bad as he is.'

'I seriously doubt that,' Sara countered. She had worked with Jeffrey for a while now, and knew that he always went out of his way to do the right thing. His integrity was one of the main things that had attracted her to him.

He said, 'I got into trouble a lot when I was a kid.'

'Most boys do.'

'Not with the police,' he countered, and she did not know what to say. He couldn't have been that bad or there was no police force in the country that would have accepted him, let alone given him the keys to the station house.

He added, 'I imagine Nell gave you an earful about my mother.'

Sara did not answer.

He started to brush her hair. 'Is that why you sucked at Trivial Pursuit? You were too busy trying to follow what Nell was saying?'

'I've never been good at board games.'

'What about other games?'

She closed her eyes, enjoying the stroking bristles. 'I beat you at tennis,' she reminded him.

'I let you,' he said, though she knew he had nearly killed himself trying to win.

Jeffrey pulled back her hair and gently kissed her neck.

'We could have a rematch?' she suggested.

He wrapped his arms around her, pulling her

closer. He did something with his tongue that made her sink back into him without thinking.

She tried to sit up but he would not let her. She whispered, 'Your mother is in the next room.'

'The toilet's in the next room,' he told her, slipping his hands under her shirt.

'Jeff —' She gasped as his hand dipped below her pajama bottoms. She stopped him before he could go any farther.

Jeffrey said, 'Trust me, she can sleep through anything.'

'That's not the point.'

'I locked the door.'

'Why did you lock it if she can sleep through anything?'

He growled at her much the way he had growled over his high school teacher. 'Do you know how many nights I laid awake in this very room when I was a kid, wishing I had a beautiful woman in here with me?'

'I seriously doubt I'm the first woman you've had here.'

'Here?' he asked, indicating the floor.

She twisted around so she could see him. 'Do you think that's some kind of aphrodisiac, telling me how many women you've had in your bedroom?'

He scooted a few inches across the floor, dragging her with him. 'You're the first one I've ever had *here*.'

She gave an exaggerated sigh. 'Finally, a way to distinguish myself.'

'Stop that,' he said, suddenly serious.

'Or what?' she teased.

'I'm not playing around.'

'According to what I've heard —'

'I mean it, Sara. I'm not having fun.'

She stared at him, not following.

'What you said to your mother,' he told her, tucking a strand of hair behind her ear. 'I'm not just having fun with you.' He paused before looking away from her, staring at the bookshelf. 'I know that's what you're doing, but I'm not, and I want you to stop saying stuff like that.'

Every warning Sara had heard over the last few months came flooding into her brain, and she bit back the raging impulse to throw her arms around him and declare her love. Instinctively, she knew that part of the reason Jeffrey was saying this to her now was because he had no idea how she felt. Sara was not foolish enough to tell him.

Her silence obviously unnerved him. She saw his jaw work, and he stared somewhere over her shoulder.

Sara tried to face him, but he would not look at her. She traced her finger along his lips, smiling as she realized he had shaved for her. His skin was smooth, and she smelled his aftershave along with something like oatmeal.

He said, 'Tell me how you feel.'

Sara could not trust herself to answer. She kissed his jaw, then his neck. When he did not respond, she kissed the palm of his hand, knowing better than to tell him that was exactly where he held her.

Jeffrey put his hands on either side of her face, his eyes intense and unreadable. He gave her a long, sensual kiss as he pushed her back, and Sara felt herself melt to the floor. He cupped her breasts, using his tongue to bring out chills along her skin. Slowly, he started to work his way down, his breath a feathery kiss across her belly, then lower. He put his tongue inside of her, and Sara felt a momentary weightlessness as everything in her body focused on that one spot. She ran her fingers through his hair, pulling him up toward her, making him stop.

His voice was a hoarse whisper. 'What?'

She drew him closer, kissing him, tasting herself in his mouth. Nothing was rushed, but Sara felt the need for urgency as she fumbled with the zip on his jeans. He tried to help, but Sara told him, 'No,' relishing the weight of him in her hand.

'Inside me,' she said, biting his ear until a guttural sound caught in his throat. 'I want you inside me.'

'Christ,' he whispered, his body shaking as he tried to hold himself back. He reached for his pocket, trying to find a condom, but she pulled his attention sharply back to focus, guiding him inside her.

She arched up as he entered her. At first, he moved slowly, almost painfully so, until Sara's entire body was tense as a violin string. The muscles along his back were equally taut, and she could not help digging her nails in as she tried to pull him in deeper. Jeffrey kept the rhythm slow, watching her every move, tuning his body to hers so that several times she was taken to the edge, only to be gently brought back. Finally the rhythm increased, his hips grinding into hers, the weight of his body pressing her to the limit until the release forced her head back, her mouth open. He kissed her, stifling the sounds she made, even as his own body shuddered against hers.

'Sara,' he breathed into her ear, finally letting himself go.

She held him inside her, and he started kissing her again, slow and sensual, his hand stroking the side of her face like a cat. Her body pulsed with after-shocks, and she slid her arms around him, holding him close, kissing his lips, his face, his eyelids, until he finally rolled to his side, resting his weight on his elbow.

She let out a short breath, feeling her body slowly come down from the high. Her head was still swimming and she could not keep her eyes open no matter how hard she tried.

He stroked his fingers along her temple, touching her eyelids, her cheeks. 'I love the way your skin feels,' he said, letting his hand slide down her body.

She rested her hand on his, letting out a content sigh. She could stay like this all night – maybe even for the rest of her life. She felt closer to Jeffrey now than she had ever felt with a man in her life. Sara knew that she should be scared, should try to hold part of herself back, but right now all she could think to do was lie there and let him do whatever he liked.

His fingers found the scar on her left side, and he said, 'Tell me about this.'

Sara's mind reeled with white-hot panic, and she forced herself not to jerk away from him. 'Appendix,' she said, though the injury had come from a hunting knife.

He opened his mouth, and she was sure he would ask how she could be a doctor and not know that the appendix was on the right side, but what he said was, 'Did it burst?'

She nodded, hoping that would suffice. Lying was not a normal habit of Sara's, and she knew better than to invent a complicated story.

'How old were you?'

She shrugged, watching him watch his finger trace along the scar. The edge was jagged, far from the precision slice of a surgeon's scalpel. A serrated blade had made the cut as the knife was buried nearly to the hilt in her side.

'It's kind of sexy,' he told her, leaning down to kiss it.

Sara put her hand to the back of his head, staring up at the ceiling as the enormity of the lie began to sink in. This was just the beginning. If she ever wanted any kind of future with Jeffrey, she should tell him now before it was too late.

He brushed his lips across hers. 'I thought we'd get out early tomorrow.'

Her mouth opened, but instead of telling him the truth, she said, 'You don't want to say goodbye to your friends?'

He shrugged. 'We can call them when we get to Florida.'

'Crap.' Sara sat up, looking for a clock. 'What time is it?'

He tried to pull her back but Sara was too fast. She rifled through her suitcase, asking, 'Where's my watch?'

He folded his hands behind his head. 'Women don't need to wear watches.'

'Why is that?'

He gave a smug, deeply satisfied smile. 'There's a clock on the stove.'

'Very funny,' she said, throwing her brush at him. He caught it with one hand. 'I told my mother I'd call as soon as we got to Florida.'

'So call her tomorrow.'

Sara found her watch, cursing under her breath. 'It's past midnight. She'll be worried.'

'There's a phone in the kitchen.'

Her underwear was still wrapped around her ankle from where she had not quite managed to kick it off. Sara tried to look as graceful as possible as she pulled them back on, followed by her pajama bottoms.

'Hey,' he said.

She looked up, but he shook his head, indicating he had changed his mind.

She buttoned her shirt as she walked toward the door. Her hand was on the knob before she realized, 'It doesn't have a lock.'

He feigned surprise. 'Is that so?'

Sara walked into the hall and pulled the door to behind her. She felt her way along the wall, stopping when she remembered the dining room table. The nightlight did not illuminate much this far from the bathroom, and Sara used her hands to feel her way toward the kitchen. Outside the room, the smell of nicotine was even stronger than she had remembered. By sheer luck, she found the telephone on the wall by the refrigerator.

She dialed her parents' house collect, whispering her name when the operator asked, hoping she would not wake up Jeffrey's mother. The call was put through and the phone rang once before her father picked up.

'Sara?' Eddie said, his voice like a croak.

She leaned against the counter, relieved to hear him. 'Hey, Daddy.'

'Where the hell are you?'

'We stopped in Sylacauga.'

'What the hell is that?'

She started to explain, but he would not let her.

'It's past midnight,' he said, his tone sharp now that he realized she was okay. 'What the hell have you been doing? Your mother and I have been worried sick.'

She heard Cathy murmur something in the background, and Eddie said, 'I don't want to hear that bastard's name. She never used to call late before him.'

Sara braced herself for a tirade, but her mother managed to wrestle the phone from her father before he could get another word out.

'Baby?' Cathy sounded equally worried, and Sara felt guilty for how she had spent the last two hours when she could have taken two minutes to call her parents and let them know she was okay.

'I'm sorry I didn't call before,' Sara told her. 'We stopped in Sylacauga.'

'And that is?'

'A town,' Sara said, still not sure she was pronouncing it correctly. 'It's where Jeffrey grew up.'

'Oh,' Cathy said. Sara waited for more, but all her mother said was, 'Are you okay?'

'Yes,' Sara assured her. 'We had a nice time with his friends. They all went to school together. It's just like home, only smaller.'

'Is that so?'

Sara tried to decipher her tone, but could not. 'We're at his mother's now. I haven't met her yet, but I'm sure she's nice, too.'

'Well, let us know when you get to Florida tomorrow if you have the time.'

'Okay,' Sara answered, still unable to read her mother's tone. She wanted to tell her what had happened, what Jeffrey had said, but she did not have the courage. What's more, she did not want to be called a fool.

Cathy seemed to read nothing into Sara's hesitation. She said, 'Good night, then.'

Sara wished her the same, and hung up the phone before her father could get back on the line. She pressed her head back against the kitchen cabinet, wondering if she should call them again. As much as she hated her mother being in her business, Sara valued Cathy's opinion. Too much was happening right now. She needed to talk to someone about it.

A loud bump came from the dining room as someone fell against the table and a woman's voice growled a curse.

'Hello?' Sara said, trying not to surprise Jeffrey's mother.

'I know you're there,' she said, her voice raspy and cold. 'Jesus Christ,' she mumbled to herself, opening the refrigerator door. In the light, Sara saw a bent-over old woman with salt-and-pepper hair. Her face was wrinkled far beyond her years, and every line in her mouth seemed devoted to smoking a cigarette. She held one there now, ash hanging off the end.

May Tolliver pounded a bottle of gin onto the counter, took a long drag from her cigarette, then turned her attention on Sara. 'What do you do?' she asked, then gave a nasty chuckle. 'That is, other than fuck my son?'

Sara was so taken aback she began to stutter. 'I . . . I . . . d-don't . . .'

'Fancy doctor,' she said. 'Isn't that right?' The laugh came again, this time even nastier. 'He'll bring you down a peg or two. You think you're the first one? You think you're special?'

'I –'

'Don't lie to me,' the old woman barked. 'I can smell him on your cunt from here.'

Seconds later, Sara was in the street. She could not recall finding the key or opening the front door or even leaving the house. The only thing she knew was that she had to put as much distance between herself and Jeffrey's mother as she could. Never in her life had another woman spoken to her that way. Sara's face burned from the shame of it, and when she finally stopped under a street lamp to catch her breath, she found that tears were streaming down her cheeks.

'Shit,' she hissed as she turned in a full circle, trying to get her bearings. She had taken a left turn at least, but beyond that, Sara was completely unsure of her surroundings. She could not even recall the name of Jeffrey's street, let alone remember what his house looked like. A dog barked as she passed a yellow house with a white picket fence, and Sara felt a chill as she realized that she did not recognize the dog or the fence. To make matters worse, her feet were burning from the hot asphalt and mosquitoes had come out in force to feast on the idiot who was walking around alone, wearing nothing but a thin pair of cotton pajamas, in the middle of the night. She did not know why she cared about finding the house. Even if she made it back, Sara would sleep in the street before she went back in. Her only hope was to backtrack from Jeffrey's to find Nell and Possum's house. There was a magnetic key safe on the undercarriage of the BMW. Jeffrey could find his own ride to Grant. Sara did not care if she ever saw her clothes or suitcase again.

Suddenly, a bloodcurdling scream cut through the night. Sara stopped mid-stride, tension filling the air like molasses. A car backfire sounded like gunshot, and adrenaline tensed every muscle in her body. In the distance, she could see a tall figure moving quickly toward her, and instinctively Sara turned, running away as fast as she could. Heavy footsteps pounded behind her, and she pumped her arms, her lungs nearly exploding in her chest as she pushed herself to get away.

'Sara,' Jeffrey called, his fingertips brushing

against her back. She stopped so quickly that he smacked into her, knocking them both down. He managed to cushion the fall with his body, but her elbow was jarred against the pavement.

'What is wrong with you?' he demanded, jerking her up by the arm. He slapped grit off the side of her pajama leg. 'Did you scream?'

'Of course not,' she snapped, suddenly angrier with him than she had ever imagined herself capable. Why had he brought her here? What did he hope to accomplish?

'Just calm down,' he said, reaching out at if to soothe her.

She slapped away his hand. 'Don't touch me' was all she could say before the car backfired again. Though this time, Sara knew it was not a car. She had been to the firing range often enough to know the sound of a weapon being discharged.

Jeffrey cocked his head to the side as he tried to figure out from which direction the sound had come. Again, there was a single gunshot, and he turned away from her, saying, 'Stay here,' as he bolted down the road toward the yellow house with the picket fence.

Sara followed as best she could, going around the fence that Jeffrey had hurdled, using a worn path in someone's garden to get to the backyard of the yellow house. There was a bright flash of light as Jeffrey kicked in the back door, followed by another scream. He ran out seconds later, and all the lights seemed to turn on in the house at once.

'Sara!' Jeffrey yelled, waving her in. 'Hurry!'

She jogged toward him, feeling a sharp sting in the arch of her foot as she crossed the grass. There were pine needles and cones in the yard, and she tried to step as carefully as she could without slowing down.

Jeffrey grabbed her arm and pulled her the rest of the way into the house. The layout was similar to Possum's, with a long hallway down the center and the bedrooms on the right.

'Down there,' Jeffrey said, pushing her toward the hall. He picked up the kitchen phone, telling her, 'I'll call the police.'

Shock overcame Sara for a moment as she walked into the master bedroom.

The ceiling fan wobbled out of balance overhead, the blades making an awkward chopping sound. Jessie stood beside an open window, her mouth moving but no noise coming out. A shirtless man lay facedown on the floor by the bed. The right side of his head was blown off. Streaks of blood led to a short-nosed gun that looked as if it had been kicked away from the area near his left hand.

'My God,' Sara breathed. Blood sprayed the area by the bed in a fine mist, spattering parts of the ceiling and the light on the fan. A chunk of skull and scalp was hanging from the bedside table; what looked like a section of earlobe was stuck to the front of the drawer.

Despite the horrific scene in front of her, Sara felt her medical training kick in. She went to the man, pressing her fingers against his neck, trying to find a pulse. She checked his carotids and found nothing, her fingers sticking to the skin when she pulled them away. There was a sheen of sweat on the body. The sickly sweet smell of vanilla filled the air.

'Is he dead?'

Sara spun around at the question.

Robert stood behind the bedroom door. He was partially bent over, leaning against the wall for support. His left hand covered a wound in his side, blood seeping out between his fingers. His right hand held a gun that was pointed toward the dead man.

Sara told Jessie, 'Get me some towels,' but the woman did not move.

'Are you okay?' Sara asked, keeping her distance from Robert. He still held the gun at his side and there was a glassy look to his eyes, like he did not know where he was.

Jeffrey entered, assessing the scene with a quick glance. 'Robert?' he said, taking a few steps toward his friend. The other man blinked, then seemed to recognize Jeffrey.

Jeffrey indicated the gun. 'Why don't you give me that, man?'

His hand shook as he handed the weapon to Jeffrey muzzle first. Jeffrey engaged the safety and tucked it into the waistband of his jeans.

Sara told Robert, 'I need to take off your shirt, okay?'

He looked at her with a puzzled expression. 'Is he dead?'

'Why don't you sit down?' she suggested, but he shook his head, leaning back against the wall again. He was a tall man and very muscular. Even in his undershirt and boxer shorts, he looked like someone who was not used to taking orders.

Jeffrey caught Sara's eye before asking, 'What happened, Bobby?'

Robert's mouth worked, as if he had difficulty speaking. 'He's dead, isn't he?'

Jeffrey stood between his friend and the body. 'What happened?'

Jessie spoke in a rush, pointing to the window. 'Here,' she said. 'He came in through here.'

Jeffrey walked along the periphery of the room, peering though the open window without touching it. He said, 'The screen's off.'

Robert hissed with pain as Sara peeled back the shirt. Still, he helped her lift it over his head so she could see the full extent of the damage. He cursed between his teeth, gripping his shirt in his hand as she tentatively pressed the wound. Blood dribbled steadily from the small hole in his side into the waistband of his boxer shorts, but he put his shirt over the area to staunch the blood before Sara could properly examine the wound. She could see an exit wound higher up in his back before he turned his body away from her. The bullet was lodged in the wall directly behind him, red pinpricks of blood forming a circle around the hole.

'Bob,' Jeffrey said, his tone sharp. 'Come on, man. What happened?'

'I don't know,' Robert said, practically grinding his shirt into the wound. 'He just . . .'

Jessie interrupted, 'He shot Bobby.'

'He shot you?' Jeffrey repeated, obviously trying to get the story from Robert. There was a surprising underlayer of anger to his tone as he looked around the room, probably trying to reconstruct the scene in his head.

Jeffrey pointed to a bullet hole in the wall on the far side of the bed. 'Is this from his gun or yours?'

'His,' Jessie said in a high-pitched voice. From the way she was acting, Sara guessed the other woman was talking loudly to try to hide the fact that she was stoned out of her mind. She swayed back and forth like a pendulum, her pupils wide enough to blind her in direct sunlight.

Jeffrey hushed Jessie with a look. 'Robert, tell me what happened.'

Robert shook his head, holding his hand tightly to his wounded side.

Jeffrey demanded, 'Goddammit, Robert, let's get your story straight before somebody puts it on paper.'

Sara tried to help, saying, 'Just tell us what happened.'

'Bob?' Jeffrey prodded, his anger still palpable.

Sara tried to be gentle, telling Robert, 'This would be easier if you sat down.'

'It'd be easier if he fucking talked,' Jeffrey yelled.

Robert looked at his wife, his mouth a straight line. He shook his head, and Sara thought she saw tears in his eyes. For her part, Jessie just stood there, slightly swaying, her robe pulled around her as if to stop a chill. She probably would not even realize how close they had both come to death until the morning.

'He came in through the window,' Robert finally told them. 'He put a gun on Jess. A gun to her head.'

Jessie's expression as he said this was unreadable. Even from this distance, Sara could see that the other woman was having difficulty following the story. At Jessie's feet were several opened prescription bottles that had probably fallen from the bedside table. Blood splotched the triangular-shaped white pills. Sara could see where her footprints had smeared into the thick pile of the carpet. Jessie had run past the body on the way to the window. Sara wondered what she had been thinking. Was she trying to escape while her husband fought for his life?

Jeffrey asked, 'What happened next?'

'Jessie screamed, and I pushed . . .' Robert glanced at the dead man on the floor. 'I pushed him back and he fell . . . and then he shot at me – shot me – and I . . .' He stopped, trying to control the emotion that obviously wanted to come.

'There were three shots,' Sara remembered. She looked around the room, trying to reconcile what she had heard in the street with the story he told.

Robert stared at the dead man. 'Are you sure he's gone?'

'Yes,' she told him, knowing that lying would serve no purpose.

'Here?' Jeffrey said, obviously trying to distract Robert from the grim truth. He pointed to the bullet hole by the bed. 'He missed the first time?'

Robert made a visible swallow. Sara could see a bead of sweat roll down his neck when he answered, 'Yeah.'

'He came in through the window,' Jeffrey began. 'He put a gun to Jessie's head.' He looked at Jessie for confirmation, and she nodded quickly. 'You pushed him off the bed and he shot at you. You got your gun then. Right?' Robert gave a curt nod, but Jeffrey was not finished. 'You keep your piece where? The closet? In the drawer?' He waited, but again Robert was reluctant. 'Where do you keep your piece?'

Jessie opened her mouth, but closed it when Robert pointed to the closed armoire opposite the bed, saying, 'There,' before Jeffrey could repeat himself.

'You got your gun,' Jeffrey said, opening the armoire door. A shirt fell out and he replaced it on the pile. Over his shoulder, Sara could see there was a plastic-molded gun safe on the top shelf. 'You keep your backup in here, too?'

He shook his head. 'The living room.'

'All right.' Jeffrey rested his hand on the open door. 'You went for your gun. He shot you then?'

'Yes,' Robert nodded, though he did not sound convinced. His voice was stronger when he added, 'And then I shot him.'

Jeffrey turned back to the scene, nodding his head as if he was having a conversation with himself, working everything out. He walked over to the window again and looked out. Sara watched him do all of this, shocked. Not only had Jeffrey changed the crime scene, now he was helping Robert concoct a plausible story for how this had all happened.

Jessie cleared her throat, and her voice shook when she asked Sara, 'Is he going to be okay?'

Sara took a moment to realize Jessie was talking to her. She was still focused on Jeffrey, wondering what he would do next. He'd had a few minutes alone with Robert and Jessie before he called Sara into the house. What had he done during that time? What had they worked out?

'Sara?' Jessie prompted.

Sara made herself concentrate on what she could control, asking Robert, 'Can I look?'

He moved his hand away from the bullet wound and Sara resumed the examination. His shirt had smeared the blood, but she thought she could make out a V-shaped sear pattern just below the opening.

She tried to wipe away the blood, but Robert put his hand back over the wound, saying, 'I'm all right.'

'I should check –'

He interrupted her. 'I'm fine.'

Sara tried to hold his gaze, but he looked away. She said, 'Maybe you should sit down until the ambulance gets here.'

Jeffrey asked, 'Is it bad?'

'It's okay,' Robert answered for her, leaning back against the wall again. He told Sara, 'Thank you.'

'Sara?' Jeffrey asked.

She shrugged, not knowing what to say. In the distance, she heard the wail of a siren. Jessie crossed her arms over her chest with a shudder. Sara wanted to see that shirt, wanted to see if the material was burned in the same pattern as Robert's skin, but he held it tightly in his fist, pressing it into the wound.

Sara had been a coroner for only two years, but the type of marking she thought she had seen was textbook quality. Even a rookie cop two days on the job would know what it meant.

The gun had been fired at contact range.

SEVEN

Lena stood in the front of Burgess's Cleaners, looking across Main Street at the police station. The tinted glass door was too dark to see anything inside, but still she stared as if she could see into the building, knew exactly what was happening. Another shot had been fired thirty minutes ago. Of the two cops missing at the start of this, only Mike Dugdale had checked in. Marilyn Edwards was still missing and Frank said he thought the attractive young police officer had been in the squad room at the start of the attack. Everyone from the Grant force was walking around like the living dead. All Lena could think was that if she had gone into work a few minutes earlier, she might have been able to do something. She might have been able to save Jeffrey. Right now, she wanted to be in that building so bad that she could taste it.

She turned around, watching Nick and Frank talking by the map table. The GBI agents were milling around the coffee machine, voices low as they waited for orders. Pat Morris talked with Molly Stoddard, and Lena wondered if Pat had been one of Sara's patients. He was young enough.

'The hell you say,' Frank told Nick, his voice loud enough to be heard over the activity. Everyone in the room looked up.

Nick indicated old man Burgess's office. 'In here.'

They both went into the small, windowless room, shutting the door behind them. The tension they stirred up was still in the room, and a few people went to the back of the cleaners, probably to go outside to smoke and talk about the outburst.

Lena took out her cell phone and waited for it to power up. It chirped twice, indicating she had messages waiting. She debated who to call, Nan or Ethan. Her uncle Hank briefly entered her mind, but considering their conversation that morning during which he practically begged her to lean on his shoulder, calling him now seemed like giving in, and Lena was not about to do that. She hated the thought of needing people almost as much as she hated having to reach out to them. In the end, she turned off the phone and tucked it back into her pocket, wondering why she had turned the damn thing on in the first place.

Frank came up beside her. His breath was sour when he asked, 'Tactical's on the roof?'

Lena pointed at the building by the station. 'Two up there that I can see,' she said, indicating the black-clad men lying on their stomachs with high-powered rifles.

'Twenty more people from Nick's office just showed up,' he told her.

'What for?'

'Stand around with their thumbs up their asses, from what I can see.'

'Frank,' Lena began, feeling a lump rise in her throat. 'Are you sure?'

'What?'

'Jeffrey,' she said, the word sticking.

'I saw it with my own eyes,' Frank said, obviously

upset by the memory. He wiped his nose with his hand as he crossed his arms over his chest. 'He just went down. Sara crawled over to him and . . .' He shook his head. 'Next thing I know, the shooter's putting a gun to her head, telling her to move away.'

Lena chewed her lip, feeling a surprising shock of sympathy for Sara Linton.

'Nick seems to know what he's doing,' Frank said. 'They just cut the power to the whole building.'

'Will the phones work without it?'

'There's a straight line to Marla's desk,' Frank said. 'The Chief put it in when he came here. Never knew why until now.'

Lena nodded, trying not to think about it too much. When he had first taken the job as Chief, Jeffrey had done a lot of things that had seemed unusual at the time but ended up making perfect sense.

Frank said, 'Phone company's made it so they can't call out unless it's to us.'

Lena nodded again, wondering who had known to do all of this. If it was left up to her, they would be storming the building right now, finding the fuckers who had started all of this and finishing it by carrying out their bodies feet-first.

She put her foot on the window ledge, retying her shoe so that Frank would not see the tears welling in her eyes. She hated the fact that she could cry at the drop of a hat now. It made her feel stupid, especially because someone like Frank would take it as a weakness, when the truth was, she was crying because she was a hairsbreadth from full-out rage. How could someone do something like this? How could they come to the station, the last place Lena held as sacred, and do this kind of thing? Jeffrey had been her rudder through all of the shit that had happened to her in the last few years. How could he be taken away from her now, when she was getting her life back?

Frank muttered, 'Goddamn media's already trying to get in.'

'What?' she asked, hiding a sniff.

'Media,' he said. 'They're trying to get helicopters down here to film it.'

'The station's within the no-fly zone,' Lena pointed out, wiping her nose with the back of her hand. Fort Grant had been shut down under Reagan, putting thousands of locals out of their jobs and running the city of Madison into the ground. Still, the military's no-fly zone was in force, and that should keep the news stations from letting their helicopters hover over the area.

Frank said, 'The hospital isn't.'

'Fuckers,' she said, wondering how anybody could do that job. They were vultures, and the people back home who watched it all live were no better than animals themselves.

Frank lowered his voice, saying, 'We gotta keep in control here.'

'What does that mean?'

'With Jeffrey gone . . .' Frank stared out into the street. 'We gotta keep our people in charge.'

'You mean you?' Lena asked, but she could read on his face that he hadn't meant it that way. She asked, 'What's wrong with you? Are you sick?'

He shrugged, wiping his mouth with a dirty-looking handkerchief. 'Me and Matt ate something bad last night.' She was startled to see tears in his eyes at the mention of Matt. Lena could not imagine what it had been like for him to watch his friend die right in front of his eyes. Frank had been Matt's supervisor when the younger man first came onto the force. Almost twenty years had passed since then and they had spent just about every working day in each other's company.

Frank said, 'We know Nick. We know what kind of guy he is. He needs all the support we can give him.'

'Is that what you were talking about in the office?' Lena asked. 'It didn't seem like you were so hot on supporting him five minutes ago.'

'We have a difference of opinion about how this should go down. I don't want some bureaucrat walking in here and fucking things up.'

'This isn't a cowboy movie,' Lena countered. 'If the negotiator knows what he's doing, then we should follow his lead.'

'It's not a guy,' Frank said. 'It's a woman.'

Lena gave him a scathing look. Frank had made it clear from Lena's first day that he did not think women belonged in uniform. It must have burned him up knowing that a woman was coming down from Atlanta to take charge.

Frank said, 'It ain't about her being a female.'

Lena shook her head, pissed off as hell that he was worried about something as stupid as this. 'You don't get into the freaking GBI baking cookies.'

'Nick trained with this gal when he first joined up. He knows her.'

'What'd he tell you?'

'He won't talk about it,' Frank said, 'but everybody knows what happened.'

Lena bristled. 'I don't.'

'They were holed up in a restaurant outside of Whitfield. Two idiots with guns looking to score off the lunch crowd.' He shook his head. 'She hesitated. The whole thing went bad in less than a minute. Six people died.' He gave her a knowing look. 'We got our people in there praying for a savior,' he jabbed a finger at the station, 'and she ain't got the balls to do it.'

Lena stared across the street. They only had six people left in the squad room.

She looked back at Frank. 'We need to find out what's going on in there.' There were parents and wives and boyfriends who were left hanging, waiting to find out whether or not their loved one was living or dead. Lena knew what it felt like to lose some-body, but at least she had found out Sibyl was dead fairly fast. She hadn't had to wait like the families were doing now. Jeffrey had told her, then they had gone to the morgue. That was that.

Frank asked, 'What is it?'

She had let her thoughts get away from her, remembering all the second chances Jeffrey had given her, including this one today. No matter what stupid thing Lena did, he never stopped believing in her. There was no one else who would ever do that again.

Frank repeated, 'What?'

'I was just thinking . . .' she said, but the sight of a helicopter swooping over the college stopped her. Lena and Frank both watched as the big black bird hung in the air over the college, then touched down on the roof of the Grant County Medical Center. The building was little more than two stories of old brick, and Lena half expected it to buckle. It obviously held, because a few seconds later Nick Shelton's phone rang. He opened it, listened for a couple of beats, then shut it.

He said, 'Cavalry's here,' but there was no relief in

his voice. He motioned for Lena and Frank to follow him outside the back of the cleaners, and they all made their way toward the hospital, the heat bearing down like a sauna.

Lena asked Nick, 'Is there anything we can do?'

He shook his head, saying, 'This's their show now. It's got nothing to do with us.'

Lena tried to get confirmation on Frank's story. 'You trained with this woman?'

His tone was clipped. 'Not long.'

'She good?' Lena prodded.

'She's a machine,' Nick said, but it did not sound like a compliment.

They were silent as he led them past the shops on Main Street. They reached the hospital in under five minutes, but with the heat and anxiety, it seemed like hours. Lena did not know what she had been expecting when they reached the hospital, but it was not the elegantly dressed woman who threw open the back exit door and walked toward them with a purposeful stride. Behind her were three burly men dressed in the requisite shirts and chinos of the Georgia Bureau of Investigation. They wore huge Glocks on their sides and walked like they had brass balls. The woman leading them was small, around five three with a slight build, but she walked toward Nick with the same swagger.

'Glad you could get here,' Nick said, a tone of resignation in his voice. He made introductions, telling Frank and Lena, 'This is Dr. Amanda Wagner. She's the GBI's chief negotiator. She's been doing this longer than anybody in the state.'

Wagner barely acknowledged them as she shook Nick's hand. She did not bother to introduce the three men she'd brought with her, and none of them seemed too upset about it. Up close, she was older than Lena had first thought, probably in her fifties. She had clear polish on her fingernails and little makeup. A simple diamond ring was all the jewelry she wore, and her hair was cut in one of those flyaway styles that took forever to fix. There was something calming about her presence, though, and Lena thought that whatever had gone on between the negotiator and Nick must have been personal. Despite what Frank had said, there was nothing hesitant about Amanda Wagner. She seemed more than ready to jump into the fray.

Wagner spoke in a cultured drawl, asking Nick, 'We've got two adult male shooters, heavily armed, with six hostages, three of them children?'

'That's correct,' Nick said. 'Phones and utilities are controlled. We're monitoring for cell transmissions, but nothing's come out yet.'

'This way?' she asked. Nick nodded and they walked back toward the cleaners as she questioned him. 'Car been found?'

'We're working on it.'

'Entrances and exits?'

'Secured.'

'Sharpshooters?'

'Standard six-point formation.'

'Minicams?'

'We'll need them from you.'

She glanced behind her, and one of the men got on his cell phone. She continued, 'The jail population?'

'Evacuated to Macon.'

Overhead, the helicopter that had brought them here took off. Wagner waited for the roar of the blades to die down before asking, 'Have you established contact?'

'I got one of my men on the phone. They haven't picked up yet.'

'Is he trained in negotiation?' Wagner asked, though surely she knew the answer. Nick shook his head, and she said, 'Let's hope they don't answer, Nicky. The first contact is generally the primary negotiator throughout the entire siege. I thought you'd learned that lesson.' She paused a moment, but when Nick did not respond, she suggested, 'Perhaps you could stop him and get me the number?'

Nick took his radio off his belt. He walked ahead of them, relaying the order. When he called out the station's phone number, one of the men from Wagner's team dialed it into a cell phone and held it to his ear.

'Who've we got inside?' she asked as they started walking again. 'Run it down for me one more time.'

Nick recited like a good student, numbering people off on his fingers. 'Marla Simms, station secretary. She's elderly. She won't be much help. Brad Stephens, foot patrol. He's got six years on the job.'

Wagner asked Frank, 'Can we count on him?'

Frank seemed surprised she had addressed the question to him. 'He's a solid beat cop.'

Lena felt the need to add, 'He's kind of shaky under stress.'

They all turned to look at her. Frank seemed angry, but Lena did not regret warning the negotiator about Brad. 'I rode in a squad car with him last year. He's not steady under pressure.'

Wagner gave her a look of appraisal. 'You've been a detective for how long?'

Lena felt a lump in her throat, and all her resolve disappeared with that one question. 'I took some time off this year for personal –'

'How lovely for you,' Wagner said, turning back to Nick. 'Who else?'

Nick continued walking and they followed. 'Sara Linton, town pediatrician and coroner.'

Her lip curled in a smile. 'That's novel.'

'She was married to our Chief of Police,' Nick said. 'Jeffrey Tolliver.'

'Just give me the names of the living.'

He stopped at the open cleaners' door, where Hemming and her fellow patrolman still stood guard. 'There's three kids in there, around ten years old and freaked the fuck out.'

'The pediatrician's probably helping. How many children were killed?'

'None,' Nick answered. 'One of them's in the hospital, might lose his foot. School's in the process of tracking down parents. A lot of them commute to Macon for work, but we've identified all the kids.' He paused to regroup. 'There's another officer inside. Barry Fordham. He was shot pretty bad from what Frank could see.'

'We have to assume he's dead,' Wagner said matter-of-factly as she walked into the cleaners. Inside, the crowd of officers and agents cleared a path for her. Wagner glanced around the room, her gaze assessing everyone from the four GBI agents Nick had brought to Molly Stoddard, Sara's nurse. She finally turned her sights back on Lena, saying, 'Would you get me some coffee, dear? Black, two sugars.'

Lena felt a flicker of anger, but she walked over to the coffeemaker to do as she was told. Pat Morris tried to catch her eye, but she ignored him.

Wagner leaned against the edge of the folding table, addressing the group. 'First is the initial assault. You've got – what – five bodies in there?'

Lena bit back her pride and provided, 'There's another patrol cop missing,' as she dumped two packs of sugar into a paper cup.

'Six bodies, then,' Wagner said. 'The whole town's lit up with this. There's only one reason he's not checking in.'

'Marilyn,' Nick corrected. 'The missing cop is a woman.'

'That's the two extra shots you heard. They're going to take out the ones most likely to resist. The Uniforms will be big bull's-eyes. Perhaps your shaky one' – she walked over to Lena and poured the coffee herself – 'doesn't seem threatening enough. That's saved your Brad his life. For now.'

Wagner checked her watch before asking, 'Do we have a ventilation plan for the station?'

Frank said, 'All the plans are at the town hall. We've already got two people searching.'

'That's our priority.' Wagner told one of her men, 'James, be so kind as to go with Nicky to help speed the search along.' Before they could leave, she added, 'Let's see about cutting the water while you're at it.'

Frank asked, 'What's the next step?'

Wagner sipped her coffee before answering. 'They'll secure the area. Put all the prisoners in one place so they can control them. Step three, they make sure no one can get in. They'll barricade the doors, and since the shooter who is obviously in charge was smart enough to bring a friend, one will always stay on point to make sure no surprises come through the front door.'

She took another sip of coffee as she seemed to calculate variables in her head. 'They've had ample time to do all of this, which means they'll soon be moving on to step four, which is to make their demands. That's where the negotiations come in. First, they're going to want the water and power back, then food. What *we* want is a chance to get inside that place.' She saw Lena open her mouth to volunteer and Wagner held up a finger, saying, 'We'll get to that when we come to it.'

Frank said, 'We got parents want to talk to their kids.'

'That won't happen,' Wagner told him. 'The goal from our end is to keep as much emotion out of this as possible. We're not going to have crying parents pleading for their children's lives. Our shooters already know how valuable the hostages are without us reinforcing the fact.'

'What else?' Lena asked. 'What happens next?'

'They'll get hungry or want to see themselves on TV. Eventually, we'll get to the point where we've traded everything we can and they'll want out of there. We need to anticipate what they'll want at that point besides money. They always want money – unmarked and small denominations.' She paused. 'We need to find their car. They didn't sprout wings and fly here, and they're certainly not planning on leaving that way.'

Lena said, 'There's a lake behind the college.'

'Private?'

'Semi,' she said. 'It's hard to get a boat in without people seeing, but you can if you want to badly enough.'

Wagner picked out one of Nick's people. 'That'll be you, okay? Take a couple of men and search the shore for boats. We're talking walking distance from the scene. They didn't plan a leisurely hike as part of their getaway.' She asked Frank, 'I suppose any reports filed on missing boats in the last week are inside the station?'

'Yeah.'

'You've rerouted 9-1-1 calls?'

'Yeah,' Frank repeated. 'To the fire station up the street.'

'Could you please see if anyone reported a missing boat this morning?'

Frank picked up one of the telephones on the counter to make the call.

Wagner looked at the two remaining men on her team. 'We'll get the children out first for food and water.' She asked Lena, 'Is there a water cooler in there?'

'In the back by the jails.'

'How many toilets?'

Lena did not understand the question, but she answered, 'One.'

She saw Lena's confusion and explained, 'Drinking water. There's around a gallon and a half of water in the tank. They'll use that between themselves.'

Frank hung up the phone. 'No missing boats,' he said. 'I put out a feeler on the radio to see if anyone remembers taking a report.'

'Good man,' Wagner said. Then, to her team, 'We'll try to get the old woman or the patrolman out after the children. They won't care about hanging onto them; the cop is still iffy and they'll see the old woman as dead weight. My guess is they'll want to keep the pediatrician.' She asked Frank and Lena, 'She's attractive?'

Lena began, 'I wouldn't say –' just as Frank answered, 'Yes.'

'I imagine she's fairly confident,' Wagner said.

'Women don't get through medical school being demure.' She frowned. 'They won't like that.'

Molly said, 'I'm her nurse at the clinic. Sara's the most levelheaded person I know. She wouldn't do anything to compromise the situation, especially with children there.'

Wagner looked at her crew. 'What do you think, boys?'

The one who held the cell phone to his ear said, 'No doubt they'll have a problem with her.'

The other added, 'They'll need to get rid of that adrenaline soon.' He started to nod. 'I'll go with them keeping the woman.'

'I concur,' Wagner said, and Lena felt her blood run cold.

Molly said, 'You don't think they'll . . .'

Wagner's incredulous tone was sharp as a tack. 'They've killed four police officers and shot at children, severely wounding one of them. Do you think they'll draw the line at sexual assault?' She turned her attention toward Frank. 'You were in there, Detective. What did they come for? What else will they want?'

He shrugged, and Lena could feel his anger and confusion. 'I don't know.'

Wagner started to interrogate him. 'What's the first thing they did?'

'They shot Matt. They shot up the station.'

'Would you say that their primary goal was to shoot Detective Hogan?'

Even though Lena had heard Nick giving someone details over the phone, she was surprised the woman knew Matt's name.

Wagner prompted, 'Detective Wallace?'

Frank shrugged again. 'I don't know.'

'You know more than we do, Detective. You were there. What did they say?'

'I don't know. They were yelling. Well, one of them was yelling. He started slapping Marla around. I went to the back of the station to call Nick.'

Lena chewed the tip of her tongue. She had never liked Marla, but there was something horrific about beating up an old lady. Considering all they had done, Lena should not have been surprised, but still, hearing about Marla took her anger up yet another notch.

'Wait a minute,' Frank said. Judging by his look, a lightbulb had gone off in his head. 'He asked for the Chief. The one who said his name was Smith. He told Marla he wanted to see the Chief. She told me, and I found Jeffrey and . . .' He had spoken in a rush until he got to Jeffrey's name.

Somehow, Wagner made sense of what he was trying to say. 'They asked for Chief Tolliver but they shot Detective Hogan?'

'I . . .' Frank shrugged. 'I guess.'

She looked around the room, finding Pat Morris over by Lena. 'You're Morris?'

He nodded, obviously uncomfortable with being singled out. 'Yes, ma'am.'

She gave him a disarming smile, as if they were old friends. 'You were there from the beginning?'

'Yes, ma'am.'

'And what did you see?'

'Same as Frank.'

Her smile thinned slightly. 'Which was?'

'I was at my desk typing up a report,' Morris began. 'The Chief came into the room and I asked him a question about how to get to the D-15 screen. I'm not that great with computers.'

'That's fine,' Wagner soothed. 'And then?'

Lena could see Morris swallow hard. 'And then Matt came in the front door. Marla said something to him, like "There you are," then Dr. Linton screamed.'

'Just screamed?'

'No, ma'am. She said, "Jeffrey," like she was warning him.'

Wagner took a breath, then let it go. She pressed her lips together and Lena noticed her lipstick had smeared a bit. 'So, we could have a case of mistaken identity.'

Frank said, 'How's that?'

'The shooter thought Detective Hogan was your Chief.' Wagner looked around the room. 'I know this is a silly question, but is there a particular perp your Chief put away who might be capable of doing something like this?'

Lena racked her brain for cases, wondering why she had not done this before. There were plenty of people she could think of who were angry enough to want to kill Jeffrey, but none of them had the balls to do it. Besides, it was never the big talkers who acted on their threats. It was the quiet ones, the ones who let their anger burn in the pit of their stomachs until it exploded, who actually showed up with a gun.

'It was worth a shot.' Wagner addressed the group again. 'Either way, mission accomplished for our two shooters. They came to kill Tolliver and as far as they know that was done in the first two minutes. Their escape was blocked by our helpful dry cleaner here, who ran into the street with his shotgun. I would guess their primary goal right now would be to get out of the building without being killed.'

'Amanda?' Nick said. He walked through the room holding a rolled-up blueprint in his hand. 'Ventilation plan.'

'Good,' she told him, spreading the schematic out on the table. She studied the layout of the ventilation system for a moment, tracing a shaft along a section of the back wall. 'This looks like the best spot,' she decided. 'We can go through the drop ceiling in the conference room to access the duct and slide a Minicam through to get a bird's-eye of what's going on.'

Frank said, 'Why can't we just go through the ceiling?'

'The tiles break too easily. We don't want dust falling down and alerting them to –'

'No,' he interrupted her, his voice excited. 'The drop ceiling goes the whole length of the station. You could just climb over that back wall and drop down and –'

'End up killing everyone in there,' Wagner finished. 'We're far from last resorts at this point, Detective Wallace. What we want now is video and sound coming out of that room. Our first step toward controlling the situation is knowing what they're up to.'

Wagner motioned her team closer, and they bent over the map, planning their point of entry. Lena watched them for a few minutes, trying to follow their jargon as they ran down the supplies they would need. She noticed Nick standing to the side, a hard look on his face. How he had left this kind of action was beyond her. There had to be more to the story of the Whitfield hostage situation than Frank knew. There was always a darker truth behind those sorts of rumors. God knows what kind of shit people had made up about Lena when she left the force.

Beside her, Pat Morris shifted against the table holding the coffee machine. He whispered to Lena, 'You following anything they're saying?'

She shook her head.

'They seem to know what they're doing,' Morris told her, and though Lena agreed, she did not comment.

'It's so weird,' Morris continued, his voice still low. 'The shooters, they can't be much older than my little brother, and he's still in high school.'

She turned to him, warning bells going off in her head. 'You're serious?' she asked. 'How young? How young did they look?'

He shrugged. 'They gotta be older, but they looked eighteen at the most.'

'Why do they have to be older?' Lena asked. She noticed that Wagner and her team had grown quiet, but she didn't care. 'Slight builds? Androgynous?'

Morris shifted uncomfortably under the pressure. 'I don't know, Lena. It happened so fast.'

Wagner broke in. 'What are you thinking, Detective Adams?'

'The last case I worked on before I left,' Lena said, the lump rising in her throat making it hard for her to speak.

Nick slammed his fist into the table, saying, 'Goddammit,' and Lena imagined the horror on his face mirrored her own. He had worked the case, too, and seen the damage firsthand.

'Oh, no,' Molly said. 'You don't think . . .'

Wagner's tone said her patience was running low. 'Let's cut the suspense, folks.'

'Jennings,' Lena finally said, the name bringing the

taste of bile to the back of her throat. 'A pedophile who's good at getting young men to do all the dirty work.'

EIGHT

Monday

Jeffrey helped the paramedics carry Robert down the front steps. He was still refusing to get onto a stretcher for his own hardheaded reasons, and every time Jeffrey tried to talk to him, Robert just shook his head, as if he could not speak.

Jeffrey offered, 'I'll be by the hospital as soon as Hoss gets here.'

Robert shook his head for the hundredth time. 'No, man. I'm okay. Just make sure Jessie gets to her mama's.'

Jeffrey patted his shoulder. 'We'll talk tomorrow when you're more up to it.'

'I'm okay,' Robert insisted. Even when they loaded him into the back of the ambulance, he only said, 'Make sure you look after Jess.'

Jeffrey walked back to the house, but he did not go in. Instead, he sat on the front steps, waiting for Hoss to show up. Clayton Hollister was the town's sheriff – had been as long as Jeffrey could remember – and when he'd called about the shooting, Jeffrey had learned that the old man had literally gone fishing. Hoss was heading back from Lake Martin, which was about half an hour's drive away. When Jeffrey had offered to go ahead and help process the scene, his old mentor had told him to hold up. 'He'll still be dead when I get there.'

Two sheriff's deputies stood outside talking to Robert's neighbors, both of them knowing better than to go inside the house until the boss arrived. Hoss ran his force with an iron fist, a management style Jeffrey had never taken to. Jeffrey knew the old man would be doubly attentive on this one; Robert and Jeffrey would likely be career criminals right now except for Hoss's early intervention. He had ridden them hard when they were teenagers, hawking their every move. Even when Hoss wasn't around, his deputies knew that the two boys were his special project, and they were just as vigilant as the sheriff, maybe even more so.

At the time, Jeffrey had resented the man's prying – he already had a father, even if Jimmy Tolliver spent more time in jail than he did at home – but now that he was a cop himself, Jeffrey understood the favor Hoss had done him as a kid. There was a reason both Jeffrey and Robert had chosen law enforcement as their careers. In his own way, Hoss had led by example. Though who knew what the hell Robert was up to now.

Sitting on the front porch watching the deputies, Jeffrey kept running back over Robert's story, trying to make sense of what he and Jessie had said. Something wasn't adding up, but that shouldn't have been surprising, considering Jeffrey was back in Sylacauga. He hated this Podunk town, hated the way every second that passed here seemed to be sucking the life out of him. He had been an idiot for coming back, and even more stupid for dragging Sara along with him. Nothing here had changed in the last six years. Possum and Bobby were still spending every Sunday together, waxing nostalgic by the pool while Jessie got drunk off her ass and Nell added her bitter quips to the mix. Sara being here had made things worse than he could have imagined.

Despite his idiotic admission last night, Jeffrey could not decide exactly how he felt about Sara. She had managed somehow to get under his skin, and part of him had asked her to go to Florida in the hopes that he would be able to fuck her out of his system once and for all. Normally, the women he dated bent over backward to please him, which generally got old after a few months and became a good justification for moving on to the next one in line. Sara was not like that. On the surface, she was the kind of woman he always thought he would end up settling down with: a perfect combination of sexuality and self-confidence that made it impossible for him to get bored. It was a case of being careful what you wished for, though, because underneath it all, she was a lot of work. She had her own opinions about things and her mind was not easily changed. To make matters worse, her mother obviously thought he was the Devil incarnate and her sister had pegged him instantly for the kind of player he'd been all his life. She had actually laughed in his face when she opened the door to Sara's house yesterday, giving him a knowing up-and-down look, telling Jeffrey his reputation preceded him.

His gut reaction was to prove them all wrong. Maybe that was the problem – and the root to his attraction. Jeffrey wanted their approval. He wanted people to think he was a good guy, the kind of guy who came from a nice middle-class, God-fearing family that stood on the right side of the law. That seemed like a lost cause now. Sara was looking at him the same way everyone else in Sylacauga did, like he was just as bad as his father.

'Hey,' Sara said, sitting down beside him on the steps.

He moved away from her. 'How's Jessie?'

'Passed out on the couch,' Sara told him, folding her arms around her knees. Her tone was reserved, like they were strangers.

'Is she on something?'

'I think her adrenaline gave out and whatever she took earlier finally caught up with her.' She stared at him, seemed to be studying him.

'What?'

'We need to talk.'

Dread washed over Jeffrey, but of the thousand things that came to his mind, what she actually said was more shocking than any of them.

'You changed the crime scene.'

'What?' He stood up, putting himself between Sara and the crowd on the street. He knew he had done nothing wrong, but still he felt defensive. 'What the hell are you talking about?'

'You left the door open.'

'The back door? How else were you supposed to get in?'

Sara tucked her chin into her chest, the way she did when she was trying to keep her calm. 'The armoire,' she said. 'You opened the door. You put the shirt back in.'

He remembered now, and for the life of him he could not understand his own actions. 'I just –' He couldn't find an answer. 'I don't know what I was doing. I was upset. It doesn't mean anything.'

Sara spoke matter-of-factly. 'A man holds a gun to his wife's head, shoots at him, and Robert runs to the armoire, grabs his gun, and shuts the door?'

Jeffrey tried to think of a logical explanation. 'He probably shut it without thinking.' Even as he spoke, Jeffrey knew he was grasping at straws. The timing didn't work.

Sara stood up, brushing dirt off the back of her pajamas. 'I'm not going to be an accomplice to this,' she told him, and it sounded like a warning.

'An accomplice?' he repeated, thinking he had heard wrong.

'Changing the crime scene.'

'That's ridiculous,' he said, heading back inside.

She followed him like she did not trust him alone in the house. 'Where are you going?'

'I'll close it back,' he answered, walking into the bedroom. He stopped in front of the armoire. The door was already closed.

When he looked at Sara for an explanation, she said, 'I didn't close it.'

Jeffrey opened the door again and stood back. He took another step back and as they both watched, it closed. He laughed with relief. 'See?' He duplicated his actions with the same result. 'The floor must be uneven,' he explained, testing the floorboards. 'When you step back here, it closes.'

A flicker of doubt crossed Sara's eyes. 'Okay,' she said, like she still was not sure.

'What?'

'Was the safe locked?'

He opened the door again, finding a black gun safe on the top shelf. 'Combination lock,' he said. 'He could have left it open. They don't have kids.'

She was staring at the dead man on the floor. 'I want to sit in on the autopsy.'

Jeffrey had somehow forgotten about the body in the room. He turned now, and looked at the corpse. The man's blond hair was matted with blood, partially concealing his face. His bare back was riddled with blood and brain, the laces of his untied tennis shoes stringing across the floor. Jeffrey never understood how people could think a dead person was just sleeping. Death changed the air, charged it with something thick and unsettling. Even with his half-opened eye and slackened jaw, there was no mistaking that the man was dead.

Jeffrey said, 'Let's get out of here,' leaving the room.

Sara stopped him in the hallway. 'Did you hear me?' she said. 'I want to sit in –'

'Why don't you do it yourself?' he interrupted, thinking this would be the only way to shut her up. 'They don't have a coroner here. The guy who runs the funeral home does it for a hundred bucks a pop.'

'All right,' she said, but the guarded look on her face was far from reassuring. Jeffrey knew if she found anything out of place, from a pattern wound to an ingrown toenail, she'd throw it back at him that she was right.

'What do you think you're going to find?' he demanded, then remembering Jessie was in the next room, he lowered his voice. 'You think my best friend's a murderer?'

'He already admitted to shooting that man.'

Jeffrey walked toward the front door, wanting to get out of the house and away from Sara. Typically, she followed him, unable to let it go.

She put her hands on her hips, her tone the same she probably used to talk to her patients. 'Think about their story, Jeffrey.'

'I don't have to think about it,' he said, but the more Sara talked, the more he did, and he did not like the conclusions his mind was drawing. He finally asked, 'Why are you doing this?'

'The time frame doesn't jibe with what we heard in the street.'

Jeffrey shut the front door, not wanting their conversation to be overheard. Through the narrow window, he could see the deputies talking to the ambulance driver who had just pulled up.

Sara said, 'There was a lag between the scream and the first shot.'

He tried to remember the sequence, but could not. Still, he said, 'That's not how it happened.'

'The shot was a few beats later.'

'What's a few beats?'

'Maybe five seconds.'

'Do you know how long five seconds is?'

'Do you?'

He saw Hoss's cruiser pull into the street. It was the same damn car he had driven when Jeffrey was a teenager, right down to the peeling sheriff's star on the side. Jeffrey and Robert had washed that car every weekend their junior year as penance for duct-taping a hapless freshman to the water fountain at school.

'All right,' Jeffrey told Sara, wanting to get this the hell over with. 'Five seconds. That goes with what they said – she screamed, Robert pushed him back, he fired. That could take five seconds.'

Sara stared at him, and he did not know if she was going to call him an idiot or a liar. She surprised him by saying, 'I honestly can't remember what they said, whether she screamed first or he pushed the guy first.' Then, probably just to be a bitch, she added, 'You might want to help Robert get that straight before he makes his statement.'

Jeffrey watched Hoss talking to his deputies. He was wearing his fishing vest and a beat-up old hat with lures pinned to it. Jeffrey felt a sense of dread overwhelm him.

He said, 'We didn't hear the second shot until I caught up with you. That's, what, another ten seconds?'

'I don't know. It wasn't immediate.'

'Robert could have been looking for his gun.'

She surprised him again by conceding, 'True.'

'Then the next shot was a few seconds later, right?' When she did not respond, he said, 'Maybe two or three seconds later?'

'About.'

'It could fit,' he insisted. 'The guy shoots at him, Robert goes to get his gun. It's dark, he can't find it at first. While he's looking for it, he's shot. He's surprised that he's shot, but he still manages to shoot back.'

She nodded, but did not seem convinced. Jeffrey knew in his gut there was something else she was holding back, and he was running out of time.

'What?' he said, wanting to shake it out of her. 'What aren't you telling me?'

'Just forget it.'

'I mean it, Sara. There's something you're not saying. What is it?'

She stared out the window, not answering.

Hoss was still standing at the end of the walk. The ambulance made a low beeping noise as it backed into the driveway. Each beep seemed to heighten Jeffrey's frustration, so that when Sara started to leave the house, Jeffrey grabbed her arm and would not let her go.

She gave a surprised 'What are you –'

'Not one word to him,' he warned, feeling like the sky was falling down and there was nothing he could do to stop it. If he could just keep Sara quiet for a few more hours, maybe he could get to the bottom of it.

Sara tried to jerk her arm back, a look of shock on her face. 'Let go of me.'

'Just promise me.'

'Let go,' she repeated, wrenching her arm away.

Jeffrey felt so angry and helpless that he punched his fist into the wall behind her. Sara flinched, like she thought he meant to hit her. Fear, then sheer hatred flashed in her eyes.

'Sara,' he said, taking a step back, holding up his hands. 'I didn't . . .'

Her mouth tightened into a thin line. When she spoke, her tone was deep, like she was fighting to keep from raising her voice. He had never seen her really angry before, and there was something about her stillness that was more threatening than if she held a gun to his head.

'You listen to me, you asshole,' she hissed through clenched teeth. 'I will not be intimidated by you.'

He tried to calm her. 'I wasn't –'

She jerked away from him. 'If you ever touch me again, I'll rip your throat open with my bare hands.'

Jeffrey could feel his heart stop in his chest. The way she was looking at him now made him feel dirty and mean, like a bully. No wonder his father always got loaded to the gills after punching up his mother. The hatred must have felt like it was eating him alive.

Outside, Jeffrey could see Hoss and the deputies starting toward the house. He swallowed the bitter taste in his mouth, trying to reason with Sara.

'All we have are questions,' he told her. 'I'll get

you into the autopsy, okay? We'll talk to Bobby and Jess tomorrow, okay? Just give me some time to figure out what the hell is going on here before you help send my best friend to the goddamn electric chair.'

She would not even look at him, but he could feel her anger ringing in his ears clear as a bell.

'Sara –'

Hoss knocked on the front door and Jeffrey put his hand on the knob, as if he could keep him out. The old man gave him a look through the window that cut right into Jeffrey, and he felt like he was fifteen years old again, caught red-handed right outside the Ben Franklin with a transistor radio he had not paid for.

Sara reached for the knob and Jeffrey opened the door.

'Hey there.' Hoss held out his hand and Jeffrey shook it, surprised by the grip. The man's hair had gone completely gray and the lines on his face were deeper, but other than that, he looked exactly the same.

Hoss said, 'Damn shame to see you again under these circumstances, Slick.' He tipped his hat to Sara. 'Ma'am.'

Sara opened her mouth to speak but Jeffrey interrupted her, saying, 'Hoss, this is Sara Linton. Sara, this is Sheriff Hollister.'

Hoss gave her one of his rare smiles. 'I hear you doctored Robert for us. Thank you for taking care of my boy.'

Sara nodded, and Jeffrey could tell she was waiting for the right moment to have her say. She was still so angry that her whole body seemed to vibrate with it.

Hoss told her, 'We can get your statement

tomorrow morning. I know it's been a hard night for you.'

Jeffrey held his breath, waiting for her to explode.

Sara cleared her throat, like she had trouble finding her voice. She surprised him by saying, 'Tomorrow will be fine.' With barely more than a glance at Jeffrey, she asked him, 'Do you think Nell would mind if I stayed on her couch tonight?'

Jeffrey looked at the ground, letting out a slow breath of relief. 'No.'

Hoss volunteered one of his deputies, saying, 'Why don't you drive the lady over to Possum's?'

Jeffrey recognized the man from church back when May Tolliver was capable of staying sober enough on Sundays to force her son to get some religion. He said, 'Thanks, Paul.'

Paul tipped his hat, giving Jeffrey a suspicious look – the same suspicious look Jeffrey had been getting since he was old enough to walk. To make matters worse, Sara gave it to him, too, walking out of the house without saying another word.

Hoss watched her go, not bothering to hide an appreciative look. Even in a pair of faded striped pajamas, Sara was an attractive woman. 'Tall drink of water.'

Jeffrey said, 'She's upset,' knowing exactly how Hoss would take his words.

'Not the kind of thing a woman should see,' he agreed. 'Jessie okay?'

'She's on the couch,' Jeffrey said, then added, 'Sleeping,' feeling like he was ten years old again and lying for his mother.

Hoss nodded, and Jeffrey knew he understood that Jessie's sleep was induced by something other than exhaustion. 'I called her mama to come over and fetch her to the house. You know Faith's the only person who can calm that girl.'

He turned back to his other deputy, who had a camera around his neck and a bright red toolbox in his hand. The man looked about twelve years old and was probably what passed for a crime scene tech around here. Jeffrey suppressed a wince of recognition as Hoss told the deputy, 'Reggie, hang out around here for Jessie's mama. We'll be right back.'

Reggie put down his toolbox, giving a respectful 'Yes, sir.'

Hoss stepped into the house, glancing around the front room. There were photos on the walls, most of them of Jeffrey, Possum, and Robert back during high school. Nell and Jessie were in some, but for the most part, it was the three men. A group photo showed Jeffrey and Robert's high school football team with a huge banner behind it announcing 'State Champs.' Sitting poolside yesterday, Possum had told Sara about their final winning game against Comer High, embellishing in a way that made Jeffrey embarrassed and sad. Possum had always been the ultimate spectator.

Hoss asked, 'What the hell happened here tonight?'

'Let me take you back to the room,' Jeffrey told him, not exactly answering the question. 'Sara and I were in the street when we heard Jessie scream.' He chewed the inside of his mouth as they walked down the hallway, lies of omission eating a hole in his stomach.

As usual, Hoss saw right through him. 'Something wrong, son?'

'No, sir,' he answered. 'It's just been a long night.'

Hoss slapped Jeffrey hard enough on the back to

make him cough; it was his way of showing other men affection. 'You're tough. You'll get through this.' He stopped outside the door of the bedroom. 'Christ a'mighty,' he muttered. 'What a mess.'

'Yeah,' Jeffrey answered, trying to see the scene the way Hoss was, for the first time. The ceiling fan overhead was still whirring, but he could tell it had been off when the man was shot; the blades had interrupted the blood spray pattern on the ceiling. There was a streak of blood where the switch for the fan had been turned on, probably by Robert. That made sense. He would have turned on the lights to see how badly he was wounded after the gunplay. It also made sense that there would be a lag between the last two shots. Robert had been handling guns since he was eight. He knew better than to fire into the dark. He had probably let his eyes adjust, tried to tell where Jessie was. Knowing her, she was standing helpless in the corner. It would be just like Robert to take his time.

Hoss looked out the window, saying, 'Screen's been knocked out.' Jeffrey didn't know if he meant from the inside or the outside, but Jesus Himself could not drag him back into the room. Jeffrey would look around outside when Hoss was gone.

Hoss asked, 'What'd Robert say?'

Jeffrey tried to think of how to answer, but Hoss waved him off. 'I'll get it from the horse.' Jeffrey's expression must have registered his surprise, because he added, 'You can give your statement tomorrow when you bring your girl in.'

From the way Sara was looking at Jeffrey when she left the house, he was not sure whether or not he would have a girl tomorrow, but he did not volunteer that information. Instead, he watched Hoss walk around the room, felt his gut constricting every time he thought about what he was keeping back. This was the main reason Jeffrey had never seriously pursued a life of crime. Unlike Jimmy Tolliver, guilt could and did keep Jeffrey up at night. He hated lying – maybe because his childhood had been riddled with lies. His mother would not admit his father was ever guilty of the crimes that put him in jail, and his father denied his mother had a problem with her drinking. Meanwhile, Jeffrey had told some whoppers of his own to anybody who would listen. He had left Sylacauga so he could stop being that person. The minute he got back, he had returned to his old ways. It was like slipping back into a pair of familiar shoes.

'Son?' Hoss said. He was still by the window. Jeffrey noticed he was standing on one of Jessie's bloody footprints. A few of her little white pills had been crushed under his heel.

'Sir?' Jeffrey said, thinking Hoss must have been as distraught as he was. Everybody showed it in different ways.

'I said it looks pretty straightforward to me,' Hoss said. He nudged the dead man's foot with the toe of his boot, and Jeffrey felt like he had been kicked in the gut seeing the casual way Hoss was dealing with this man's death. That was how it had always been for Hoss, though. There were good guys and bad guys, and to protect one, you did what you had to do to the other. He had always been hard on Robert and Jeffrey, but he was the only man in town allowed to say anything bad about them.

Hoss squatted down, looking at the corpse. Greasy blond shoulder-length hair covered most of the face. Still, Hoss asked, 'Recognize him?'

'No, sir,' Jeffrey said, kneeling down for a better

look. He was still in the doorway, and down close to the carpet, he could see backsplatter fanning from the body. The edges of the fan led to where Jeffrey knelt. Robert must have been trying to find the light when he was shot.

'Luke Swan.' Hoss stood, looping his thumb in his belt.

The name was familiar to Jeffrey if not the face. 'We went to school with him.'

'He dropped out before y'all graduated,' Hoss said. 'Remember?'

Jeffrey nodded, though he didn't. His high school life had been spent in an insulated clique of football players and cheerleaders. Luke Swan was hardly the athletic type. He looked like he weighed ninety pounds wet.

'Been in and out of trouble ever since,' Hoss said, a sad note to his voice. 'Drugs, alcohol. He's slept off more than a couple of good times at the station.'

'Did Robert ever arrest him?'

Hoss shrugged off the question. 'Hell, Slick, we only got eight deputies on the street any given shift. All of us have seen the boy one time or another.'

'He ever do anything like this before?' Jeffrey asked. When Hoss shook his head, he added, 'Armed B&E is a big step up from just getting in and out of trouble.'

He crossed his arms. 'You saying something? Should I be concerned?'

Jeffrey looked at the body. He still could not see all of the man's face, but the thin blue lips and small build gave him a youthful quality. 'No, sir.'

Hoss came toward him, not bothering to look where he was walking. He told Jeffrey, 'That lady of yours seemed like she had something to say.'

'She's a coroner in our town.'

He gave a low whistle, impressed, but not for the obvious reason. 'Y'all can afford a full-time coroner?'

'She's part-time,' Jeffrey told him.

'She charge much?'

Jeffrey shook his head, though he had no idea what Sara made. Judging by her house and her car, she made a hell of a lot more money than he did. Of course, it was a lot easier to make money when you came from it. Jeffrey had seen the truth of that his entire life.

Hoss tilted his head toward the body. 'Think she'd do this one for us?'

Jeffrey felt his chest tighten again. 'I'll ask her.'

'Good.' He turned back around, looking at the room. He said, 'I want to get this mess cleared up and Robert back on the street as soon as possible.'

Then, as if to put an end to any further discussion, he reached over and turned off the light.

NINE

Sara woke in a sweat, her head spinning as she sat up too fast. She looked frantically around the room, trying to remember where she was. The Auburn memorabilia was almost comforting. Even the orange and blue blanket Nell had given her last night was a welcome sight. She sat back on the couch, tucking the blanket up around her neck as she adjusted to the quiet sounds of the neighborhood. Coffee was brewing in the kitchen, and somewhere, a car horn beeped.

Sara pulled her legs up, resting her chin on the top of her knees. She had not dreamed about Atlanta in a long time, but seconds ago, she had been back there – back in that bathroom at Grady Hospital where she had been raped. Her attacker had handcuffed her arms behind her and defiled Sara in ways she could still feel if she let her mind stay there long enough. Then he had stabbed her in the side and left her to bleed to death.

At the memory, her throat constricted again, and Sara closed her eyes, trying to breathe through her emotions.

'You okay?' Nell asked. She stood in the doorway with a cup of coffee in her hand.

Sara nodded, trying to find her voice.

'Possum's gone to open the store. Jeffrey went to check on Jessie. He's a fool if he thinks she'll be out of bed before noon.' She paused when Sara did not respond. 'He said to tell you to be ready to go at eight-thirty.'

Sara looked at the clock on the mantel. It was half past seven.

Nell said, 'Coffee's ready when you are,' and left Sara alone in the room.

Sara sat up, hitting her toe on her suitcase. Jeffrey had put it there a few hours ago while she pretended to sleep. He had sneaked in like a thief, and she had watched him go, wondering exactly what she had gotten herself into. Jeffrey Tolliver was not the man she thought he was. Even Cathy Linton would have been surprised by his behavior last night. Sara had felt threatened, and at one point she had been frightened enough to think that he would actually hit her. She could not let herself get involved with someone like that. There was no denying that she had feelings for Jeffrey, maybe she was even in love with him, but that did not mean she had to put herself in a situation where she was afraid of what might happen next.

Sara pressed her lips together, looking at the framed magazine cover of Jeffrey on the wall. Maybe being back home had altered him in some way. The man Sara had seen last night was nothing like the Jeffrey Tolliver she had grown to know over the last few months.

She found herself trying to reason out his behavior. Prior to this, there had been nothing in his personality that would have pointed to last night's outburst. He was frustrated. He had punched the wall, not her. Maybe she was overreacting. Maybe the circumstances had brought him to the edge, and she had done nothing but help push him over. He had grabbed her arm, but he had also let it go. He had warned her not to talk, but when the sheriff came, he had done nothing to stop her. In the light of day, Sara could understand his anger and frustration. Jeffrey was right about one thing: Alabama was a death-penalty state, and not just a death-penalty state, but almost as gung-ho about it as Texas and Florida. If Robert was found guilty, he could be looking at the electric chair.

Though she was punch-drunk from lack of sleep, Sara tried to go over in her mind again what she had seen in Robert's bedroom last night. She was no longer certain about what she had heard in the street, nor was she sure about the sear pattern she had seen when Robert had removed his hand. He had been fast about it, and had done a very good job of smearing blood around the wound. What it came down to was that Sara had to ask herself why he had gone to such great lengths to cover the entrance wound if there was nothing to hide.

If she was correct, the muzzle of the gun that shot Robert had been placed at an upward angle against the skin. The hot metal had seared a V-shaped impression of the muzzle into the flesh. Either the person who shot him had been in an inferior position, squatting or kneeling, or Robert had held the gun to his own side and pulled the trigger. The second theory would explain why so little damage was done. The abdomen contained seven major organs and around thirty feet of intestines. The bullet had managed to miss them all.

Sara would have voiced her suspicions to the sheriff last night, but after taking one look at the man, she knew that, like Jeffrey, he was going to do everything he could to give Robert the benefit of the doubt. Clayton 'Hoss' Hollister screamed good ol' boy, from his nickname to his cowboy boots. Sara knew exactly how his kind operated. Her father certainly wasn't part of Grant's network of powerful old men – he hated doing favors because he *had* to – but Eddie Linton played cards with most of them. Sara had learned how they worked her first week as coroner, when the mayor explained to her that the county had an exclusive contract to order all their medical supplies through his brother-in-law's company, no matter how much he charged.

Today, Sara wanted to see Robert's wound again, and even if Jeffrey wouldn't – or couldn't – keep his promise to let her do the autopsy, she wanted to watch while whoever was in charge examined the slain man – or victim, depending on how you looked at it. After that, all she wanted to do was get the hell out of Sylacauga and away from Jeffrey. She needed time and some distance so she could get her head together and figure out exactly how she felt about him in light of last night's explosion.

Sara tested her weight on her feet. Her soles were bruised from the impromptu run last night, and something sharp had taken a chunk of skin out of her heel. She would stop to buy Band-Aids once she got on the interstate.

Nell offered a faint smile when Sara limped into the kitchen. 'Kids won't be up for another hour.'

Sara tried to be polite. 'How old are they?'

'Jared's ten, Jennifer's ten months younger.'

Sara raised an eyebrow.

'Trust me, I got my tubes tied the second she was out.' Nell took a coffee cup out of the cabinet. 'You like it black?' Sara nodded. 'Jen's the smart one. Don't tell Jared I said that, but Jen's a full grade ahead of him in school. It's his own damn fault – he's not stupid, he's just more interested in sports than books. Boys that age just can't sit still for anything. You probably know all about that with your job.' She put the cup down in front of Sara and poured coffee as she spoke. 'I guess you want a houseful of kids when you settle down.'

Sara watched steam rise from the cup. 'I can't actually have children.'

'Oh,' Nell said. 'There's my foot in my mouth again. You'd think I loved the taste of leather.'

'It's okay.'

Nell sat down across from Sara with a heavy sigh. 'God, but I'm nosey. It's the only thing my mother says about me that's true.'

Sara forced a smile. 'Really, it's okay.'

'I won't press you for details,' Nell said, but her tone of voice implied she would be more than open to hearing them.

'Ectopic pregnancy,' Sara provided, though she went no further.

'Does Jeffrey know?'

She shook her head.

'You could always adopt.'

'That's what my mother keeps saying,' Sara said, and for the first time she voiced the reason why she couldn't bear the thought of adoption. 'I know this sounds horrible, but I take care of other people's children all day. When I get home . . .'

'You don't have to tell me,' Nell said. She reached over and squeezed Sara's hand. 'Jeffrey won't mind.'

Sara gave her a tight smile and Nell breathed out a

heavy sigh, saying, 'Well, shit. Can't say I didn't see that coming, but I was hoping it would last a little longer.'

'I'm sorry.'

'Forget about it.' Nell slapped her thighs as she stood. 'Nothing bad between you and me. Jeffrey's loss is my gain. First damn time that's ever happened, I can tell you.'

Sara stared down at her coffee again.

'You want pancakes?'

'I'm not that hungry,' Sara told her, even as her stomach grumbled.

'Me neither.' Nell took out the griddle. 'Three or four?'

'Four.'

Nell put the griddle on the stove and went about preparing the batter. Sara watched, thinking she had seen her mother do this same thing thousands of times. There was something so comforting about being in a kitchen, and Sara felt the nightmares from the night before start to fade.

'Stupid neighbor,' Nell said, tossing a cheery wave at someone outside the window over the sink. A car door slammed, followed by an engine starting. 'He's gone every weekend with some whore he met in Birmingham. Watch it,' she said, tossing Sara a look over her shoulder to make sure she was paying attention. 'Soon as he pulls out of the driveway, those dogs will start barking and they won't shut up till he comes back around ten tonight.' She stood on the tips of her toes and craned her head to see into the neighbor's yard. 'I've talked with him ten times about getting those poor things some shelter. Possum even offered to build him something. God, they howl when it rains.'

The dogs started barking on cue. Just to keep her talking, Sara asked, 'They don't have a doghouse?'

She shook her head. 'Nope. He kept having to come home because they jumped the fence, so he put them on chains. So, of course every morning like clockwork they knock their water bowls over and I have to trudge over there and fill 'em back up.' She handed Sara a carton of eggs and a bowl, saying, 'Make yourself useful,' before continuing, 'Boxers are so damn ugly. They're not even the cute kind of ugly. And Lord, do they slobber. It's like taking a spit bath every time I go over there.'

Sara broke the eggs into the bowl, not listening to Nell's words so much as the cadence of her voice. She was thinking about Jeffrey and trying to put logic to what had happened last night. Sara knew that both her biggest strength and her biggest weakness was that she saw things clearly in black and white, but right now, for the first time in her life, she was seeing the gray. She had been tired last night, and upset by everything that had happened. Had she really seen the sear mark? The more she thought about it, the more she convinced herself that she had not. But her gut still told her to go with what she had first thought. And why would Robert keep covering the wound unless he really had something to hide?

'Sara?' Nell said. She had obviously asked a question.

'I'm sorry,' Sara apologized. 'What?'

'I asked did Robert recognize the man?'

Sara shook her head. 'I guess not or he would've said something.'

'It hasn't made the papers yet – we only get a weekly here and it's not due until next Sunday – but I heard on my walk this morning that it's Luke Swan.

The name won't mean anything to you, but we all went to school with him. He used to live a couple of houses over.' She pointed toward the backyard. 'Possum was born here and I grew up across the street – did I tell you?' Sara shook her head. 'We moved in after his mama died. I couldn't stand the woman –' she knocked three times on the wooden cabinet under the sink, 'but it was nice of her to leave the house to us. I thought Possum's brother would make a stink, but it all worked out.' She paused for breath. 'Where was I?'

'Luke.'

'Right.' She turned back to the stove. 'He lived here a few years before his father lost his job, then they moved over by the school. He didn't exactly run with our crowd.'

Sara could guess she meant the popular crowd. The same groups had been at her own school, and though Sara had been far from popular, she was lucky enough not to have been picked on for it.

Nell continued, 'I heard he's a troublemaker, but who knows? People say all kinds of things after somebody's dead. You should hear Possum talk about his mama like she was Mary Poppins, and that woman was never happy a day of her life. She was a lot like Jessie that way.' Nell poured four pancakes onto the griddle. 'I heard Jessie's at her mama's.'

'Yes,' Sara confirmed.

'Good Lord,' Nell mumbled, taking the bowl of eggs from Sara. She beat them with a fork, then dumped them into a frying pan. Even though Sara had graduated in the top ten percent of her class at one of the toughest medical schools in the country, she always felt inadequate around women who could cook. The one meal she had prepared for her last boyfriend had resulted in the throwing away of two pots and a perfectly good garbage can.

Nell said, 'I ebb and flow with that woman. Maybe it's because Robert and Possum throw us together all the time and expect us to make happy. Sometimes I think she's not that bad and sometimes I just want to pop her upside the head to knock some sense into her.' She tapped the fork on the edge of the pan before setting it on a napkin. 'Right now I just feel sorry for her.'

'It's an awful thing to have happen.'

Nell flipped the pancakes with a spatula. 'Bobby's a real doll but you never know what they're like until you get them home and take them out of their packages. Maybe he sucks his teeth. Possum started doing that a few years ago until I threatened to beat him with a bat.' She put the pancakes and some of the eggs onto a plate and handed it to Sara. 'Bacon?'

'No thank you.'

Nell took three strips of bacon out from under a napkin and put them on Sara's plate. 'I was hating her something awful until a few months ago. She had a miscarriage. I was over at her house every day making sure she didn't do something stupid. Liked to tore the both of them up. She's wanted a kid ever since I met her. We're talking back in junior high school. Never been able to have one, though.'

Sara poured syrup onto the pancakes. They were all perfectly round and the same thickness. 'What stupid thing did you think Jessie would do?'

'Take too many pills,' Nell said, flipping the pancakes one by one. 'She's done it before. If you ask me, it was just to get attention. Not that Robert seems all that inattentive, but you just never know, do you?'

'No,' Sara agreed around a mouthful of bacon. Until last night, she never would have guessed that Jeffrey was capable of threatening her. She could still feel the breeze from his fist passing just a few inches from her head as he punched the wall. 'Would she ever cheat on him?'

'Ha,' Nell laughed, filling up her plate. She sat down across from Sara, pouring a liberal amount of syrup over the pancakes as she talked. 'If she did, it'd have to be with somebody up in Alaska. Robert knows everything that goes on in this town. He'll probably take over for the sheriff if the old fart ever retires. Hoss has held the office since before dirt. I think the only way he'll leave is feet-first. Hell, knowing this town, people'd still vote for him, even if he was dead.'

'You don't have a police force, it's only the sheriff's office?'

Nell took a bite of egg. 'You know how small this town is? If we had both, there wouldn't be anybody left to work at the gas station.' She stood up. 'Juice?'

'I'm fine.'

Nell got two glasses out of the cabinet and put them on the table. 'Mind you, if Jeffrey was around, Hoss would have retired years ago.'

'Why is that?'

She poured the juice. 'Heir apparent. Robert's father was half useless, but better half useless than being stuck with Jimmy Tolliver. That man was a monster. Jeffrey won't talk about it, but that scar under his shoulder came from his daddy.'

Sara had seen the scar, but not wanting to open a conversation about scars, she had never asked about it. Now she asked, 'How?'

Nell sat back down. 'I was standing right there,'

she said, taking a bite of pancake. Sara waited while she chewed, wishing for once that Nell would get on with it. Finally, she swallowed. 'May said something smart-ass and Jimmy just laid into her. I mean like a fury. I've never seen anything like it. Never hope to see it again, knock wood.' She rapped her knuckles on the table.

Sara swallowed, though she had nothing in her mouth. 'He hit her?'

'Oh, hon, he hit her all the time. It was like she was his own private punching bag. Jeffrey, too, when he was home. Not that he was home much. He spent most of his time out by the quarry, trying to get away from it. He'd just sit out there and read until the sun went down. Sometimes he'd sleep out there unless Hoss found him, then he'd make Jeffrey sleep at the station.' She drank some juice. 'Anyway, this one time I was there, they were hauling off on each other and Jeffrey tried to step in between them. Jimmy backhanded the shit out of him and Jeffrey went flying – and I do mean flying – across the room. Cut his back open on the stovetop. This was back when they had those knobs with the sharp metal edges, not like now where it's all just buttons and dials.'

After a while, Sara said, 'I didn't know.' She tried to imagine what it must have been like for Jeffrey growing up in that kind of environment and could not. Like most pediatricians, she had seen her share of abused children. Nothing made her more angry than a cowardly adult who took out his or her frustrations on a child. As far as Sara was concerned, they should all be left to rot in jail.

'Takes a hell of a lot to get Jeffrey angry,' Nell continued. 'I guess that's a good thing, though maybe not. You've got to wonder about him holding that in all the time. He hates to argue. Always has. You know he had an academic scholarship to Auburn?'

'Jeffrey?' Sara asked, trying to absorb this new information.

'Part of it was football, but they don't give you a full ride to warm the bench.' She gave a surprised laugh, as if she could not believe what had just come from her mouth. 'Don't ever tell Possum I said that, but it's the God's truth. The minute Jeffrey got to Auburn, he hated football. He would have quit the team if Hoss'd let him.'

'What did Hoss have to do with it?'

Nell put down her fork. 'You know why Jeffrey's called Slick?'

'I can take a wild guess.'

She snorted a laugh. 'Yeah, he's slick, I'll give him that, but the name came because no matter what kind of trouble he got into, he was real slick at getting out.'

'What kind of trouble?'

'Oh, not anything big when you consider what kids get up to today. Stealing things from the five-and-dime, borrowing his mama's car while she was passed out on the couch. The same kinds of things his daddy probably did when he was that age. We're talking ten or twelve. You gonna finish that?' Sara shook her head and Nell reached over with her fork and took the last bite of pancake. 'Jeffrey'd probably be where his daddy is if Hoss hadn't come along.'

'What did Hoss do?'

'Made him cut the grass at the jail instead of spending a couple of nights locked up in it. Sometimes, he'd take Jeffrey back in the cells and make him talk to some of the guys who were hard cases. Basically, he scared the shit out of him. Robert, too, but he didn't need as much scaring. He's always been more of a follower, and with Jeffrey straightened out, you got Robert, too.'

'It's a good thing Hoss came along.'

'Sometimes I wonder,' Nell said, sitting back with her coffee. 'Jeffrey's got a tender heart. I guess you noticed.'

Sara did not answer, though she wondered if Nell had an accurate picture of him. A lot could happen in six years. A lot could happen in one night.

'I always saw him ending up teaching, maybe coaching football at the high school. After Jimmy went up for life, he changed. Maybe Jeffrey thought joining the force and being a cop would make up for the fact that his daddy was a criminal. Maybe he thought it'd make Hoss happy.'

'Did it?'

Nell pushed away her plate. 'Like you wouldn't believe.'

Sara saw Jeffrey walk by the kitchen window and she stood from the table, telling Nell, 'I should get dressed.'

Jeffrey opened the back door. He seemed surprised to find Nell and Sara eating breakfast.

Sara said, 'I was just going to get changed.'

He gave her a quick glance, saying, 'You look fine,' even though she was still in the pajamas she had been wearing when she ran out of his mother's house last night.

Nell asked, 'How's Jessie and them?'

'Like you'd think.' He indicated their cleaned plates. 'That smells good.'

'I didn't marry Possum to cook for you,' she said, standing up. 'There's plenty of batter left in the bowl and the eggs shouldn't be too cold. I've gotta go check-see if those stupid dogs have knocked over their water bowls yet.'

Nell took all the conversation with her when she left the room. Not knowing what else to do, Sara sat back down at the table. She felt like the pancakes she had eaten were expanding in her stomach. The coffee left in her cup was lukewarm, but she managed to swallow it.

Jeffrey chewed a piece of bacon as he poured himself a cup of coffee. He put the pot on the warmer, then took it out again, holding it up to see if Sara wanted more. She shook her head no, and he put it back, eating another piece of bacon as he stared at the kitchen faucet.

Sara took up her fork and traced it around the syrup in her plate, wondering what, if anything, to say. Really, the burden to speak was on him. She put down the fork and crossed her arms, staring at Jeffrey, waiting.

He cleared his throat before asking, 'What are you going to say today?'

'What do you want me to say?' she asked. 'Or are you going to threaten me again?'

'I shouldn't have done that.'

'No, you shouldn't have,' she told him, her anger coming back in sharp focus. 'I'll tell you this right now, between the way your mother talked to me last night and your threats, I could leave right now and never look back.'

He looked down at the floor, and she could feel his shame without seeing it. His voice caught as he tried to speak, and he cleared his throat before he could manage, 'I've never hit a woman in my life.'

Sara waited.

'I'd cut off my own hands before I did anything

like that,' he told her, his jaw working as he obviously tried to fight the emotions welling up inside. 'I watched my daddy beat my mama every day of my life. Sometimes she pissed him off, sometimes he did it just because he could.' He kept his face turned away from her. 'I know you don't have any reason to believe me, but I would never hurt you.'

When Sara did not answer, he asked, 'What did my mother say to you last night?'

Sara was too embarrassed to repeat it. 'It doesn't matter.'

'It does,' he said. 'I'm sorry. I'm sorry I brought you here to this . . . this place.' He chanced a look at her, and she could see his eyes were bloodshot. 'I just wanted you to see . . .' He stopped. 'Hell, I don't know what I wanted you to see. Who I really am, I guess. Maybe you're seeing that now. Maybe this is who I really am.'

She felt sorry for him, and then she felt stupid for doing so.

He pulled out the chair Nell had vacated, dragging it a few feet from the table before he sat. 'Bobby wouldn't talk to me this morning.'

Sara waited for the rest.

'I walked in the room and he was getting dressed to go home.' Jeffrey paused, and she sensed rather than saw his feelings of helplessness. 'I told him we needed to talk and he just said no. Just like that, "No," like he has something to hide.'

'Maybe he does.'

He tapped his fingers on the table.

'Was Jessie with him?'

'No. She wasn't even awake yet when I dropped by the house to check on her.'

Sara chewed her lip, debating whether or not to tell him what she had seen.

'Go ahead,' he said. 'Go ahead and say whatever it is that I'm not seeing.' He slammed his palm against the table, frustrated. 'Jesus, I'm not doing this on purpose, Sara. No matter how many years have passed, he's still my best friend. It's not exactly easy for me to be a cop right now.'

Sara took a deep, calming breath. She had flinched when he hit the table, and her first response had been to get up and leave. Just because he came from a violent family did not mean Jeffrey was a violent man, but she could not help but see him differently now. His broad shoulders and well-muscled body, which she had once found so attractive, only served to remind her of how much stronger than her he was.

He must have sensed this, because he moderated his tone. 'Please don't look at me like that.'

'I just –'

When she said nothing, he prompted, 'What?'

Sara tucked her chin into her chest, not ready to have this conversation. She directed him back toward the problem at hand, saying, 'I want to see Robert's gunshot wound again.'

'Why?'

'I'm not sure, but . . .' she began, but even as she said it, she *was* sure. 'There was a sear mark at the bottom of the wound.'

'You're not sure?'

'I don't want to be, but I am.'

He gave a humorless laugh. 'He kept covering it with his hand.'

'He used the shirt to stanch the blood.'

'Did he let you see the shirt?'

She shook her head. If the gun had been held at contact range, the sear mark as well as soot would be on the shirt.

He said, 'They probably threw it away at the hospital.'

'Or he did.'

'Or he did,' Jeffrey conceded. He shook his head again. 'If he'd talk to me, try to explain what'd happened . . .'

'What are we going to do?'

He kept shaking his head. 'Why won't he talk to me?'

Sara did not volunteer the obvious answer.

He said, 'Luke Swan could have been going for him. His body was only a few feet away.'

'Probably three or four feet.'

'Robert pushed him,' Jeffrey said. 'Swan would have been crouched or on his knees.'

'Could have been.'

She could hear the strain in his voice as he tried to explain it all away. 'Swan could have heard Robert getting his gun. He moved toward him. Maybe he held his gun up and in front of him.' Jeffrey illustrated, holding out his hand, his fingers in the shape of a gun. 'He shot Robert, then Robert shot him.'

Sara tried to see the holes in his theory. 'It's possible.'

His relief was palpable. 'Let's see what the autopsy says, okay? We'll just keep this to ourselves until then. The autopsy will show what happened.'

'Did you ask if I could sit in?'

'Hoss wants you to do the exam.'

'All right.'

'Sara . . .'

'I'm already packed,' she said, standing. 'As soon as it's finished, I want to leave.' Then, to make herself clear, she said, 'I want to go home.'

TEN

The ringing telephone grated like nails on a black-board. Sara's hearing started to play tricks on her, the ringing fading in and out like a retreating police car. To pass the time, she would count the seconds between rings, sometimes losing count, sometimes sure that it had stopped, only to hear the startling bell again. And it was a bell, not the usual computer-generated bleep from the digital phones. The black telephone was so old Sara was surprised that it did not have a rotary dial. It didn't have any sleek lines or shiny buttons. Between cell phones and cordless phones and the digitization of noise, she had almost forgotten what a real telephone sounded like.

She used the back of her hand to wipe sweat off her lip. The heat from outside had started encroaching on the poorly ventilated squad room from the moment the power was cut. Now, over an hour later, the air was heavy, almost suffocating. To make matters worse, the bodies scattered around the room were starting to smell.

Brad's uniform shirt and pants were off, stuffed into the air-conditioning grates by Smith, probably to block prying eyes on the part of the police. Brad sat in his white boxer shorts and black socks, his embarrassment long past. Smith trusted Brad for some reason and he was the only one of them allowed any sort of freedom. Sara had sneaked him Jeffrey's wallet while he was taking the girls to the bathroom. She had no idea where he had hidden it. Her only hope was that he had done it well.

Stress had finally drained two of the remaining little girls, and they both slept with their heads in Brad's lap. Marla sat at a distance from the group, her mouth open, staring blankly at the floor. Sara was terrified the older woman would have another fit and tell Smith Jeffrey's true identity. She realized with cold clarity that if a choice had to be made, she would do whatever she needed to do to protect Jeffrey.

She leaned her head against the wall, allowing herself to look at Smith. He was pacing again, muttering under his breath. He had taken off his coat and she could see that every inch of his body was built, the muscles of his arms and shoulders bulging under his short-sleeved T-shirt. A huge blue tattoo of an eagle covered his right bicep, and on every second pass he took across the room Sara tried to decipher the words underneath to no avail.

Like his accomplice, he wore thick nighttime camouflage pants with his combat boots. The Kevlar vest must have felt like a straitjacket in this heat, but he kept it strapped tightly to his chest. Animal aggression sweated from Smith's every pore, but it was the second shooter, the quiet one, who scared Sara most. He was the one who followed orders, who did whatever he was told to do, whether it was to shoot at small children or blow a hole through a police officer's head. This personality type was hardly uncommon among young men – the military actively recruited for it – but adding Smith to the mixture made him even more volatile. If something happened to Smith, the second shooter was a wild card. Cut off the head of the scorpion and the tail could still sting.

Jeffrey stirred in Sara's lap, and she put her hand on his good shoulder to still him, saying, 'It's all right.'

He rubbed his eyes like a sleepy child. A fold in the material of her dress had creased his face, and she wanted nothing more than to kiss the line away.

'What time is it?'

She looked at her watch. 'Half past one,' she told him, stroking his hair off his forehead. 'Do you remember where we are?'

He took a deep breath, then let it go. 'I was dreaming about the first time I really made love to my wife.'

Sara pressed her lips together. She wanted so much to be back in that place that tears came to her eyes.

He continued, 'We were in the house where I grew up, on the floor in my room . . .'

'Shh,' she shushed, not wanting him to say too much.

He understood, but he closed his eyes for a moment like he did not want to let the memory go. When he opened his eyes again, Sara could tell how much pain he was in. Still, he did not complain about his wounds. Instead, he told her, 'Goddamn phone is driving me crazy.'

'I know,' she said, illogically wishing they would just unplug it if they were not going to answer. She waited for the next ring to finish before asking, 'Are you in much pain?'

He shook his head no, but she knew he was lying. Sweat poured off his body, and not just from the heat. The wound had clotted, but the blood could be pooling on the inside. His arm was cold to the touch, the pulse still thready. She guessed the bullet was between a torn artery and a nerve. Whenever Jeffrey moved, the nerve pinched, causing shooting pains that must be unbearable. Any movement also brought the risk of dislodging the bullet. Because the wound was so high up, she could not apply a tourniquet. The only thing keeping him from bleeding out was the pressure from the bullet. If he didn't get help soon, Sara did not know how much longer he could hold on.

'I was thinking,' she said, her voice barely more than a whisper, 'how much you . . .' She looked at Smith, but he was talking to his accomplice. 'How much has changed,' she said. He was so different from the man she had first fallen in love with, yet so much about him was the same. Time had done nothing but smooth his character, polishing it like a stone.

'Where are they?' he asked, trying to sit up.

She pressed gently on his shoulder and he stayed where he was. The fact that he had so little fight in him was alarming. 'They're in the front,' she said. 'They have Allison.'

'Ruth Lippman's daughter?' he asked, managing to raise his head. She let him see the girl before gently pushing him back down. Allison sat on the front counter, her legs dangling in the air. There was a long gash down the front of her shin where she'd slid down the sidewalk after attempting a particularly silly stunt on her bicycle last week. Sara had put in two sutures and extracted a promise in exchange for a lollipop that the little girl would be more careful the next time.

Smith had stopped pacing and was standing beside

Allison, his shotgun in the crook of his arm. On the other side of the girl stood the second shooter, his rifle resting on the counter, still pointing toward the front door. Smith watched them carefully, and Sara knew that he could hear everything they said.

She told Jeffrey, 'I'm worried about your arm.'

'It's okay,' he said, trying to sit up again.

'Don't,' she told him, then, 'Please. You shouldn't move any more than you have to.'

Jeffrey must have heard the concern in her voice because he stopped struggling.

He asked, 'Have they said what they want?'

She shook her head, trying not to make eye contact with Smith. Sara had worked in pediatrics most of her life. Even though Smith was not a child, he had all the markings of a twenty-something-year-old who had not quite grown up. She knew how aggressive young men could behave when they were challenged, especially if there was someone around to impress. She did not want to get shot in a case of one-up between Smith and his friend.

Jeffrey shifted to get more comfortable, and she prayed he wouldn't do any more damage to his arm. He lowered his voice, asking, 'One of them seemed to know you. Do you recognize him?'

She shook her head again, wishing to God she could tell him she knew exactly who the two shooters were and why they were here. She had moved back to Grant from Atlanta almost fifteen years ago, and would surely remember Smith if he had been a patient. Then, if Smith was a patient she could not recall, why was he here to kill Jeffrey? Or was he here on orders from his friend? Sara craned her neck, trying to get a better look at the second man. His ball cap was pulled low to hide his face, but the flash of sunlight coming in from the partially open front door showed Sara his eyes. They were empty, like a stagnant pool of water.

Sara realized Smith was watching her stare at his buddy, and she forced herself to smile at Allison. The little girl was slumped against the back of the counter with her skirt bunched up around her knees. Tears streamed down her face. Ruth Lippman had been Sara's tenth-grade English teacher. The woman was a perfect combination of tough and challenging, and Sara had loved her for it.

'He doesn't have much of an accent,' Jeffrey said, and he was right. There was a definite Southern twang when Smith let his temper get out of control, but for the most part, he spoke in the flat, unaccented English of a military brat. Or, maybe Sara was just making that fit the mold. For all she knew, he could be a wanna-be, someone whose father had been career military, but whose own criminal record or psychological profile had washed him out of the military before he even made it to his first week of boot camp.

Jeffrey closed his eyes.

'Why don't you try to sleep?'

'I shouldn't,' he said, but his eyelids fluttered and stilled.

Sara looked up at Smith, who had taken all this in with a watchful eye. She tried to keep her voice strong, but couldn't suppress the tremor in her voice. 'He needs medical attention. Please let him leave.'

Smith twisted his lips to the side as if he was actually considering her request. Beside him, the second shooter shifted. He said something under his breath and Smith walked over to the phone and picked it up mid-ring.

He said, 'We'll trade the old lady for sandwiches and bottled water. None of it better be fucked with. We can test it.' He listened to the response, his head to the side. 'No, I don't think so.' There was another pause, and Smith turned around, facing Allison. He held the phone in front of her face and Sara sensed he was smiling at her. She willed the girl not to trust him, but she saw Allison smile back just before Smith pinched her leg. Allison screamed, and Smith put the phone back to his ear.

He gave a steely laugh. 'That's right, lady. We're gonna hold on to the kids.' He turned back around, his eyes scanning the remaining hostages. 'We want some beer, too.'

His partner's head jerked around, and Sara got the impression that Smith had deviated from the script. So, she thought, maybe Smith wasn't completely in charge of this after all.

Smarting from the reprimand, Smith took his anger out on the person at the other end of the phone. 'One hour, bitch. You take any longer than that, the body count's gonna get a lot higher.'

ELEVEN

Sara drove to the funeral home, Jeffrey giving her directions from the passenger seat. Normally, she liked to have time alone before an autopsy to get a sense of the task in front of her, but there was no time for that luxury. She had called her mother before they left Nell's and told Cathy she would be back home in Grant that evening.

'Here,' Jeffrey said, indicating a long U-shaped building on the side of the highway. Nothing else was around except a small flower shop across the road. Eighteen-wheelers stirred the hot air as Sara got out of the car. In the distance, there was a grumble of thunder, which perfectly reflected her mood.

She winced as she stepped onto the asphalt, a loose rock digging through the thin sole of her sandals.

Jeffrey asked, 'You okay?' and she nodded, walking toward the entrance.

Paul, the deputy who had taken her to Nell's last night, stood at the doorway smoking a cigarette. He stubbed it on the side of the trash can and left it in the sand on top.

'Ma'am,' he said, opening the door for Sara.

'Thank you,' Sara answered, noticing the suspicious look the deputy gave Jeffrey.

Jeffrey asked, 'Where are they?'

When he answered, he looked at Sara instead of Jeffrey. 'They're down that hall in the back.'

The deputy walked between them as they headed toward the back of the building, and Sara could hear his keys jangling and the leather of his gun belt squeaking with every step. The funeral home was almost institutional, with painted cinder-block walls and fluorescent lighting giving a yellow cast to everything. Sara could smell embalming fluid and some sort of air freshener that might have been pleasant in a living room or office but here was almost sickening.

Paul indicated, 'Through here,' reaching ahead of her to open the door at the end of the hall. She chanced a look at Jeffrey, but he was staring past her into the room, his jaw set. Embalming equipment surrounded a concave metal table where the body had been placed. Covering the dead man was a clean white sheet, the edges blowing gently in the breeze generated by a loud window air-conditioning unit. The air was so cold it was stifling.

'Hey there,' Hoss said, holding out his hand to Sara. She went to shake it, too late realizing he meant to put his hand on her elbow and guide her into the room. Sara knew that men of Hoss's generation generally did not shake hands with women unless it was in jest. Her grandfather Earnshaw, whom she dearly loved, was the same way.

Hoss introduced her to the men in the room. 'This is Deacon White, the funeral director.' A rotund, dour man with a receding hairline gave Sara a curt nod. 'That's Reggie Ray.' Hoss indicated the second deputy who had been at Robert's house last night. The young man still had a camera around his neck, and Sara wondered if he slept with it.

'Slick,' Hoss said, addressing Jeffrey. 'Don't think I mentioned this last night – Reggie's Marty Ray's boy.'

'That so?' Jeffrey said, without much interest. Still, he offered the other man his hand. Reggie seemed reluctant to take it, and Sara wondered again why the deputies were so cagey around him.

Hoss said, 'Got Robert's statement this morning,' and Sara saw the surprised look on Jeffrey's face. 'Neighbors pretty much backed up his story.'

Sara waited for Jeffrey to ask what Robert had said, but he stared at the floor instead.

After a few moments of awkward silence, Deacon White indicated a door behind Sara. 'We keep our protective clothing in the storage room. You're welcome to anything we have.'

'Thank you,' Sara told him, getting a solemn nod in return. She wondered if the man was annoyed she was taking over. Grant County's funeral director had been a childhood friend of Sara's and more than happy to relinquish the responsibility of town coroner, but Deacon White was a lot harder to read.

She walked over to the storage room, which was little more than a glorified closet. Still, she shut the door. The moment she did, the men started talking. She could hear Hoss's deep baritone mixing with Paul's. From what she could gather, they were discussing a recent basketball game at the high school.

Sara opened a surgical gown and slipped it on, feeling foolish as she spun like a dog chasing its tail trying to tie the back. The gown was huge on her, obviously meant for Deacon White's pronounced midsection. By the time she had slipped on a pair of paper shoes and a hair protector, Sara felt like a clown.

She put her hand on the door, but did not open it. Closing her eyes, she tried to block out all that had happened in the last twenty-four hours. Focusing on her belief that Robert's wound was self-inflicted might shadow her findings during the autopsy, and Sara wanted to make certain she only went with known facts. She was not a detective. Her task now was to give her professional opinion to the police and let them decide how to proceed. The only thing she could control was how well she performed her job.

The men grew quiet as she walked back into the room. She thought she saw a smile on Paul's face, but he looked back down at his notebook, writing something with a well-chewed nub of pencil. Deacon White stood by the body, and Jeffrey and Hoss both leaned against the wall with their arms crossed over their chests. Reggie was by the sink, his camera gleaming in the light. An air of expectancy filled the room, but despite this, Sara got the distinct impression that this was merely a case of going through the motions.

Still, she asked, 'Where are the X rays?'

Deacon exchanged a look with Hoss before saying, 'We don't normally do X rays.'

Sara tried to cover her shock, knowing how it would look to come into their backyard and start treating them like a bunch of yokels. X rays were standard procedure for an autopsy, but they were especially important when dealing with a head wound. The bullet punched out bone as it entered the skull, and X rays of bone chips would provide conclusive evidence of the path the bullet had taken. Excising the wound could distort the path or even create false tracks.

She asked, 'Have you found the bullet?'

'From his head?' Reggie asked, sounding surprised. 'I got two twenty-twos out of the walls. I didn't find anything near his head except for . . . head.'

'The bullet could still be in there,' Sara told him.

Hoss cleared his throat politely before saying, 'Maybe ol' Reg here missed it on his sweep through the room. I'm sure we'll find it when we look again.'

Reggie seem to bristle a bit at this, but he had regained his composure by the time Hoss looked his way. He gave the sheriff a slight shrug as if to say it could happen.

Sara tried to phrase her words carefully. 'Sometimes, brain tissue can slow a bullet down enough so that it has insufficient velocity to exit the skull.'

Hoss pointed out, 'The right side of his head has been blown out.'

'That could be from a fracture.' Knowing the policeman's ammunition of choice, she made an educated guess, asking Reggie, 'We're talking a nine-millimeter hollow-point, I would assume?'

He flipped back through his notebook, reading, 'The Beretta had twenty-two long rifle, the Glock had hollow-point.'

Sara said, 'That could exert enough force to fracture the bone out through the scalp.' She did not add that an X ray would easily show this.

Hoss said, 'All right.'

She waited for him to say more, but when he did not, Sara pulled back the sheet. She should not have been surprised to find the body faceup, and hoped she managed to hide her irritation. Livor mortis had shifted to the back of the head, which meant blood could have seeped into the soft tissue of the scalp.

Any evidence of confluent bruising would be difficult to tell from antemortem bruising. Unless there was a laceration or some sort of pronounced abrasion in the scalp, it would be almost impossible for Sara to tell whether the bruises came from the man's own pooling blood or from someone hitting him in the head.

Rigor mortis had set in, fixing the body in a casketing position. Swan's hair was plastered to most of his face with sweat and blood. Still, she could see his mouth and eyes were slightly open, and there was a purple-blue cast to the side of his face where it had rested on the carpet. His chest was narrow, his ribs pronounced. His hands had not been bagged to preserve evidence from the scene, such as gunpowder residue or any fibers he might have clutched in his hand – and 'clutched' was the right word in this case; Swan's right hand was in a tight fist.

Reggie said, 'I tried, but I couldn't get his hand open.'

'That's fine,' Sara said, thinking that if she was able to find gunshot residue, there would be no proving whether or not it came from Reggie's or the dead man's hands. 'Do you have photographs of the scene yet?'

He shook his head no. 'I've got my drawings here,' he said, taking a folded mailing envelope out of his pocket. Inside were three sheets of paper with crude diagrams of the crime scene. He seemed apologetic when he showed them to Sara. 'I was gonna do 'em up better this morning.'

'That's fine,' she repeated, smoothing out the papers on a table by the sink. The bed and armoire were two lopsided rectangles across from each other. Luke Swan had been reduced to a stick figure with two X's for eyes. His right hand was under his body, the other out to his side. She asked, 'He was lying on his right hand?'

Reggie nodded again. 'Yeah. It was stuck like that when we turned him over.'

Deacon added, 'Rigor mortis was extremely pronounced.'

'What time did you get there?'

'About two hours after the accident,' he said, and Sara tried not to dwell on the fact that the man who would have performed the autopsy was already calling it an accident.

'Did you have trouble moving him?'

'We had to break the rigor to get him on the gurney.'

'Arms and legs?' she asked, and he nodded yes. Rigor mortis generally started in the jaw and worked its way out to the extremities. The body would take anywhere between six and twelve hours before it became fixed.

Jeffrey spoke for the first time, saying, 'Maybe he panicked. Maybe he was high on something that got his heart rate going.'

'We'll do a tox screen.'

Hoss broke in with strained politeness, 'Wanna explain that for those of us who didn't go to college?'

Sara told him, 'Rigor mortis can be brought on more quickly by strenuous exercise before death. A depletion of adenosine triphosphate, or ATP, would cause the muscles to stiffen more quickly.'

The sheriff nodded, though she could tell from his expression that he had not absorbed the information.

Sara opened her mouth to explain again, but something about Hoss's posture told her it would do no good. He was so much like her grandfather Earnshaw that she caught herself smiling.

Reggie said, 'These're the casings from the bullets,' indicating a line he had drawn near the door. Two more were marked beside the victim. 'The twenty-twos were here and here. The nine-mil is here by the door.'

Jeffrey cleared his throat, seemingly reluctant to speak. 'Did you fingerprint the casings?'

Reggie let his rancor show this time. 'Of course I did.' He added, 'And the guns. We traced the Glock back to Robert. It's his service weapon. The Beretta had the serial number shaved off.'

Hoss nodded, tucking his hands into his pockets.

Sara asked Deacon, 'Gloves?' and he took a box down from the cabinet by the sink. All the men watched Sara as she pulled on two pairs of surgical gloves, one over the other. Deacon rolled over a mayo tray, and she glanced down at the instruments, relieved to find a breadloafing knife, scissors, scalpels, and the other requisite tools for autopsy.

Deacon said, 'I'll help you with this,' and together he and Sara folded back the sheet covering the lower half of Luke Swan's body. His jeans and underwear had already been removed, which meant she could only guess by the lack of blood spatter from the head wound as to where the pants had been on the body.

Swan was a small man, probably no more than five seven and around a hundred sixty pounds, his body containing none of the grace his last name implied. Though he kept his blond hair long to the shoulder, he was far from hirsute, with a sparse patch of pubic hair around his groin. His penis was slightly tumescent, the swollen testicles showing signs of petechiae. His legs were spindly, and a large scar ran down the side of his left thigh. Sara guessed the wound had come during childhood. At the time it must have been a significant injury. For some reason, she thought of the scar on Jeffrey's back, and wondered what had been going through Jeffrey's mind when his father had hit him.

She asked Paul, 'Do you mind taking notes for me?'

'No, ma'am,' he said, turning to a fresh page in his notebook.

'He's how old?'

Paul said, 'Thirty-four.'

She nodded, thinking that fit the man in front of her. She called out her findings so far, pausing to give Paul time to write. Back in Grant, she used a Dictaphone for her reports, and she was not used to having to pause the natural cadence of the exam.

'Skin is slightly dry, probably due to lack of nourishment,' she said, running her hand down his arm. 'Track marks, probably a few years old, along the right arm.' On a hunch, she examined the area between his toes, saying, 'Fresh needle marks.'

'What's that?' Hoss interrupted.

Jeffrey explained, 'He was using the area between his toes to shoot up to try to hide the fact that he was using.' To Sara, he said, 'That would explain the ATP.'

'Depending on what he was using, it might.' She asked Deacon, 'Have you taken blood and urine?'

The man nodded. 'It'll take a week or two to get it back, though.'

Sara held her tongue, but Jeffrey said, 'Can we get a rush on that?'

Hoss said, 'It'll cost.'

Jeffrey shrugged, and Hoss gave a slight nod to Deacon, indicating it was okay.

Sara examined the surface of the body, finding nothing remarkable other than a star-shaped scar below the right ankle.

She asked Deacon, 'Can you help me open his hand?'

He put on a pair of gloves, and as they all watched, Deacon tried to pry open the fingers. The hand would not give, and he adjusted his footing, giving himself a wide stance as he tried to press his thumb into the small opening between Swan's thumb and index finger. When he put his shoulder into it, the finger broke open. The next was easier, and one by one he broke back the fingers and thumb. The snaps sounded like twigs breaking.

'Nothing,' Deacon said. He was leaning over the hand, and he moved out of the way so that Sara could see. Fingernail grooves cut into the meaty flesh of Swan's palm, but it appeared empty.

Deacon asked, 'Death spasm?'

'Those are very rare,' Sara answered, looking back at the chest where the fist had been. 'He was lying on his fist. The weight of his body could have closed the fingers and the rigor fixed it in place.' She looked around, finding a rolling lamp in the corner. 'Do you mind getting that so I can take a closer look?'

He did as he was asked, unwrapping the cord and getting Paul to plug it into the wall socket. The bulb flickered a few times but easily illuminated the empty palm.

Using the sharp edge of the tweezers, she scraped under his fingernails, removing dry skin as well as some larger, unidentifiable flakes. She put them in a specimen bottle, along with some nail clippings, and watched Paul seal them with a strip of bright green tape.

While Reggie took photographs, Sara held a ruler next to the scars and other identifying marks she had found. They progressed to the head, and she used her fingers to pick out pieces of skull and gray matter before pushing the hair back off Swan's face and exposing the entrance wound on the left side of his head.

Jeffrey had been quiet through all of this, and when he said, 'Powder tattooing,' his voice was so low Sara was not sure if he had spoken the words or she had heard them in her own head.

He was right. There was a scatter-shot of reddish brown lesions surrounding the entrance wound where hot powder grains from the gun had burned the skin. Sara held the ruler as Reggie took photographs. She lightly combed her fingers through the hair and checked the surrounding skin for telltale markings. Finally, she said, 'There's no soot that I can see.'

'Did he bleed it off?' Jeffrey asked, standing beside her.

'Not from this side,' she told him, feeling slightly relieved. The head was a mess, but she could see it clearly under the light now. Powder tattooing with the absence of soot most likely indicated an intermediate-range wound, meaning Robert was standing at least eighteen to twenty-four inches from the man when Swan was shot.

Jeffrey asked, 'What'd he have in the Glock again?'

Paul was thumbing back through his notes. 'Federal, one-fifteen grain.'

'Ball powder,' Jeffrey said, with palpable relief. He told Hoss, 'Ball powder travels faster. That puts Robert anywhere from two to four feet away.'

'Goes with what he said this morning,' Hoss told them. 'Had a hangfire when he pulled the trigger.'

'Hangfire?' Sara repeated, though not because she did not understand the word. A hangfire meant there was a delay between Robert pulling the trigger and the bullet being fired from the gun.

Jeffrey asked, 'Did he say how long it took?'

'He wasn't sure,' Hoss answered. 'Maybe half a second or so.'

Jeffrey looked at Sara, and she wondered if her own expression of disbelief mirrored his. There was no scientific way to prove or disprove how the gun had fired or when. Bullets did not come with a time stamp, and whether or not the gun had in fact had a hangfire was impossible to prove with any scientific accuracy.

Sara turned her focus back to the head, combing through the hair for debris and setting it aside on the tray for collection. She tried to keep her mind on the task, but all she could think was how quickly excuses were being made for every question the evidence raised. If the situation had been reversed and Robert was lying on the table in front of her, she knew that all the men here would track down Luke Swan like a rabid dog.

As if he knew what she was thinking, Jeffrey asked Hoss, 'Where's Robert now?'

'He's with Jessie at her mama's,' Hoss provided. 'Why?'

'I thought I'd check in on him. See how he's doing.'

'He's fine,' Hoss said, looking at his watch. 'This is running a little later than I thought it would. I need to step out for a meeting.'

Jeffrey asked, 'Do you want Paul to take our statements?'

Hoss seemed to have forgotten about this, but he answered, 'No, I'll do that. Let's meet back at the station around three.'

Jeffrey told him, 'We were planning on leaving before then.'

'That's fine,' Hoss told them, giving Jeffrey a hard pat on the back. 'Y'all drop by the station on your way out of town. I'm sure it won't take long.'

Paul waited for his boss to leave before saying, 'I need to get back to some paperwork myself.' He gave Sara a polite nod, then left the room. Deacon White was next, making an excuse about a lunch appointment. Sara wondered if he noticed the clock in the room read ten.

Reggie put down his camera and leaned against the sink, his expression plainly stating he had nowhere to go and even if he did, he did not trust Jeffrey alone in the room with the corpse.

Jeffrey made it worse by asking Reggie, 'What did Robert's statement say?'

Reggie shrugged. 'Why are you so curious?'

Jeffrey returned the shrug.

Sara did not know how Reggie would handle this, but still, she told Jeffrey, 'I don't want to dig around for the bullet. We need X rays first or I'll destroy any evidence.'

Reggie said, 'There wasn't another bullet in the room. I checked. It was just the two twenty-two LRs in the walls and casings on the floor like I drew.'

Jeffrey seemed cautious, like he was feeling Reggie out. 'What did Robert carry for backup?'

Reggie stared without answering.

Sara added, 'A twenty-two would have less velocity than a nine-mil. It would be more likely to stay in the skull.'

Reggie's chin dropped slightly. His eyes went from Jeffrey to Sara. 'I think we should find that bullet.'

Jeffrey nodded his agreement, saying, 'Yeah.'

Sara changed into a fresh pair of gloves, thinking she hardly had the authority to do this, but also knowing that this was the only way to find the truth. Carefully, she probed around the exit wound in the skull with her fingers, not wanting to use the forceps because they could scratch or change the markings on the metal.

'Nothing,' she finally said. 'It could be deeper in.'

Reggie told her, 'Hoss won't let us take him back for X rays.'

'Luke,' Jeffrey said. 'His name's Luke Swan. You ever have him in your cruiser?'

'Hell,' Reggie snorted. 'About a million times.'

'For what?'

'Mostly breaking and entering, but he always made sure the houses were empty. Usually, he picked when he thought folks were at church.'

'Last night was Sunday.'

'Church is over by eight. Even if he was stoned, he would've seen the cars in the driveway and known.'

'You ever find a weapon on him?'

'Not once.'

'He ever do anything violent?'

'No.' Reggie paused as if to think it over. 'He was small-time, usually just taking what he could carry

189

out in a pillowcase.' He added, 'But you never know, do you? I bet the people said the same thing about your daddy before he hooked up with them fellas who shot my uncle Dave.'

Sara saw Jeffrey's throat work as he swallowed.

Reggie continued, 'You never know what some people are capable of. One minute they're stealing lawn mowers, the next minute they're murdering a sheriff's deputy in cold blood.'

Sara felt the need to say something, though she could not think what. Jeffrey's fists were clenched like he wanted nothing more than to beat Reggie to a pulp. Making things worse, Reggie tilted his chin up, practically begging Jeffrey to take a swing.

Sara asked, 'Reggie, would you mind taking notes?'

Reggie took his time breaking eye contact with Jeffrey. 'No, ma'am,' he said, taking out his note-book. He glanced back at Jeffrey. 'Anything to help.'

While he wrote, Sara went back through her findings, not wanting to track down Paul for his earlier notes and delay leaving this god-awful town a minute longer than necessary. Out of the corner of her eye, she caught Jeffrey staring at Luke Swan and wondered what he was thinking. He had not told her that the shooting his father was involved in resulted in the death of a cop. Reggie's words had obviously hit their mark, and she could feel Jeffrey's anger melt into a sadness that felt almost like a fourth presence in the room.

The rest of the autopsy was as routine as was possible with any gunshot victim. There were no remarkable findings and no clues that pointed to anything other than what Robert had told them last night. Long-term drug use was obvious, as was a fatty diet that left deposits of calcium in Swan's heart. His liver was larger than expected, but considering Sara found alcohol in the man's stomach, it made sense. As for the missing bullet, maybe Reggie had overlooked it at the house or maybe it was buried deeper in the brain. Sara had not opened Swan's head, wanting to leave the option of X rays open should Hoss later be persuaded to actually investigate the case.

Sara was closing the Y-incision with the usual baseball stitch when she remembered to ask about clothing.

Reggie supplied, 'They're in a bag at the station.'

'They're not here?' Sara asked, thinking that was odd.

'Hoss took them for evidence this morning,' Reggie said, flipping back through his notes. 'Pair of twenty-nine-thirty Levis, pair of Nike sneakers and white socks, wallet with six bucks in it and a license.'

'No underwear?' Sara asked.

He reread the notes. 'Guess not.'

'Car keys?'

'He never drove himself anywhere. Lost his license on a DUI coupla three years back.'

'DUI doesn't mean he stopped driving,' Jeffrey pointed out.

Reggie shrugged. 'Never caught him on the street. Car belonged to his grandma, anyway. She's crazy as a loon. Hoss caught her driving the wrong way a couple of times, then she ran through that stop sign over on Henderson and tore off the front end. Even if he wanted to drive after that, the car wouldn't start.'

Sara took off her gloves. 'Is there somewhere I can sit to write out my report?'

'I'll go fetch Deacon,' Reggie offered. 'I'm sure he won't mind you using his office.'

Sara went to the sink to wash her hands, feeling Jeffrey watch her every move. She tried to catch his eye again, but Deacon came into the room and he looked away.

'Well,' Deacon said, shuffling through some papers. 'I guess these are probably what you're used to.'

Sara glanced down at the autopsy forms. 'Yes, thanks.'

'I usually fill them out in here,' Deacon added, rolling a chair over to the counter by the sink.

'That's fine.'

Jeffrey said, 'I'll be out by the car when you're ready,' and left the room.

Deacon said, 'I'll leave you to it.'

Sara pulled up the chair and Reggie walked over, looking over her shoulder as she wrote in her name and the various details the state required. She recorded Luke Swan's address and home phone number, then the various weights and measurements of organs and other landmarks she found on the body. She was writing her conclusion when Reggie cleared his throat. Sara looked up, waiting for him to speak.

For some reason, she anticipated a treatise against Jeffrey. What she got was, 'This look pretty straightforward to you?'

Sara tried to measure her words, not knowing whether or not to trust the man. 'I don't think any shooting is straightforward.'

'That's true,' he agreed, his tone just as cautious as hers. 'How long you known Jeffrey Tolliver?'

For some reason, Sara felt the need to take up for Jeffrey. 'A while. Why?'

'Just asking,' he said.

'Was there something else?'

He shook his head no and she went back to the report.

A few minutes later, Reggie cleared his throat again, and she looked up, expectant.

He said, 'The Beretta takes seven rounds in the magazine.'

'Then you should have found five bullets in the magazine.'

'Six if he had one in the chamber.'

Sara waited, thinking this was like pulling teeth. 'How many did you find?'

'Six.'

She put down the pen. 'Reggie, are you trying to tell me something?'

His jaw worked just like Jeffrey's did when he was angry. Sara was getting tired of drawing out information from reluctant men.

She said, 'If you've got something to say, then say it.'

Instantly, she knew she had pushed him in the wrong direction, but Sara was no longer worried about stepping on people's feelings. 'Reggie, if you think there's something suspicious about this shooting, then you need to speak up. All I can do is fill in these forms. I'm not a cop and I'm not your mama.'

'Lady,' Reggie began, his voice shaking with anger, 'you don't know what you're getting yourself into here.'

'That sounds an awful lot like a threat.'

'It's a warning,' he said. 'You seem like a nice enough person, but I don't trust the company you keep.'

'You've made that abundantly clear.'

'You might want to think about why people keep warning you off him.' He tipped his hat to Sara as he headed toward the door. 'Ma'am.'

TWELVE

The heat slammed into Sara like a brick as soon as she opened the door to leave the funeral home. Overhead, she could tell a storm was coming, but the rolling clouds did nothing to cool the air. Her skin seemed to contract for a few seconds before it adjusted, and by the time she got to Jeffrey standing by the car, she could feel sweat dripping down her back. Despite this, she told him, 'Let's go for a walk.'

He did not ask questions as they made their way through the cemetery behind the building. There was no breeze as they climbed a sloping hill, and Sara felt slightly dizzy from the heat. Still, she kept going, absently reading markers as they walked toward the wooded area at the rear of the cemetery. There was a gate in the fence, and Jeffrey held it open for her.

The sky darkened even more as they walked into the forest, and Sara did not know if it was from the canopy of trees overhead or the impending thunderstorm. Either way, the temperature seemed to drop about ten degrees in the shade, and for that she was thankful.

They walked along a narrow path, Jeffrey ahead of her pushing back branches and kicking debris out of the way. Birds called overhead, and she heard a buzzing sound that could belong to a cricket or a snake, depending on how much she let her imagination get away from her.

Finally, she broke the silence. 'I know this is a crazy question considering we're in Alabama, but has anyone thought to ask why Luke Swan wasn't wearing a shirt?'

Jeffrey pulled a twig off a low-hanging branch. 'I don't think anybody's asking much of anything.' He glanced at her over his shoulder. 'There weren't any footprints outside the window.' Seemingly as an afterthought, he added, 'Of course, the ground was dry. You could make the argument that nothing would leave footprints.'

'It seems to me arguments are being made to dismiss a lot of things,' she said, flinching as a tree root dug into her heel.

He stopped, facing her. 'I couldn't tell if the screen was pulled off from the outside or pushed from the inside.'

'What are you going to do?'

'Hell,' he said, throwing the twig into the woods. 'I don't know.' He knelt down and started to untie his shoes.

'What are you doing?'

'You might as well be walking barefoot in those sandals.' He slipped off his tennis shoe and handed it to her.

Sara hesitated, and he added, 'I've had my mouth on every part of your body, Sara. You think I haven't noticed your feet are the same size as mine?'

'They're not that big,' she mumbled, putting her hand on his shoulder to steady herself as she slipped her foot into his shoe. To her embarrassment, the fit was nearly perfect.

She looked down to see if he had noticed, and he smiled up at her. 'I love the way you blush.'

'I'm not blushing,' she said, though she could feel it in her cheeks.

He helped her into the other sneaker. She started to kneel down to tie the laces, but Jeffrey did it for her, saying, 'I keep waiting for somebody to say something. There's no way they're all buying this story.'

'I think Reggie has some questions,' she said, watching him double-knot the laces. He had such large hands, but they were soft, and his touch was always so gentle. For some reason, the anger Sara had felt toward him this morning had dissipated, and all she could think was that twenty-four hours ago she had been on the verge of falling in love with this man. As much as she wanted to change her mind, she could not alter how she felt about him.

'There.' He stood, holding her sandals in one hand. 'Okay?'

She took a step, lying, 'They're a little loose.'

'Yeah, right.' He continued, walking in his socks. 'Did Reggie mention I dated his sister?'

'I just assumed you'd dated every woman in town.'

He gave her a look.

'Sorry,' she said, and she really was. They walked for a few more minutes before she asked, 'Why is everyone so against you?'

'My dad wasn't exactly in the Rotary Club.'

'It goes back further than that,' she said, wondering what he was hiding. She had her own secrets, though, and she was hardly in a position to fault him for being reticent.

He stopped, facing her again. 'I want to stay in town another day.'

'Okay.'

'And I want you to stay with me.'

'I don't –'

'You're the only person here who doesn't think I'm some kind of criminal.'

'Hoss doesn't.'

'He will after I give my statement.'

'What are you going to say?' she asked, wary of his answer.

'Exactly what you'll say: the truth.' He resumed walking and she followed. 'Maybe it'd be different if Robert was talking.' He stopped, pointing behind Sara. She turned, looking at the mountains on the horizon.

'That's Herd's Gap,' he said. 'All the rich people live there. Jessie's family included.'

Sara shaded her eyes, taking in the view.

'I know it doesn't look like much, but it's right at the foot of the Appalachian Mountains. You can't see them from here, but up that way,' he indicated the space to their left, 'are the Cheaha Mountains.' He started walking again. 'And underneath us, there's thirty-two miles of the hardest, whitest marble in the world. It goes about four hundred feet down.'

Sara watched his back, wondering why he was telling her this. 'Is that so?'

'Sylacauga marble is in the Washington Monument and the Supreme Court building,' he continued. 'I remember when I was a kid the windows would shake from all the blasting.' He stepped over a fallen tree and held out his hand to help Sara over. She could see his socks were getting filthy, but he did not seem to care.

He said, 'There's an underground river that cuts through the city. Between the river and the blasting in the quarry, there are sinkholes all over town. A few years ago one of them opened up at the Baptist church and the back half of the building dropped about ten feet underground.'

'Jeffrey –'

He stopped again. 'That's what I feel like, Sara. I feel like this whole town is sinking, and I'm going right down with it.' He gave a harsh laugh. 'They say you can't get any lower than the ground, but this is the one place you can.'

She took a deep breath, and breathed out, 'I can't have children.'

He did not speak for what seemed like an eternity, then he gave her a neutral 'Okay.'

'I gather we're supposed to pretend you didn't say what you said last night before . . .' she threw a hand into the air, '. . . before all hell broke lose.'

'No,' he stopped her. She believed him when he told her, 'I meant what I said.'

'Then tell me,' she asked. 'Tell me why Reggie doesn't trust you.'

Droplets of rain splattered against the leaves overhead, and Sara looked up at the sky just as the bottom dropped out. In seconds, they were both soaked. The rain was so dense she reached out to take Jeffrey's hand for fear she would lose him.

'This way,' he yelled over the downpour. He walked fast, then started jogging when a bolt of lightning cracked the sky. The tall trees all around them that had been so beautiful before were nothing more than lightning rods now, and Sara picked up the pace along with him, wanting to find shelter before the storm got worse.

The sky grew darker, and Sara looked up just as Jeffrey pulled her down into a squatting position.

Carefully, he pushed back a clump of hanging vines and rotted old boards before leading her through a four-foot-wide opening into a cave. Inside, the air turned almost cold, and she put her hand against the rough rock of the ceiling, trying to get her bearings. Even with her knees bent, Sara could not stand up straight. She curved at the waist, reaching out with her hands, trying to feel her surroundings as Jeffrey pulled her farther into the cave. There was nothing but empty space to her left and right, but overhead the ceiling sloped up so that she could straighten a bit more. Still, she had to keep her head and shoulders down so she would not scrape against the ceiling.

In the distance, she could hear the muffled rain as well as a constant dripping. Just enough light came in through the vines and cracked boards at the entrance to keep them from total darkness, but somehow that was no comfort. Even as her vision adjusted, she could not see the back of the cave.

'You okay?' Jeffrey asked.

'Fine.' Sara shuddered, but not from the cold. She kept her hand against the ceiling, feeling claustrophobia overwhelm her.

'Jesus, it smells in here.' He passed by her again, doing something at the entrance of the cave. More light came in as he kicked out the boards, but it was still too dark for comfort.

Sara blinked a few times, making out a long bench seat like the kind they used to put in cars. Stuffing and springs jutted out of the vinyl upholstery. In front of the seat was an old coffee table with hemp rope around the edges, scuffs showing where people had sat with their feet propped up. Jeffrey brushed something out of his hair as he walked over to the seat. He searched under the bench, and over the steady hush of the rain she heard him laugh.

'They're still here,' he said, sounding pleased.

She stepped closer to him, unsettled by the darkness. A musty odor was in the air, and underneath that the scent of decay. She wondered if there were any animals in here, or perhaps an animal was on his way back home, looking to get out of the storm.

Jeffrey struck a match, and the cave was briefly illuminated before the flame flickered out. Like her, he was standing with his shoulders hunched against the ceiling. Unlike her, he seemed perfectly at ease. She felt embarrassed for being so frightened. Sara had never been afraid of the dark before, but the closed space had a feel to it that she could not quite name.

He struck another match. The fire burned down just as quickly as it had with the first, casting the cave back into darkness. He said, 'I guess they got wet.'

Sara spoke before she could stop herself. 'I don't like it in here.'

'The storm will pass soon,' he told her, taking Sara's arm and leading her to the seat. 'It's okay,' he soothed. 'We used to come here after school.'

'Why?' she asked, thinking this was as close to being buried alive as she ever wanted to come. Even sitting down, she could feel the cave looming over her. She reached out, grabbing Jeffrey's hand.

'It's okay,' he repeated, finally sensing her fear. He put his arm around her and kissed the side of her head.

Sara leaned into him, asking, 'How did you find this place?'

'It's near the quarry,' he told her. 'Robert came

across it one day while we were out looking for arrowheads.'

'Arrowheads?'

'This area was filled with Indians. Creek at first, then Shawnee warriors. They called it Chalakagay. DeSoto's records mention the town in the early 1500s.' He paused. 'Of course, the government came in around 1836 and moved them all out west.' He stopped again. 'Sara, I don't want kids.'

The sound of rain filled the cave, sounding like a thousand brooms sweeping across the rock.

'I didn't exactly have the best role models growing up, and who knows what the hell my genes will pass on.'

She put her fingers to his lips. 'Tell me more about the Indians.'

He kissed her fingers, then asked, 'Why, you want something to help you sleep?'

Sara laughed, and she realized with a start that she could stay here forever as long as he kept talking. She repeated, 'Tell me more.'

He paused, probably trying to think of what to say. 'You can't see it, but there's a lot of marble in here. Not enough to get the quarry folks interested, but you can see the veins along the back wall. That's why the air is so cool. Are you cold?'

'No, just soaking wet.'

He pulled her closer and she put her head in the crook of his neck, thinking that everything would be okay if they could just stay this way until the storm passed.

He continued, 'We stole this bench seat from an old car out in the junkyard. Possum's probably still got the scars on his ass from the dog we had to wrestle for it. The coffee table was out by the road for trash pickup. We carried it two miles up the highway to get it here.' He laughed good-naturedly. 'We thought we had it made.'

'I bet you brought girls here all the time.'

'Are you kidding? They were afraid of spiders.'

'Spiders?' She stiffened.

'Don't tell me you're suddenly afraid of spiders.'

'I'm just afraid of things crawling on me that I can't see.' He stood up, and she asked, 'Where are you going?'

'Hold on,' he told her, and she could hear his hand feeling along the wall of the cave. 'We used to keep a coffee can . . .' He stopped, and she heard the jangle of metal against metal. 'Aha. More matches. Possum got them out of the back of a comic book. They're supposed to be waterproof.'

Sara tucked her feet underneath her, keeping her back flat to the seat. Crazy as it was, she had the unnatural fear that something – or someone – would reach out and touch her shoulder.

'Here we go,' he said, striking a match. She could see his face in the light as he held the flame to a small utility candle. There was a flicker, and she held her breath, not breathing until the wick caught.

'I can't believe it still works after all this time.'

In the flickering light, Sara saw a form behind him. Her heart jumped into her throat and she gasped so loudly that Jeffrey startled, banging his head against the ceiling.

He looked behind him, shouting, 'Jesus Christ!' In his haste to get away, he tripped against the coffee table, unable to catch himself before he hit the ground.

Sara panicked, reaching out for the candle. Hot wax burned her hand, but she managed to keep the flame from blowing out. Her heart was pounding so hard that her ribs ached.

'Christ,' Jeffrey said, brushing dirt off his jeans. 'What the fuck is that?'

Sara forced herself to stand, and walked over to the skeleton that had scared her so much seconds before.

The remains were laid on a rock that jutted out like a seat. Though the bones looked yellowed with age, sinew remained in a few areas, probably because of the coolness of the cave. Part of the left leg down to the foot was missing, as well as some fingers on the right hand. Even in the dim candlelight, Sara could see the teeth marks where some kind of rodent had gnawed skin from the bone. She held the candle up to the head, which had tilted sideways and become lodged in a crevice between two rocks. The skull was fractured on the right side, the bone collapsed into the braincase from the force of what must have been a very heavy object.

She looked back at Jeffrey just in time to see him slip something into his pocket.

His tone was defensive. 'What?'

Sara turned back to the skeleton. 'I think this person was murdered.'

THIRTEEN

Lena was gritting her teeth so hard her jaw hurt. Wagner wasn't saying much into the phone, but Lena and probably everyone in the cleaners could hear the shooter screaming on the other end.

Wagner said, 'Why don't you tell me your name?' Only to be answered with a barked laugh. When she asked about the children, the only response she got was a little girl yelling into the phone. The sound echoed in the room, and Lena fought the urge to cover her ears.

Wagner remained calm. 'I take it that means you're holding on to the children?'

The answer was mumbled, but the shooter's last demand was loud and clear, especially since Wagner held the phone a few inches from her ear to deflect the sound. 'One hour, bitch. You take any longer than that, the body count's gonna get a lot higher.'

Despite the threat, Wagner smiled as she closed her cell phone. 'Well,' she said. 'They want beer.'

Lena opened her mouth to restate her offer to volunteer, but Wagner held up a finger for silence, saying, to Frank and Nick, 'Gentlemen, if I could have a moment of your time?'

The two men followed her into Bill Burgess's office. Wagner smiled at Lena before shutting the

205

door. It was a cat's smile, and Lena could not tell if the woman was being polite or warning her off. Either way, Lena would fight tooth and nail to be the one to go into the station. She had to do her part. Jeffrey had allowed her back on the force despite what everyone in town was saying. The worst crime was that he was lying dead right now and Lena was alive.

Molly Stoddard had been leaning against the folding table, but she stood up and knocked on the door to Burgess's office. She entered without waiting for a reply, closing the door behind her.

Lena watched Wagner's guys for a reaction, but they seemed uninterested. One of them was talking so low on his cell phone she wondered if he was just moving his lips, and the other two were leaned over a map of the station, pointing to different areas like they were hatching a plan. They had not been able to get a camera into the air-conditioning vent because the shooters had blocked them with clothing.

She walked over to see what they were planning. The guy on the cell phone ended the call. He told her, 'Jennings was killed in a six-car pile-up outside Friendswood, Texas, last year.'

'You're kidding,' she said, feeling like all the wind had been knocked out of her.

The guy added, 'There were two kids in the back. One of them walked away from the accident. That's good, right?'

'Yeah,' Lena said, though she doubted the kid felt lucky. She had seen the kind of damage Jennings was capable of firsthand. That the animal had died in such a seemingly normal way was just wrong.

The office door opened and Amanda Wagner came out followed by Frank. Nick and Molly were still inside, and Lena could see that Molly was using the phone on old man Burgess's desk. Her head was bent down and she had her hand wrapped around the back of her neck like she wanted to keep the conversation private.

Wagner's man repeated the information about Jennings. His boss said, 'Well, it was a long shot anyway.' She motioned Lena toward the office. 'Follow me.'

Nick waited until they were all inside before shutting the door. Molly looked up at Lena, a flash of irritation in her eyes. Into the phone, she said, 'Baby, Mama has to go now, okay?' She waited a beat. 'I love you, too.'

Lena had not given Sara's nurse much thought beyond noticing her around the clinic, and it had never occurred to Lena that the woman was a mother. She was probably a good one, too – always calm, always there for her kids. She did not seem to have a selfish bone in her body. Some people were just made for that kind of life.

'Detective Adams,' Wagner began. 'We've selected you to go into the building.'

Nick said, 'I want to repeat that I'm against this.'

Lena went on the defensive. 'I know what I –'

'Not you,' Nick interrupted. 'Her.'

'Wait a minute,' Lena said, finally understanding what Molly had done. 'She's going, too?'

Wagner provided, 'We'll send you in as paramedics under the guise of offering medical assistance.'

'You said Barry was probably dead.'

Molly looked at Nick as she spoke. 'Some of the kids could be hurt. Sara could need me.'

Nick's mouth went into a straight line, and Lena

wondered why he was so vehement. His objection seemed more personal than professional.

'Just for the record,' Wagner began, 'I'm a little hesitant to send you in, Detective, but Nicky assures me you're up to the challenge.'

Lena bit back the defensive remark that wanted to come. Instead, she swallowed her pride and said, 'If you're not certain . . .' She tried to find the words, struggling with her emotions. 'If you think someone else is more qualified, then I'll step down.'

'That's just it,' Wagner answered. 'There isn't anyone more qualified. If I send in one of my boys, the shooters will know immediately what's going on. I think our best plan of action is to send in both of you. They'll be more comfortable with women.'

'Or they'll take you both hostage,' Nick added. 'Or just shoot you.'

'He's right,' Wagner said. 'There's nothing to keep them from doing either or both.' She crossed her arms. 'Are you still so eager to get into that building?'

Lena did not hesitate. 'Yes.'

They all looked at Molly.

'Ms. Stoddard?' Wagner asked.

Molly exchanged a look with Nick. 'Yes.'

Wagner said, 'Your resolve seems to have slipped a little.'

'No.' Molly stood. 'I'm ready.'

2:15 P.M.

Lena washed her hands in the bathroom sink of the Grant Medical Center. Her hands shook slightly, but that was nothing new. Her hands had been shaking off and on for the last two years, ever since she was abducted. Sometimes, Lena thought the shaking was because of the scars in her hands that her attacker had made, but her doctors assured her there was no nerve damage.

'You okay?' Molly Stoddard asked. She was watching Lena's hands like they told a story.

'I'm fine,' Lena told her, snatching a paper towel off the roll.

'It's okay to be nervous,' Molly said. 'As a matter of fact, I'd feel better if you did.'

'Right,' Lena answered. She took the EMT uniform off the counter and went into a stall to change.

'*I'm* nervous,' Molly said. She was obviously waiting for Lena to speak, but when she did not, Molly drew out an 'O-okay.'

Lena took off her jacket and hung it on the hook on the back of the stall door. She was unbuttoning her shirt when a knock came at the bathroom door.

Nick Shelton asked, 'Y'all decent?'

Molly said yes as Lena said no.

'Sorry,' Molly apologized, but Lena could already hear Nick in the room. She sat on the toilet, not wanting to be undressed with him in the room, even though there was a locked stall door between them.

'I wanted to say,' Nick began, his voice sounding hesitant. 'I just . . .'

'We'll be fine,' Molly said, as if she knew exactly what was bothering him. Lena peered through the crack in the door and she saw that Molly had her hand on Nick's face.

Molly whispered again, 'I'll be fine.'

'You don't have to do this,' Nick said.

'If I was in there and Sara –'

'Sara doesn't have two kids at home, and that's

exactly what she'd be telling you now if she was here.'

Molly looked Lena's way, and Lena stood to continue changing so they would not think she had been watching. Her pants dropped to the floor and she heard a muffled clank as the knife she always kept in her back pocket hit the tile. Lena looked out the crack to make sure Molly and Nick had not seen. They were still whispering, as if the fact that she was three feet away meant nothing. Nick clearly did not want Molly to go into the station. Lena couldn't blame him. There was no guarantee the shooters weren't looking for more hostages.

Lena opened her pocketknife and ran her finger along the sharp blade. The knife was little more than three inches long, but she could do some damage with it. The only question was where she could hide it in case the shooters frisked her.

Nick raised his voice to include Lena. 'They capitulated too easily,' he said. 'Usually, hostage takers are unstable. They're emotional. You have to deal with them for a while, get their trust, before they make concessions. They're sending Marla out too soon.'

Lena slipped on the pants for the paramedic's uniform. They were about one size too big, which was a better fit than she had hoped. She suggested, 'Maybe they're hungry.'

'There's something not right here,' Nick insisted. 'They obviously know what we're doing. They wouldn't have blocked the vents just for the hell of it. They knew we would have cameras and that standard operating procedure is to try the vents first. This could be a trap to get more hostages.'

Lena slid off her sneaker and dropped in the

pocketknife. She stepped back into the shoe, wiggling the knife around until it was snug against the arch of her foot.

'Lena?' Nick prompted.

'I know the dangers, Nick,' Lena snapped, thinking he was treating her like a ten-year-old instead of a seasoned cop. She put on the white paramedic's shirt, which was tight across her chest. The badge over the pocket read MARTIN, and she wondered if Martin was a skinny guy or a flat-chested woman.

When she opened the door, Molly moved away from Nick as if they had been caught. Lena checked herself in the mirror, thinking that with the buttons stretched across her chest she looked like some slut out of a porn movie. Considering some of the Grant paramedics she had seen around town, she fit right in.

She told Nick, 'I know you don't trust Wagner.'

'Do you know why?' Nick asked, but he did not let her answer. 'I know the rumor, but let me set it straight. I'm the one who hesitated. She didn't hesitate. She never hesitates. She's ice. And I'll tell you another thing.' He gave Molly a meaningful look. 'She doesn't like women.'

Lena blew air out through her lips.

'It's true,' Nick said. 'She doesn't mind using them as bait. That's exactly what she's doing here, no matter what you think. That's what happened in Ludowici. She sent in a female cop and the shooters kept the woman. She was dead ten minutes later.'

'Because *you* hesitated?' Lena asked. She could see the guilt flash in his eyes and she regretted her words – not because she didn't mean them, but because the situation was stressful enough without having Molly Stoddard pissed off with her, too.

Nick said, 'This won't go down like you think. You've been on the job long enough to know something isn't right here. You feel it in your gut. You know that, Lena.'

'I'll be outside,' Lena told him, thinking it would be best to leave them alone. She walked out of the bathroom and ran into one of Wagner's men. He was built like a brick wall, and he grabbed her in surprise. His hands stayed on her body a little too long, and she pushed him back, trying not to show her anger. She walked toward Wagner, who was standing at the end of the hallway with a cell phone to her ear. She ended the call as Lena reached her.

Wagner said, 'What's in your shoe?'

'It's just tight,' Lena said. 'Kind of like this shirt.'

'Better too tight than too big,' Wagner countered. 'What happened to your lip?'

Lena put her hand to her mouth, a second later realizing she had given herself away. 'Accident,' she said, but the lie sounded weak even to her.

Wagner seemed to be taking all of this in, but she did not challenge Lena. 'I don't quite trust you, Detective Adams, but I'm letting you go in there because you're familiar with the layout and because they'll see you as less threatening.'

'Thanks for the vote of confidence.'

'You don't need any more confidence from me, Detective,' Wagner shot back. 'Listen closely: you're to deliver the food and get Marla Simms out of there as quickly as possible.'

'All right.'

'I don't need heroics, and I certainly don't need you exchanging yourself for any hostages.'

Lena looked down, trying to hide her expression. That had been exactly what she was planning.

'It might seem like a good idea, but you're more useful to me out here than you are in there. You're trained to appraise dangerous situations. I need your expert opinion.'

She seemed like a frank person, so Lena decided to say what was on her mind. 'That sounds like you're blowing smoke up my ass.'

Wagner's lip curled up in a smile, and she got a look in her eyes that Lena had seen several times before in other people; the woman realized she had underestimated Lena. 'Maybe a little of it's smoke, but you worked with Brad Stephens. Maybe he can communicate something to you. I know partners pick up on each other's codes.'

'He wasn't my partner.'

'I don't have time for your ego,' Wagner reprimanded. 'What I want from you when you come out of that place is a detailed drawing of where everyone is. I need to know how many desks and filing cabinets are against the doors and I need to know exactly how they're armed. What are they using, Sig, S&W, Glock? Detective Wallace thinks the shotgun is a Wingmaster. Did they bring extra ammo? What caliber? Are they still wearing Kevlar? How are they getting along? Is one getting a little too big for his britches? Maybe the other one can be turned or distracted. I need to know every weakness in their armor, and I can't get that from you if you stay inside.'

Lena nodded. All of that would be useful, and there was no way Molly Stoddard would even begin to know how to tell the difference between a twenty-two and a nine-mil, let alone give an accurate assessment of available firepower.

Lena asked, 'Should I try to pass them anything?'

'No,' Wagner said. 'Not at this point. We need to establish some trust. They're going to pat you down head to toe.' She glanced at Lena's shoe. 'If they find anything, they're going to be angry, and they're going to take it out on someone. This someone might not be you, so before you take any risks, you need to ask yourself if it's worth jeopardizing the lives of the people around you.'

'Okay,' Lena said, shifting her weight. 'I'm ready.'

Wagner stared at her for a beat. She smiled ruefully. 'Sweetheart, you can piss on my face, but don't tell me it's raining.'

Lena was caught out, but she tried not to show it.

Wagner glanced down at Lena's shoe again. All she said was, 'Be careful.'

FOURTEEN

Monday

Jeffrey trudged back through the woods, his socks bunching from the wet earth. He stopped by a tree, using it to lean on while he peeled them off. The rain was barely more than a memory, and the air was filled with mist as the sun evaporated it up to the clouds. Jeffrey wiped sweat off his forehead with the back of his hand as he walked into the cemetery. The sun was sharper in the open graveyard, and the sloping hill with its jutting white markers seemed like teeth in the big mouth that was trying to swallow him.

Reggie was sitting in his cruiser with the door open, a cigarette hanging from his lips. He stayed where he was, making Jeffrey come to him. The asphalt was blistering against Jeffrey's bare feet, but he was damned if he'd show it.

Reggie gave a leisurely glance down at the wet athletic socks Jeffrey held in his hand. His lip curled up in a sarcastic sneer, but Jeffrey didn't let him get out whatever shitty thing he wanted to say.

'Take me to the station,' Jeffrey ordered, climbing into the passenger seat of the cruiser.

Reggie took one last suck on his cigarette before closing the door. He cranked the engine and let it idle for a few minutes. 'Where's your girl?'

'She's fine,' Jeffrey told him. Despite the fact that she had been scared out of her mind seconds before finding the bones, Sara had insisted on staying with them while Jeffrey went to get help.

Reggie rested his hand on the shift for a moment before putting the car in gear. He took his time merging onto the interstate and drove the posted speed limit into town, waving at folks out the window like he hadn't a care in the world. Jeffrey tried not to show his irritation, knowing Reggie was doing all this on purpose, but as they crawled past the high school at twenty miles per hour, he had to let off some steam or he would explode.

'Is there a reason you're going this slow?'

'Just to piss you off, Slick.'

Jeffrey stared out the window, wondering how much worse this day could get.

Reggie said, 'You wanna tell me what's going on here?'

'No.'

'That's your prerogative.'

Jeffrey gave a low whistle. 'Big word.'

'I thought you might be impressed.'

'Your sister teach you that?'

'You shut up about my sister.'

'How's Paula doing?'

'I said shut up, you fucker,' Reggie said, his voice a low warning. 'Why don't you ask me how my cousins are doing? How they're getting by without their father? How it feels for all of us when we get together and my uncle Dave's not there?'

Jeffrey felt all the guilt his words could bring and more. Still, he said, 'I'm not my father's keeper.'

'Yeah,' Reggie said, making a sharp turn into the sheriff's station parking lot. 'That's real convenient for you. I'll tell that to my cousin Jo when she graduates this fall and her daddy's not around to congratulate her. I'm sure it'll be a real comfort.'

Jeffrey grabbed his wet socks off the floorboard and got out of the car before Reggie cut the engine. He walked into the building, ignoring the secretary and the deputy who was leaning over her desk as he went back to Hoss's office, opening the door without knocking.

Hoss looked over the newspaper he was reading when Jeffrey closed the door. 'What is it, son?'

Jeffrey wanted to sit down, but something stopped him. Instead, he leaned against the wall for support, the weight of his fears catching up with him. He looked at Hoss's office. Like the man, nothing had changed in the last decade. The fishing trophies and photographs of Hoss on his boat were still around, and the folded American flag that had been on his brother's coffin when they brought his body back from Vietnam was still given a place of prominence on the shelf by the window. After his brother had died, Hoss had tried to join up, but his flat feet had kept him out. He always joked that the Army's loss was Sylacauga's gain, but Jeffrey knew he did not like to talk about it, as if having flat feet made him less of a man.

Hoss prompted, 'Jeffrey?'

'We found some bones.'

'Bones?' Hoss asked, creasing his newspaper in a tight fold.

'In the old cave me and the boys used to use when we were in junior high.'

'Out on the edge of the quarry?' Hoss asked in a careful tone. 'Probably just a bear or something.'

'Sara's a doctor, Hoss. She knows what human

bones look like. Hell, even if she didn't, the damn thing was laying out on the rocks like she was taking a nap.'

'She?' Hoss asked, and all the air went out of the room.

A knock came at the door.

'What is it?' Hoss demanded.

Reggie opened the door. 'I was just –'

'Give us a minute,' Hoss barked, his tone inviting no dissention.

Jeffrey heard the click of the door, but his eyes were on Hoss. The old man seemed to have aged about a hundred years in the past few seconds.

Jeffrey reached into his pocket and pulled out the chain he had found in the cave. He held it up, letting the gold heart-shaped locket twirl in the light.

'It doesn't prove anything,' Hoss said. 'She went to the cave a couple dozen times. Everybody knows that. Hell, she told them herself.'

'Sara won't let this go.'

'I thought y'all were leaving this afternoon?'

'I talked her into staying another day before all this happened,' Jeffrey told him. 'Even without that, she'll want to see this through.'

'I don't see giving her a choice.'

Jeffrey felt the heat of his remark and the underlying warning. 'I don't have anything to hide,' he said, hearing the false bravado in his own voice.

'It's not a matter of hiding anything, Slick. It's about burying the past and getting on with your life. You and Robert both.'

'No matter how much of a bitch Lane Kendall is, she deserves to know this.'

'Know what?' Hoss asked. He stood from his chair and walked to the window. Like Jeffrey's, his office had a stellar view of the parking lot. 'We don't know anything right now.'

'Sara will find out soon enough.'

'Find out what?'

'Her head was bashed in,' Jeffrey said. 'Someone killed her.'

'Maybe she fell,' Hoss suggested. His posture was ramrod straight, his back to Jeffrey. 'You ever think of that?'

Jeffrey said, 'Then we should let Sara figure it out.'

'Could be it's not even her,' Hoss tried. He turned back around and seemed to have collected himself. He reached out to Jeffrey, asking for the necklace.

Jeffrey handed it over, saying, 'She wore it all the time. Everybody saw it.'

'Yep,' Hoss agreed. He took out his pocketknife and pried open the heart-shaped locket. He palmed the charm and held it out for Jeffrey to see. Baby pictures had been crudely cut into the shape of the heart and glued into either side. A strand of blond hair curled around the photograph on the left, a small piece of twine holding the ends together.

'Two different babies,' Jeffrey said. One photo was in color and the other in black and white, but it was still easy to tell that the child on the right had a shock of dark black hair, while the one on the left was fair.

Hoss turned the necklace around to look at the photos. He gave a heavy sigh and closed the locket before handing it back to Jeffrey, saying, 'Hold on to this.'

Jeffrey did not want to, but he took the necklace and tucked it back into his pocket.

Hoss said, 'I told Reggie to wait for you back at the funeral home.'

'Why's that?'

'You need to go talk to Robert.'

'He didn't seem too interested in talking to me this morning.'

'He is now,' Hoss said. 'He called the station looking for you.'

'Sara's waiting back at the cave with the body.'

'I'll run go fetch her.'

'She won't give up on this,' Jeffrey repeated.

'On what?' Hoss asked. 'Could be some bum walked into the cave and forgot to come out. Could be somebody fell and hit their head. Could be a lot of things, right?' When Jeffrey did not answer, he reminded him, 'You've got nothing to hide.'

Jeffrey remained silent. They both knew that he did. Things were going downhill faster than he could keep up with.

Hoss gave him a hard pat on the shoulder. 'I ever let anything bad happen to you, son?'

Jeffrey shook his head, thinking that the words were no great comfort. Hoss had proven more than a few times that he was not above bending the law to keep Jeffrey and Robert out of trouble.

Hoss flashed one of his rare smiles. 'It'll be fine.' He opened the door and waved in Reggie as he asked Jeffrey, 'What happened to your shoes?'

Jeffrey looked down at his bare feet. They should be digging in the sands of Florida by now. He should be rubbing suntan lotion on Sara's back and front and every other part of her body while she laughed at his jokes and looked at him like he was the second coming.

Hoss asked, 'What size are you?'

'Ten.'

'I'm an eleven and a half.' He asked Reggie, 'What size shoe do you wear?'

Reggie looked embarrassed, as if his answer would be the punch line to a joke. Still, he said, 'Nine.'

'You're stuck with mine, then.' Hoss took a set of keys out of his pocket and handed them to Reggie. 'Run go fetch my boots out of the back of my truck.'

FIFTEEN

Hoss's boots smelled like he had worn them ankle-deep in fish guts. Considering the dried scales stuck to the soles, Jeffrey guessed that was exactly what he had been doing in them. Steel-toed with leather uppers, they were hot as hell and heavy as lead. Jeffrey did not even have to look at them to hate them. If he could have gotten away with not wearing anything, he would have gladly gone barefoot.

Growing up, Jeffrey had always been forced to wear hand-me-downs or used shoes and clothing bought cheap from the Baptist church's quarterly yard sale. He hated wearing other people's stuff, and when he was old enough, most of his shoplifting was done at the Belk's in Opelika. Sometimes when the shoe department got busy, the clerks were not able to keep up with who got what, and Jeffrey's first pair of new shoes that actually fit had been part of his most brazen shoplifting stunt ever: he had walked out of the shoe department bold as God, a pair of gleaming new fifteen-dollar black loafers hugging his feet, the soles so new he nearly slipped on the polished marble floor. His heart had been beating like a snare drum the whole time, but showing up at school the next day looking and feeling like a million bucks had made it all worthwhile.

In Hoss's shoes, Jeffrey felt like he was wearing two blocks of cement. Loose blocks, since they were a size and a half too big. There was already a blister working on his heel, and the arch of his foot felt like it had a piece of grit stuck in it, probably something from a fish.

Reggie drove the car through town just as slowly as before, managing an irritating crawl as they got stuck behind a tractor for what seemed like a hundred miles. He kept his scanner turned down low as he listened to country music on the radio, one hand on the wheel, one hand on the center console, lightly tapping along with Hank Williams.

Jeffrey chanced a look at the other man as they headed up Herd's Gap toward Jessie's mother's house. Reggie Ray was of average height, but he was a little on the scrawny side. He could not have been more than twenty-five or -six, but his dirty brown hair was already receding at the temples. A spot in the back looked a little fluffier than it should have been, and Jeffrey guessed he was combing over to hide a thinning area. Reggie would probably be bald by the time he reached his mid-thirties.

Jeffrey ran his hand through his own hair, thinking the only good thing his father had ever given him was a full head of hair. Even at close to sixty, Jimmy Tolliver still had the same thick, wavy hair he'd sported in high school. He still kept it in the same style that was popular at the time: a slicked-back variation of a pompadour. In his prison stripes, he looked like an extra from an Elvis movie.

Reggie said, 'What's so funny?'

Jeffrey realized he had been smiling at the memory of his old man, but he was not about to share that with Reggie, especially considering the mark Jimmy had left on the Ray family.

He said, 'Nothing.'

'Those boots smell like shit,' Reggie said, rolling down the window. Hot air sucked into the cab like a furnace. 'What happened to your shoes?'

'I left them with Sara,' he said, offering no further explanation.

'She seems like a real nice woman.'

'Yeah,' Jeffrey said. Then, to beat him to the punch, he added, 'Don't know what the hell she's doing with me.'

'Amen,' Reggie agreed. He tilted his hat back as they crested a hill. In the distance, Jeffrey could see people standing out on the golf course at the Sylacauga Country Club. Jeffrey had caddied a few times for some of the players, but he had quickly grown irritated by the condescending way the rich men treated him. Besides that, he had never understood the lure of golf. If he was going to spend a few hours outside, Jeffrey would rather be running and using his muscles for something other than chasing a little white ball around in a tiny clown car.

Reggie cleared his throat, and Jeffrey could tell it took something out of him to ask, 'What's going on?'

'What do you mean?'

'Why's Robert wanna talk to you?'

Jeffrey was honest but only because he knew Reggie would not believe the truth. 'I don't know.'

'Right,' Reggie said, skeptical. 'Why'd Hoss want me to drive you out instead of him?'

That was a good question, one Jeffrey had not considered when Hoss had volunteered to help Sara back at the cave. That was more the type of scut work Hoss usually gave to his deputies. Hoss would normally be more likely to drive out to see Robert with Jeffrey than trek through the forest looking for Sara. Maybe he thought he would be able to distract her somehow. Jeffrey wished him luck, but he knew Hoss was bound to fail.

'Slick?' Reggie prompted.

'I wish you wouldn't call me that,' Jeffrey told him, knowing even as he said it that Reggie would now call him Slick until the day he died. 'Hoss went back to find Sara.'

'She lost?'

'No.' Jeffrey did not debate long on whether or not to tell Reggie what was going on. The deputy would find out soon enough. 'She found something. We found something. There's this cave near the quarry –'

'The one with the boards over it,' Reggie said. He must have noticed Jeffrey's surprised look, because he added, 'Paula told me about it.'

'How'd she find out?' Jeffrey asked, knowing he had never taken Reggie's sister to the cave. It was an unwritten rule between him, Robert, and Possum that no girls were allowed. Except for that one time, he knew that they had all kept to it.

Reggie shrugged, not giving an answer. 'What'd you find?'

'Bones,' Jeffrey said, trying to gauge the other man's reaction. 'A skeleton.'

'Well.' His jaw relaxed, and he glanced over at Jeffrey. 'This ain't your week, is it, Slick?' He gave a raspy chuckle that turned into a full-on laugh. 'Oh, me,' he managed through laughter. He even slapped his thigh.

'That's real professional of you, Reggie,' Jeffrey said, relief washing over him as they turned onto Elton Drive. Jessie's mother was out in the yard watering some flowering plants. Behind her was a two-story white house with large columns holding up a second-story balcony. Jasper Clemmons was probably retired by now, but he had worked in senior management at the local mill and his home reflected his position. The first time Jeffrey had seen the place, he had been reminded of something out of *Gone With the Wind*. Now he thought it looked more like a low-rent Tara. The place had been kept up, but to Jeffrey's more seasoned eye, he understood that the house was trying too hard. Considering Jessie's family, it was a perfect fit.

Faith Clemmons had never liked Jeffrey. Despite popular opinion, Jeffrey had not dated every woman in town, and Faith seemed to take it personally that Jeffrey had passed on her daughter. There was no denying Jessie had been gorgeous – hell, even now she was still a beautiful woman – but there was something about her that was too desperate for Jeffrey's liking. He did not like clingy women, and even as a teenager, he had recognized Jessie for what she was: a bottomless pit of need.

At first, Jeffrey had been worried when Jessie set her sights on Robert, but now he knew that they were a perfect couple – if you could call two people who needed each other more than they loved each other a perfect couple. Robert liked rescuing people. He liked being the good guy and feeling like he was doing the right thing. Jessie, a constant damsel in distress, was the perfect excuse for him to get on his white horse and come to the rescue. Some men liked that kind of thing, but the thought of it made Jeffrey feel like he had a noose around his neck.

'Hey, Faith.'

'Jeffrey,' she said, spraying water on the plant bed between them. 'Robert's inside.'

'Thanks,' he answered, but she had already turned her back to him.

Reggie gave a tight grin, murmuring, 'Another one of your fans.'

Jeffrey ignored him as they walked to the house. The blister on his heel was starting to throb, but Jeffrey would be damned if he limped around Reggie.

To take his mind off the pain, Jeffrey thought about Sara back at the cave. Hoss had probably shown up by now. What was he telling her? What story was he weaving to try to protect Jeffrey? Sara would get sick of this, he knew. She wasn't the type of woman who put up with being lied to, and last night's business had nearly chased her away forever. Soon, she would probably start to realize that there was some truth to what everyone was saying. The part that hurt most was that it was Jeffrey's own damn fault. Bringing her here had been like swallowing a live grenade. Jeffrey was just waiting for it to explode.

Through the screen door, Jeffrey could see the long hallway that ran to the back of the house. The place had been built back when mansions were the real thing: something for the elite to own and not just big empty boxes that echoed when you walked into them. Jeffrey had only been to Jessie's house a handful of times, but he remembered there was a formal parlor as well as a sitting room, on either side of the front hall, with a dining room, kitchen, and huge family room at the back. He raised his hand to knock on the door just as Jessie came out of the kitchen. She had a glass in her hand and he guessed from the color of the liquid and the clinking ice as she walked that she was drinking straight scotch.

Reggie noticed, too. He made a show of looking at his watch. 'Barely past noon.'

Jeffrey started to make an excuse for her, but stopped himself at the last minute.

'Hey, boys,' Jessie said. She was a good drunk in that she never slurred her words or turned sloppy. As a matter of fact, drinking did nothing but sharpen her edges. Underneath Jessie's flawless skin and perfect figure was a bitter woman who saw only the bad in things. Alcohol brought the acid to the surface.

Jeffrey asked, 'Is Robert here?'

'Not like we could go home,' Jessie said, pushing open the door. She stepped to the side but still blocked the doorway enough so that Jeffrey had to brush past her to get into the house. Reggie was denied the same treatment. She cut him off at the door, saying, 'Y'all can wait in the parlor. I'll go get Robert.'

Jeffrey watched her go. She was teetering on heels so high that it did not seem possible she could walk in them. How she managed to accomplish the balancing act three sheets to the wind was beyond the laws of science.

Reggie cleared his throat. He had his arms crossed over his chest like a disapproving schoolmaster. Of course he had taken Jeffrey's appraisal of Jessie the wrong way. 'She's your best friend's wife.'

Jeffrey ignored him as he walked into the front parlor. Like the rest of the house, nothing had changed much here. Two long couches covered in burgundy-and-white-striped silk faced each other, a spindly coffee table between them. Wingback chairs framed a large picture window at the front of the room, facing a massive fireplace you could roast a small man in. All of the furniture looked delicate enough to fall over with a sneeze, but Jeffrey knew better. He sank into one of the couches to wait for Robert while Reggie stood at the door with the same snide look on his face.

Jeffrey stared at the white carpet, which looked like it had been vacuumed to within an inch of its life. He could see his footprints making a pattern toward the couch, and wondered if the odor in the air was from the dead fish on Hoss's boots or the bowl of potpourri on the coffee table. He thought again of Sara and what she was doing now. He wanted to be with her, to try to control what she was thinking, to make her believe he wasn't a monster. If only it was within his power, he would snap his fingers and they would magically be somewhere, anywhere, other than here.

Reggie asked, 'You got a thing with the mother, too?'

'What?' Jeffrey realized his gaze had ventured out the window to where Faith Clemmons was watering her azaleas. 'Jesus Christ, Reggie. Lay off it, okay?'

He crossed his arms over his chest. 'Or what?'

Footsteps slowly padded down the stairs, and Jeffrey felt all the steam go out of him as Robert entered the room. He had looked bad this morning, but now he looked as if he had been hit by a truck. His shoulders were stooped and he kept one hand to his side, much the same way he had the night before.

Jeffrey stood, not knowing what to say. He settled on 'Why don't you sit down?'

'I'm okay,' Robert said. 'Reggie, can you give us a minute?'

'Sure,' Reggie answered, his tone slightly guarded. Still, he tipped his hat before leaving the room.

Robert waited until the screen door had shut before he spoke. 'You found her body in the cave.'

Jeffrey was stunned by Robert's certainty. He had not asked a question; rather, he had made a statement. Her body had been found.

'Hoss called me,' Robert said, carefully sinking into one of the wingback chairs. 'He thinks it might be some bum or something – fell and hit his head. You know it's Julia Kendall.'

The name brought a heaviness to the room. Jeffrey felt sweat break out on his brow despite the air conditioning. He dug around in his pocket and pulled out the necklace with the heart-shaped charm. 'I found this by the bench seat.'

Robert reached out for the necklace and Jeffrey gave it to him. Using the nail on his thumb, Robert pried the locket open and looked at the photographs. 'Jesus. Julia.'

Jeffrey looked out the window to where Faith had turned off the hose and was talking to Reggie. They were probably having a good time comparing notes on what an asshole Jeffrey was. Reggie might even be telling her about Julia. News would be around town before Jeffrey even had a chance to tell Sara. She would get the story from somebody else, somebody who would get it all wrong. He slumped back into the couch, thinking he could not take it if she looked at him again the same way she had last night.

Robert asked, 'What did you tell Sara?'

'Nothing,' Jeffrey said, feeling remorse wash over him. That would have been the time to tell her, in the cave. He wasn't sure if she had seen him find the necklace and put it into his pocket. He should have said something right then and there instead of acting like he was guilty of something.

Jeffrey said, 'I hid the necklace from her.'

'Why?'

'Because I've got enough people in town telling her I'm some kind of animal without proving it.'

'What does this prove?' Robert asked, handing the necklace back to Jeffrey. No one wanted to keep the damn thing, and Jeffrey was irritated that it kept coming back to him.

Jeffrey said, 'It's going to stir up all that shit all over again. Jesus, I hate this fucking place.'

Robert stared at his hands. 'Everyone said she just ran away.'

'I know.'

They were both quiet, each of them probably thinking the same thing. For Jeffrey's part, he had a sick feeling in his gut like his life was about to turn upside down and there was nothing he could do to stop it.

Robert said, 'You know what they do to cops in jail?'

Jeffrey felt his throat close. 'We're not going to jail,' he managed. 'Even if they found something . . . some way to connect us to this . . . it was such a long time ago –'

'No,' Robert said. 'I'm asking you. I have no idea except what I've seen on television, and that's enough to make your blood turn. What do they do to cops in jail?'

'Robert –'

'I'm serious, Jeffrey. What do they do to them? What should I expect?'

Jeffrey looked at his friend maybe for the first time since the other man had entered the room. Except for a few lines around his eyes, Robert looked the same way he had in high school. He was still fit and a little lanky, but the way he slouched into the chair and bounced the heel of his shoe up and down was new. On the football field, Jeffrey had known every thought going through the other man's mind, but now he had no idea what Robert was thinking.

Jeffrey finally asked, 'What are you trying to say, Bobby?'

'I'm not trying, I'm telling. I shot Luke. I shot him in cold blood.'

Jeffrey was sure he had heard wrong.

'He was having an affair with Jessie.'

Shock stopped Jeffrey for another moment. 'What are you –'

Robert's tone was matter-of-fact, like he was talking about killing ants in his garden instead the death of another human being. 'I went to the store to pick up some things, then I came home and found them together. He was . . . shit, I guess you know what he was doing with her.'

It was too much; Jeffrey couldn't handle anything else today. 'Robert, why are you saying this? It's not true.'

'I got out my gun and shot him.' He shook his head. 'Not like that. I saw them first, then I went back to get my gun. I came back into the room and Jessie screamed. I asked them what the hell they were doing. He tried to make excuses and I just pulled the trigger.'

Jeffrey stood up. 'Don't say anything else to me.'

'His head . . . it just exploded.'

'Robert, shut the fuck up. You need a lawyer.'

'I don't need a lawyer,' he said. 'I need something to wipe this out of my mind. I need something that'll help me forget what it was like seeing his head just –'

'Robert,' Jeffrey interrupted, making his voice firm. 'You don't need to tell me this.'

'Yeah,' he said. 'I do. I'm confessing. There wasn't a break-in. The second piece is my backup. I used it to shoot myself. Sara knows, she saw where I held the gun. Jesus, that was stupid, but I did it. I wasn't thinking. I didn't have a lot of time. The lights were already turning on next door. You get called out on these things as a cop and you think, "Christ, what a fucking idiot," but the truth is when it happens to you, you don't have time to think. Maybe it's shock or fear or some kind of stupid thing that just kicks in, but you make mistakes. You don't *want* to get caught, but you can't think how not to.' He indicated the chair. 'Sit down, Jeffrey. You're making me nervous.'

Jeffrey sat. 'Why are you doing this?'

'Because it's not right,' he answered. 'I talked to Hoss this morning, gave him my statement just like I told you last night. It's like back when we were in school. Any old story we reel out, he bites.'

'He doesn't know any of this?'

'No, I wanted to tell you first. I owed you that much.'

'Robert,' Jeffrey said, thinking the man had done him no great favor. Despite the sense it made, Jeffrey could not believe the story. He had grown up with this man, spent countless hours listening to records with him, talking about girls, planning the cars they were going to buy when they turned sixteen.

Robert said, 'I've got to take responsibility for my actions. That man is dead because of me, because I couldn't control myself – all my anger and hatred and

233

. . . everything. It just came up to the surface and the next thing I knew, he was dead on the floor.' He started to tear up. 'I killed him. He's dead. He was screwing my wife and I killed him.'

Jeffrey pressed his fingers into his temples, not knowing what to say.

'Did you know Jessie had a miscarriage a few months ago?'

Jeffrey tried to talk past the lump in his throat. 'No.'

'Would've been a boy. How do you like that? It's the one thing that would have finally made her happy, and God just wouldn't let it happen.'

Jeffrey doubted seriously anything could make Jessie happy, but he still said, 'I'm sorry.'

'It was my fault,' Robert said. 'Something about me . . . I don't know, Slick. Something about me never works for her. I'm just poison.'

'That's not true.'

'I'm not a good man. I'm not a good husband.' He gave a heavy sigh. 'I've never been a good husband. People stray for all kinds of reasons, I guess, but in the end . . .' He looked up. 'I haven't been much of a friend to you.'

'That's not true,' Jeffrey repeated.

Robert just stared at Jeffrey, a kind of despair on his face. He slumped back farther in the chair as if he did not have the strength to sit up. He kept staring at Jeffrey, his eyes moving back and forth like he was reading a book.

'It was me,' Robert finally said. 'It was all me. I killed Swan and I killed Julia, too.'

Jeffrey felt like all the breath had been sucked from his lungs.

'All that other stuff – I did that, too.'

'No, you didn't,' Jeffrey insisted. What the hell was he talking about? There was no way Robert had killed anybody.

'I used a rock to hit her in the head,' Robert told him. 'It was pretty quick.'

'You didn't do that,' Jeffrey said, either anger or fear making his voice waver. This was just too much. 'Everyone thought she ran away. You said it yourself less than five minutes ago.'

'I lied,' he countered. 'I'm telling you the truth now. I threw the rock in the abandoned quarry. You'll never be able to find it, but my confession should be good enough.'

'Why are you saying this?'

He stood up, wincing from the pain in his side. 'Go get Reggie.'

'I won't. Not until you tell me why you're lying.'

Robert knocked on the window and motioned Reggie inside. 'I want Reg to take me in.'

'That's not –'

'It's better this way, Slick. Simpler. Now we've got everything tied up all neat. It's finally over and done with.' Robert wiped his eyes. 'Look at me crying like a girl.' He gave a humorless laugh. 'Reggie sees me like this he'll think I'm some kind of pansy.'

'Fuck Reggie,' Jeffrey said, just as the deputy walked in. Reggie's eyebrow shot up, but for once, he kept his mouth shut.

Robert held out his hands to the deputy. 'You need to cuff me.'

Reggie looked back and forth between the two men. 'This some kind of stupid joke?'

'I killed Luke Swan last night,' Robert said, putting his hand in his front pocket. For some reason, Jeffrey's first thought was that he was going to pull

235

out some type of weapon. Instead, Robert showed them a spent bullet.

Reggie examined the casing. 'Federal,' he noticed, just like the bullets Robert had in his Glock.

Robert told him, 'It was just sticking out from his head.' He put his index finger to the area beneath his ear. 'Just the tip of it, right here. You wouldn't think a bullet would be like that, just peeking out like someone put it there, but it slid right out. I didn't even have to pull much.'

Reggie still wouldn't buy it. He handed the bullet back to Robert, but Robert wouldn't take it. 'Y'all are shitting me, right?' He snorted a laugh. 'This one of your practical jokes, Bubba? You trying to get me in trouble with Hoss again?'

'Stop dicking around, boy,' Robert demanded, his tone harder than Jeffrey had ever heard it. Robert was Reggie's superior, and he was giving him an order when he said, 'Cuff me and read me my rights. Do it by the book.'

Jessie came in, her drink topped off to the rim. 'Y'all want something to . . .' Her voice trailed off as for once she noticed that she was not the center of some drama. Her eyes locked onto Robert's, and in the split second before she managed to control herself, she looked terrified. She recovered quickly, but still put her hand to the doorjamb like she needed something to keep her from falling over. 'What did you tell them?'

Robert's eyes watered again, and his voice was full of regret as he said, 'The truth, baby. I told them the truth.' Again, he held out his hands to Reggie. 'Luke Swan was having an affair with my wife. I came home and found them together, and I shot him.' He shook his hands. 'Come on, Reggie. Get it over with.'

Jessie murmured, 'Oh, Jesus.'

Robert said, 'Cuff me.'

Reggie put his hand to the back of his belt, but he did not get his handcuffs. 'I'm not cuffing you,' he said. 'I'll take you to the station to talk to Hoss, but no way I'm putting handcuffs on you.'

'Reggie, I'm ordering you.'

'No fucking way,' Reggie said. 'Not that I wouldn't love to see you riding in the back of my car, but I ain't gonna have Hoss come down on me for something you did.' He added, 'Not this time, anyway.'

'You need to do this by the book,' Robert told him.

Reggie would not relent. 'I'll go crank up the car, let it cool down a little. You come out when you're ready.'

'I'm ready now,' Robert said. When Jeffrey moved to follow them, he held up his hand. 'No, Jeffrey. Let me do this alone.'

Jessie was still in the doorway, and Robert had to pass his wife to leave. Jeffrey watched as Robert kissed her cheek, saw the way Jessie flinched away from his touch, try as she might to pretend she wasn't. Jeffrey wanted to grab her and shake her, to throw her to the ground and throttle the life out of her, for treating Robert this way. There was no way he had killed a man. Jeffrey did not buy it. Something was not right here.

Still, when Robert asked Jeffrey, 'Look after Jess for me, will you?' Jeffrey nodded.

He told Robert, 'I'll be up at the station later.'

'Jess,' Robert said. 'Give him the keys to my truck.' He managed a sad smile. 'I don't guess I'll be needing it for a while.'

'Don't say anything to them, not even Hoss,' Jeffrey coached. 'We need to find you a lawyer.'

Robert left the room without responding. Seconds later, the screen door popped shut.

'Well,' Jessie said, then took a long drink. The glass had been nearly full when she started and she had left little more than the ice cubes. Jeffrey watched her throat work as she drank it all down, wondering how she could appear to be so calm with her husband on the way to being charged with murder.

Jessie sucked an ice cube into her mouth before dropping it back into the glass. 'This must be the best day of that old hick's life.' She waited for Jeffrey to say something, but he did not oblige. 'Reggie's been waiting like a hawk lo these many years, looking for the day Robert stumbled. I'm sure he's planning on swooping in tomorrow and getting that promotion that has so long eluded him.'

'Doesn't sound like Robert's the one who stumbled to me,' Jeffrey told her, letting all the bile he felt rise out in his tone. This was her fault. She had brought this down on Robert. She had brought this down on all of them.

'Oh, that's just perfect, Slick. So damn typical. He shoots and kills a man and somehow you manage to paint me in the black.'

'Why'd you cheat on him?' Jeffrey demanded. 'Why?'

She shrugged like it was a casual thing. There was something nervous about her, almost twitchy.

'He was good to you.'

'Now, don't go getting on your high horse, Jeffrey Tolliver. You're forgetting who you're talking to.'

'I never cheated on anybody,' he said, disgusted by the knowing look she gave him. Jeffrey might have

238

done his share of fucking around, but he made certain the women he was involved with knew exactly what they were – or were not – getting into.

He said, 'When I make a promise to someone, I keep it. I sure as shit wouldn't run around on my wife.'

'Easy to say now,' Jessie said, sucking the liquor off another ice cube. She smacked her lips. 'You're the worst kind of cheat because you think you're too good to let it happen.'

'Don't you even care that he's going to jail? This is a death-penalty state, Jessie. He could end up getting a needle in his arm.'

She looked down at her glass, swirling the ice around.

'How'd it start?' Jeffrey demanded. 'Were you buying drugs from him?'

'Drugs?' She looked startled. 'Robert?'

'Luke Swan,' he said. 'He was using. Is that how it went down?' He grabbed her arm, looking for needle marks. 'You two shot up together and it went from there?'

'You're hurting me.'

He pushed up her sleeve, checked the crease of her elbow and under her arm.

'Stop it!'

He checked her other arm, spilling ice onto the floor. 'What made you do it, Jessie? What?'

'Goddammit, Slick,' she screamed, pushing him away. 'Where the hell do you get off?'

'I don't have time for this,' Jeffrey said, thinking if he did not get away from Jessie right now he'd really hurt her. With Sara last night, the thought repulsed him, but now he wanted nothing more than to smack some sense into Jessie.

He said, 'Give me Robert's keys.'

She held his gaze for a second longer, then said, 'They're in my purse in the kitchen.' She waited a beat, like she wanted to make sure he knew she was making a choice. 'I'll go get them.'

Jeffrey paced in the doorway as he waited for her. He was sick of this crap. It was one thing for Reggie to break his balls, but he sure as shit wasn't going to take it from Robert's cheating wife.

'Here go,' Jessie said, coming back from the kitchen with a full drink in one hand and the keys in the other.

'You're some piece of work,' he said, holding out his hand for the keys.

She gave him a strange look that he could not quite read. 'I should have married you.'

'I don't recall asking.'

She laughed like what he had said was the funniest thing she'd heard all day. 'You watch, Slick.'

'Watch what?'

'That Sara of yours sure seems to have you tied around her little finger.'

'Leave her out of this.'

'Why, because she's better than me?'

It was true, but Jeffrey didn't want to get into it. He had learned the hard way that you could not reason with a drunk. 'Give me the damn keys.'

'You're gonna marry her, and then you're gonna fuck around on her.'

'Jessie, I'm only going to tell you one more time.'

'There's gonna come a day when you realize you're not the center of her world anymore, and then you're gonna run out sniffing around for something new. Mark my word.'

Jeffrey kept his hand out, forcing himself not to speak.

She held the keys over the palm of his hand and dropped them as she said, 'Come see me in a couple of years.'

'I'd rather watch my dick rot off.'

She smiled, holding up her glass in a toast. 'Until then.'

Robert's truck was the same piece-of-shit '68 Chevy he had been driving since high school. The gears were temperamental, and the whole truck groaned each time Jeffrey tried to shift. There had to be some art to making the truck move, but that knowledge was lost on Jeffrey. At each stop sign, he lurched like a sixteen-year-old kid just learning to drive, the engine cutting out more often than not as he tried to get the damn thing into first.

Once he drove out of Herd's Gap, he did not know where to go. Sara was probably at the funeral home going over the bones. Hoss was at the station booking Robert. Jeffrey could go home, but his mother would be there for lunch and the last thing he needed was to watch his mother fortifying herself with cheap vodka before she started her second shift at the hospital. Dealing with one alcoholic a day was enough. He was heading toward Nell's, thinking she'd probably already know about Robert's arrest by now, when he remembered Possum.

That was the way it had always been with Possum: he was an afterthought. Unlike Robert, who was on the football team with Jeffrey and could carry his own socially, Possum was a third wheel, someone who tagged along as a buffer between his two ultra-competitive friends. He laughed at their jokes and kept score between them. Not that Possum was completely altruistic. Sometimes he got lucky and managed to snag some of Jeffrey's and Robert's castoffs.

Nell was definitely one of Jeffrey's castoffs, and one he had been glad to get rid of. Even as a teenager, she had known exactly what she wanted and was not afraid to speak her mind. That her mind was usually focused on what she saw as Jeffrey's many faults was the biggest problem he had with her. She was very outspoken and could be downright nasty when it came to giving her opinion on his latest transgressions. If not for the fact that she was one of the few respectable girls in school who still put out, he would have dropped her after their first date.

Jeffrey would be the first to admit that he liked a challenge, but Nell was the sort of person you could never win with. In the end, he had to admit that Possum was a better fit for her – he didn't mind being told what to do and gladly accepted any sort of criticism at face value – though Jeffrey had been surprised to learn the month after he left for Auburn University that they had gotten married. It made him wonder what had been going on behind his back. Nine months later, he realized exactly what had been going on. If he let himself think about it, it still stuck in his craw, but in all fairness, he had told Nell they should date other people when he moved away. The problem was, he had imagined her pining away for him, not jumping into the sack with his best friend.

Jeffrey forced the truck into second as he turned into the parking lot of Possum's store. The place was still run-down and depressing, with faded Auburn flags banking either side of the door. Signs in the windows advertised cold beer and live bait; two things essential to any small-town country store.

The bell over the door clanked loudly as Jeffrey

entered the building. Wooden floors that had been installed back during the Depression squeaked underfoot, dirt from sixty years of wing tips and work boots and now sneakers filling the grooves.

Jeffrey walked straight to the back and pulled out a six-pack of Bud from the walk-in cooler. Before the door closed, he pulled out a second six-pack and walked to the front of the store.

'Hello?' Jeffrey called, putting the beer on the front counter. The cash register was the older kind that didn't take much to get into, and there was a coin dispenser with around a hundred dollars in change ready for the taking. Typical Possum to rely on other people's honesty.

'Possum?' Jeffrey said, taking one of the beers out of the cardboard pack. He used the Coca-Cola opener on the side of the counter to open the bottle. The beer was bitter, and Jeffrey tossed it back, trying to bypass his taste buds. He walked around the counter, looking at the photographs Possum had taped up around the cigarette displays. Like Robert, he had a lot of pictures from their high school days. Unlike Robert, there were photos of kids at various stages in life. Jennifer went from a red face in a bundle of blankets to a precocious girl. Jared grew from a little baby to a tall and rangy-looking kid. Jeffrey guessed he was about nine now, and felt genuine empathy for the kid; at that age, Jeffrey had been all hands and feet, like a colt just learning how to walk. Jared had dark hair like Nell and the same haughty tilt to his chin. There was nothing about Possum in the kid, but Jennifer was very much her father's daughter. She had his eyes, and her shoulders were hunched in that good-natured, nonthreatening way that had saved Possum from getting his ass kicked on more than one occasion.

Jeffrey took a healthy swig of beer, his tongue anesthetized to the taste by now. He thought about Robert, and what hell he must have gone through when Jessie lost their kid. Marriages were perplexing animals, always changing, sometimes gentle, sometimes vicious. When Jeffrey was a beat cop, he had hated domestic disturbance calls because there was always something, some indefinable connection that attached a husband to a wife and turned them from wanting to kill each other to wanting to kill whoever was interfering, in this case the cops. One minute they could be wailing on each other, calling each other every name in the book, the next minute they could be throwing themselves in front of the squad car to keep their spouse from going to jail.

Children always made things worse, and as a patrolman, Jeffrey had done his best to keep them out of the fray. This was always difficult because most kids thought they could help take some of the heat off their parents by getting in the middle of things. Jeffrey had done this often enough with his own parents, and he knew what drove kids to get involved. He also knew how futile it was. There was nothing more horrible than getting a domestic call and going out to find some kid whimpering in the corner with a black eye or a busted lip. On more than one occasion, Jeffrey had set a father straight. He knew he was channeling some of his own fury when he took on an abusive parent, and up until a few years ago, Jeffrey had considered that to be one of the perks of being a cop.

Jeffrey dropped his empty into the trash and got

out another bottle of beer. He used the edge of the counter to pop open the top and gathered from the scratch it made in the wood that Possum used the counter for the same thing.

He leaned his head back, taking a long swig of beer. His stomach grumbled in protest, and Jeffrey realized he had not eaten anything since the bacon he'd had at Nell's that morning. At this point, Jeffrey did not care. He was halfway through the bottle when he heard a toilet flush in the back.

'Hey, Slick.' Possum came out of the bathroom, buttoning up his pants. He saw the beer. 'Go on and help yourself.'

'Good thing I didn't,' Jeffrey said, hitting the No Sale button on the cash register. The drawer popped open, showing neat rows of cash. 'There's at least two hundred dollars in here.'

'Two fifty-three eighty-one,' Possum said, taking one of the beers. He popped the top off on the counter and took a pull.

Jeffrey finished his beer and took another. Possum glanced at the two empties but held his tongue.

Jeffrey said, 'Guess you heard about Robert?'

'What's that?'

Jeffrey felt a sinking in his gut. He took a healthy drink, trying to push his brain to a point where none of this mattered anymore. 'He turned himself in.'

Possum coughed as beer went down the wrong way. 'What?'

'I was just at Jessie's mama's. He said he did it.'

'Did what?'

'Shot that man.'

'Luke Swan,' Possum whispered. 'Jesus wept.'

'Jessie was cheating on him.'

Possum shook his head. 'I don't believe that.'

'You don't have to believe me. Talk to Robert. He said he walked in on the guy banging her.'

'Why would she cheat on him?'

'Because she's a slut.'

'There's no need to talk like that.'

'Talk like what, Possum? The truth?' Jeffrey took another swig of beer, then another. 'Jesus, you haven't changed a damn bit.'

'Come on, now.'

'Possum,' Jeffrey said. 'That's what you are, playing dead until it all passes over and then coming out like nothing's wrong.' He finished his beer, waiting for that buzz in his head that took away some of the pain. 'He said he killed Julia, too.'

Possum leaned against the counter, his mouth slightly open. 'That's just crazy talk.'

'Yeah, it's crazy. This whole damn town is crazy.'

'Do you believe him?'

Jeffrey was surprised by the question, mostly because Possum never questioned anything. 'No,' he said. 'Hell, I don't know.'

'Damn,' Possum said.

Jeffrey reached for another beer. Possum's hand caught his, and he told Jeffrey, 'Maybe you oughtta pace yourself.'

'I've already got a mama.'

'She's as good a reason as any to slow down a bit.'

Before he could stop himself, Jeffrey punched Possum in the jaw. His aim was off, but the power behind his fist was enough for Possum to lose his balance and fall back against the store safe.

'Ow!' Possum said, more surprised than outraged. He put his hand to his mouth and looked at the blood. 'Jesus, Slick, you near about broke my tooth.'

Jeffrey raised his fist to hit him again, but the look

in Possum's eye stopped him. Possum wouldn't hit back. He never hit back. He never got angry and he never thought anything Jeffrey did was wrong.

Jeffrey reached into his pocket and took out a couple of tens for the beer.

'No,' Possum said, pushing the money away even as blood dribbled down his chin. 'Forget about it.'

'I pay my own way,' Jeffrey said, throwing the money on the counter. He picked up the remaining bottles and the other six-pack.

'Listen, Slick, lemme give you a ride –'

'Fuck off,' Jeffrey said, pushing him away.

Still, Possum followed him to the door, saying, 'You don't need to be driving like this.'

'Like what?' Jeffrey asked, opening the passenger door to Robert's truck. He put the beer in and walked around to the driver's side, his foot catching on a loose bit of pavement. He grabbed the hood ornament, keeping himself up.

Possum said, 'Jeffrey, come on.'

Jeffrey climbed in behind the wheel, feeling his eyes blur as the world turned upside down. The truck turned over with a rewarding purr, and he pulled out of the parking lot, jerking the wheel at the last minute so he would not take out the gas pumps.

SIXTEEN

2:50 P.M.

Molly climbed into the passenger's seat of the ambulance, looking Lena up and down. 'They didn't have a tighter shirt?'

'Guess not,' Lena said, knowing the other woman was trying to lighten things up but unable to play along. Her hands were sweating and her nerve, usually as strong as steel, was failing her. Things would be okay once she got inside the station. Lena was the type of person who faced her fears head-on. Jitters were understandable, but once the show was on, she would be ready to perform.

Molly took a deep breath. When she let it go, her shoulders dropped like a deflating balloon. Her stethoscope was wrapped around her neck, and she grabbed either end in her fists and said, 'All right, I'm ready.'

Lena tried to put the key in the ignition, but she could not keep her hand steady enough. After a couple of tries, Molly leaned over, saying, 'Here.'

'It's from the scars,' Lena said as the ignition caught. 'Nerve damage.'

'Does it bother you much?'

Lena gassed the engine, feeling the vibrations through the floor. 'No,' she said, then, 'Sometimes.'

'Did they have you do physical therapy?'

Lena did not understand why they were having this stupid conversation, but she kept it up as she put the ambulance in gear, liking the chatter. 'About three months,' she said. 'Paraffin soaks, playing with a tennis ball, putting pegs in holes.'

'For dexterity,' Molly said, staring straight ahead at the street.

'Yeah,' Lena said. The Grant Medical Center was less than three hundred yards from the police station, but the closer they got, the farther away it seemed. Lena felt like they were following a tunnel into a black hole.

'I had to do PT for my knee a while back,' Molly said. 'Hurt it running up the stairs after my youngest.'

'You have two kids?'

'Two boys,' she said, a note of pride to her voice.

Lena steered the van over a steel plate covering a hole in the road, the heavy ambulance barely registering the rough terrain. She wondered if there was a baby growing inside of her, and whether it was a boy or a girl. What would happen if she had a kid? If she married Ethan, she would never be able to get away from him.

Molly said, 'Twins.'

'Shit,' Lena said, though not for the reason Molly was probably thinking. Twins. Twice as much responsibility. Twice as much danger. Twice as much pain.

'You okay?' Molly asked again.

'It's my birthday today,' Lena said, not really paying attention to where she was going.

'That so?'

'Yep.'

Molly said, 'Here should be a good spot,' and

Lena realized she had nearly passed the station. Nick had said not to block the door, but they had figured the best place to park would be closer to the dress shop, not the college.

Lena considered backing up, but it was too late. 'Guess it'll have to do.'

'Right,' Molly said, rubbing her hands on her thighs. 'Well, this should be routine, right? Just go in with the food and get out with Marla, yes?'

'Yes,' Lena agreed, her hand slipping on the gear-shift as she put the van in park. She cursed under her breath, trying to psych herself into doing this. She was never afraid of things. Lena had seen more horror in the last few years than anyone should see in a lifetime. What did she have to be afraid of? What was waiting in that building that could be worse than what had happened to her two years ago?

'Listen,' Molly began, a tinge of hesitancy to her voice. 'Nick told me not to tell you this . . .'

Lena waited.

'Standard procedure is to have a time limit. If we don't come out, they come in.'

'Why didn't he want me to know?'

'Because he was afraid they would find out,' she said, meaning the gunmen.

'Right,' Lena said, understanding. Nick didn't trust her to be in there. He had said as much to Amanda Wagner. He thought she was going to do something stupid, something that would get them all killed. Maybe she would. Maybe without even think-ing, Lena would screw this up like she had screwed up everything else in her life. Maybe this was it. The end of everything.

'We'll be okay,' Molly said, reaching over and taking Lena's hand.

For lack of anything better to do, Lena looked at her watch.

Molly followed suit, saying, 'We synchronized mine to his,' as she showed Lena the large Snoopy watch she wore. Lena adjusted her digital watch to Molly's, wondering if this would come to anything.

'They'll come in exactly forty minutes after we walk through the door.' She checked her watch again. 'I guess that'll be 3:32.'

Lena said, 'Okay.'

Molly put her hand on the door handle. 'We'll get you back in time for your party.'

'Party?' Lena asked, wondering what the hell she meant.

'For your birthday,' Molly reminded her. She opened the door a few inches. 'Ready?'

Lena nodded, not trusting herself to speak. They both got out of the van and met at the back, where Wagner's men had loaded boxes of cold water and prewrapped sandwiches they had gotten from one of the gas stations on the outskirts of town. As they walked toward the station, Lena concentrated on the sandwiches. She read the labels, wondering who would actually pay money for a ham salad sandwich on white bread. The expiration date on the pack read three months from now. There were probably enough preservatives in one bite to pickle a horse.

'Here we go,' Molly said, just as the door was pushed open from the inside.

Lena suppressed a gag as Matt's body flopped back onto the ground. What was left of his head made a splattering sound as it hit the concrete, blood and brain spilling out onto the sidewalk. Most of his face was gone, his left eye dangling from a nerve like a fake Halloween mask. The bottom part of his jaw was exposed, and she could see everything – his teeth, his lolling tongue, the way the tendons and muscles held the whole thing in place.

'Slow,' said the man standing just inside the doorway. He was wearing a black knit ski mask that had almond-shaped slits for the eyes and mouth but no nose. He reminded Lena of something out of a horror movie, and she felt a cold shock of fear that nearly paralyzed her. Frank had not mentioned masks. The men had put them on specifically to hide their identity from the paramedics. What that meant for the hostages who had already seen them, Lena did not know.

'Nice and easy,' he said, motioning them in. In one hand he held a shotgun – the Wingmaster Frank had seen – and in the other was a Sig Sauer. His Kevlar vest was tight to his chest, and she could see another pistol sticking out of the waistband of his fatigues.

Lena realized she had stopped walking when Molly whispered, 'Lena!'

By sheer force of will, Lena managed to get her feet moving. She tried to step over Matt without actually looking at him, her stomach in such a knot the whole time that she felt the urge to double over. Her sneakers left tracks in his blood.

Inside, the temperature of the station was at least twenty degrees hotter than on the street. There was a second shooter standing behind the counter, an AK-47 resting on the surface in front of him. He wore a ski mask, too, but his had more of an hourglass shape to it, leaving ample room to breathe. His eyes were flat, almost lifeless, and he barely glanced at Lena and Molly as they entered the lobby.

The first one, probably Smith, tried to shut the door but Matt was in the way. He slammed the door into the body, but it would not move. 'Fuck,' he mumbled, viciously kicking Matt in the side. His boots were steel-toe military issue, and Lena heard something break, probably Matt's ribs. They snapped like twigs.

Smith said, 'Come move this fucker.'

Lena stood there, the box of sandwiches in her hands, frozen to the floor. Molly gave her a panicked look before setting down the box of bottled water. She walked over to Matt and grabbed his ankles to pull him back into the station.

'No,' Smith said. 'Outside. Get this fucker outside.' He wiped at his mouth with the back of his arm. 'Fucker stinks.' As Molly walked toward the head, Smith gave Matt another solid kick to the chest. 'Fucking prick,' he said, an edge to his voice that stopped Molly in her tracks. He raised his foot again, kicking Matt in the groin. The dead weight did not resist, and the sound of boot hitting flesh reminded Lena of the noise Nan made when she would hang the rugs from the house on the laundry line and beat them with the broom.

Smith's anger was spent fairly quickly, and with one final kick, he told Molly, 'What the fuck are you waiting for? Move the fucker.'

Molly looked like she did not know where to touch him. Matt was wearing his usual short-sleeved white shirt with a tie that had gone out of style when Jimmy Carter left the White House. Blood from his head wound saturated his shirt, and there were fresh rents along his arms where Smith had kicked him. These newer wounds were a strange purple color, and they did not bleed.

Smith pushed Molly with his boot. It was not a threatening gesture in and of itself, but considering his earlier display, Molly seemed to take it for the threat it was. She tried to pull Matt by his shirt, but it just came untucked, the buttons popping off and tapping against the floor like hail, his white fish-belly rounding over his pants. Finally, she grabbed him under his arms and pulled.

The body would not move, and Smith was about to give it another kick when Molly said, 'No.'

Smith was incredulous. 'What did you say?'

'I'm sorry,' Molly said, looking down. The front of her uniform was covered in black blood. She looked at Lena. 'For God's sake, give me a hand.'

Lena looked around, like she did not know where to put the box she was holding. She did not want to touch him. She could not touch his dead body.

Smith leveled the Wingmaster on her. 'Do it.'

Lena put down the box, feeling her lungs shake in her chest as she tried to breathe. She clamped her jaw shut, trying to keep her teeth from chattering. She had never been so scared in her life. Why was she afraid? There had been times in the past when she had welcomed death, even begged it to come to her door, but now she was terrified by the thought of being killed.

Somehow, she managed to kneel at Matt's feet. She stared at his cheap black loafers, the frayed cuffs of his worn pants, the white athletic socks that had a dirty brown cast to them. Molly counted to three, and they lifted him. The pant cuff slid up on his left leg, and Lena saw his ankle jutting out, the pasty white, hairless skin around the bone wrinkling as the foot flexed flat against Lena's abdomen. She thought of the baby inside her, wondered if he knew how close he was to a dead man. Wondered, too, if it was catching.

They set him out on the sidewalk away from the front door, Smith watching their every move. His mouth was twisted into an expression of deep satisfaction as he watched them, and Lena fought the urge to run as she followed Molly back into the station. She did not realize what had happened until they were back inside. Smith had the food and water. He could have shut them out right then and there. He could have shot them in the face or told them to fuck off, but he hadn't.

'That's better,' Smith said. 'Tolliver was stinking up the room.'

Molly's head jerked around, her mouth open.

'What?' Smith asked, pointing the Sig at Molly's forehead. 'You want to say something else, bitch? You want to mouth off?'

'No,' Lena answered for her, surprised she was capable of saying the word.

Smith's smile behind the mask was horrifying. She saw his eyes crawl up and down her body, paying specific attention to her breasts; the glint told her he liked what he was seeing. He pushed the muzzle of his gun into Molly's head one last time before turning his attention to Lena. 'That's what I thought.' He motioned for her to turn around. 'Hands against the wall.'

The phone started ringing, a shrill bell that cut through the air like a knife.

Smith repeated, 'Turn around.'

Lena pressed her palms between two framed photographs from the 1970s Grant County police force. They were all men, all in blues, all with shaggy mustaches. Ben Walker, then the Chief of Police, was the only one who looked out of place with his military crew cut and clean-shaven face. Farther down was a photograph with Lena in it. She held her breath, hoping to God Smith did not notice.

'You hiding anything?' Smith's hands were like a sledgehammer as he patted her down. He pushed her flat to the wall, pressing himself against her. 'You hiding anything?' he repeated, deftly unbuttoning her blouse with one hand.

She was silent, her heart pounding in her chest. She tried not to look at the photograph less than two feet from her nose. She had been so young then, so open to her future and what it held. Being a cop like her old man had been Lena's life plan for as long as she could remember. The day that photograph had been taken was one of the best days of her life, and now it might end up killing her.

Smith slipped his hand into her open shirt, his palm cupping her breasts. 'You got something good in here?' he asked. 'Heart sure is beating fast.'

She stood as still as she could, eyes squeezed shut as his hand moved to her other breast. His breath was heavy, his pleasure evident.

Lena should have been terrified, but she was not. Something was eerily familiar about the threat of his body pressed into hers. Smith was a small man, compactly built. Muscles rippled along his arms and chest, and if Lena let herself consider it, he reminded her of Ethan. She knew how to handle Ethan, how to keep him walking that tight line between anger and control. Seeing how far she could push her lover was almost a game by now. The problem was that sometimes she lost. Lena had the split lip to prove it.

Smith whispered, 'You got something good?' his breath hot in her ear. She could feel him pressing harder into her, making his intentions obvious. Lena felt herself floating somehow, like her soul was in another place while her body remained at the station.

Then there was another voice that Lena did not recognize. The second shooter had said, 'Stop that,' with little authority, but Smith still backed away, his hand lingering for as long as it could.

Smith ordered Lena, 'Take off your shoes.' Then told Molly, 'You next. Up against the wall.'

Molly's trepidation was obvious, but she followed suit, leaning her hands against the wall between the photographs. Lena buttoned her shirt as she watched Smith give Molly a solid pat-down without copping any feels. She moved away from the photographs and sat on the floor to untie her shoes. She had taped the knife to the indentation just behind her ankle bone, underneath her sock. The tendon throbbed, and she tried not to show her nervousness as she handed Smith her shoes. The high tops had covered her ankle when he frisked her. If he did not frisk her again or ask her to remove her socks, she would be okay.

Smith turned her shoes upside down, looking at the soles and peering inside. He did the same with Molly's shoes, then dropped them both back on the floor. Molly went to put on hers, but Smith stopped her.

He rummaged through the boxes, looking for contraband, then said, 'Pick these up and tote 'em in the back.'

Lena knelt down and picked up the box, covering her chest in the process. She waited for Molly to pick up the drinks before pushing open the swinging doors to the squad room. Lena had managed to slip her sneakers on but had not tied them. Her feet were sweating, but she could feel the surgical tape holding the knife. How could she pass it along? How could she leave it where it would do anyone any good?

She concentrated on the things that she could control, checking out the room. The station was turned upside down, but Lena was glad to find that the map Frank and Pat had drawn was pretty accurate. Clothes had been shoved into the air vents, and the filing cabinets and desks were shoved against the doors. Brad stood in the center of the room wearing his boxer shorts and a white undershirt, his hairless white legs looking like matchsticks poking out of his black socks and regulation shoes. Beside him, the three girls were on the floor tucked under Marla's arms like a flock of chickadees. At the rear of the room, Sara sat with her back to the wall. A man lay with his head in her lap, the bottom soles of his shoes facing Lena. She stumbled, dropping the box. The man was Jeffrey.

'Here,' Brad said, picking up sandwiches and putting them back in the box. His eyes were open wider than usual, and he spoke in a deep baritone. 'Matt was shot in the shoulder,' he said.

'What?'

'Matt,' Brad said, his eyes going to Jeffrey. 'He was shot in the shoulder.'

Her mouth said, 'Oh,' as if she understood, but Lena could feel her brain stretching to make the connection.

Sara's voice was a hoarse whisper, her concern obvious. 'He's in and out. I don't know how much longer he can hold on.'

Molly asked, 'Can we do anything to help him?'

Sara had trouble speaking. She cleared her throat, then said, 'You could get him out of here.'

'That ain't gonna happen,' Smith said, rifling through the sandwiches, reading the labels. 'Man, this is ass.' He seemed to be showing off, and Lena

258

guessed it was for her benefit. She was becoming one of those women she hated seeing as a cop. She would go to their houses when their boyfriends got out of hand, and they would beg and cry to keep the bastard out of jail. There was something about them, something about the way they held themselves and looked at the world like they were waiting for one more punch. They gave off some kind of scent or something that invited the kind of guy who liked to hit women.

Sara said, 'He needs medical attention.'

Molly took her stethoscope and headed toward the back.

Smith said, 'You going somewhere?'

'I was going to –'

'That's okay,' Smith stepped aside with a slight bow. He saw Lena watching and gave her a wink.

Lena knew what was expected of her, and she said, 'Thank you,' without giving it another thought.

She started unpacking the sandwiches, handing them to the children and asking them each in turn if they were okay. Still, she felt that same disconnection, as if someone else was in the room handing out sandwiches and Lena as floating overhead, watching the scene.

The phone was still ringing, and Smith walked over, picked up the receiver and slammed it back down.

One of the girls jumped at the noise. She cried, 'I want my daddy.'

Lena soothed, 'I know. It won't be long.'

The girl started crying in earnest and Lena gave her a bottle of water, feeling helpless and angry at the same time. 'Don't cry,' she said, sounding more like she was pleading. Lena had always been horrible with kids. Still, she tried, 'It's going to be okay.'

Marla gave a low moan, her eyes glassy as she stared at Lena.

Lena tried to get the old woman's attention, saying, 'Are you all right?' She tried to act like a paramedic, putting her hand on Marla's shoulder, asking, 'Are you okay?'

Smith was over near Molly and Sara. He obviously did not like what he was hearing, because he finally said, 'That's enough. Get out of here. Take the old bitch.'

Molly said, 'He needs help.'

'What about me?' Smith asked, indicating a small strip of white cloth wrapped around his arm. Blood spread out from the center, nearly saturating it.

The phone started ringing again. Wagner had probably freaked when they carried Matt outside.

'There are supplies in the ambulance,' Molly said. 'Let Matt go and I'll stay here and suture you.'

'Got a couple of heroes here,' Smith said to his partner, and Lena realized he meant her as well.

Lena was kneeling by Marla, and Smith practically swaggered as he walked toward them. Without a word, he jerked up one of the girls by her wrist and yanked her toward the front of the room. She yelled, but he must have twisted her arm enough to shut her up. He took the crying child with him and talked to his partner. Lena was still on her knees, and she turned to watch them, putting her feet behind her. Slowly, she moved her hand to her ankle, feeling the pocketknife. She felt someone's hand over her's, but dared not turn around. Brad was to her right, so she knew it wasn't him. The children were too frightened to move. Marla. It must have been Marla whose fingers worked so deftly with the tape and removed the pocketknife.

Smith said, 'We got a doctor, couple of paramedics. Why not?'

His partner gave a wary shake of his head, but seemed resigned to whatever Smith had planned.

Smith walked back to Lena, dragging the girl. 'Go get your case out of the ambulance.'

'What?' she said, not understanding.

He looked at his watch, which was the kind she had seen in magazines, advertising the fact that Navy SEALs used the same brand. He said, 'Get your case and get back here.' He pressed the Sig to the little girl's head. 'You've got thirty seconds.'

'I don't –'

'Twenty-nine.'

'Fuck,' Lena cursed. She scrambled to stand and bolted toward the door, her heart lurching in her chest. At the ambulance, she threw open the back doors, looking for anything that resembled a case.

'Officer?' a man called. She knew it was one of the cops by the cruisers but she did not have time. 'Officer?'

'It's okay!' she yelled, panic filling her voice. 'It's okay!' There was a long plastic case strapped into the side of the ambulance. She had been on accident scenes enough to know this was the first thing the EMTs brought with them. Her fingers fumbled with the buckle and she said, 'Fuck-fuck-fuck,' trying to remember how long she had been out of the building.

The man kept pushing. 'Do you need help?'

'Shut up!' she screamed, throwing open the case. There were all kinds of drugs and boxes. She hoped it had everything they would need. At the last minute, she grabbed another bag and the defibrillator.

She ran through the front door, startling the second shooter. He reared up but did not pull the trigger on her. Lena rushed to the back, where Smith still had the gun pressed to the little girl's head. He was looking at his watch, smiling, and she felt such seething hatred for him that she dropped the gear and reached for the little girl, snatching her away.

The muzzle of Smith's gun caught Lena in the forehead, stunning her for a moment. She dropped to her knees and he kicked her in the chest. She fell back just as Brad tried to come to her aid. Smith trained the Sig on Brad and pressed his foot into Lena's sternum.

He said, 'I knew you would try to be a hero.'

'No,' Lena said, the pressure from his boot pushing the life out of her.

Smith pressed harder. 'You want to be a hero?'

'No,' she said. 'Please.' She tried to pry up his boot but that just made him press harder. 'Please,' she repeated, thinking about the child inside her, wondering what this was doing.

Smith exhaled sharply, like he was disappointed. 'All right,' he said, removing his foot. 'Let that be a lesson.'

Brad helped Lena stand. She found that her knees were weak and she felt sick all over. Had the pressure done something? Had Smith broken her inside?

Smith used his foot to push the plastic case toward Sara. 'This should be enough to do it,' he said. 'Field surgery, just like on TV.'

Sara shook her head. 'It's too dangerous. There's no way –'

'Sure there's a way.'

'He should be in an operating room.'

'This'll have to do.'

'He could die.'

Smith indicated his gun. 'He might die anyway.'

'What do you have against...' Sara stopped, obviously trying to control her emotions. They seemed to get the better of her, though, and she demanded, 'What do you have against us? What did we do to you?'

'It's not you,' Smith told her. He picked up the phone, shouting, 'What the fuck do you want?'

'Then Jeffrey,' Sara said, her voice catching again. Smith would not look at her, so she addressed her words to the second gunman. 'What did Jeffrey ever do to you?'

The second shooter turned toward Sara, his rifle still aimed at the door.

'Shut the fuck up,' Smith barked into the phone. 'We're just gonna perform a little field surgery here. That's why you sent the medics, right?'

Sara would not let go. 'What?' she demanded. 'What's the point? Why are you doing this?' she begged, sounding desperate. 'Why?'

The second shooter kept staring at her, and Smith put the phone to his chest, waiting to see if his partner would answer. The young man had a quiet voice, but it carried when he answered, 'Because Jeffrey's his father.'

Sara looked as if she had seen a ghost. Her lips trembled when she asked, 'Jared?'

SEVENTEEN

Sara counted off the rings on the phone, waiting for her parents' answering machine to pick up. Eddie hated answering machines, but he had gotten one when Sara came back from Atlanta just to help her feel safer. After the sixth ring, the machine whirred on, her father's voice gruff as he asked the caller to leave a message.

Sara waited for the beep, then said, 'Mama, it's me –'

'Sara?' Cathy said. 'Hold on.' Sara waited while her mother went to turn off the machine, which was upstairs in her parents' bedroom. There were only two telephones in the house: the one in the kitchen that had a fifty-foot cord and the one in the master bedroom that had become off-limits to Sara and Tessa as soon as they had reached dating age.

Sara let her gaze fall to the skeleton on the table where just this morning Luke Swan had lain. Hoss had brought three cardboard boxes to transport the bones, and though Sara had been shocked by his lackadaisical attitude, she was not in a position to question the man's methods. She had painstakingly put the skeleton together, trying to find clues that would help identify her. The whole process had taken hours, but she was finally certain

264

about one thing: the girl had, in fact, been murdered.

Cathy came back on the line. 'You okay?' she asked. 'Is something wrong? Where are you?'

'I'm fine, Mama.'

'I was out buying sprinkles for cupcakes.'

Sara felt a tinge of guilt. Her mother only made cupcakes when she was trying to cheer Sara up.

Cathy continued, 'Your daddy got called away to the Chorskes' again. Little Jack flushed a handful of crayons down the toilet.'

'Again?'

'Again,' she echoed. 'You wanna come on over and help me with the frosting?'

'I'm sorry,' Sara told her. 'I'm still in Sylacauga.'

'Oh.' The word managed to convey disappointment as well as disapproval.

'There was a problem,' Sara began, wondering whether or not to tell her mother what had happened. This morning, she had told Cathy about Robert and the shooting, but left out her suspicions about who had pulled the trigger. Now Sara realized as she talked that she could not hold back, and told her mother everything, from the sear mark to Reggie's warning to her worries about whatever Jeffrey had put in his pocket.

'Was it a bracelet or something?' Cathy asked.

'I don't know,' Sara said. 'It looked like a gold chain.'

'Why would he do that?'

'Good question,' Sara said. 'I've been looking at the bones all day.'

'And?'

'Her cranial sutures haven't fully closed.' Sara leaned against the table, looking at the girl,

265

wondering what had brought her short life to such a tragic end. 'The knobbed ends of her long bones haven't completely fused, either.'

'Which means?'

'She was probably in her late teens or early twenties.'

Cathy was silent, then, 'Her poor mother.'

'I put in a call to the sheriff to ask if there are any open missing persons.'

'And?'

'I haven't heard back from him. I haven't heard from anyone all day, as a matter of fact.' Even Deacon White had barely spoken to her when she had returned with the skeleton. Sara added, 'In a town this small, I don't imagine there's a long list of missing people.'

'Do you think it's recent?'

'Recent as in ten, maybe fifteen years,' Sara guessed. 'I've been working on putting the skeleton together for the last five hours. I think I know what happened to her.'

'Did she suffer?'

'No,' Sara lied, hoping she sounded convincing. 'I don't know what's going to happen next. I'm not sure we'll be able to come home tomorrow.'

'You're going to stay with Jeffrey, then?'

Sara bit her bottom lip. She had gotten this far and decided that she might as well continue. 'It seems like the more people say bad things about him, the more I want to . . .'

'Take care of him?'

'I wouldn't say that.'

'Defend him?'

'Mama . . .' Sara began, her voice trailing off. 'I don't know,' she said, and that was the truth. 'It

266

bothers me that you're so set against us.' She paused, thinking of her father. 'It bothers me that Daddy hates him so much.'

'I remember,' Cathy said, 'back when you were four or five.'

Sara pressed her lips together, waiting for the lecture.

'We were all down at the Gulf, and your father took you fishing just to get away, the two of you. Do you remember?'

'No,' Sara said, though she had seen the pictures often enough to think she did.

'You were fishing with rubber worms, but the crabs kept coming along and clamping onto them, thinking it was food.' She laughed. 'I heard your daddy screaming and cussing up a storm, yelling at the crabs to let go, that they were just holding on to worthless nothing.' She waited a beat, probably to make sure Sara understood. 'He tried everything to get them to let go. He even beat them with a hammer, but their claws just kept clamped down on the line no matter what he did. He finally ended up cutting bait and letting them go.'

Sara let out a slow breath. 'Am I the stubborn crab or the worthless bait?'

'You're our little girl,' Cathy said. 'And your father will come around. Eventually, he'll cut bait and let you go.'

'What about you?'

She laughed. 'I'm the hammer.'

Sara knew this all too well. She told her mother, 'I just know what my gut tells me.'

'What's it saying?'

'That I . . .' She was about to say that she loved Jeffrey, but Sara could not bring herself to do it.

Cathy picked up on it anyway. 'So much for your fucking around.'

She could not put into words exactly what had happened in the cave, but she tried, 'I don't know why, but even with all that's happened, I trust him. I feel safe with him.'

'That's no small thing.'

'Yes,' Sara agreed. 'I suppose you know me better than I think.'

'I do,' Cathy said, giving a resigned sigh. 'But I should trust you more.'

Sara said nothing.

'I can't protect you from everything in the world.'

'I don't need you to,' Sara told her. 'I may *want* you to, but I don't need you to.' To soften her words, she added, 'But I love you for being there.'

'I love you, too, baby.'

Sara let out her own sigh, feeling everything catch up with her. Usually, when things got bad she wanted nothing more than to sit in her mother's kitchen and listen to her talk. Cathy had been her touchstone for as long as Sara could remember. Now all she wanted to do was to fall asleep with her head on Jeffrey's shoulder. The transition was startling. She had never felt this way about a man in her life. Even with Steve Mann, back when she was a teenager and everything was so emotional and desperate, Sara had not felt this same burning need to be with him. Jeffrey was like some drug that she could not get enough of. Sara was caught, and there was nothing she could do but wait it out and see what happened next.

Sara said, 'I need to go, Mama. I'll call you tomorrow, okay?'

'Take care,' Cathy said. 'I'll save some cupcakes for you.'

Sara waited until her mother had hung up the phone. She went to do the same, but there was a noise on the line – someone breathing – then a second click.

Someone had been listening in on the conversation.

Sara went to the door and looked out the window into the hallway. The lights had been turned off hours ago when Deacon White had gone home. She knew there was an intern named Harold who lived in an apartment over the garage, but she was told that after hours he pretty much kept to himself unless he was called to transport a body.

She picked up the phone again and pressed the button marked 'Apt.'

There were six rings before the man picked up with a bleary-sounding 'Hello?'

'Harold?'

'Uhn,' he grunted, and she heard him moving around. Obviously she had awakened him. He repeated, 'Hello?'

'Were you just on the phone?'

'What?'

Sara tried again. 'This is Sara Linton. I'm in the building.'

'Oh . . . right . . .' he managed. 'Mr. White said you were staying late.' He paused and she guessed from the sound he was yawning. 'I'm sorry,' he said, then under his breath, 'Jeesh.'

Sara stretched the phone cord so she could see through the window again. A car turned into the parking lot and a pair of headlights lit up the hallway. She shielded her eyes, trying to see who it was. The car had pulled into the handicap space next to her BMW, lights on high beams.

Harold sounded irritated. 'Hello?'

'I'm sorry,' Sara apologized. 'I wanted to leave and –'

'Oh, right,' he said. 'I'll come lock you out.'

'No, I –' she tried, but he had already hung up.

Sara looked into the hallway again, narrowing her eyes past the bright headlights, trying to see if anyone came to the door. A few minutes passed before a figure cut the glare. Harold stood in the middle of the hall, shielding his eyes as Sara had done. He was dressed in his pajamas and had his mouth open in a wide yawn when Sara joined him.

'Who the heck is that?' Harold asked, walking to the front door.

'I was –' She stopped. The car was a truck, and she could see Jeffrey climbing out of the driver's seat. He had the radio blaring with some country music station, and she suppressed a curse, telling the intern, 'Thank you for letting me out.'

'Yeah,' he said, giving another yawn that was so wide Sara could see his back molars. He twisted the lock and opened the door.

Sara started to leave, but could not help but ask the intern, 'Is there anyone else in the building?'

Harold looked over his shoulder. 'Nobody breathing.' He yawned again, one yawn too many, and Sara wondered if he had really been sleeping when she called.

She opened her mouth to question him, but he tossed her a wave as he locked the glass door, giving another yawn for her benefit.

Sara could smell Jeffrey from ten feet away; it was like walking past a brewery. Even without the overwhelming stench of beer, he was weaving as he walked toward her. Sara was slightly taken aback. She had not considered Jeffrey a teetotaler, but neither had she ever seen him drink more than a glass of wine or an occasional beer. Knowing what she did about his mother, this made sense, and the fact that he had chosen tonight to get drunk sent up warning signals Sara did not quite know how to read.

She gave a cautious 'Hey.'

He had a silly grin on his face, and he held his finger in the air for silence as Elvis Presley's 'Wise Men Say' came on the radio.

'Jeffrey . . .'

He put his arm around her waist and pulled her toward him, making sloppy work of leading her in a dance.

She looked at the truck, which was probably older than she was. A long bench seat like the kind she had seen in the cave stretched from door to door, a single gearshift sticking up from the floorboard.

She asked, 'Did you drive here?'

'Shh,' he said, the smell of beer on his breath so overpowering that she turned her head away.

'How much have you had to drink?'

He hummed with the song, picking up the line 'Falling in love . . . with . . . you . . .'

'Jeff.'

'I love you, Sara.'

'That's nice,' she said, gently pushing him away. 'Let's get you home, all right?'

'I can't go to Possum's.'

She put her hands on his shoulders, aware that she was literally keeping him upright. 'Yes, you can.'

'They arrested Robert.'

Sara absorbed this information, but did not offer an opinion. 'We'll talk about it when you're sober.'

'I'm sober now.'

'Sure you are,' she said, glancing back to see if Harold was watching.

'Let's go somewhere,' Jeffrey said, trying to climb into the truck headfirst.

'Hold on,' Sara said, catching him when he fell back. She braced her hands against his butt and pushed him in.

He slurred his words, saying, 'Shh-ure been a long day.'

'I can't believe you drove like this.'

'Who's gonna arrest me?' he asked. 'Hoss wouldn't't've arrested Robert if it wasn't for me.' He put his hands on the wheel. 'Jesus, I'm bad luck. Whole town goes to hell when I show up.'

'Scoot over,' she said, giving him a nudge.

'Men don't let women drive.'

Sara laughed, giving him more of a push than a nudge. 'Come on, big boy. You'll still be a man in the morning.'

Beer bottles clanged onto the floor as he slid onto the passenger's side. He leaned down, rummaging through the bottles. 'Shit,' he said. 'We need more beer.'

'We'll get some,' she told him, climbing into the truck and closing the door. The metallic clang echoed in the cab. She reached down to crank the engine, but the keys were gone.

'He'll probably get the needle,' Jeffrey said, and she could hear the pain in his voice. 'Oh, Jesus,' he said, putting his hand to his eyes.

Sara stared at the front entrance of the funeral home, not knowing what to say. Thanks to her stint at Grady Hospital's emergency room, she had dealt with more than her share of drunks. There was no use trying to reason with them when logic was the last thing on their mind.

She asked, 'Where are the keys?'

Jeffrey leaned his head back against the window and closed his eyes. 'In my pocket.'

Sara stared at him, feeling torn between wanting to slap him and wanting to tell him everything was going to be okay. She settled on saying, 'Scooch down on the seat a little.' When he did, she put her hand into his front pocket.

He smiled, and moved her hand a little closer to center. Considering his lack of sobriety, she was surprised to find his libido none diminished.

'Hey,' he protested when she found the keys and removed her hand.

'Sorry,' she said, her tone contrary to the word as she looked for the ignition key.

'How about a blow job?'

Sara laughed as she found the clunky key. 'You're the one who's drunk, remember? Not me.' She cranked the engine, relieved when it caught on the first try. 'Put on your seatbelt.'

'There aren't any seatbelts,' he said, sliding closer to her.

Sara engaged the clutch and put the truck into reverse. Jeffrey had positioned himself so that he was straddling the shift. She asked, 'How much have you had to drink?'

'Too much,' he admitted, rubbing his eyes.

The sign on top of the building lit up the cab as she backed up, and Sara saw at least eight empty beer bottles rolling around on the floorboard. Jeffrey was wearing black boots she hadn't seen before, and one of the legs of his jeans was pulled up, showing his hairy calf.

She waited until they were on the highway to ask, 'When did they arrest Robert?'

'A little while after I left you,' he said, his head bumping back against the glass. 'He wanted me to come see him. I was just glad he was talking to me.'

He went quiet, and she prompted, 'What did he say?'

'That he did it,' Jeffrey said, throwing his hand into the air as if in resignation. 'I was standing right there in their goddamn stupid front parlor and he looked me in the eye and said he did it.'

Sara was having a hard time following him, but she said, 'I'm sorry.'

'Came back from the store and just shot him. No questions asked.'

Sara could only repeat, 'I'm sorry.'

'You were right.'

'I didn't want to be.'

'Is that true?'

She chanced a look at him. He seemed to be getting back to himself, but his breath was enough to make her turn her head back toward the road. 'Of course it's true.' She put her hand on his leg. 'I'm sorry it happened this way. I know you did everything you could.'

'You won't believe me,' he said. 'I know you said Robert was lying before, and I said you were wrong, but now I think you're right. I mean – I think he's lying now.'

Sara stared at the road ahead.

'You're thinking it's because he's my friend, but it's not. I know it adds up. I know his story makes sense, but he's a cop. He's had time to think about it and get it right so that it all matches up.' He tapped his finger to his head, missing a few times. 'I know it here. I've been a cop too long to not know when people are lying.'

'We'll talk about it tomorrow,' she told him, knowing this was useless.

He rested his head on her shoulder. 'I love you, Sara.'

She had ignored him the first time, but now she felt the need to comment. 'You've just had too much to drink.'

'No,' he disagreed, his breath hot on her neck. 'You don't know how it is.'

She squeezed his leg before shifting into fourth. 'Try to sleep.'

'I don't want to sleep,' he said. 'I want to talk to you.'

'We'll talk tomorrow.' She slowed at an intersection, trying to remember which way to turn. A billboard pointing to a bank looked familiar, and she took a left.

She asked, 'Is this the right way?'

'People only say what they mean when they're drunk,' he told her. 'I mean, being drunk doesn't make you say things you don't mean.'

'I don't know about that,' she said, glad to recognize a gas station from this morning. The store was dark and, like everything else in town, had probably closed hours ago.

'I love you.'

Sara laughed because that was all she could do.

'Turn here,' he said. When she didn't turn quickly enough, he grabbed the steering wheel.

'Jeffrey!' she said, her heart jumping into her throat. He had turned them onto a gravel road.

'Just keep going straight,' he told her, pointing ahead.

Sara slowed the truck. 'Where are we?'

'Just a little farther.'

She leaned closer to the steering wheel, trying to make out the road ahead of her. When she saw a fallen tree in the distance, she stopped. 'The road's blocked.'

'Little more,' he said.

Sara put the truck in neutral and stepped on the parking brake before turning to him. 'Jeffrey, it's late, and I'm tired, and you're dru—'

He kissed her, but not the way she was used to. He was rushed and sloppy, his hands clumsy on the buttons of her jeans.

'Hold on –'

'I want you so much.'

She could tell, he was like a piece of steel against her thigh, but even though Sara could feel her body reacting to his, sex was the last thing on her mind.

'Sara,' he sighed, and kissed her so deeply that she could not breathe.

She managed to soften the kiss, and when his lips moved to her neck, she said, 'Slow down.'

'I want to be inside you,' he said. 'I want it like last night.'

'We're parked in the middle of nowhere.'

'Let's pretend,' he said. 'Let's pretend we're at the beach.' He scooped his hands under her bottom and she gave what could only be called a yelp as she suddenly went horizontal, her feet splayed out against one door and her head bumped into the other. Sara had not been flat on her back in a parked truck since the tenth grade.

Jeffrey tried to move down on her, but considering they were both two grown adults of above average height stuck in a space that was barely five feet long, his attempt was far from successful.

'Sweetheart,' she said, trying to reason with him. She forced his head up to look at her, surprised to see the raw need in his eyes.

'I love you,' he said, leaning up to kiss her again.

Sara returned the kiss, trying again to slow him down. He took the hint, and his kiss was not as probing. When he came up for breath, he moaned, 'I love you.'

'I know,' she said, stroking the back of his neck.

He looked up at her again, and she watched as his eyes seemed to focus on her for the first time since she had walked out of the funeral home. He looked forlorn, like the world had abandoned him and Sara was his only hope. 'Is this okay?'

She nodded, not knowing what else to say.

He repeated, 'Is it okay?'

'Yes,' she said, helping him slide down her jeans.

Even though her body was ready for him, Sara braced herself when Jeffrey entered her. She put her hand behind her, trying to keep her head from bumping into the armrest as he moved inside of her. Overhead, she could see an index card tucked into the sun visor. A woman's hand had hastily scribbled a grocery list on the card, and Sara read the items silently to herself between thrusts. *Eggs . . . milk . . . juice . . . toilet paper . . .*

She turned slightly, trying to keep the gearshift from stabbing her thigh. That was all Jeffrey needed to finish the job, and he collapsed like dead weight on top of her.

Sara dropped her hand to her forehead, wondering how she had gotten herself into this. She said, 'Well, that was romantic.'

Jeffrey did not respond, and when she put her hand on his back he turned his head and let out a heavy breath.

He was asleep.

Sara woke up with a pounding headache that started at the back of her neck and worked up her head like a vise. She could not begin to imagine what Jeffrey felt like this morning, but part of her hoped he was in agony. God knew that she'd had some bad sex in her life, but last night ranked right at the top of what was, thankfully, a rather short list.

She felt for her shoes as she rose from the couch, wondering what time it was. Sunlight was streaming in through the windows and Sara guessed it was almost ten. The clock told another story: it was nearly noon.

'Crap,' Sara mumbled, stretching her arms up to the ceiling. Her back felt as if all the muscles were knotted into bows, and her spine probably resembled a hook from the way she had slept on the couch.

She continued to stretch her back and shoulders as she walked through the house, looking for Nell. The kitchen was empty, pots and pans drying in the sink. She looked outside and saw Nell standing in the neighbor's yard with an ax raised over her head. As Sara watched, Nell brought down the ax on the chain that staked the dogs to a tree.

'What was that?' a voice behind Sara asked. She spun around and saw a young, dark-haired boy standing in the doorway. He was dressed in shorts with no shirt, his skinny chest concave in the center.

'Jared?'

'Yes, ma'am,' he said, looking around the room. 'Where's my mama?'

'She's outside,' Sara told him, wondering if Nell would want her son to know what she was up to. Truth be told, Sara was a little curious herself.

Jared walked to the back door, his sneakers shuffling across the floor. Sara was more than familiar with this curious phenomenon that plagued young boys – most of them did not learn to pick up their feet when they walked until they reached their twenties.

Sara trailed him outside, keeping well back to avoid the dust his shoes were stirring up. He reminded her of Pigpen in the Peanuts comics.

Nell was on the back porch at the neighbor's, putting leashes on the dogs. She saw Jared and said, 'What are you doing out of bed?'

'I'm bored.'

'You should've thought about that before you said you were too sick to go to day camp.' Nell smiled at Sara. 'Did you introduce yourself to Dr. Linton?'

'Doctor?' he asked, a hint of fear in his voice.

Nell said, 'You best get back in that bed before I make her take your temperature.'

There was something so familiar about his reaction – the set to his mouth, the annoyance that flashed in his eyes – that Sara caught herself staring at the boy, her mouth open.

'What?' Jared asked, giving her another familiar look.

Sara shook her head, not trusting herself to speak. His resemblance to Jeffrey was startling.

Nell saw the look on her face, and shooed Jared away. 'Go on, now. Take Mama's ax.'

He shuffled back to the house, dragging the ax behind him, and Sara pressed her lips together, biting back the obvious question.

Nell clicked her tongue and tugged on the leashes. The dogs stood at attention. 'You look like you've got something to say.'

'It's none of my business.'

'That's never stopped me.' Nell led the dogs around to the front of the house as she told Sara, 'Jeffrey doesn't know.'

Sara nodded, acknowledging that she had heard her but still not trusting herself to comment.

At the front of the neighbor's house, Nell sat on the porch with a sigh. 'Possum and I got married a few weeks after Jeffrey moved away to Auburn.'

'You didn't tell him?'

'So he'd come back and marry me?' she asked, petting one of the dogs. 'Not much point in that; we would've both killed each other the first week. I got on his nerves because I was always telling him he was wrong, and he got on mine because he wouldn't admit that I was right.'

Sara could only stare.

'He would've done the right thing,' Nell said. 'And I didn't want anybody to marry me because it was the right thing.' The dog rolled on its back, and Nell scratched his stomach. 'I love Possum. I liked him at first, but then he stepped in when Jeffrey was gone and we had Jared and Jen came later – not much later.' She gave a private smile. 'But we have a family now, a life together. Possum is a good man. He works less than five minutes away and he still calls if he's gonna be late. He doesn't mind picking up Motrin or tampons for me at the Piggly Wiggly and he's never said anything makes me look fat, even when I wore overalls for three years straight after I had Jen. I know where he is every second of the day, and I know if I fart in church he's gonna take the rap.' She gave Sara a pointed look. 'I like my life exactly how it is.'

'You don't think Jeffrey has a right to know?'

'To what end?' she asked, and she had a point. 'Possum's Jared's father. He changed that boy's diapers and walked the floor with him while I was passed out from exhaustion. He signs his report cards and coaches the Little League. There's nothing either of them wants for, and no reason to rock the boat.'

'I understand.'

'Do you?'

'I won't tell him,' she said, wondering how she could keep such a secret.

'It's not good for Jeffrey being back here right now,' Nell said. 'God knows I was mad at him for staying away so long, but there's too much history here. Too much has happened.' She slipped off her flip-flop and scratched the other dog with her toes. 'Jeffrey's turned out all right. He really has. There's something about him inside that's good, just like with Possum, only you have to scratch the surface to get to it. I don't know what you'd call it, but he's grown into the person I always thought he could be if he just got away from . . .' She indicated the street. 'From this place where everybody thinks they know your story and they don't give a never-you-mind about filling everybody else in on what they think about it.'

'Reggie Ray gave me an earful.'

'Don't listen to that old redneck,' she chastised. 'He's the worst of the lot. Keeps saying he was born again. He needs a couple of more rebirths before he turns into a decent human being.'

'He seemed all right.'

'Then you weren't looking close enough,' Nell

said, an edge of warning to her tone. 'There's two things you need to know about this town, Sara: the Rays think their shit don't stink and the Kendalls are pure white trash.' She indicated her own front yard. 'Not that I can say much with all that crap Possum put in the yard, but at least my kids show up to school in clean clothes.'

'Who are the Kendalls?'

'They run the fruit stand outside of town,' she said. 'Mean bastards, every one of them.' She added, 'Don't get me wrong, there's nothing wrong with being poor – me and Possum's brought it to an art form – but that doesn't mean you can send your kids out with dirt on their faces and muck under their fingernails. You see them at the store and you have to hold your breath, they're so filthy.' Nell paused, shaking her head in disapproval. 'A few years ago, one of them showed up to school with lice. Infected the entire ninth grade.'

'Has anyone called children's services?'

Nell snorted. 'Hoss has been trying to run the whole family out of town for years. The old man was horrible. Beat his wife, beat his kids, beat his dogs. Best thing he ever did was drop dead of a heart attack mowing the grass back behind the seed store.' She shook her head again. 'Still left his wife with one in the oven, and that one's the worst of all. Thank God he's not in Jared's grade. He gets thrown out of school every other day for fighting or stealing or God knows what. Punched a girl last week. Little bastard's just like his father.'

Sara said, 'Sounds horrible,' but still, she could not help but feel sorry for the child. She often wondered if kids like that could straighten themselves out with the right parent around. She had never completely bought the 'bad seed' theory, though Nell's appraisal that the apple had not fallen far from the tree was probably shared by everyone in town.

Nell changed the subject, saying, 'Y'all got in late last night.'

'I hope we didn't wake you up.'

'I was already up with Possum,' she said. 'Fool man slammed his chin against the counter at work. Don't ask me how he did it, but it gave him a toothache all night long. Tossing and turning till I about strangled him.'

A car with a woman and a young boy coasted by the house, the woman holding a sheet of paper in her hands like she was trying to read directions.

Sara said, 'Jeffrey had a little too much to drink.'

Nell's surprise was obvious. 'I've never seen him drink much.'

'I don't think it's a habit.'

Nell studied her, like she was trying to figure Sara out. 'Was it about Julia?'

'Who's Julia?'

Nell looked out into the street, where the car that had coasted by earlier had backed up and was parking in front of the driveway.

'Who's Julia?' Sara repeated. 'Nell?'

Nell stood up. 'You need to talk to Jeffrey about that.'

'About what?'

She waved to the woman getting out of the car, saying, 'You found it.'

The woman smiled as her son ran up to the dogs and threw his arms around them. 'They look just like the pictures.'

'This one's Henry,' Nell said, indicating one of the dogs. 'This is Lucinda. Truth be told, she only comes

283

to Lucy.' She held out the leashes to the boy, who gladly took hold.

The woman opened her mouth, looking like she was about to protest, but Nell reached into her pocket and pulled out a wad of cash. 'This should cover the cost for having them fixed. My husband and I never got around to it.'

'Thank you,' the woman said, the cash obviously helping to make up her mind. 'Is there any particular food they like?'

'Anything,' Nell said. 'They just love to eat and they love kids.'

The boy said, 'They're great!' with that enthusiastic tone children use when they're trying to convince their parents they will become future astronauts or presidents if only they get the thing they are asking for.

'Anyway.' Nell looked at Sara then back to the woman. 'I should be going. We've got to finish packing up the house. Movers will be here at two.'

The woman smiled. 'It's a shame you can't keep them in the city.'

'Landlord won't allow it,' Nell told her, holding out her hand. 'Thank you kindly.'

'Thank you,' the woman said, shaking her hand. She shook Sara's, too, then told the child, 'Honey, say "Thank you."'

The boy mumbled a 'Thank you,' but his attention was squarely set on the dogs. Sara watched them bound toward the car, the boy jogging to keep up with the rambunctious animals.

Sara waited until the woman was in the car, but Nell held up a hand to keep her from speaking. 'Put an ad in the paper,' she said. 'No sense letting those dogs waste away out back when there's people who know how to care for them.'

'What are you going to tell your neighbor when he gets home from work?'

'I guess they broke their chains,' Nell shrugged. 'I'd better go check on Jared.'

'Nell –'

'Don't ask me questions, Sara. I know I talk too much, but there's some things you need to hear from Jeffrey.'

'He doesn't seem interested in telling me much of anything.'

'He's over at his mama's,' Nell said. 'Don't worry, she won't be home for another few hours. She grabs lunch at the hospital on Tuesdays.'

'Nell –'

Nell held up her hand, walking away.

After walking up and down the street twice, Sara realized she could always look at the mailboxes instead of trying to remember what Jeffrey's mother's house looked like. She found the one marked 'Tolliver' five houses down from Nell's and hoped to God no one had been watching her make a fool of herself. She felt especially stupid when she recognized Robert's truck parked in the driveway.

In the daylight, the house looked more run-down than Sara had thought the first time she had seen it. Several coats of paint had been added over the years, giving the siding a rippled effect. The lawn was a depressing brown and the spindly tree in the front yard looked like it was about to fall over.

The front door was wide open, the screen door unlocked, but still she knocked, saying, 'Jeffrey?'

There was no response, and Sara walked into the house just as she heard a door slam in the back.

She repeated, 'Jeffrey?'

'Sara?' he asked, coming into the family room. He had a handheld propane torch in one hand and an adjustable wrench in the other.

'Nell said you were here.'

'Yeah,' he said, not exactly looking at her. He held up the torch. 'The pipe in the kitchen burst about two years ago. She's been washing dishes in the bathroom ever since.' She did not respond, and he motioned her back to the kitchen. 'I'm gonna finish up with this, then go over to the jail and check on Robert. I just don't buy what he said yesterday. I know there's something he's not telling me.'

'Lot of that going around,' Sara mumbled.

'What?'

She shrugged, looking at the mess on the floor. He had taken apart the entire faucet just to replace the pipe. She asked, 'Did you turn off the water?'

'That's what I was doing outside,' he told her, sitting on the floor. He took some sand cloth and sanded an end piece of copper pipe with the methodic precision of an amateur.

Sara sat across from him, trying not to be critical of the work he had already performed. Had her father been here, he would have called Jeffrey a girl.

There was a note of pride in Jeffrey's voice when he said, 'I went ahead and replaced everything.'

'Hm,' she mumbled. 'Need help?'

He cut his eyes at her, and she gathered this was something like driving in that only men did it. Considering her father had taught both Sara and Tessa safety procedures for using propane and acetylene torches before they could comfortably say the words, this was more than slightly insulting.

Still, she let it pass, saying, 'I didn't tell you last night –'

'About that,' he interrupted. 'I'm really sorry. I promise you, I don't usually drink like that.'

'I didn't think you did.'

'As for the other . . .' His voice trailed off, and Sara picked up the can of flux, needing to do something with her hands.

She said, 'Don't worry, I'm not going to hold you to it.'

'Hold me to what?'

She shrugged. 'What you said.'

'What did I say?' he asked, his tone of voice wary.

'Nothing,' she told him, trying to open the can.

'I was talking about what we did,' he said, then corrected, 'I mean, what *I* did.'

'It's okay.'

'It's not,' he said, taking the flux and opening it for her. 'I'm not . . .' He paused, as if searching for a word. 'I'm not usually that selfish.'

'Forget about it,' she told him, but somehow his half-ass apology made her feel better. She dipped the brush into the flux and daubed it onto one of the elbows he had already sanded. 'I want to talk to you about the skeleton.'

His attitude changed completely, and she could see his defenses go up. 'What about it?'

'It's a woman. A young woman.'

He gave her a careful look. 'Are you sure?'

'The shape of the head is obvious. Men usually have larger skulls.' She took the measuring tape and measured the distance from the sink to the cutoff valve at the floor. 'Men's skulls are heavier, too. Usually with a bony ridge above the eyes.' She measured a length of pipe and clamped the cutter at the correct spot. 'Men have longer canine teeth and wider vertebrae,' she continued, spinning the cutter until the pipe broke. 'Then there's the pelvis. Women's are wider for childbearing.' She lightly sanded the pipe. 'Plus, there's the sub-pubic angle. If it measures less than ninety degrees, then it's male, more than ninety, it's female.'

He put flux on the pipe as Sara slipped on a pair of safety glasses. His face remained blank as he shoved the elbow onto the pipe, and he waited until Sara had used the flint striker to light the torch before asking, 'How do you know she was young?'

Sara adjusted the torch before waving the flame over the pipe, heating it enough to make the flux boil. 'The pelvis tells the story. The public bones meet in the front of the pelvis. If the bone surface has bumps or ridges, that means it belongs to a young person. Older people have smoother bones.'

She turned off the torch and threaded out the solder, watching it melt into the joint. She continued, 'There's also a depression area in the pubic bone. If a woman has given birth, there's a notch where the bones separated in order to allow room for the baby's head.'

Jeffrey seemed to be holding his breath. When Sara did not continue, he asked, 'Did she have a baby?'

'Yes,' she told him. 'She did.'

Jeffrey put the pipe down in front of him.

'Who's Julia?'

He exhaled slowly. 'Didn't Nell tell you?'

'She said to ask you.'

Jeffrey sat back against the cabinet, leaning his hands on his knees. He would not look at her. 'It was a long time ago.'

'How long?'

'Ten years, I guess. Maybe more.'

'And?'

'And she was . . . I don't know, it sounds bad now, but she was kind of like the town slut.' He wiped his mouth. 'She did things. You know, touched you.' He glanced at her, then looked away. 'Rumor was she'd give a blow job if you bought her something. Clothes or lunch or whatever. She didn't have much, so . . .'

'How old was she?'

'Our age,' he said. 'She was in the same class as me and Robert.'

Sara saw where he was going with this. 'Did you ever buy her anything?'

He looked offended. 'No,' he said. 'I didn't have to pay for that kind of stuff.'

'Of course not.'

'Do you want to hear this or not?'

'I want you to tell me what happened.'

'She just left one day,' he said with a forced shrug. 'She was there one day and gone the next.'

'There's more to it than that.'

'I can't . . .' He let his voice trail off. 'I found this yesterday in the cave,' he said, taking something out of his pocket. Sara saw a necklace with a charm on it.

'Why didn't you tell me then?'

He opened the locket and looked inside. 'I don't know. I just –' He stopped. 'I just didn't want you to know one more bad thing about me.'

'What bad thing?'

'Talk,' he said, meeting her eyes. 'It's just talk, Sara. The same old bullshit that's been following me around since I got here. You get to a point where you're guilty of one thing and people think you're guilty of another.'

'What do they think you're guilty of?'

Jeffrey held out the chain. 'I showed it to Hoss. He didn't want anything to do with it.'

Sara looked at the cheap gold heart and the pictures inside. The children were still infants, probably only a few weeks out of the hospital.

Jeffrey said, 'She wore it all the time. Everybody saw her with it, not just me.' He gave a harsh laugh. 'The thing was, nobody knew what she had done to get it. No one would cop to it, you know? She'd show up in a new dress at school one day and we'd start talking shit about who bought it for her, what she did to get it. This' – he indicated the necklace – 'she showed it to everybody. She didn't know any better. She thought it was expensive. It's not even solid gold, it's plate.' His shoulders dropped. 'There's no telling what she did for it.'

'It looks old to me,' Sara told him. 'Not an antique, but old.'

He shrugged.

'What about the photographs?'

He took back the locket and looked at the pictures inside. 'I've got no idea.'

'So, yesterday in the cave, you knew it was her?' Sara asked, wondering why he had not said anything at the time.

'I didn't want to think it was her,' Jeffrey said. 'I've been feeling guilty all my life for things I didn't do. Things I had no control over.' He gave a long, sad sigh. 'My parents, the house I lived in, the clothes I wore. I always felt so ashamed of everything, wanted to show people a better part of me than my circumstances.' He looked around the kitchen. 'That's why I left here, why I was so anxious to get away and never come back. I was sick of being Jimmy Tolliver's son. I was sick of walking down the street and feeling everybody's eyes on me, waiting for me to mess up.'

Sara waited.

'You see the better part of me.'

She nodded, because she could not deny this, despite what reason would dictate.

'Why?' he asked, and he seemed like he really wanted to know.

'I don't . . .' She let her voice trail off, giving a shrug. 'I wish I could say. My brain keeps telling me all these things. . . .' She did not elaborate. 'I just feel it in here,' she said, tapping her fingers to her chest. 'The way you make me feel when you make love to me and the way you double-knot my shoes so they won't come untied and the way you listen – you're doing it now, really listening to what I have to say because you honestly want to know what I'm thinking.' She thought of the soldier's letter he had read to her what seemed like a lifetime ago, and couldn't explain it any better than, 'I guess that you see me, too.'

He put his hand over hers. 'This thing with the bones. It's going to blow wide open.'

'How?'

'Julia,' he told her, and it seemed to take great effort for him to say her name. 'I need you here, Sara. I need you seeing me the way I really am.'

'Tell me what's going on.'

'I can't,' he told her. She thought she saw tears in his eyes, but he looked away. 'It's a mess,' he said. 'I thought maybe Robert had . . .'

'Robert had what?'

She saw his throat work as he swallowed. 'Robert says he killed her.'

Sara put her hand to her chest. 'What?'

'He told me yesterday.'

'Morning?'

'No, after we found the bones.' Sara started to tell

him that the sequence did not make sense, but Jeffrey continued, 'I showed him the necklace and he said he bashed her head in with a rock.'

Sara sat back, trying to absorb what he was saying. 'Did you tell him that her skull was broken?'

'No.'

'Then how did he know?'

'He might have gotten it from Hoss. Why?'

'Because that's not how she died,' Sara said. 'The skull fracture came at least three weeks before she died.'

'Are you sure?'

'Of course I'm sure,' Sara told him. 'Bone is living tissue. The fracture was already healing when she was killed.'

'It looked like she'd been hit in the head.'

'That was from something else. Maybe a rock fell in the cave or an animal . . .' She did not want to tell him what the animals could have done. 'Absent scalp and tissue, I can't tell you whether or not she was hit in the head immediately before she died, but even with that, her hyoid bone was broken.'

'Her what?'

'The hyoid,' she said, putting her fingers to her throat. 'It's here, a U-shaped bone in the center. It doesn't just break on its own. There has to be significant pressure there, some sort of blunt force or manual strangulation.' She watched Jeffrey, trying to gauge his reaction. 'It wasn't just fractured, it was broken in two.'

He sat up. 'Are you sure?'

'I'll show you the bone if you want.'

'No,' he said, tucking the necklace back into his pocket. 'Why would he say he killed her when he didn't?'

'That was my next question.'

'Maybe if he's lying about that, he's lying about the other night.'

'Why?' Sara asked. 'Why would he lie about either?'

'I don't know,' Jeffrey told her. 'But I've got to find out.' He indicated the sink. 'Can you finish this?'

Sara looked at the mess. 'I guess.'

He started to leave, then turned around. 'I meant it, Sara.'

She looked up. 'Meant what?'

'What I said last night,' he told her. 'I do love you.'

Despite the horrors of the last few days, she felt a smile on her face. 'Go talk to Robert,' she told him. 'I'll finish this and meet you back at Nell's.'

EIGHTEEN

Tuesday

Jeffrey pulled down the visor of Robert's truck, trying to get the sun out of his eyes. He was not exactly hungover, but a small headache was sitting right behind his nose like a hot dime. Like her husband, May Tolliver had passed on one thing to her son for which Jeffrey was grateful: unless he got rip-roaring drunk, he never got hungover. It was a gift as well as a curse. In college, while Jeffrey had been able to drink anyone under the table and still be able to perform at football practice the next day, most of the guys had stopped their heavy drinking by the end of the first quarter for fear of getting kicked off the team. Jeffrey had taken a few years more. After waking up in a hospital outside of Tuscaloosa with his hand in a cast and no memory of how he had gotten there, Jeffrey had decided to bring his drinking days to an end.

Reggie Ray was sitting at the front desk when Jeffrey walked into the sheriff's station. He said, 'What are you doing here?'

Jeffrey did not have time for pleasantries. 'Fuck off, you little pissant.'

Reggie stood so fast his chair fell over. 'You wanna say that to my face?'

Jeffrey had walked past the desk, but he turned around. 'I thought I already had.'

They both waited in that stupid game of chicken that men were supposed to outgrow by this age. Even knowing this, Jeffrey stood his ground. He was sick of being treated this way. No, it went further than that. He was sick of *letting* people treat him this way. Talking to Sara, Jeffrey had finally realized after all these years that the guilt and shame he had experienced had been his own damn doing. Sara did not see him as his father's son. Even now, hearing the worst she could from all kinds of people, she stood by her original view of him. She had known him the least amount of time, yet she seemed to know him better than all of them rolled together, even Nell.

Jeffrey crossed his arms, asking Reggie, 'Well?'

'Why is it every time you're in town something bad happens?'

'Luck, I guess.'

'I don't like you,' Reggie said.

'Is that all you can come up with?' Jeffrey asked. 'Well, guess what, you little shit, I don't like you, either. I haven't liked you since you walked in on your sister giving me a blow job in your father's garage.'

Reggie took a swing, but Jeffrey caught his fist in the palm of his hand. The impact sounded harder than it was, making a loud smack in the empty room. Jeffrey squeezed Reggie's hand until the other man's knees bent.

'Asshole,' Reggie hissed, trying to get his hand back.

Jeffrey jerked the other man forward, banging him against the desk before he let him go. The front door opened and Possum walked in, glancing at Reggie, who was doubled over, before giving Jeffrey a friendly smile as if nothing had happened the day before.

'Possum,' Jeffrey began, feeling like a total bastard when he noticed the bruise running along the bottom of Possum's chin.

Possum held his friendly smile, just like always. 'No big thing, Slick,' he said, patting Jeffrey on the back. 'I got your change from yesterday. Don't let me forget to give it to you.'

'No,' Jeffrey said, thinking he had never felt so bad in his life.

Possum moved on. 'You talk to Robert?'

'I was just going to try.'

'Bail was set this morning,' Possum said, taking a thick envelope out of his pocket.

Jeffrey saw a wad of cash in the envelope and took Possum a few feet down the hall. Not that Reggie Ray wasn't listening, but he felt better having some distance from the other man.

He said, 'Possum, where'd you get that money?'

'Borrowed it against the store,' Possum said. 'Nell about had a heart attack, but we can't leave Robert locked up like that.'

Jeffrey felt his shame return. He had not even considered the possibility of Robert making bail, let alone helping out. 'Jessie's family's got plenty of money,' he said. 'You should let them do this.'

'They already said they won't,' Possum told him, and for once he looked angry about something. 'I tell you, Slick, it hurts my heart the way she's treating him. No matter what was going on, he's still her husband.'

'Did you talk to her?'

'Just came from there.' He lowered his voice. 'She was drunk as a mop and it's not even noon yet.'

'What did she say?'

'Said he could rot in hell for all she cared,' Possum

told him, his tone as bitter-sounding as possible in such an affable man. 'Can you believe that? They've been together longer than dirt, and she just writes him off.'

'She *was* having an affair,' Jeffrey reminded him.

'How long?' he asked, and Jeffrey thought that was a good question. 'It doesn't make sense to me, is the thing. Mean as she could be, how could she tool around town making the nasty and nobody ever finds out and tells Robert?'

'Maybe somebody told him,' Jeffrey said, giving Reggie a glance. The deputy was staring at them with open hatred, and Jeffrey wondered if he was about to snap.

Possum must have noticed this, too. He put himself between the men, asking Reggie, 'Where do I pay bail?'

'In the back,' Reggie said. 'I'll take you.'

He shifted his gun belt as he walked toward Jeffrey, his hand resting on the butt of his gun like he wanted to remind him he could do something with it. When he bumped his shoulder against Jeffrey, Jeffrey let it go, thinking he had started enough fights lately without getting into it again so soon. When the two men were gone, he knocked on Hoss's office door, not waiting to be asked in.

'Hey,' Hoss said, standing up from his desk. Robert was sitting in front of him, hands on his lap, shoulders rolled in like he was waiting for the executioner.

'Possum's here bailing you out,' Jeffrey told him.

Robert's shoulders slumped even more. 'He shouldn't be doing that.'

'He took out money against the store.'

'Christ,' Robert breathed. 'Why'd he do that?'

'He couldn't see you staying here,' Jeffrey said, trying to get Hoss's attention. The old man stared out at the parking lot. Jeffrey got the feeling he had interrupted something. 'I've gotta say I'm not too crazy about it myself.'

Robert said, 'I'm okay.'

Jeffrey waited for him to turn around, but he would not. 'Bobby?'

He gave Jeffrey a quick glance, but that was enough to show that he had a black eye and a split lip. Jeffrey walked around the chair, trying to get a better look at him. Bruises peeked out of the top of his orange jail uniform and his left arm had a large bandage wrapped around it. Jeffrey's fists clenched without thinking about it, and he had trouble asking, 'What happened?'

Hoss answered for him. 'Got a little rowdy last night.'

'Why wasn't he sequestered?' Jeffrey demanded.

'He didn't want special treatment.'

'Special treatment?' Jeffrey repeated, not bothering to hide his outrage. 'Good God, that's not special treatment, that's common sense.'

'Don't question me, boy,' Hoss warned, his finger pointed in Jeffrey's direction. 'I can't make any man do what they don't want to do.'

'That's bullshit!' Jeffrey countered. 'He's a fucking inmate. You can make him sleep in his own shit if you want to.'

'Well, I wasn't here to do it!' Hoss raged. 'Goddammit, I wasn't here.' He used the back of his hand to wipe his mouth, and Jeffrey could feel the misery radiating off him like a bad smell. Whatever Jeffrey was feeling at this moment, he knew that Hoss felt worse.

'Who did it?' Jeffrey asked Robert. 'Was it Reggie Ray? If he's the one –'

Robert interrupted, 'It wasn't Reggie's fault.'

'If he –'

'I asked to be put in,' Robert said. 'I wanted to see what it was like.'

Jeffrey still could not find the words to express himself.

Hoss shifted his belt much as Reggie had done. 'I'm gonna walk outside and give you time to cool your temper,' he told Jeffrey. His tone was even enough, but the way he slammed the door behind him sent a clear message.

Jeffrey went to the source, asking Robert, 'What happened?'

Robert shrugged, wincing as it caused him obvious pain. 'I was sleeping. They woke me up and moved me into general population.'

Jeffrey felt sick at the thought of cops doing this to one of their own. There was a code, and even now Robert was upholding it despite what the bastards had exposed him to.

'Why didn't you call for help?'

'From who?' Robert asked, a sadness in his tone. 'They've all been waiting for something like this,' he said, indicating the deputies in the station with a nod of his head. 'It's the same as when we were kids, Jeffrey. Not a damn thing has changed. Every guy in here was just waiting for me to fuck up so they could throw me to the lions.' He gave a sad laugh. And Jeffrey could only imagine how horrible his night had been. The other inmates had probably thought it was Christmas, having a cop to take out all their hostilities on for the night.

Robert continued, 'All these years ... I really

thought some of those men were my friends, that I had proven myself.' He paused, obviously trying to control his emotions. 'I had a wife. I was part of a family. Hell, I even coached Little League. Did you know that? We got to the quad-A championship last year. Liked to won but one of the Thompson boys overthrew to home.' He smiled at the memory. 'Did you know that? We made it to the big stadium over in Birmingham.'

Jeffrey shook his head. He had grown up with this man, spent every day of his boyhood with him, yet he knew nothing about his life as an adult.

'You just never know what people think about you, do you?' Robert asked. 'You go to ballgames and picnics and watch their kids grow up and hear about their divorces and affairs and it doesn't mean shit. They smile to your face while they're stabbing you in the back.'

'You should've called Hoss last night,' Jeffrey said. 'He would've come down and straightened all of this out.'

'It'd just make things worse the next time.'

'Worse?' Jeffrey said. 'What's worse than getting the shit beat out of you?' His mind answered his own question, and he sunk down in the chair beside Robert before his knees gave out. 'They didn't . . . ?'

Robert's voice sounded like it was coming out of a dead man. 'No.'

Jeffrey put his hand to his stomach, a hot sickness churning in his belly. 'Jesus . . .' he whispered, as close to a prayer as he had come in twenty years.

Robert's hands started to tremor, and Jeffrey noticed the handcuffs keeping them together. His fingers were as beaten up as his face, deep gashes on his knuckles where his fists had met something hard.

He looked as if he had fought for his life last night.

Jeffrey asked, 'Why are you cuffed?'

'I'm a dangerous criminal,' Robert reminded him. 'I've killed two people.'

'You didn't,' Jeffrey said. 'Robert, I know you didn't do this. Why are you lying?'

'I can't do this,' Robert said. 'I thought I was strong enough, but I'm not.'

Jeffrey put his hand on Robert's shoulder, but pulled it away when the other man flinched. He wondered if Robert was telling him the truth about last night, though if he really thought about it, Jeffrey did not want to know a damn thing.

Jeffrey said, 'We'll get you a lawyer.'

'I don't have any money,' he said. 'Jessie's family wouldn't piss on me if I was on fire.'

'I'll pay for it,' Jeffrey told him, even as he racked his brain to think of where he could find that kind of money. 'I don't have enough equity in my house, but I've got a retirement plan I can cash out. It's not much, but it'll be a retainer. Between me and Possum, we can find a way to do this. I'll work security, get another job if I have to.' He cast about for something concrete. 'I can move back to Birmingham and drive down on the weekends.'

'I can't let you do that.'

'You don't have a choice,' Jeffrey told him. 'You can't spend another night in jail.'

Robert shook his head, an overwhelming sadness filling the room. 'I've never had much of a choice about anything, Jeffrey. I'm so sick of living this life. Just plain dog tired of everyone and everything in it.' He closed his eyes. 'Jessie's finished with me. She was finished with me a long time ago.'

'Is this because of the miscarriage?' Jeffrey asked,

thinking that was enough to put a strain on any relationship. There had to be a reason Jessie went out on her husband. People did not cheat for no reason.

'It goes back further than that,' Robert said. 'It goes back to that day Julia came to school, saying I raped her. She never trusted me. Not after that.'

Jeffrey felt all of his senses strain. 'Did you tell Jessie what happened?'

'She never asked,' Robert said. 'There's things she knows in her head, but she never asks the question. Why don't people ask the question?'

'Maybe they don't want to know the answers,' Jeffrey told him, thinking he was just as bad as Jessie. Still, he said, 'Jessie didn't believe those rumors. Nobody who really knew you believed it was true.'

'They believed it about you,' Robert said. He looked up at Jeffrey, his eyes watering. 'I let them think that all this time.'

'Think what?'

'That you raped Julia,' he said, his eyes shifting around, like he wanted to take in every part of Jeffrey's reaction. 'I let them think it was you in the woods. I let them think you raped her.'

Jeffrey felt all the saliva in his mouth go dry.

'I was just protecting myself,' Robert said. 'You went away, but I had to stay here, had to live with them all bearing down on me, thinking they knew my nature.' He looked away. 'Every Sunday at church, I could feel Lane Kendall staring a hole into me, like she could see what was going on, like she knew what happened that day.'

'What happened, Robert?' Jeffrey waited, but he did not answer. 'Tell me what happened,' he repeated.

'I've never asked you before because I believed you were innocent. If you're saying you're guilty now, then tell me what happened.'

Robert cleared his throat a few times, then reached out with both hands to get a cup of water off the desk. He took a sip of water and winced as it went down, his Adam's apple jerking in his throat. Jeffrey saw the bruises around his neck and knew that someone had tried to strangle him. Or had they put their hands around his neck to keep him from calling out? The bruises darkened as they wrapped around the front of his neck. Had someone stood behind him, squeezing his throat shut? What were they doing that was so bad they needed to make sure Robert could not call out?

'Robert,' Jeffrey whispered, trying to find his voice. 'Tell me what happened.'

He shook his head. 'Go home, Slick.'

'I'm not leaving you.'

'Go back to Grant County and marry Sara. Start a life. Have some kids.'

'I'm not gonna do that, Robert. I'm not gonna leave you a second time.'

'You didn't leave me the first time,' Robert said, anger flashing in his eyes. 'Look, I raped her. That's just what I'm going to tell them: I took her to the cave and I raped her, and she started screaming, saying she was going to tell everybody. I panicked, just like I panicked the other night. I took a rock and smashed the side of her head in.' He gave Jeffrey a hard look. 'Does that satisfy you?'

'Which side?' Jeffrey asked. 'Which side of her head did you hit her on?'

'Hell, I don't know. Look at her damn skull. It's the side that's broken.'

'You didn't kill her,' Jeffrey said. 'She was strangled, she wasn't beaten.'

'Oh.' Robert could not hide his surprise, but he recovered quickly. 'Yeah, I strangled her, too.'

'You didn't.'

'I did,' he insisted. 'I strangled her just like this,' he said, the cuffs clinking as he wrapped his hands around an imaginary neck.

'You didn't,' Jeffrey countered.

Robert dropped his hands, though he would not admit defeat.

'I was just talking to her at first, trying to be nice,' he said, his voice getting smaller. His eyes glazed over as he went somewhere else, and he spoke so softly that Jeffrey had to strain to listen. 'When she looked away, I hit her in the head, and when she fell over, I got on top of her, behind her. She screamed, and I started choking her to shut her up.' He used his hands again to illustrate. 'She wouldn't stop screaming, and it got me mad just hearing her, and it got me excited, too – excited like I don't know. I kept one hand on the back of her neck.' He put his hand palm down, like he was there. 'I knew she was scared – terrified. I was scared, too. I thought somebody would come, somebody would see me like that, like some animal. And I couldn't stop. I couldn't get anybody to help me. My throat . . .' He put his hand to his neck. 'My throat felt like I swallowed a handful of tacks. I just couldn't breathe. I couldn't even make a sound more than a whimper, but in my mind, I could hear them laughing about it, egging me on, like it was some kind of game to see how far I could go before I broke.' He let his hands drop to his lap, his breath coming in sharp rasps. Jeffrey did not know if he was talking about Julia anymore or what had happened to him last night. 'I just wanted to go somewhere in my head, somewhere safe where I was okay, but it was all so horrible that I couldn't do anything but bite down on my tongue and pray to God it would be over soon.' His lips trembled, but there were no tears.

'Robert,' Jeffrey said, reaching out again to touch him.

Robert pulled away as if Jeffrey had slapped him. He curled into himself as much as he could. 'Don't touch me,' he whispered. 'Please don't touch me.'

'Robert,' Jeffrey repeated, trying to keep his voice controlled. If he had a gun, he'd go back to the jail right now and kill every one of those fucking bastards. He'd start with Reggie and work his way up the food chain until – what? – until he put the gun to his own head and pulled the trigger? He was just as guilty in all of this as the others were.

Still, he had to know, 'Why are you lying to me about Julia?'

'I'm not lying,' Robert said, anger flaring up again. 'I raped her.' He gave Jeffrey a steady look. 'I raped her and then I killed her.'

'You didn't kill Julia,' Jeffrey insisted. 'Stop saying you did. You didn't even know how she died.'

'What does it matter?' Robert said. 'I'm going to get the needle anyway.'

'You're not,' Jeffrey said. 'Not if you cop to manslaughter. You can be out in seven years. You can still have a life.'

'What kind of life?'

'I'll help make a life for you,' Jeffrey said, and in that moment, he was certain he could make it work. 'You can come to Grant with me. Work on the force.'

'Not with a felony rap.'

'We'll find something else, then,' Jeffrey told him.

'We'll get you the fuck out of this town. You can start over, have a new life.'

'What kind of life?' Robert repeated. He raised his hands, indicating the station. 'What kind of life can I have after this?'

'We'll get to that when the time comes,' Jeffrey said. 'Just stop talking to people, okay? Don't talk to anybody but the lawyer – not even Hoss. We'll get the best guy we can. We'll go to Atlanta if we have to.'

'I don't want a lawyer,' Robert said. 'I just want some peace.'

'You're not going to find peace in a prison uniform, Robert. You have to know that by now.'

'I don't care anymore,' he said. 'I really don't.'

'That's just for right now,' Jeffrey told him. 'That's just because of last night.'

'Nothing happened last night,' Robert said. 'We got into a scuffle, but that was it. They knew better after I got finished with them.'

Jeffrey sat back in the chair.

'I beat the shit out of them,' Robert said, his teeth showing in what he probably wanted to be a smile but looked like more of a snarl. 'Three on one, and I beat the ever-loving shit out of them.'

'That's good,' Jeffrey said, knowing he could not disagree. Three on one. Robert hadn't had a chance.

Robert's false bravado continued. 'I punched one of 'em so hard he was begging for his mama.'

'There you go,' Jeffrey said, his heart breaking even as he said the words. 'You showed 'em, Bobby. You showed 'em all.'

Robert took a deep breath, sitting up straighter, squaring his shoulders. 'All right,' he said, like he was bracing himself. 'It's all right. I can do this.'

'You don't have to do it alone,' Jeffrey told him. 'I'm here. Possum's here.'

'No,' Robert said, like his mind was made up. 'I'm going to do this, Jeffrey. It's the least I can do.'

'Least you can do for what?'

'For you,' he said, giving Jeffrey a knowing look. 'I know what really happened.'

Jeffrey felt as if he had been threatened, but he did not know why. 'What do you mean?' he asked.

'I saw you in the woods with Julia that day. I saw you both going to the cave.'

Jeffrey shook his head. They had been alone that day. He had checked.

'I'm willing to take the rap for everything,' Robert said, tears welling back into his eyes. When he spoke, his voice shook from the effort. 'I'll say I did it, take the blame for all of it and let you walk away. Just tell me, Slick. Tell me the truth. Did you kill her?'

NINETEEN

Sara was sitting in a chair on Nell's front porch as Jeffrey pulled into the driveway. He had exchanged Robert's truck for her BMW, and she was glad to see it back in one piece. She walked toward him as he got out of the car, but something about his expression stopped her.

'What's wrong?' she asked.

'Nothing,' he told her, though he was obviously lying. 'Let's go to Robert's house again.'

'Okay,' she agreed. 'Let me go tell Nell where I'm going.'

He grabbed her hand, pulling her back toward the street. 'She'll figure it out.'

'Okay,' she repeated, wondering what was going on. He held on to her hand as they walked down the street. There was a slight breeze in the air, which made the day more bearable, but it was still hot on the black asphalt, and Sara could not help thinking back to two short nights ago when she had run down the street trying to get away from Jeffrey. Maybe he was thinking about the same thing, because he squeezed her hand.

She asked, 'Are you okay?'

He shook his head, but did not elaborate.

'Why do you want to look at the house again?'

'Something's not right,' he said. 'It doesn't add up.'

'What did Robert say?'

'Nothing new,' Jeffrey told her. 'He's still taking the rap for it. Taking the rap for everything.' His jaw tightened, and he was quiet a beat. 'He's lying about Julia. It makes me wonder what else he was lying about.'

'Like what?' Sara said, thinking that it was pretty clear what had happened in the bedroom that night. 'All the evidence backs what he's saying.'

'I just want to look at it again,' he said. 'I want see for myself that it works out.'

'What specifically do you think doesn't add up?'

He let go of her hand as they approached Robert's house, not answering her question. The yellow clapboard looked freshly painted and the white picket fence gave the place a surreal effect, like it was a Hollywood version of what a home should be.

There was a bright yellow strip of police tape on the door. Jeffrey took out his Swiss Army pocketknife, prying up the blade with his fingernail. 'He was attacked last night.'

'In the jail?'

He nodded.

'By whom?'

Jeffrey sliced through the police tape. 'He won't say.'

'How could Hoss let that happen?'

'It wasn't Hoss,' Jeffrey told her, closing the knife. 'Robert won't say who put him in general population, but I have a feeling it was Reggie.'

'Why didn't he just paint a target on his back?'

'If I see that stupid redneck fuck again, I'm going to rip his head off.'

Sara had a hard time reconciling Reggie with these actions, but Nell had said he was not to be trusted.

She asked, 'Is Robert all right?'

Jeffrey opened the door and stepped back, letting Sara enter the house first. 'I tried to get him to talk to me, to tell me what went down, but he wouldn't.'

'Was he badly beaten?'

'It's not that I'm worried about,' Jeffrey said, and she read everything on his expression in a moment.

'Oh, no,' she said, putting her hand to her chest. 'Is he okay?'

He closed the door behind them. 'He says he's fine.'

'Jeffrey,' she said, wrapping her hand around his shoulder. He looked down the hallway, not at her, and she could tell he was struggling to maintain his composure.

'Possum was down there this morning to bail him out,' he said. 'I didn't even think about doing that.'

'How could he make bail?'

'Hoss must have pulled some strings,' Jeffrey told her. 'It's not like he's a flight risk. Where would he go?'

'I'm so sorry,' she told him, feeling his sadness wash over her.

He put his arms around her, and she held him, trying to offer comfort when she knew there was little else she could do.

'Oh, Sara,' he breathed, burying his face in her neck. His whole body relaxed, and despite all that had happened, she felt an overwhelming sense of happiness knowing that just by holding him she could bring him such peace.

He said, 'I just want to get away with you.'

'I know,' she told him, stroking the nape of his neck.

'I want to take you dancing,' he said, and she laughed because they both knew she had the co-ordination of a just-born colt. 'I want to walk on the beach with you and drink piña coladas out of your belly button.'

She laughed again, pulling away, but he would not let her. Sara kissed his neck, letting her lips linger on his skin. He tasted salty, like the ocean, and she could smell the musky odor of his aftershave. 'I'm here,' she said.

'I know,' he told her, finally breaking the embrace. He gave a heavy sigh, indicating the house with a toss of his hand. 'Let's just get this over with.'

'What are we looking for?' she asked, following him into the living room.

'I don't know,' he said, opening one of the drawers in the coffee table. He rummaged around inside, then closed it. 'Where did he keep his backup gun?'

'I think he said the living room?' Sara said, more of a question because she could not remember.

'There should be a safe,' he said. 'If he was telling the truth about where he kept it.'

Sara was not sure if anything Robert said could be trusted, but she opened the doors on the television cabinet. Except for a large TV and a bunch of videotapes, she saw nothing. She bent down to go through the drawers, saying, 'They don't have kids in the house. He could've just kept it in a drawer.'

'Robert knows better than that,' Jeffrey said, getting on his hands and knees to look under the couch. 'Hoss taught us both that you always secure your weapon.' He sat back on his heels, a sad look in his eyes. 'Robert coached Little League,' he said. 'He probably had kids in here all the time. He wouldn't have left a gun laying around.'

'Jessie had an episode,' Sara told him. 'Nell told me around the miscarriage she took too many pills.'

'Another reason for him to keep it hidden,' Jeffrey pointed out.

Sara rummaged through a stack of instruction sheets for every piece of electronic equipment in the house. She found several old remote controls, a few spent batteries, and a fingernail file, but no gun safe. She asked, 'Where do you keep your backup?'

'By my bed,' he answered. 'When I'm home, my service piece is in the kitchen.'

'Why there?'

'I've never thought about it,' he said, running his hand under the coffee table. 'Just seemed logical. One upstairs, one downstairs.'

'Where in the kitchen?' Sara asked, walking toward the back of the house.

'Cabinet over the stove,' he called, then, 'Shit.'

'What?'

'Got a splinter.'

'Try to be a little more careful,' she advised him, walking down the hall. The bedroom was directly across from the kitchen, but she did not let herself look. The stench of dried blood was overpowering, and Sara knew that it would linger in the house long after Robert and Jessie found someone who could clean it. She could not imagine how Jessie could go on living here after what had happened.

Sara opened the cabinet over the stove, finding a stack of Tupperware bowls with their lids neatly piled beside them. She stood on the tips of her toes, peering all the way to the back, but there was nothing even resembling a gun. She went around the room, opening and closing all the cabinets, with the same results. She even checked the refrigerator, which had a full gallon of milk, juice, and the usual staples, but no gun.

'Find anything?' Jeffrey asked. He stood in the doorway with one hand cradling the other.

'Does it hurt?' Sara asked.

'Not much,' he said, holding out his hand. She turned on the light and saw a thick splinter in the palm of his hand.

'They must have some tweezers,' she said, opening the drawers. A quick search found nothing but common kitchen utensils. 'I'll check the bathroom.'

She headed toward the master bathroom but stopped when she caught sight of a sewing basket sitting on the highboy beside the dining room table.

She told Jeffrey, 'Come in here, the light's better,' as she searched the basket. 'These will work,' she said, finding a pair of straight-edged tweezers among the pins and needles.

'You want me to open these?' Jeffrey asked, but he was already twisting the rod to open the blinds. He looked out into the backyard, saying, 'It's nice here, huh?'

'Yes,' she said, taking his hand in hers. She wore glasses sometimes at work, but she had been too vain to bring them along on the trip. 'This might hurt.'

'I can take it,' he said, then, 'Ow, shit.' He jerked back his hand.

'Sorry,' she said, trying not to smile at his reaction. She held his hand closer to the window, taking advantage of the light. 'Just think about something else.'

'That won't be hard,' he told her sarcastically, wincing as the tweezers grew near.

'I haven't even touched it,' she said.

'Are you this mean to your kids?'

'Usually they're a little braver.'

'That's nice.'

'Come on,' she teased him. 'I'll give you a lollipop if you're good.'

'I'd rather give *you* something to suck on.'

She raised an eyebrow, but did not respond. Slowly, she worked at the splinter, trying to get it to come out in one piece.

Jeffrey asked, 'Did you notice something weird about Swan?'

'Weird how?' She groaned as the splinter broke.

'Like . . .' He made a hissing sound as she dug into the skin. 'He's the exact opposite of Robert.'

She shrugged. 'Maybe that was the point. She wanted something different. A change.'

'Am I different from the guys you usually date?'

Sara worked on the splinter, trying to come up with a good answer. 'I can't say that I've given it much thought.' She smiled as the splinter came out. 'There.'

He put his hand to his mouth, something Sara saw kids do at the clinic, as if some genetic imperative convinced them that their mouth could cleanse a wound.

'Let's look in the bedroom,' Jeffrey said.

'You think he was lying about keeping a backup in the living room?'

'I don't know.'

'He could have kept it in his truck.'

'Maybe.'

'What else is bothering you?' She decided not to let him brush it off. 'I'm not stupid, Jeffrey. Something's bothering you. Either tell me or not, but don't keep denying it.'

He put his hand on the windowsill. 'Yes, something is bothering me. I just can't talk about it.'

'Okay,' she agreed, glad that she had at least gotten him to admit it. 'Let's finish in here. Maybe then we can go back to Nell's and try to make some sense of all this.'

The bedroom door was slightly ajar, and the hinges squeaked when she opened it. Light was streaming in through the windows, and Sara was surprised to find that her memory of what the room had looked like the night Swan had been shot was completely skewed. Somehow, her mind had exaggerated everything so that whenever she tried to imagine the room, she saw blood everywhere. In actuality, except for the splatter fanning out to the door and ceiling and the pool of blood and matter where Swan had lain, the room was clean.

Jeffrey opened the armoire and searched the shelves as Sara went to the bedside table opposite the side Swan had been shot. Everything in the room had been dusted for prints, black powder showing specks of dirt and ridges on every available surface. She assumed Reggie had lifted whatever evidence he needed, but still Sara tried not to touch the black powder on the cabinet door, knowing from experience how difficult it was to wash off. She opened the door from the top, stepping back as a baby-blue vibrator fell out onto the floor.

Jeffrey was looking over her shoulder. 'That explains a lot,' he said in a knowing tone.

'What does it explain?' Sara asked him, taking a

tissue to use as she returned the machine to its resting place. 'Every woman I know has one of these.'

He seemed surprised. 'Do you?'

'Of course not, honey,' she joked. 'You're more than man enough for me.'

'I'm serious, Sara.'

'What?' she asked, glancing in the cabinet before shutting the door. There was a small tube of personal lubricant, but she thought better than to tell Jeffrey. She said, 'It doesn't mean anything. Sometimes couples use them. What sort of smoking gun are you looking for here?'

'I don't know,' he said, sounding defeated. 'He's not telling me the truth. We've got to either prove he's lying or prove he's not.' He shrugged his shoulders. 'Either way, I'm going to support him through this.'

Sara told him, 'Sometimes when people lie, they sprinkle in the truth so that it sounds believable.'

'Meaning?'

'Robert might have told us a bit of information that we're just not hearing.' Sara suggested, 'Let's take it from the beginning and go over what Robert and Jessie said happened the first time.'

'You mean what they told us when Luke was shot?'

She nodded.

'All right,' he said, looking around the room. 'Let's take it from the top. We were in the street. I heard the shots and ran through the backyard to here.' He stood in the doorway. 'I saw what had happened, or at least saw the dead guy. Robert groaned and I turned around. He was here,' Jeffrey pointed behind the door. 'Jessie was over here,' he said, indicating the area by the window.

'Then what?'

'I asked Robert if he was okay, then I went to get you.'

'All right,' Sara began, taking up the narration. 'I came in and you went to call the police. I checked Swan's pulse, then I went to help Robert.'

'He wouldn't let you look at the wound,' Jeffrey provided. 'Jessie kept interrupting while I tried to get the story.'

'Which was,' Sara took over, 'they were in bed. Swan came in through the window.'

Jeffrey walked over to the window. He looked out into the backyard. 'Someone could have sneaked in through here.'

'Did Robert ever say he knocked the screen out?' She clarified, 'As part of his new story where he says he did it. Did he say that he knocked out the screen?'

'No.'

Sara glanced around the room, trying to remember how things had looked that night.

'So, Swan has a gun,' Jeffrey said, picking back up on Robert's first explanation. 'He crawls to the bed. Jessie wakes up and screams. Robert stirs and Swan shoots at him.'

'He misses,' Sara provided. 'Robert runs to the armoire and gets his gun.' She stood in front of the armoire. 'He shoots at Swan, but the gun hangs.'

Jeffrey finished, 'Swan shoots him, then Robert's gun goes off and shoots Swan in the head.'

Sara looked down at where she was standing. The blood-spray pattern did not point to the armoire.

She said, 'He would've had to have been here,' walking to the door and lining herself up with the pattern. 'Look at this,' she said, indicating blood in the carpet where Swan had fallen. 'Robert had to have been standing here.'

'Why?'

'He shoots,' she said, holding out her hand with her thumb and index finger forming the shape of a gun. 'The bullet hits Swan in the head, and there's backsplatter from the bullet. It's basic science: for every action, there's an equal and opposite reaction. The bullet goes in, the blood sprays back. Look at the pattern of the blood.'

Jeffrey stood beside her, looking at the carpet. 'Okay,' he said. 'I see it. He was standing here.'

'Hold on,' she told him, leaving the room before he could ask why. She got the sewing basket and came back, saying, 'This isn't exactly scientific.'

'What are you doing?'

She found a spool of yellow thread, thinking that would show up best. 'Blood's subject to gravity, just like anything else.'

'So?'

'So,' she said, opening a box of straight pins. 'You can tell from the shape of the drop which way the blood fell. If it was splattered, if it fell straight down.' She pointed to the bullet hole behind the door. 'See?' she told him. 'You can tell from the pattern that Robert was standing near the wall when the bullet exited his body. The blood drops are almost perfectly round except at the top, where you can see they've got a slight teardrop shape to them. That means the bullet was on an upward trajectory.'

'But it looks scattered,' Jeffrey said, pointing to the hairline ribbons of red radiating from the circular drops.

'The blood hit the wall straight on, but it still splattered back.' She used a straight pin to point this out. 'This is where the bulk of the impact took place.'

'All right,' he agreed, though she could tell he still did not buy it. 'What can the rest of this tell us?'

'Watch,' she told him, picking at the end of the thread. She pulled it out a few yards, then bent to the carpet to match it to the blood. 'I'm just guessing at the angle, and of course I'll have to adjust it – probably up – for the parabolic, but I –'

'What are you talking about?'

'Basic trigonometry,' she answered, thinking it was obvious. 'I really don't have the right equipment, so this is just a hunch, but the formula goes something like, the ratio of width and length of the bloodstain equals the angle of impact. . . .' She had lost him again, so she said, 'Go find some tape.'

'Masking? Duct? Scotch?'

'Anything sticky.'

While Jeffrey searched the house for tape, Sara went about lining up the thread. She used the pins to attach the ends to the carpet and spun out the thread in lengths of ten to twelve feet.

'Will this work?' Jeffrey asked, handing her a roll of electrical tape.

'It should,' Sara said, peeling off strips of tape and sticking them to her arm. She found the major splatters on the bedside table, careful not to touch the chunks of flesh that remained. She wished she had put on a pair of gloves before starting this, but it was too late now.

She told Jeffrey, 'Stand here,' pointing to the foot of the bed.

'What are you going to do?'

'There's nothing to attach the thread to on this end,' she said. 'I need to use you.'

'Okay,' he agreed, and she went back to each piece

of thread, probably thirty in all, and judging the angle as best she could without the proper instruments, she followed the angle of the splatter, pinning the ends of the thread to Jeffrey's clothing. She used the black tape to highlight where the yellow threads crossed. By the time she had finished, Sara had worked up quite a sweat in the closed room, but it was well worth the effort.

'His head was here,' Jeffrey said, indicating the point at which all the string converged. The black electrical tape represented the area of impact, like some sort of forensic spider on a web, showing the exact spot where the bullet exploded out blood, bone, and brain.

Sara had already gotten her jeans dirty crawling around on the bloody carpet, but she was hesitant to put herself where Swan had been kneeling when he was shot. He must have been a few feet from the bed when the bullet hit. She said, 'He was a little shorter than I am, so his head must have been about here, give or take a few inches because of miscalculations on my part.'

'Jessie was in bed,' Jeffrey said, not moving because of the string. 'Swan must have been on his knees in front of her.'

Sara saw what could have been an outline of a handprint. 'Here,' she said. 'Do you see this?'

'Yeah,' he nodded. 'Swan must have had his hand there. Maybe he was leaning against the bed, using it for balance.'

'He was facing this way,' Sara said, indicating the bed. 'The bullet entered the side of his head, here,' she put her fingers to the space above her ear. 'It came out low on the other side.' She indicated the glob of flesh still stuck to the bedside table. 'This is his earlobe.'

'So it fits,' Jeffrey said. 'Robert was standing over here about where I am and Swan was kneeling beside the bed, doing whatever.'

'He was facing Jessie.'

Jeffrey's shoulders slumped, and the string went with him. 'What he said was right, then. He didn't even give him a warning. He just shot him in cold blood.'

'Let's get these off,' Sara said, meaning the pins. 'This doesn't tell us why.'

'The why is clear enough,' he said, helping her with the pins. 'He saw another man fucking his wife. I'd feel the same way.'

'You wouldn't shoot someone.'

'I don't know what I'd do,' Jeffrey said. 'If I saw you with somebody else . . .'

'Robert saw them first,' Sara said, still trying to think it through. 'He wasn't carrying his gun when he walked in the first time.'

'No,' Jeffrey agreed. 'He must have gone back out into the room or his truck or wherever the fuck it is he keeps his gun.'

'Then he came back,' Sara continued. 'That's premeditation.'

'I know,' Jeffrey said, dropping some pins into the plastic box.

She wound up the string, wondering what they were going to do now. Robert had already confessed. Their purpose here had been to try in some way to break his story. They had done nothing more than proven he had shot the man with premeditation. It was the difference between ten years with early release and death row.

Car tires screeched outside, and Jeffrey said, 'I wonder what –' just as a door slammed. They both walked to the front of house to see who was there. Jeffrey threw open the door just as a woman was raising her fist to bang on it.

'You!' she screamed, her voice reminding Sara of a gravel truck. 'You fucking bastard, I knew you'd be here!'

Jeffrey tried to close the door but the woman inserted herself in the house. The smell of her hit Sara first, the metallic tinge of menstrual blood, though the woman was well past that time in her life. She was enormous, probably a hundred pounds overweight, with a face that was a mask of sheer rage.

'You fucking pig!' the woman screamed, punching her hand into Jeffrey's chest.

'Lane –' he began, holding up his hands to stop her.

'You killed my daughter, you murdering bastard!' she bellowed. 'You and your fucking friends aren't going to get away with this!'

Jeffrey tried to push her out the door, but she was able to keep it open by sheer force of weight. She punched her hands into Jeffrey's chest again, this time hard enough to knock him back into the house. The door flew open as he fell to the floor.

Sara went to him, telling the woman, 'Stop!' before she could help herself.

She turned on Sara, giving her the kind of up-and-down appraisal that she would probably give a leper. 'I heard about you,' she said. 'You fucking slut. You don't even know what kind of trash you're with.'

Jeffrey had managed to stand, but he was breathing hard, and Sara wondered if the force of the punch had broken one of his ribs.

Sara hissed, 'Who is this?'

'Eric!' the woman called back into the yard. 'Get in here. You, too, Sonny.'

Jeffrey leaned hard against the wall, like he needed help to stay up. Sara was about to ask him what was going on when she saw two young boys walking up the porch stairs. They were pitiful creatures, undernourished and filthy. Sara was reminded of two baby birds who had fallen out of their nest and been abandoned by their mother, and she felt angry just looking at them. What sort of person could allow such neglect? Who could treat two children this way?

The woman grabbed one of the boys by the back of his neck and thrust him toward Jeffrey. 'Say hello to your father, you little bastard.'

Sara caught the boy before he fell. Under his dirty gray shirt she could feel his ribs poking through.

The woman said, 'This is the asshole who raped your mama.'

Sara felt as if her throat had closed. She looked at Jeffrey but he would not meet her gaze.

'Rape?' Sara managed, the word echoing in her head like a bell.

'You pig,' the woman told Jeffrey. 'Be a fucking man and take some responsibility for once in your pathetic life.'

'Please,' Sara said to the woman, trying to concentrate on the things she could control. 'Don't do this in front of the children.'

'Don't do what?' the woman demanded. 'Boy needs to know his father. Ain't that right, Eric? Don't you wanna meet the man who raped and killed your mama?'

Eric looked up at Jeffrey, curious, but Jeffrey's face was stone, and he did not even glance at the child.

'Are you okay?' Sara asked the boy, using her

323

fingers to push his dirty hair out of his eyes. He was tall enough to be Jared's age, but there was something sickly about him. She could see odd-looking bruises on his arms and legs. She asked, 'Are you sick?'

The woman answered for him. 'He's got bad blood,' she said. 'Just like his piece-of-shit father.'

'Get out of here,' Jeffrey growled, his voice a warning. 'You don't belong here.'

'You're gonna let Robert pay for this,' she said. 'You fucking coward.'

'You don't know anything about it.'

'I know I got medical bills out the ass,' she yelled back. 'Nobody on my side of the family's ever had this kind of shit.' She gave the boy a look of pure hatred, like she could not stand being near him. 'You think I'm made of money? You think I can afford to rush this'un up to the hospital for a transfusion every time he falls down?'

Jeffrey warned, 'Get the fuck out of here before I call Hoss.'

She stood her ground. 'Bring him on! Bring him on right now and we'll settle this once and for all.'

'There's nothing to settle,' Jeffrey shot back. 'Nothing's changed, Lane. You can't do anything now.'

'The hell you say,' she told him. 'Everybody knows you raped her.'

'The statute of limitations on that ran out three years ago,' he told her, and the fact that he knew this sent a cold shiver through Sara's spine. 'Even if you had something, they couldn't touch me.'

The woman shoved her fat finger into Jeffrey's face. 'I'll fucking kill you myself, you goddamn bastard.'

'Ma'am,' Sara tried, keeping her hands on Eric, not wanting to let him go. He seemed a million miles away, as if he was used to adults behaving this way. The boy who remained in the yard was playing with a plastic toy truck, his lips making engine noises. Still, Sara said, 'Let's not do this in front of the children.'

'Who the fuck are you?' she laughed. 'Just who the fuck do you think you are?'

Sara stood up, anger compelling her to speak. 'I know that this child is sick. He's filthy. How can you let him get like this?' She indicated the other boy. 'Him, too. I should call child services on you.'

'Go ahead and call them,' she said. 'You think I give a shit? Two less mouths to feed.' Still, even as she said this she reached out her hand, indicating Eric should come to her. The boy followed the command, and Sara reached to stop him, her fingers brushing his arm. She could feel raised welts where the black and blue marks riddled his skin.

The woman told Sara, 'Your boyfriend here raped my daughter.'

Sara felt light-headed. She put her hand out to the wall to keep herself steady.

'He raped her and got her pregnant, and when she asked him for help, he killed her, and left me to raise his little bastard of a son.' The woman shoved her finger back in Jeffrey's face. 'This isn't over.'

'Yes,' he said. 'It is.'

'You tell that fucking buddy of yours if I see him in the street, he's a dead man.'

'Why don't I tell Hoss and he can run you in for making threats?'

'You fucking coward,' she said, her lips twisting into a sneer as she coughed in the back of her throat. Before Jeffrey could move away, she spit on his face.

'This isn't over,' she repeated, grabbing Eric by the wrist. He already had bruises up and down his arm, but the child did not protest. The other boy in the yard trotted back to the car, looking for all the world as if his mother had told him they were going for ice cream.

Jeffrey took out his handkerchief and carefully unfolded it. He patted his face, wiping off the spit.

Sara took several minutes to find her voice. She kept hearing the woman's accusation over and over in her head. Finally, she managed, 'Do you want to tell me what that was about?'

'No.'

She threw her hands into the air, feeling angry and vulnerable. 'Jeffrey, she said you raped her daughter.'

'Do you believe her?' he asked, looking her right in the eye. 'Do you believe I raped somebody? That I killed somebody?'

She had been too shocked to let her mind fully consider the possibility. The accusation had hit her like a hammer, knocking her senseless.

'Sara?'

'I don't . . .' She shook her head. 'I don't know what I believe anymore.'

'Then we don't have much to say to each other,' he told her, walking away.

'Wait,' she told him, following him down the driveway. 'Jeffrey.' He did not turn around, and she had to run to catch up with him. 'Talk to me.'

'Looks like you've already made up your mind.'

'Why won't you tell me what happened?'

He stopped, turning to face her. 'Why won't you let it be, Sara? Why can't you just trust me?'

'It's not a matter of trust,' Sara told him. 'My God,

that woman says you raped her daughter. She says you have a son.'

'That's bullshit,' he snapped. 'You think I could have a kid and not know it? There's no way.'

Sara remembered Jared, and bit back the urge to throw Nell's secret in his face.

'What?' he demanded, mistaking her reticence for something more sinister. 'You know what? Fuck this.' He continued to walk down the street, obviously exasperated. 'I thought you were different. I thought you were somebody I could trust.'

'It's not an issue of trust.'

' "Issue," ' he repeated. 'Fuck that.'

'Oh, that's really mature,' she said, mocking him. ' "Fuck that." '

She tried to grab his shoulder to stop him but he jerked away, advising, 'You wanna leave me alone right now.'

'Why?' she asked. 'Are you going to rape me, too? Strangle me?'

He had been angry before, livid, but she read his hurt like an open book, immediately regretting her words.

Sara tried to take it back, but he shook his head like he did not trust himself to talk. He held up his finger to her, as if to make a point, but still he said nothing. Finally, he shook his head again and continued down the street, walking toward his mother's house.

'Shit,' Sara whispered, tucking her hands into her hips. Why did everything have to be so difficult between them? The minute things were going well, something – usually someone – came along and ruined it. Rape. She could handle anything they said about him but this. Why had he not told her before?

327

Why hadn't he trusted her? Probably for the same reasons she did not completely trust him.

Nell was sitting on the front steps when Sara walked up to the house, and she stood, holding her hand out to Sara, saying, 'I saw Lane Kendall's car up at Robert's. What did that old cow say to you?'

Sara opened her mouth and to her surprise burst into tears.

'Oh, honey,' Nell said, leading her into the house. 'Come here.' She pulled Sara toward the couch. 'Sit down.'

Sara sat, and Nell hugged her. She felt ridiculous and grateful at the same time, and her words came in jagged murmurs between sobs as she let everything out that she had wanted to tell Jeffrey. 'Those poor children.'

'I know.'

'They looked so dirty, so hungry.'

Nell shook her head, tsking.

'I don't want to feel this way.'

'Oh, now,' Nell said, stroking her hair. 'Shh . . .'

'What happened?' she begged. 'Please just tell me what happened.'

'Come on,' Nell soothed, taking a Kleenex out of the box. She held the tissue to Sara's nose and said, 'Blow.'

Sara did as she was instructed, feeling silly for her outburst. She sat up, wiping her eyes with another tissue. 'Oh, God, I'm so sorry.'

'It's a wonder you haven't broken down before this,' Nell said, taking another tissue to wipe her own eyes.

'Those children . . .' Sara murmured. 'Those poor boys.'

'I know. It makes my stomach ache every time I see them.'

'Why can't anyone *do* something?'

'Don't ask me,' she said. 'I'd put an ad in the paper if I thought someone would take them.'

Sara tried to laugh, but she could not. 'What about children's services?'

'You wanna know something funny?'

Sara waited.

'She used to work for them.'

'No,' Sara said. She could not believe it.

'She did,' Nell confirmed. 'About fifteen years ago she was a caseworker at the Department of Family and Children's Services. Then she got into a car accident on the way to do a house visit and sued the county and the state and anybody else she could get her hands on. Between her disability and whatever she got from the settlement, she's not hurting for money.'

'Where does she spend it?'

'Not on any of her kids,' Nell answered ruefully. 'The upshot is, she knows all the rules. She knows how to get around having those kids taken away. D-FACS is scared of her. If it wasn't for Hoss making drop-bys every now and then, she'd probably put those two boys in a closet and throw away the key.'

'What's wrong with the youngest?'

'Some blood thing,' Nell said. 'He's always having to get transfusions.'

'Hemophilia?' she asked, thinking Nell probably meant infusions. Even in a town as small as Sylacauga, the doctors would know better.

'No, something else like that, but not hemophilia,' Nell told her. 'State pays all the bills, I'm sure.'

Sara sank back into the sofa, feeling an overwhelming exhaustion. The two women sat there in silence, and for some reason Sara told her, 'I was raped.'

For once, Nell did not respond.

'I've never said that out loud,' she said. 'I mean, the actual words. I always say I was attacked or I was hurt. . . .' She pressed her lips together. 'I was raped.'

Nell let her take her time.

'It was when I worked in Atlanta,' Sara said, adding, 'Jeffrey doesn't know.' She picked at a piece of string on the cushion.

Nell gave Sara a moment before saying, 'I guess we've each got our secrets from him.'

'I've never felt like this with a man,' Sara said. 'Not about anybody.' She tried to find a way to articulate it. 'I feel totally out of control, like no matter what my brain tells me, there's this little thing in the back of my head saying, "No, don't listen to them. You can't live without him."'

Nell repeated, 'He has that effect on women.'

'I just want . . .' She threw her hands into the air. 'I don't know what I want.' She picked at the string again. 'I can't even tell him to his face that I love him, but every time I see him or even think about him . . .'

Nell took another tissue and handed it to Sara. 'I never believed it,' she told her. 'What they said about him and Julia.'

'What exactly did they say?'

'That Jeffrey and Robert raped her in the woods.'

Sara bit her bottom lip. Nell had said the words matter-of-factly, but they still had power. The word 'rape' in and of itself was the most obscene sort of profanity.

'She was a slut,' Nell said. 'Not that that's any

excuse. Hell, my sister Marinell was a bigger slut, but she knew better than to brag about it.'

'Tell me everything,' Sara said. 'Jeffrey won't.'

Nell shrugged. 'She did things with boys. I don't know, it sounds like no big deal today, but back then, you just didn't put out.' She amended, 'Well, you did it, but you sure as shit didn't let everybody know about it.'

'I remember,' Sara said. Fear had kept her from giving in to Steve Mann, and shame had kept her from really enjoying it when she finally did.

'Julia wasn't pretty,' Nell said. 'She wasn't plain, either, but there's a quality girls like that have that makes them ugly. I guess it's some sort of desperation, where they grab onto anybody they think can make them feel better about themselves.' She stared at the pictures of her family that lined the wall. 'I look at Jen and it just makes me cringe sometimes because I see this need in her. She's not even a teenager yet and she's got this unquenchable thirst for approval.'

'Most girls are like that.'

'Are they?'

'Yes,' Sara said. 'Some are better at hiding it.'

'I try to tell her she's pretty. Possum's just crazy about her. Went to the father-daughter dance with her at the end of school last year. My God, but that man can carry off a baby-blue tux like nobody you've ever seen.'

Sara laughed, imagining Possum in the tuxedo.

'She's doing sports now,' Nell said. 'Basketball, softball. It's making a difference.'

Sara nodded. Girls who participated in sports had more self-confidence; it was a proven fact. She said, 'I look back and thank God I had my mother.' Sara laughed at herself. 'Not that I ever believed a word she said, but she was always telling me I could do anything I wanted to do.'

'Obviously, part of you was listening,' Nell pointed out. 'You don't get to be a doctor just because you're pretty.'

Sara felt a tinge of a blush at the compliment.

'Anyway,' Nell said, folding and unfolding the tissue. 'Julia was kind of loose. She didn't make a secret of it, either. She thought it meant something that the boys would go with her, like they thought she was special or they loved her. Like blowing them behind the gym after school made her some kind of special. She actually bragged about it.'

'Did she ever go with Jeffrey?'

'The truth?' Nell asked.

Sara could only nod.

'The truth is, I can't tell you. I don't see why he would. I was giving it to him pretty regular then.' She laughed at herself. 'You never know with boys that age, though. A sixteen-year-old boy is gonna pass up on getting laid? Hell, most grown men wouldn't pass that up. Sex is sex, and they'll do just about anything to get it.'

'Did you ever ask him about what happened?'

'I didn't have the guts,' Nell said. 'I wouldn't have a problem now, but you know how it is when you're young. You're scared to say something that might piss him off and make him leave you for the next hot thing.'

'Who was the next hot thing?'

'Jessie, I thought, but in retrospect I know that he never would have done that to Robert.' Nell tucked her feet under her legs. 'I don't think he did, if you want my gut reaction. Even then, Jeffrey had this thing about him, this sort of guide that let him know the difference between right and wrong.'

'I thought he was in trouble all the time.'

'Oh, he was,' Nell said. 'But he knew he was wrong. That's what I kept after him about. He just knew better than to do the crap he did. He had to get to that point where he made the decision to listen to his gut.' She added, 'Your gut's a lot smarter than you think.'

Sara thought of her conversation with her mother yesterday. 'My gut tells me to trust him.'

'Mine, too,' Nell said. 'I remember when Julia came to school the next day after she said she was raped. It was horrible. She told anybody who would listen. The details just filtered through so that by lunchtime we were all thinking she was bruised and battered.' She paused. 'Then I saw her in the hall, and she didn't look that upset to me. She seemed to be enjoying the attention.' Nell gave another shrug. 'The thing was, she lied all the time. Lied for attention, lied for pity. No one believed her. She probably didn't even believe herself.'

'What did she say exactly?'

'That Robert took her to the cave, gave her some beer, loosened her up.'

'Where does Jeffrey come in?'

'Later,' Nell answered. 'The story took on a life of its own, just like these things always do. He swore up and down he was with Robert when it happened, and she said sweet as you please that, by the way, Jeffrey was there, too. Said they both took turns on her.'

'She changed her story?'

'From what I heard, but gossip goes both ways. She could have been saying they were both involved from the beginning and I just heard it wrong. It was a mess.

By the end of the day there were rumors she'd been gang-raped by a group of boys from Comer. Some of the football team was talking about going after them. People just go crazy with that kind of thing.'

'Were the police –' Sara stopped. 'Hoss.'

'Oh, yeah. Hoss was called. Some teacher at the school overheard Julia crying about it and they called in Hoss.'

'What did he do?'

'He interviewed her, I guess. God knows he knew where she lived. Right before her father died, Hoss was there every weekend breaking up a fight between him and Lane.'

'Did he interview Jeffrey and Robert?'

'Probably,' Nell said, not sounding certain. 'Julia backed off the story real quick after Hoss was called in. Stopped talking about it at school, stopped acting like the injured party. People tried to get her to say something – not because they were concerned but because it was a good scandal – but she wouldn't talk. Wouldn't say a thing. She was gone a month or so later.'

'Gone where?'

'To have that baby, I'd guess,' Nell said. 'Fat as Lane is, no one made a connection when she told everybody she was pregnant again. Her husband had just died and we all felt sorry for her.' Nell paused. 'Now, there was a blessing, that old man dying. He was a terror, worse than Lane ever thought to be. Worse than Jeffrey's dad, I'd say. Just a mean, nasty piece of work.'

'How many children did she have?'

'Last count, six.'

'Is the one I saw today – Sonny – her youngest one?'

'He's a cousin. I don't know why she took him on. Probably for the extra money the state gives her.'

'That's unbelievable,' Sara said, wondering how anyone could allow that woman to raise a child, let alone two.

'Julia came back nine or ten months later and there was Eric, her new brother.'

'No one said anything about the timing?'

'What were they going to say?' Nell asked. 'And then a few more weeks later, she was gone again. It was just easier to say that Lane was the mother and Julia had run off somewhere. Dan Phillips, one of the boys who'd been on the football team, ran off around that time. There were all kinds of rumors, but they died off pretty quick. It made it easier for everybody, I guess.'

Nell sat up on the couch and took a photo album out from under the coffee table. She thumbed through some of the pages until she found what she was looking for. 'That's her, there in back.'

Sara saw a photograph of Possum, Robert, and Jeffrey standing in the bleachers of a football stadium. They were all wearing their letterman jackets with their last names stitched on the front above their football jersey numbers. Jeffrey had his arm around Nell, and she leaned into him like a love-struck young girl. Inexplicably, Sara felt a stab of jealousy.

'Bastard never would give me his jacket,' Nell said, and Sara laughed, but felt secretly relieved for some reason. In high school, wearing a boy's letterman jacket was right up there with wearing his class ring. It was not so much a symbol of the boy's love, but a way for the girl to make the rest of her friends jealous.

As if reading her mind, Nell asked, 'Whose ring did you wear?'

Sara felt herself blush, but more from shame than anything else. Steve Mann's class ring had been a hulking chunk of gold with a hideous chess knight on the side – nothing like the football and basketball rings the athletes wore. Sara had hated wearing it and took it off as soon as she moved to Atlanta. Three months passed before she got up the nerve to mail it back to him along with a note explaining that she wanted to break up. To her credit, she had apologized to him years later, but Sara wondered if she would have given it a second thought had she not been forced to move back to Grant after what happened in Atlanta.

Nell took her silence for something else, probably assuming someone like Sara had not dated much in high school. She said, 'Well, it's stupid anyway. Jeffrey didn't have a class ring – couldn't afford it – but all the other girls wore theirs like a damn wedding ring.' She laughed. 'The only way they could get them to fit was by wrapping half a roll of tape around the band.'

Sara allowed a smile. She had done the same thing.

Nell returned to the photo album, saying 'There' as she put her finger beside a blurry image of a young girl standing behind a picture of Possum and Robert. 'That's Julia.'

Sara had been expecting something horrible from Nell's description, but Julia looked like any other teenage girl from that time period. Her hair was straight to her waist and she was wearing a simple dress with a floral pattern. She looked sad more than anything else, and as sudden as her previous stab of jealousy, Sara felt a sharp sense of sympathy for the teenager.

Nell leaned over to look. 'Now that I'm seeing her again, she wasn't that bad. You really can't judge personality in a picture, can you?'

'No,' Sara agreed, thinking the girl was fairly attractive. Yet, that had not been enough to help her transcend the circumstances of her family life. She asked, 'Was her father abusive?'

'He beat the crap out of them.'

'No,' Sara said. 'The other way.'

'Oh, you mean . . .' Nell seemed to think about it. 'I have no idea, but it'd make sense.'

'Do you know who the father of her child might have been?'

'No telling,' Nell said. 'If you wanted a list of everybody she'd been with, it'd end up being half the town.' She gave Sara a pointed look. 'Reggie Ray included.'

'He was younger than her.'

'So?'

Sara conceded the point, then said, 'From what Lane said, it sounds like Eric has to go to the hospital a lot to get treatments. So he has to have some sort of clotting problem with his blood.' She tried to think of other possibilities. 'There has to be an autosomal recessive or dominant transmission.' She saw Nell's perplexed expression and said, 'Sorry, it means that the disorder is genetic. It has to do with one of the two proteins that make up clotting factors.'

'Is that supposed to make sense?'

'Bleeding disorders are passed from parent to child.'

'Ah.'

'Do you know if Julia had anything like that?'

'I wouldn't think so,' Nell said. 'I remember one time during home ec, she sliced her finger open pretty bad with a pair of scissors. Whether or not it was an accident, I don't know, but she didn't seem to bleed any longer than a normal person would.'

'If she had something like von Willebrand's disease, then having a child without proper medical supervision would have been life-threatening,' Sara said. 'There would also be other people in her family who were affected, and Lane pretty much said that wasn't the case.'

'So you're saying it had to come from the father?' Nell asked. 'I can't think of anyone in town with that kind of problem.' She added, 'Not Robert, especially. He got pretty banged up on the football field and never seemed the worse for it.'

'Jeffrey, too,' Sara said. She remembered drawing his blood sample. The puncture had bled no longer than usual. Even as she considered this, Sara felt ashamed. She had never genuinely thought Jeffrey could be guilty of either crime, but some part of her was glad that there was irrefutable proof.

'I could ask around,' Nell offered.

'It comes in degrees,' Sara said. 'Some people have it and don't even know it. It's not as easy for women because of their menstrual cycles. Generally, they know there's a problem. My bet would be it came from the father.'

'A needle in a haystack,' Nell pointed out. 'Who knows, maybe Dan Phillips has it.' She reminded Sara, 'The one who ran off about the same time Julia did.' She reached over and paged through the album. 'Here,' she said, indicating a young man standing in the back row of the football team photo.

'He doesn't look like a football player,' Sara said.

338

Phillips was on the thin side and his dark hair was combed straight back off his head. He looked healthy enough, though one photo could not give the full story.

'He mostly played tackle dummy,' Nell said. 'Just being on the team and wearing the letterman jacket was all most of these guys wanted. Go down to the hardware store on game day and you can still hear them talking about it like they were in the damn Super Bowl.'

'Glory days,' Sara said. It was the same in Grant. She turned the page, looking at the other pictures. There was a black-and-white snapshot of Jared from a few years back, and she said, 'He's growing up to be a handsome boy.'

'You're not going to tell Jeffrey, are you?' Nell tried to smile. 'Don't answer that.' She put the album back under the table. 'You still leaving town?'

'I don't know.'

'Stick around.' Nell patted her leg. 'I'm making cornbread tonight.'

'Where's Robert?'

'Possum took him to the store to buy him some clothes,' she said. 'Robert didn't want to go back to the house and God only knows what Jessie did with the stuff at her mama's.'

'What about Robert?'

'He'll be okay.'

'No,' Sara said. 'Robert. We've only been talking about Jeffrey. Did you ever think he was involved in what happened to Julia?'

Nell took her time answering. 'He was always secretive.'

'About what?'

'Maybe "secretive" is the wrong word. Makes him

sound shifty. He's just private. Doesn't talk about his feelings much.'

'Jeffrey doesn't, either.'

'No, not like that. Like he doesn't want anyone to get too close to him.' She sat back on the couch, her back slumped into a C. 'Everybody thought it was Possum who was on the outside, but I think it was Robert. He never seemed to fit in. Not that Jeffrey treated him that way, but it's that same thing we were talking about earlier. He always waited to see what Jeffrey did before he acted.'

'That's not uncommon for teenagers.'

'It was more than that,' Nell said. 'If Jeffrey got into trouble, Robert would take the blame. He was like Jeffrey's safety net and Jeffrey let him do it.' She looked at Sara. 'The minute Jeffrey left, Robert did the same thing with Hoss. He'd take a bullet for either one of them, and I'm not exaggerating.'

Sara debated before telling her, 'Robert is saying that he killed Julia.'

Something in Nell's face shifted, though Sara could not pin down what. Her voice had changed, too. 'I don't know about that.'

'No,' Sara said. 'Me neither.'

TWENTY

Jeffrey found his mother's Impala parked in her usual space in front of the hospital. She could have easily walked to work and back, but May Tolliver would never add more minutes to the time it took for her to get that first drink after her shift in the hospital cafeteria ended.

As usual, she had left the windows down to keep the car from turning into an oven. Jeffrey smelled stale cigarette smoke wafting through the air as he opened the door. She always kept a spare key in the glove compartment, and he found it underneath a bunch of religious tracts and brightly colored pamphlets that must have been stuck under the windshield wiper of the car at some point. She might have been a chain-smoking drunk, but May never littered.

The engine turned over after he pumped the gas several times, and Jeffrey brushed cigarette ash off the gear console as he shifted the car into drive. The windows were foggy from nicotine, and he took out his handkerchief, wiping the windshield as he drove out of the parking lot. If his mother left the hospital before he got back with the car, she would easily put two and two together and realize that with Jeffrey in town he had probably borrowed her car. He had 'borrowed' it often enough as a teenager, and May had never mentioned it to a soul. The two times Jeffrey had been pulled over by sheriff's deputies, May had insisted she had loaned the car to her son.

Jeffrey drove aimlessly through downtown, not heading in any particular direction. He felt sick in his gut, like someone had died. Maybe someone had. He was sinking back into that old feeling that his life was totally out of control. He was the eye of a storm that caused nothing but destruction.

He could not get over the fact that all these years Robert had even for a minute entertained the thought that Jeffrey had killed Julia Kendall. Back in Hoss's office, when Robert had asked the question, Jeffrey had been too shocked to show anything but anger. Even when he denied it, tried to tell Robert what had really happened, the other man had simply shaken his head, like he did not want to hear whatever yarn Jeffrey had concocted to explain his actions.

'It doesn't matter,' Robert had kept saying. 'I'll take the rap.'

Jeffrey realized he was close to the funeral home, and he took a last-minute turn across the highway, pulling into the lot. He parked in the back, hoping Deacon White would not have the car towed. Jeffrey was sick of borrowing people's cars and shoes and whatever else he'd taken these last few days. He wanted to be in his own home in his own bed. He wanted to be alone. The cave was the closest thing he could think of that might bring him some peace.

No one came out of the building to warn him off, so Jeffrey got out of the car and walked the back way to the cemetery. He had a grandfather buried some-where on the hill, but Jimmy Tolliver had never mentioned the man's name. Knowing how these things worked, Jeffrey guessed that Jimmy's old man had taught him everything about parenting that he knew; which was to say, not a lot. Jeffrey had never felt that genetic urge that some men feel, like they had to get a woman pregnant and pass on their heritage. Maybe nature was correcting an error. Some people were not meant to pass on their blood.

As he walked into the woods, Jeffrey could not help but think of Sara and the way she had talked to him. She obviously believed everything Lane Kendall had said, no matter the fact that the woman was lying trash. Jeffrey still felt the burn of shame Lane had brought him all those years ago, the way she had talked around town, letting everyone know that she was sure Jeffrey had raped her daughter, even though Julia's story had changed so many times even she could not keep up with it.

But what was rape? People always thought of it as something violent and vicious, some deranged psychopath forcing a woman to spread her legs under threat of harm. Julia had been with plenty of boys, and Jeffrey was certain she had not wanted any of them. She had been looking for love and acceptance, and seen sex as a way to get that. Probably most of the guys who went with her knew that, but at that age, it was hard to care. If a girl was more than half willing, you were halfway there. Being sweet to Julia before she lifted her skirt or holding her for a few minutes afterward was the price you paid to get laid. Some of the boys even joked about it, trying to guess who had done what to get in her pants. The jokes had flown the day Julia had shown up with that damn necklace, acting like she had finally convinced someone to love her. The poor fuck who'd given it to her had probably been shitting in his pants when she started showing that thing off.

Maybe some guy had felt guilty for taking advantage of her, figured out after coming in her mouth that maybe she wasn't exactly enjoying it. Of course, what man hadn't had sex with a woman who wasn't exactly into it? Drunk as he was the other night, Jeffrey had known Sara wasn't in the mood, but he had somehow managed to get her to say yes. He had been so desperate for that release, for that moment when everything seemed okay, that he had ignored the fact that she was doing him a favor.

Julia Kendall had called it doing a guy a favor. Jeffrey could still remember the way she looked at him, twirling that stupid cheap necklace around her finger, saying, 'Hey, Slick, you want me to do you a favor?'

In the forest, Jeffrey stopped at the mouth of the cave. The boards had been broken away, probably where Hoss had come in to get the bones. Julia's bones. Jeffrey hesitated before going in, thinking this was a grave, no longer his boyhood hideout. Still, he went in, thinking there was no better place for him to be right now.

He sat on the bench, his mind again going back to Sara. She thought he was guilty, and why not? The things people had been telling her were horrible – and some of it was true. God only knew what Nell was putting into her head right now. Back when Julia disappeared, Nell had started acting differently around him. She had started to pull away, like she did not quite trust him anymore. Three weeks before graduation, she had broken up with him in the gymnasium, yelling at him like he was a dog. God, she had hated him that day, and Jeffrey still did not know what he had done.

He had left the gym and run into Julia. She was back from wherever she had run off to, come home to help her mother with the new baby. Lane Kendall's husband was dead and she needed all the help she could get. Even with the false charges Julia had made against Jeffrey and Robert, when he ran into her – and he had literally run into her, she had been standing right outside the gym doors – and she asked if he wanted her to do him a favor, he had said, 'Sure.'

The rape allegations had died down when Julia left town the first time. No one really believed her, anyway. She had slept around too much for people to think she was not a willing participant, and why the hell would a man rape her when she was giving it up easily enough?

'I'm sorry about what I said,' Julia had told him, following him through the woods, the back way to the cave. 'I didn't mean to get y'all in trouble.'

'You didn't get us in trouble.'

She laughed. 'I bet not,' she said. 'That old Hoss can't abide anybody doing you wrong.'

Jeffrey had not responded. They had reached the cave, and he held back the vines.

'It's dark in there.'

'You gonna do this or not?' he said, giving her a push toward the cave. At seventeen, Jeffrey had not yet learned the fine art of seduction. Hell, he hadn't even learned how to keep his brain working when all the blood in his body rushed to that one place. Standing outside the cave, knowing that in a few minutes Julia was going to be doing the one thing

Nell refused to do, his pants had been so tight across the front that he could barely move.

'You still mad at me?' she asked, a curious smile at her lips as she glanced down at his crotch. 'Maybe I shouldn't go in there.'

'Suit yourself,' he said, going into the cave ahead of her, his erection so painful he was surprised he could speak.

Jeffrey looked around the cave now, trying to remember what it felt like to have Sara in here. Certainly, better than when Julia was there. She had finally followed him inside and within minutes she had started crying, telling him she had made a mess of her life, apologizing for what she had said about Robert and Jeffrey. He had gotten angry because all he wanted was a blow job, not her fucking life story.

Julia had wanted him to kiss her, but Jeffrey had refused. There was something ugly about the shape of her mouth, and all he could think about was how many other guys had been there. In the end, he had told her to go away. When she would not go, he left the cave. The next time he saw Julia Kendall, Sara was there and Julia was nothing but a skeleton, laid out on the rocks as if she had gone to sleep that day, waiting for Jeffrey to come back.

The question was, did Robert really kill her? God knew he hated the girl for spreading that rumor that they had raped her. Unlike Jeffrey, who just chalked it up to Julia trying to get attention, Robert had seethed with the kind of hatred that burns you from the inside. Maybe it was because Jeffrey knew that he would be going away to Auburn in the fall, or maybe it was because he knew how baseless the allegations were, but he had not taken Julia's charges to heart the way Robert had. In retrospect, Robert could have been angry because he felt guilty. Someone had made that baby.

Jeffrey took a deep breath and slowly let it go. Robert could not have killed her. He did not even know how she had died. Someone out there did, though. Someone had been in this cave with Julia. An argument had sparked or maybe whoever did it had just had enough of her. Jeffrey had seen this kind of thing all the time when he was a cop in Birmingham. It was depressing when you heard firsthand the stupid excuses people could come up with to try to justify the fact that they took another life. Was there a man out there right now, going to church on Sundays, playing ball in the yard with his kids after work, telling himself he was still a good guy because Julia Kendall had asked for it? The thought made him sick.

He rested his foot on the coffee table and looked around the dank cave. The first time they had found this spot, he had thought it was the best place in the world. Now it just looked like a damp hole in the ground. More than that, it was a tomb.

He stood as best he could and walked out into the sunlight. Slowly, he made his way back toward the funeral home, trying to think about what to do next. He wanted answers to all of this, wanted it solved once and for all. Robert was not going to help him with anything, but being a cop, Jeffrey was used to noncooperation from the chief suspect. Maybe that's what Jeffrey needed to do now, think about this case like a cop instead of as Robert's friend. Looking at it that way, he had forgotten an important step: talking to the victim's family.

A few years before he moved to Grant County, Jeffrey had spent two weeks driving around the

South, looking at all the historic homes he could only read about when he was growing up. The trip was born of impulse and the need to get out of Birmingham while a certain assistant district attorney he had been dating cooled her heels over Jeffrey telling her there was no way in hell they were going to get married. Looking back, it had been one of the best times of his life.

Among other sights on the trip, he saw the Biltmore House, Belle Monte, and Jefferson's Monticello. He toured battleships and historic battlefields and walked the same path Grant took to Atlanta. Wandering through downtown after viewing The Dump, an old apartment building that really was a dump yet held the distinction of being where Margaret Mitchell had written most of *Gone with the Wind*, he happened upon a classically designed mansion called the Swan House.

Like everyone else of any rank in Georgia, the Inman family had got its money from cotton and decided to build a house that celebrated their wealth. They had hired a local architect named Philip Trammell Shutze to design their mansion, and he had come up with nothing short of a masterpiece. The Swan House had some of the most beautiful rooms Jeffrey had ever seen, including a bathroom with floor-to-ceiling pink marble that had been painted over to look like white marble; the lady of the house had not liked the original color. Long after the tour had ended, he had managed to sneak into the opulent library and just stare at the old books on the shelves. Jeffrey had never stood in such a room in his life, and he felt at once in awe and humbled.

In great contrast, Luke Swan's house was the kind of shack even Jeffrey had looked down on when he was a kid. As a matter of fact, the house was so bad that somewhere along the way the Swan family had simply abandoned it and moved into a trailer home parked in the driveway. Stacks of newspapers and magazines stood on the porch, just waiting for a stray cigarette or match to bring the whole place down. It stank of poverty and hopelessness, and Jeffrey thought not for the first time that there were still large chunks of the rural South that had not yet fully recovered from Reconstruction.

As Jeffrey parked on the dirt road in front of the house, six or seven dogs ran out to the car – the standard redneck house alarm. A majestic-looking mailbox stood at least four feet high in front of the driveway, fancy script giving the street numbers. Just to be certain, Jeffrey checked the numbers against the page he had ripped out of the phone book he had found dangling from a wire by the pay phones outside Yonders Blossom. The book was at least ten years old, but people in Sylacauga did not tend to move around much. There were only two Swans listed in town, and Jeffrey had taken the wild guess that Luke was not associated with the ones who lived near the country club.

'Git back!' a woman yelled at the dogs as Jeffrey got out of the car. The animals scattered and the old woman stood on the cinder block porch outside the trailer, leaning heavily on a wooden cane. Her cheeks were sunken in, and Jeffrey guessed she had left her teeth in a glass somewhere inside the trailer.

She asked, 'You come about the cable?'

'Uh . . .' He looked back at his mother's car, wondering what she must have been thinking. 'No, ma'am. I came to talk to you about Luke.'

She clasped her housedress together with a gnarled

old hand. He walked closer and he could see her rheumy eyes were having trouble focusing.

As if she knew what he was thinking, she said, 'I got the cataracts.'

Her accent was so heavy that he had trouble understanding her. 'I'm sorry.'

'Not your fault, is it?' she asked, no menace in her tone. 'Come on in,' she said. 'Mind that first step. My grandson was gonna fix it for me, but then, well, I guess you know what happened.'

'Yes, ma'am,' Jeffrey said, testing the bottom step. The cinder block shifted, and he could see where rain runoff from the trailer had eroded the soil underneath. He kicked some dirt and stones under it, making it a bit more level, before following her into the trailer.

'Not much,' the old woman said, the understatement of the century. The place was a pigsty, the narrow design making it seem like the walls were closing in. More newspapers and magazines were piled around the room, and Jeffrey wondered what she was doing holding on to all this stuff.

'My late husband was quite the reader.' She indicated the piles of magazines. 'Couldn't bear to part with his things when he passed.' She added, 'The emphysema got him. Don't smoke, do you?'

'No, ma'am,' he said, trying to follow her into the main room, a combination kitchen/dining room/living room that was little more than ten feet square. The trailer smelled of chicken fat and sweat, with a slightly medicinal undertone that older people got when they stopped taking care of themselves.

'That's good,' she said, putting her hands out in front of her to feel her way toward her chair.

'Smoking's horrible. Kills you something bad in the end.'

Beside him, Jeffrey saw a stack of *Guns & Ammo* along with magazines of a considerably more adult nature. He glanced at the old woman, wondering if she was aware that a copy of the 1978 Christmas edition of *Penthouse* sat less than three feet from where she stood.

She said, 'Go on and sit if you can find a place. Just move that stuff aside. My Luke used to sit there and read to me.' She put her hand behind her, feeling for the chair. Jeffrey took her elbow and helped her sit. 'I like the *National Geographic,* but the *Reader's Digest* is getting a little too liberal for my liking.'

He asked, 'Do you have someone who comes in to take care of you?'

'It was just Luke,' she told him. 'His mama done run off with a door-to-door salesman. His daddy, that was my youngest boy, Ernest, well, he never amounted to much. Died in the penitentiary.'

'I'm sorry,' Jeffrey said, walking across the sticky carpet. He considered the chair, but remained standing.

'You sure do apologize a lot for things that ain't got nothing to do with you,' the woman said, feeling around on the table beside her. He saw a plate of crackers, and wondered how she chewed them. She put one in her mouth and he saw that she didn't chew them so much as let them melt on her tongue while she talked.

She told him amidst a spray of crumbs, 'Cable's been out for two days now. I liked to had a fit when it went off – right in the middle of my program.'

Jeffrey started to say he was sorry again, but he

caught himself. 'Can you tell me about your grandson?'

'Oh, he was a good boy,' she said, her whiskered mouth trembling for a moment. 'They got him down at the funeral home still?'

'I don't know. I guess.'

'I don't know where I'm gonna get the money to bury him. All I got is my social security and the little bit I get from the mill.'

'You worked there?'

'Up until I couldn't see no more,' she said, smacking her lips. She paused a beat as she swallowed the soggy cracker in her mouth. 'That was four, five years ago, I'd say.'

She looked about a hundred, but she could not be that old if she was able to work in the mill that recently.

'Luke wanted me to get that surgery,' she told him, indicating her eyes. 'I don't trust doctors. I've never been to a hospital. Wasn't even born in one,' she said proudly. 'I say take the burdens God gives you and go on.'

'That's a good attitude,' Jeffrey said, though he wondered at choosing blindness for the rest of your life.

'He took care of me, that boy,' the old woman said. She reached for another cracker, and Jeffrey looked back at the small strip of a kitchen, wondering if that was all the food she had.

He asked, 'Was Luke into anything bad that you know about? maybe hanging out with the wrong kind of people?'

'He made money cleaning people's gutters and washing their windows. Nothing wrong with an honest day's work.'

She had said 'win-ders' for windows, and Jeffrey smiled, thinking he hadn't heard that word in a while. 'No, ma'am.'

'He had some trouble with the law, but what boy around here hasn't? Always something he was into, but the sheriff was real good about being fair. Let him make restitution to folks.' She put the cracker in her mouth. 'I just wished Luke'd found him a good woman to settle down with. That's all he needed was somebody to look after him.'

Jeffrey thought that Luke Swan had needed a hell of a lot more than that, but he kept this opinion to himself.

'I hear he was going with that deputy's wife.'

'That's what they say.'

'He always did have a way with the women.' She found this hilarious for some reason. She patted her knee as she laughed, and Jeffrey saw her bare gums as well as bits of cracker in her open mouth.

When she had finished, he asked, 'Did he live here with you?'

'Back in the back. I slept here on the couch or in my chair sometimes. Don't take much to get me to sleep. I used to sleep out there in that tree when I was a little girl. My daddy'd come out sometimes and holler, "Girl, you git down from that tree," but I'd sleep right through it.' She smacked her lips again. 'You wanna see his room? That's what the other deputy wanted.'

'Which deputy?'

'Reggie Ray,' she said. 'Now, there's a good man. He sings in the choir at church sometimes. I swear, that man has a voice like an angel.'

Again, Jeffrey held back his opinion, though he wondered why Reggie did not mention before that he had been to Luke Swan's house. Considering Reggie was a deputy, the visit was routine, but still, Jeffrey wondered.

He asked, 'Did Reggie find anything?'

'Not that I know of,' she said. 'You're welcome to go back and look around.'

'I appreciate it,' Jeffrey told her, patting her shoulder before heading back into the trailer.

He had to close the bifold door to the bathroom to get down the hall, but before he did, Jeffrey saw the filthiest toilet he had ever seen in his life. The walls were molded plastic shaped to look like tiles, and there were splatters of God knew what all around the tiny room. Only a blowtorch could have cleaned it off.

The old woman called, 'You see anything?'

'Not yet,' Jeffrey said, trying to breathe through his mouth. He pushed back another bifold door, thinking nothing could be worse than the smell in the hallway. He was wrong. Luke Swan's room was a stinking mess. The sheets were pulled back and there was a stiff-looking patch at the center of the twin bed. A single bare lightbulb dangled over the bed, suspended from a wire looped across the ceiling. He could not believe Jessie could be interested in anyone who lived in a place like this. She was too damn picky. He hated to admit it, but Jessie had a little more class.

Two plastic storage boxes by the bed seemed to hold the bulk of Luke Swan's clothes. The plastic was clear, and Jeffrey was thankful he did not have to touch anything to see inside. Spiderwebs and the kind of dirt that took years to accumulate were under the bed, but except for a filthy-looking white sock, there was nothing else there.

The closet had a locker shoved into it, the same kind you would find in a school. Stained underwear and socks were thrown onto the top shelf, shirts and jeans on the bottom. Jeffrey strained to see into the back, not wanting to put his hand into the locker. Just looking at Luke Swan's room made him feel like he had something crawling on him. Finally, he gave up and brushed the clothes out, hoping nothing bit him. Other than a pair of Speedos with a tear in the crotch, he found nothing.

Jeffrey turned around, looking back at the room. He was not about to touch the mattress, even if there was a letter explaining everything that had happened tucked underneath. Reggie would have done that, anyway. If he had found something incriminating, he sure as shit would have thrown it in Robert's face a long time ago.

Using his foot, Jeffrey kicked Swan's clothes back into the closet. After he had shoved everything back in, he changed his mind and pulled it back out. Hoping he did not get some sort of disease, Jeffrey put his hands on either side of the locker and pulled it out from the closet.

The metal made a horrible groaning noise, shaking the whole room, and the old woman called, 'You okay in there?'

'Yes, ma'am,' he told her, but then, looking behind the locker, seeing what was hidden in the back of the closet, he suddenly was not okay at all.

'How . . .' he began, but could not ask the question. He could only sit on the nasty bed and stare, his mind reeling for a moment, trying to come up with some kind of explanation or story – something that would help put Robert in the clear instead of pointing the finger right back at him. He kept coming back to the same conclusion, though, and he wanted a drink, several drinks, so bad he could taste the alcohol burning its way down to his belly.

'No,' he said, like saying it out loud would make it true. 'No,' he repeated, but he still could not stop himself from asking, 'Robert, what have you done?'

TWENTY-ONE

'Jared?' Smith said, slamming down the phone. 'Who's Jared?'

Sara looked panicked, and Lena tried to distract him, saying, 'You said you'd let Marla go.'

'Shut up,' he told her, sauntering toward Sara. 'Who's Jared?' he repeated. 'Who is he?'

Sara kept her mouth closed, like she was wondering how far she could push him.

Smith placed the shotgun against her ear. 'I'm'a ask you one more time,' he said, his accent thicker as his voice dropped a few octaves. 'Who's Jared?'

Jeffrey spoke, his voice thick with pain. 'Jeffrey's son,' he said, but even Lena could hear his uncertainty. He wasn't confirming it, he was asking Sara a question.

'He didn't know,' Sara told Smith, her hand pressing to Jeffrey's good shoulder. 'Jared has a father who raised him.'

Smith pulled the gun away, resting it on his shoulder. 'Fucker,' he spat, turning around to his accomplice. 'You hear that, Sonny? He's got another kid.'

Lena was watching Sara, and the other woman's face went slack as if she was having a small seizure. She knew, Lena thought. She knew who they were.

357

Sonny was pissed that he had been given away, and he snapped. 'Thanks a lot, *Eric*.'

Smith ran over to his partner, and they spoke in harsh whispers to each other. Lena strained to hear them, but they were being too careful. She chanced a look back at Marla, and the old lady had a glint in her eye. Lena realized she had been playing the part all along. She glanced down at Marla's hands, trying to see where she had hidden the knife.

'Fuck off!' Smith screamed, and Sonny pushed him hard enough so that Smith stumbled and fell.

Glass and debris scattered as Smith scrambled to get up. He ripped off his mask, which sent a sharp fear through Lena, as if someone had reached into her chest and grabbed her heart. Smith got back in Sonny's face, screaming obscenities, and all Lena could think was that they were all going to die now. He had shown his face. He did not care who saw him, which meant he did not think anyone would be alive to make an ID.

Sara screamed, 'Look down! Don't look at him.'

Molly did as she was told, but Lena was too late. Smith reeled around, his heavy boots crunching glass. They made eye contact, and Lena thought she had never seen anyone so dead in her life. Smith ran toward the back of the room, gun raised. She tried to grab him but he shrugged her off like a blanket.

'Don't look at his face,' Sara repeated, just as Smith slapped her hard enough to knock her over. Still, she told Molly, 'Don't look at him. Close your eyes.'

Smith kicked Sara's shin, cutting a gash. He demanded, 'What are you doing?'

'She hasn't seen you!' Sara screamed back, scrambling to sit up. 'Molly hasn't seen you! Close your eyes!' She reached out to Molly, touching her leg before Smith pushed them apart.

'She has two children,' Sara said, panic making her voice shrill. 'Two boys at home. Let her go. She hasn't seen you.'

Molly sat where she had been since this all started. She held Jeffrey's hand in her own, her eyes tightly closed. She might have been praying.

'She hasn't seen you,' Sara repeated, her voice shaking. 'She hasn't seen you. Let her go.'

Smith stared at them, his eyes moving back and forth, and Lena could see him struggling to think this through. He glanced over his shoulder at his partner, but did not invite his opinion.

Lena said, 'You could let her go. Let her take Marla.'

Smith seemed to consider this, too. 'What about my arm?' he asked. He turned back to Molly, who still had her eyes closed. 'You said you'd suture it.'

'I need the lidocaine,' she said. 'I need . . .' She turned and looked at Lena oddly. 'Give me thirty-three cc's of the two percent lidocaine.' Her tone was sharp, her tongue carving each letter like a razor as she repeated herself, 'Thirty-three cc's of two percent.'

Sara's confusion came too quickly to hide. Lena saw her brow knit, but Smith obviously knew enough to say, 'You trying to put me out?' He pushed her with the toe of his boot. 'Huh?'

'No,' Molly answered. Still keeping her eyes averted from Smith, she managed to glance at the clock on the wall, reminding Lena that they would come at 3:32. Lena gave a tight nod, letting her know she understood. Twenty minutes to go.

Smith pushed the shotgun into Molly's face, even

jumpier now. 'Get out of here,' he said. 'I don't trust you. Take the old lady, too.'

Molly stood, Sara with her.

'What are you doing?' Smith asked.

'She's my friend,' Sara told him, embracing the nurse. 'Tell my family . . .' Sara began, but obviously could not finish.

Molly went to Marla and tried to help her stand, but the old woman was too afraid to do anything.

'It's okay,' Lena told her, reaching under Marla's arm to assist her. Marla's hand brushed across her ass, and Lena was confused until she realized that Marla had tucked the pocketknife into her back pocket.

Lena hazarded a look at Smith, but he had not seen anything. Likewise, Sonny seemed unaware.

'All right,' Smith said, indicating the door. 'Move it.' He waved his gun at Marla. 'Come on, get going before I change my mind.'

Molly kept her head down as she walked with Marla toward the front door. Lena could see her whole body was practically vibrating with fear, and she knew that Molly had realized that her back was a target until she was safely across the street.

Smith strolled after them, his gait still casual. He whispered something as he passed Lena that she was glad she could not hear. She kept her expression neutral, wondering how she could get the knife out of her pocket and drive it deep into Smith's heart.

'Psst,' Brad said. She lifted her chin, letting him know she was listening.

'What did she mean?'

Lena kept her voice as low as she could. 'Time.'

Brad thought for a moment. 'Three thirty-two?' he whispered, and she nodded. 'On your signal.'

'Get ready,' Smith told his partner, and Sonny leaned over the counter, lining up his rifle for a shot. 'Now!'

Lena saw what they were doing and lunged toward the front of the room, screaming, 'No!' just as the gun went off.

She had been several feet away, and Smith had ample time to ward off her blow. He looked annoyed, and pushed her away like he had done before, like he was swatting a fly. Lena stood quickly, but not to challenge him. She looked out the front windows, seeing Molly kneeling over Marla. The old woman had been shot in the back. SWAT swarmed, giving them both cover as they were dragged to the cleaners.

'Marla,' Lena said, still looking out the window. 'They got Marla.' She turned on Smith, her fists raised. 'You fucking bastard!' she yelled, pounding into him. It was just like with Ethan – he was nothing but a wall of muscle.

'Whoa,' Smith said, stepping back, taking her with him. He caught her hands easily, laughing at her anger. 'You're a feisty one,' he said, wrapping his hand around her ass and pulling Lena into him. 'You like that, lady? You like that big cock?'

Lena clenched her jaw shut. 'You killed her,' she hissed, digging her fingernails into his arms. 'You killed that old lady.'

He put his lips close to her ear. 'I might kill you, too, honey, but don't worry, we'll have a little fun first.'

She jerked away, her hand catching on the bandage he had tied around his bicep. She threw the bloody cloth on the ground, then wiped her hands down her legs as if she could get the filth off herself.

'You bastard,' she said. 'You murdering bastard.'

He had his hand to his arm, and she could see the blood pooling through his fingers. 'That's not good,' he said.

Sonny put down his gun and took a bandana out of his pants pocket. He said, 'Here,' and Smith took the cloth.

'Wrap this around my arm,' Smith ordered, holding it out to Lena.

'Fuck off,' she said, and he gave her an open-palmed slap that sent her to the floor.

'Do it,' he told her, handing her the bandana again.

Lena stood and took the cloth. His arm was bleeding profusely, though from what she could tell, the wound was not deep. Still, she tied a tourniquet around his upper arm, pulling it tight, wishing she was squeezing it around his neck.

'What are you looking at?' Smith asked Sara, pushing Lena away as he walked to the back of the room. Sonny had his gun raised again, and he gave Lena a look of warning before turning back to the door.

Smith repeated, 'What are you looking at?'

'Nothing,' Sara told him, kneeling by Jeffrey again. She put her hand to his face, and Lena saw he stirred, but did not wake. 'He needs to be in a hospital.'

'We're gonna take care of him right here,' he said, using his foot to push over the case from the ambulance. He told Lena, 'Grab that other shit.'

She got the defibrillator and the IV kit, casting a look over her shoulder for Sonny's benefit. Brad had moved closer to the other man, but not enough to crowd him.

'I'm not a vascular surgeon,' Sara said.

'You'll do,' Smith told her, taking the bag from Lena.

Sara kept trying. 'The axillary artery has been hit. I won't be able to see anything.'

'Doesn't bother me,' he said, kneeling down beside Jeffrey.

'I can't do a block under these circumstances,' she told him. 'I'm not an anesthesiologist.'

'You keep making excuses, I'm gonna think you don't want to do this.' Smith dumped the IV kit onto the floor.

'What are you doing?'

'Might as well give him a fighting chance,' Smith said, unbuttoning Jeffrey's shirt cuff.

'I can do that,' Sara told him, but Smith waved her off.

Sara demanded, 'Why are you doing this?'

'Why not?' he shrugged as he rolled up Jeffery's sleeve. 'Nothing better to do.' Still, he gave Lena a look over his shoulder, and she wondered again if he was showing off for her benefit or if he just liked playing these games. Maybe it was a little of both.

'You should insert the cannula . . .' Sara began, but Smith shot her a look of warning.

Lena watched as he wrapped the rubber tourniquet around Jeffrey's upper arm. He was by no means an expert, but he managed to get the needle inserted into the vein on the third try.

Smith laughed at his failed attempts. 'Good thing he's passed out.'

'You've seen this done before,' Sara said. 'How often do you need infusions?'

He looked up at her, and Lena could see his crystal blue eyes registering first alarm, then something that looked like joy. They both stared at each other for a few beats, before Smith laughed.

He said, 'Took you long enough.'

'You've got it wrong,' she told him, and Lena wished to God she knew what Sara was talking about. 'You've got it all wrong.'

'Maybe,' he said, glancing at his accomplice. The other man was staring out the front window as if he had no concern about what was going on in the rest of the room. Lena knew that he was watching them, though. Sonny, or whatever his name was, had eyes in the back of his head.

Smith connected the IV, then called Lena over. 'Hold this,' he said, meaning the drip bag. 'Make yourself useful.'

Lena sat down, her back against the wall. She kept one hand tucked behind her as the other held the IV. Smith was less than a foot away from her, but Lena had no idea what she could do.

Smith opened the medical case. 'Tell me what to give you.'

Sara said, 'I can't do this.'

'Lady,' Smith told her, 'you don't have a choice.'

She sat back, shaking her head. 'I refuse.'

'I'll kill a kid for every minute that you don't do this,' he said. When she did not respond, he took the gun out of his waistband, held it up, and aimed the muzzle toward one of the girls.

Brad moved in front of the child, and Smith said, 'I'll shoot you, too.'

'And then what?' Sara asked. 'You shoot them all, and it's just me left?'

He nodded toward Lena without looking at her. 'I can think of some other things to do,' he said. 'What do you think about that, Doctor? You wanna watch that, too?'

'You wouldn't,' Sara said, though surely she knew he would.

He asked her, 'You think that kind of thing runs in families?'

Sara looked down, something like shame passing across her face.

Lena could not keep herself from asking, 'What are you talking about?'

'Don't you know?' Smith responded. 'Of course you don't know. It's not like he's gonna advertise he's a fucking rapist, is it?'

'Who?' Lena said, just as Sara told Smith, 'No.'

'Don't like that, do you?' Smith asked. He kept the gun pointed toward Brad, saying, 'How about you, Skippy? You like hearing that?'

Brad shook his head. 'It's not true.'

'What's not true?' Lena asked.

Smith looked back at Sara. 'Tell them, Doc. Tell them why we're all here.'

'No,' Sara insisted. 'You've got it all wrong.'

Smith's lips peeled back in an awful smile as he told Lena, 'Your boss? Big Chief Tolliver lying out there with his head blown off? He raped my mother, and I'm the bastard that paid for it.'

TWENTY-TWO

Tuesday

Sara woke from a hard sleep, no dreams to frighten her this time. She was in Jared's small bed, looking at a life-size rubber eagle, one of Auburn University's mascots, suspended by piano wire over her head. How the boy managed to sleep with that thing hovering, as if it was going to pounce at any moment, was a mystery. Little boys were strange creatures, as evidenced by the bug-eyed iguana hungrily staring at her from its glass cage.

She sat up, rubbing the sleep out of her eyes. The air conditioning was on, but she was hot from the afternoon nap. Sara had never liked sleeping in the middle of the day, and as if to remind her of this, her right temple throbbed with a dull pain.

In the kitchen, she found a Coke and some aspirin. Between the caffeine and the drugs, she hoped to chase away what was beginning to feel like a migraine headache. Maybe the cotton mill or the quarry spat toxic fumes into the air. Sara had been nursing a headache from the moment she got to Sylacauga.

She padded to the back of the house, feeling a bit like the walking dead. Naps were supposed to be replenishing, but she felt like she hadn't slept a wink. Maybe she had dreamed and just could not remember. If it was bad enough to make her body feel this way, Sara was glad she had forgotten whatever nightmare her mind had come up with.

Nell had warned her not to use the children's bathroom, and after a quick glance, Sara saw why. Towels and clothes were strewn about and there was a suspicious number of toys in the bathtub, considering Jen's and Jared's ages.

She walked through the master bedroom, thinking Nell had surprisingly good taste when given a palate that did not include orange and blue. A huge sleigh bed with a homemade quilt was angled out from the corner, giving a great view of the sunny backyard. An antique rocker was in the corner, and a large chest of drawers had a television on top.

Like the bedroom, the bathroom was neat and tidy. The towels matched the quilt on the bed, and the throw rugs on the floor complimented everything. Sara put the Coke bottle on the edge of the tub as she used the toilet, covering a large yawn with the back of her hand. She was trying to peel off a piece of toilet tissue from the roll when she heard someone in the house. Like some sort of barn animal, Sara had left the bathroom door open, and she rushed to wipe and pull up her pants just as a loud crash came from the front room. Without thinking, she opened her mouth to ask if anyone needed help, but stopped when she heard a suspicious-sounding noise.

Carefully, she walked into the bedroom as another loud crash echoed through the house. Whoever it was had made it to the kitchen. Doors slammed closed one after the other as someone searched the cabinets, just as Sara had done in Jessie's kitchen the day before.

She glanced around, realizing she was trapped in the back of the house. The bathroom led to the bedroom, and other than the window, the only way out was through the hall. Footsteps padded down the hallway as she considered this, and Sara ran back to the bathroom and jumped into the tub, hiding behind the curtain just as the intruder walked into the bedroom.

Whoever was here was looking for something – that much was obvious. The closet door was opened and stuff was shoved off the shelves and onto the floor. Sara felt a bead of sweat roll down her back as the intruder entered the bathroom.

She could see the shadow of a large man standing by the toilet, a few inches from where she hid. The light cast him in shadow, and even though Sara knew he could not see her, she felt exposed, as if any minute she would be found. The man reached down and took something off the edge of the tub. The Coke bottle. He would see that there was condensation, feel the refrigerated drink inside.

He said, 'Who's there?'

Sara put her hand to the back of the shower, feeling the cool tiles. Her mind flashed back to that bathroom in Atlanta, where her attacker had left her handcuffed to the stall. She could not forget the sensation of the cold tiles pressing into her bare knees. She had stared at those tiles for what seemed like hours as she waited to be found. Her mouth had been taped shut to keep her from screaming, and there was nothing she could do but watch her life bleed out onto the floor.

The curtain screeched back on the rod, and she jumped, pressing her back to the wall.

Robert stood there with the Coke in his hand. He was obviously angry to see her. 'What are you doing here?'

Sara put her hand to her chest, relief washing over her like a flood. She lost it quickly, though, as she realized that she was not the one who did not belong in the house. Why was Robert here? What was he looking for?

She tried, 'I was . . .'

Robert looked around, as if an excuse were hidden somewhere in the bathroom. 'Get out of there, Sara.'

She wanted to do as he said, but her feet would not move.

'What do you want?' he asked her. When she did not answer, he put the bottle down on the counter and started rooting through the bathroom cabinet.

'Nell should be back soon,' Sara told him as he threw towels and boxes onto the floor.

He glanced at her over his shoulder. 'Possum took them all to see the dollar movie and out to eat.'

Sara finally managed to move. Robert would not hurt her; he was Jeffrey's friend. She lifted her foot over the edge of the tub, saying, 'Jeffrey should –'

'He won't be back for a while,' Robert said, then, 'Don't go anywhere, Sara.'

Still, she kept moving, heading toward the door. 'I'm just –'

'Don't move!' he ordered, the sound of his voice echoing off the walls. There was a wild look to his eyes, and she slowly realized how desperate he was.

She fought back the panic welling inside of her. 'I have to go.'

He stood, blocking her way. 'Go where?'

'Jeffrey's waiting on me.'

'Where?'

'At the station.'

He stared a hole right through her. 'You're lying, Sara. Why are you lying to me?' When she did not answer immediately, he yelled, 'Why are you here, goddammit? You're not supposed to –'

'I-I . . .' she stammered, looking for the right words. She had never felt scared of Robert before, but like a lead weight, it fell on her that he was wanted for murder. Looking at him now, she wondered if Jeffrey was wrong. Maybe if he was backed into a corner, Robert *was* capable of killing.

'Come with me,' he said, grabbing her by the arm, not giving her a choice. He threw Sara toward the rocking chair, ordering, 'Sit down.'

Sara tried to refuse, but her knees gave out and she sank into the rocker.

Robert went to the large chest of drawers under the window, close enough to stop her if she tried to move. The television had tinfoil-wrapped clothes hangers bent awkwardly to form antennae. Robert opened the top drawer and the tinfoil made a dry, scritchy noise.

'What are you looking for?' she asked. 'Money? Do you need money? I can give you –'

He was on her in a flash, his hands grasping the arms of the rocker, his face less than an inch from hers. 'I don't want your fucking money! Do you think money's gonna solve this? Is that what you think?'

'I –'

'Dammit!' He pushed away from her, the chair rocking violently. In a flash, his calm returned, and he went back to the chest of drawers. Sara watched as he opened the bottom drawer and pulled out a small black box that she instantly recognized as a gun safe.

She jumped out of the chair, but stopped when he turned on her, the same angry expression on his face. She pressed into the wall, trying to edge her way to the door as he dialed the combination on the safe. She should move faster. Why wasn't she running? Why couldn't she move?

He seemed calmer now that he had found what he was looking for. 'Where're you going?'

'Why do you need a gun?'

'I'm leaving town,' he said, using his thumb to dial in the combination. The safe popped open, and he took out the gun. 'Six–thirteen, the final score for the last game we played against Comer.'

'I should –'

He pointed the gun at her. 'Don't go, Sara.'

Again, her mind flashed back to the terror she had endured in the bathroom at Grady Hospital, bleeding from everywhere, unable to move her arms or legs, unable to get help. She would not – could not – be trapped like that again. There would be no surviving after that.

He ordered, 'Sit down,' indicating the chair.

She wanted to be calm, but her heart would not obey. 'I won't tell anyone,' she told him, realizing that she was begging.

'I can't trust you to do that,' he said, using the gun to wave her back to the chair. 'Come over here and sit down.' He waited for her to comply. When she didn't, he added, 'I'm sorry about before. I shouldn't have yelled at you.'

She stared at the gun, willing her words to be true. 'It's not loaded.'

He pulled back the slide with a sharp, metallic click. 'It is now.'

She stayed where she was. 'What are you going to do?'

'Nothing,' he told her, then, 'Tie you up.'

Sara's heart jumped into her throat. She could not

be tied up. She would go crazy if she was confined like that. She tried to take a breath, but realized that was the problem. She was breathing too much, too hard.

'I need a head start,' he told her, though she had not asked. He pointed the gun at her again. 'Get away from the door, Sara. I *will* shoot you.'

'Why?' she asked, praying that logic would kick in, but also wondering if this was the last thing Luke Swan saw before his head was blown apart.

'I don't want to hurt you,' he said, as if that would reassure her despite the fact that he was pointing a gun at her chest. 'But you'd tell Jeffrey and he'd find me.'

Sara felt her hands start to tremble. She would hyperventilate soon if she did not get her breathing under control. 'I don't know where Jeffrey is.'

'He'll be back here soon enough,' Robert told her, going through the closet again, still keeping the gun trained on her. He kicked out a small toolbox. 'He can't leave you alone. I've never seen anything like it.'

Sara gauged the distance to the hallway. Robert was still an athlete. He could make a dash as quickly as she could. A bullet would be even faster, but she had to take the chance. She took a small, almost imperceptible step, closing her distance to the door.

Robert snapped open the toolbox with one hand. He kept his eyes on Sara even as he pulled out a roll of silver duct tape.

Her mouth opened, but she could not take a breath. Her attacker had used the same kind of tape to keep Sara quiet while he raped her. She had been unable to scream as he assaulted her.

'I wish there was something else I could use,' Robert said. 'This is going to hurt when it comes off.'

'Please,' she said, her voice shaking. 'Lock me in the closet.'

'You'll still yell.'

'I won't,' she promised him, her legs shaking so badly she thought her knees might give out. 'I swear I won't yell,' she repeated, tears streaming down her face at the thought of the tape touching her skin. Somehow, she managed to take another step toward the door. She held out her hands to him, saying, 'I promise I'll be quiet. I won't say a word.'

The fact that she was on the verge of being out of control seemed to make him even more calm, and he spoke to her in what sounded like a reasonable voice. 'I can't trust you to do that.'

She barked a sob. 'Oh, please, Robert. Please don't do this. Please . . .'

'Don't –'

Sara bolted toward the door, heading into the hallway. Robert went from a crouch to a dead run, and she felt his fingertips brush against her arm as she passed by. Sara dared not look over her shoulder as she rounded into the living room. She was almost to the front door when hands clamped around her waist, slamming her into the coffee table as Robert tackled her from behind. Possum's Auburn memorabilia fell to the ground and shattered, the thick glass top of the table cracking it neatly in two underneath their combined weight. The wind was knocked out of Sara, and she felt her lungs lurch in her chest.

'Goddammit,' Robert said, jerking her up by the waist. Sara's arms flew up, and her feet scattered glass all over the room as he dragged her back toward the bedroom.

'Please –' she begged, digging her fingernails into the back of his hand. She clawed for anything to stop him, hanging onto the wall, knocking down pictures and plants. She grabbed onto the doorjamb as he tried to force her into the bedroom and she felt her fingernails tear as he finally managed to shove her inside.

'Jesus,' Robert yelled, dropping Sara onto the floor as she raked a chunk of skin off his arm. She scrambled to get up, screaming in her head but unable to make any noises come out of her mouth. Her hands were bleeding, but she would fight him more if she had to.

'Stop it!' he warned, kicking her feet out from under her. She crawled on her hands and knees toward the door and he picked her up by the middle again.

Sara finally managed to yell, 'Let me go!' just as Robert threw her back on the floor. Her head banged against the wood and she felt her stomach roll, her eyelids flutter.

'Sara,' he said, helping her sit up. He cradled her head in his lap, saying, 'Stop this. I don't want to hurt you.'

'Robert, please . . .' she begged, fighting not to be sick. She tried to get up but there was no strength left in her body. All of her muscles felt useless and she could not make her eyes focus on anything.

Robert rested her head back onto the floor and dragged the rocking chair from the other side of the room. 'I didn't want to hurt you,' he said, gently picking her up off the floor. Her arms and legs flapped like a rag doll's as he placed her in the chair. She tasted vomit in the back of her throat, and without warning, the room began to pitch again.

'Don't pass out,' he told her, though she wondered how he could stop her. Sara had never passed out in her life, but her head was reeling so much that she thought she might be concussed.

She took deep breaths even though her ribs ached from the effort. Robert stared at her, watching her every move. After what seemed like several minutes, Sara's vision cleared, and her stomach stopped feeling so tight.

'Just got the wind knocked out of you,' Robert said, obviously relieved. Still, he kept his hand on her chest for a minute, making sure she could sit up on her own. He kept a careful eye on her as he stretched out a strip of tape. He pulled down her sock, then wrapped the tape around her ankle and the leg of the chair.

Sara watched, incapable of doing anything to stop him.

'I can't go to prison,' he said. 'I thought I could, but I just can't. I can't have another night like last night.'

He taped her other leg to the chair, which began to rock. Sara felt her stomach turn, but he stopped the rocking, then sat back on his heels, looking at her. 'I want you to tell Possum I'll send him money when I get settled. He's worked his ass off to get that store, and I'm not going to have him lose it because I jumped bail.'

Sara strained her legs against the tape, feeling her circulation being cut off. 'Robert, please don't do this.'

He fed out another strip of tape. 'Put your hand on the arm of the chair.'

Sara did not move, and he lifted her arm by the wrist and put it on the chair for her.

'I can't do this,' she said, feeling like the life was seeping out of her. 'I can't do it.'

He stared at her with curiosity, as if she was overreacting. He offered, 'I won't tape your mouth if you promise not to yell for help.'

She broke into tears again, so grateful for this small concession that she would have done anything for him.

'Please don't cry,' he said, taking out his handkerchief to wipe her tears. She thought of Jeffrey and his handkerchief, and how gentle he was with her. Sara started to cry even harder.

'Jesus,' he whispered, as if Sara was punishing him. 'It won't be long,' he said. 'Don't be like this, Sara. I won't hurt you.' He looked startled for a moment, saying, 'You cut your eye.'

She blinked, just now noticing the blood clouding her vision.

'Damn, I'm so sorry,' he said, wiping the blood. 'I didn't mean for this to happen. I didn't mean for anybody to get hurt.'

She swallowed, feeling some of her strength come back. Maybe she could reason with him. Maybe she could talk him into stopping now. She would promise not to yell, not to call anyone, if he would just leave her arm free.

Robert folded the handkerchief into a neat square. She tried to think of a way to get to him, to make him see that she was not a threat. 'I'll tell Possum about the money,' she said. 'Who else? Who else do you want me to talk to? What about Jessie?'

He tucked his handkerchief back into his pocket and picked up the tape. 'I tried to write a letter, but I've never been much good at that kind of thing.'

'She'll want to know,' Sara insisted. 'Tell me, and I'll tell her.'

'Jessie doesn't care about me.'

'She does,' Sara pressed. 'I know she does.'

He exhaled slowly, using his teeth to cut off a strip of tape.

Sara bit her lip hard enough to draw blood.

'I tried to make things work,' he told her, taking her wrist. Sara tried to jerk away, but he forced her hand down to the arm of the chair.

She stared at his fingers as he taped her arm, feeling such deep despair that it almost took her breath away.

He sat back on his heels again. 'That's not so bad.' He reached out his hand to touch her mouth. 'You bit your lip,' he told her. Sara jerked away without thinking, and a look of hurt flashed in his eyes, as if he had not been the one responsible for all of this.

'I'm not what you think,' he said. 'I really did love her.'

'Please let me go,' she begged.

He rubbed his hands on his thighs. The gun was on the floor beside him, but Sara was hardly in a position to reach down and grab it. He had taped her tightly to the chair.

He repeated, almost to himself, 'I really did love her.'

Sara stared at the gun as if she could will it into her hand. She tried to fight the tremor in her voice when she said, 'You say that like you don't anymore.'

'I don't know what went wrong.' He gave a weak smile. 'What tells you in your heart that you love Jeffrey?'

'I don't know,' Sara answered, unable to take her eyes off the gun. Finally, she forced herself to look at him, saying, 'Robert, please. Don't leave me like this. I can't do it. I can't take it.'

'You'll be okay.'

'Not like this,' she said. 'Please. I'm begging you.'

'Tell me what it is that makes you love Jeffrey,' Robert asked, as if striking some sort of bargain. 'What is it that makes you know?'

'I don't know.'

'Come on,' he said, and she realized that he was trying to help her calm down so that it would be easier for him to do what he needed to do.

'I don't know,' she repeated. 'Robert –'

'Has to be something,' he said, giving her a forced smile, as if they were a couple of good people brought together under bad circumstances. 'Don't tell me it's his sense of humor and great personality.'

Sara racked her brain for something to tell him. There had to be a right answer, an answer that would make him free her from the chair and let her go, but she could think of nothing to say.

'You don't know?'

She told him the only thing she could think of. 'It's the little things. That's what Nell says it is with Possum – the little things.'

'Yeah?'

'Yeah,' she echoed, trying to keep her panic down, trying to remember what Nell had said. Sara's voice sounded muted in her ears, as if she was talking underwater. 'He's always home when he says he'll be and he doesn't mind going to the grocery store for her.'

Robert gave a sad smile as he stood. 'Maybe I should've gone to the grocery store for Jessie.'

Sara felt her brain trying to make a connection but she could not understand why. Still, her mouth kept talking. 'I'm sure you did sometimes.'

He spooled out an extra-long strip of tape, using his teeth to tear it, letting the roll drop to the floor.

378

'Never did,' he told her, wrapping the tape around her chest and upper arms, fixing her back flat to the chair. 'She said she liked doing that stuff. Made her feel like she was taking care of me.'

'You never went to the grocery store?' Sara asked. Something Jeffrey had told her the night before clicked into place, and she felt an eerie sort of calmness spread over her.

He looked around for the tape. 'Damn,' he said, wincing as he knelt down in front of the bed. He put his hand to his stomach where he had been shot. 'Rolled under the bed,' he told her, bracing his hand against the mattress as he bent to retrieve the tape.

'You never went to the store for her?' Sara repeated, watching him kneel in front of the bed. His hand was still on the mattress, and in her mind she saw the bloody outline around Luke Swan's hand on the bed.

'Never went to the store,' he assured her, sitting back up, breathing heavily. 'Shit, that hurt.'

Despite the fact that she could not move, Sara suddenly felt herself gaining some control over the situation. 'Did she drive your truck much?'

'That's a funny question,' he said, but still answered, 'Yeah. She hated to, but if I parked behind her in the driveway, it was easier than backing them both out.'

Sara strained her wrist against the tape, trying to see if there was any give, saying, 'It wasn't you who went out to the store that night, was it, Robert? It was Jessie. She went in your truck.'

He stretched out another long piece of tape. He would not look at her, and instinctively she knew that he wanted her to continue.

'The night Luke was shot,' she said, almost dreading his answer. 'Sunday. Was Jessie in your truck on Sunday?'

The strip was too long and the tape had folded on itself. He tried to pick it apart. 'I don't know what you're talking about.'

'Jessie was in your truck,' Sara told him, more sure of herself now. '*She* went to the grocery store that night. There was milk and juice in your refrigerator. I saw the grocery list in your truck.'

He continued to pick at the tape as if it could be saved.

'If it was Jessie who went to the store, then it was Jessie who came home. You told the truth, but you swapped things around. It was Jessie who came home, and it was you –' She stopped, astonished. 'It was you in the bedroom,' she said. 'You were with Luke Swan, not Jessie.'

Robert gave a forced laugh, giving up on the strip of tape and wadding it into a ball.

Sara continued to press, still certain of what had happened. 'You were on the floor, kneeling in front of the bed.'

'Maybe one will be enough,' he said, picking up the roll of tape.

'Was Luke behind you when he was shot?'

He tore off a four-inch strip. 'I'm going to have to cover your mouth.'

She fought back her fear, needing to know the truth. 'Just tell me what happened, Robert. You didn't kill him. I know you didn't kill him. Was it Jessie? Did she find you? Robert, you have to tell someone. You can't just leave it like this.'

He started to put the tape over her mouth, but stopped at the last minute. Sara stared at him as he tried again, but something would not let Robert cover her mouth.

He walked back a few steps, sitting on the bed with obvious discomfort. He held the tape in his hands, cradling it like he was afraid it would explode.

Sara forced herself to speak gently, not knowing how far she could push him. She asked, 'You were with Luke that night, weren't you?'

Robert stared at his hands, his silence enough of an answer to keep her going.

'Did Jessie know before that night?' She paused, then asked, 'Robert?'

He slowly shook his head. 'I tried so hard with her,' he finally said. 'She was the only woman in the world I thought I could be a husband to.' He looked out the window into the backyard. Sara wondered if he was thinking of family barbecues and picnics, playing catch with the son he could never have. 'She was supposed to be gone for a while,' Robert continued. 'Said she was going to her mama's, then to the grocery store, like she did every Sunday night.'

'What happened?'

'She got into a fight with her mama.' He let out a weary sigh. 'She came home early, had time enough to put up all the groceries. Some kind of cop I am, huh? Didn't even hear her in the kitchen.'

'Did she walk in on you?'

'She thought I was still over at Possum's watching the game.'

'Did she walk in on you?' Sara repeated.

'I kept it hidden,' he said, still not answering her question. 'I kept it hidden for all these years.' He rubbed his eyes with his fingers. 'I made a deal with God. I promised Him I wouldn't do it anymore if He would give Jessie a baby.' He dropped his hand.

'That's all we needed, see, was to be a family. I would've been a good father.'

Obviously, he expected some sort of confirmation, because he looked away when Sara would not give it. 'God just knew better than to let it happen. Maybe He knew I couldn't hold up my end of the bargain.'

'God doesn't make those kinds of deals.'

'No,' he said. 'Not for men like me.'

'Being gay doesn't make you a bad person.'

He winced at the word.

Sara strained her leg against the tape, trying to see if there was any chance of escape.

'Everything I did with her turned to poison,' he said. Inexplicably, a genuine smile came to his lips. 'You know what it's like to be in love for the first time in your life?'

Sara did not answer.

'Dan Phillips,' he said. 'Damn, but he was beautiful. I know you wouldn't think a boy could be that way, but he had these baby-blue eyes that . . .' He put his hand to his mouth, then dropped it. 'Does that make you sick to hear?'

'No.'

'It made *me* sick,' he said. 'Julia caught us behind the gym. Hell, I never took any of her favors. Dan, neither. We didn't know that was where she met boys.' He gave a harsh laugh. 'It was our first time. First and last.'

'What did she do?'

'Screamed to high fucking hell,' he said. 'I've never felt so ashamed in my life. Threw up for the next week, just thinking about how she looked at us. Like we were filth. Hell, we *were* filth. Dan ran off. Just left town. Couldn't take seeing my face anymore.'

'Is that why you killed her?'

He looked wounded, as if she had insulted him. 'If that's what you want to think, go ahead.'

'I want to know the truth.'

He stared at her for a beat. 'No,' he said. 'I didn't kill her. For a while, I thought Jeffrey might have, but . . .' He shook his head. 'Jeffrey didn't do it. There's probably a long list of men in this town who hated her for one reason or another, but he's not like that.'

'You didn't rape her, either.'

'No. That was just her way of torturing me, spreading that damn rumor. She thought I'd say what I was, try to defend myself by letting everybody know.' His face turned into a scowl. 'Like I'd do that. I'd rather die than let anybody know.'

Sara had to ask. 'And Jeffrey?'

'She thought I'd take up for him. Some friend I was, huh? Let people think Jeffrey raped her just to hide my secret.' He paused, making sure she was listening. 'I told you, Sara. I would rather die than have it get out.'

He looked her in the eye when he said this, and Sara understood the threat.

She had to keep him talking. 'Is that why you took the blame for shooting Luke?'

Robert stared at her, silent. 'It was the same thing all over again.'

'What was?'

'He knew,' he said. 'Takes one to know one, I guess.'

'Luke?'

'I had him in the back of my car one night. Picked him up on a loitering charge down by the bowling alley.' Robert looked out the window again. 'He was cold, so I gave him my jacket. One thing led to another. I don't even really remember how it happened . . . just that it felt so good, and then the next day, it felt so horrible.'

Sara could see the anguish on his face, and despite the situation, she found herself feeling sorry for him.

'I don't know how, but he kept my letterman jacket. Maybe he stole it out of the car when I wasn't looking. Doesn't matter how he got it, but my name's on it big as day. He called me at the station the next morning. Said he was going to wear it around town, tell everybody he was my *girlfriend*.' He snorted in disgust at the word. 'He kept following me around, flirting with me like a damn girl.' His jaw worked, and he stared down at his hands.

'You could have just told him to go away,' Sara pointed out. 'No one would have believed him over you.'

'That's not how it works here,' he said, and part of her knew that Robert was right. Gossip was currency in a small town. Even a rumor that seemed improbable had more value than the boring truth of an everyday, normal life.

She asked, 'What happened, Robert?'

He took his time answering, the truth more horrible to him than the lie he had been telling for the last few days. 'I was weak. I just wanted somebody to comfort me, to feel right with.' He looked back up at Sara, as if he expected her to any moment voice some kind of revulsion. 'I called him up, told him to come over. Told him I wanted him to fuck me. You like hearing that? You know what we were doing, don't you? Fucking up the ass like two fairies.'

Sara was unfazed. 'Were you in love with him?'

'I hated him,' he said, and she could tell by Robert's tone of voice that he really did. 'He was like holding up a mirror, looking at myself. All the ugly things about me.' Under his breath, he added, 'Fucking fairy. Faggot.'

'Is that why you killed him?'

A car pulled up outside and they both waited as a door was closed. Seconds later, they heard Nell's next-door neighbor go into his house and slam the door. If he noticed the dogs were missing, he did not seem to care.

Sara prompted, 'Robert?'

Again Robert paused before answering. 'Jessie came in on us,' he finally said. 'She heard us. The noises we were making.' He looked back at Sara as if to gauge her reaction. 'She got my gun because she thought somebody had broken into the house. Didn't even bother to call the police.' He jumped to a tangent. 'That was what the fight with Faith was about. That's why she was home early.'

Sara waited, not understanding.

'The fight with her mama. They were arguing because Jessie showed up stoned out of her mind. Drunk on something, taking pills, whatever. Her mama always blamed me for that even though Faith's drunk most days, out there swigging out of a flask when she's supposed to be watering the garden. That's how Jessie got through her life with me. That's how she dealt with my failures. She took pills to keep the pain back.'

Sara heard the next-door neighbor slam his front door again. Sara waited, hoping he would come over to ask about his dogs, but the car started and she heard him reverse down the driveway.

'Jessie meant to shoot me,' Robert told Sara, looking out the window, probably watching the neighbor head down the street. 'She pulled the trigger because she was so shocked. She didn't exactly think it through, but she meant to shoot me, not him. At least that's what she told me later. Said she was so drunk that first she thought there were two of me and I'd finally managed to go fuck myself.' He ran his tongue along his top teeth. 'I didn't even know she was there. I hear Luke saying in my ear, "Hey, how about it? You wanna join the party?" I didn't know what the hell he was talking about. Later, I figured he was talking to her. Provoking her, even though he had to see she had a gun in her hand. That's what he did with people, just pushed and pushed until they were over the edge.'

'She shot him.'

'I was wearing my T-shirt, but . . .' His voice trailed off, and he swallowed hard before continuing. 'I felt this spray on my back, like this kind of mist. I didn't hear the sound until later, like two or three seconds later. It must have been faster than that, but my brain just kind of slowed it down. You know how it does that?'

Sara nodded. She knew from her own experience that trauma slowed things down, as if pain was something to be savored rather than endured.

'There was this kind of pop, like a balloon or something.' He took a deep breath. 'Then he slumped against me, and I felt this wet . . .' He shook his head at the memory. 'He slid down my back.'

Sara remembered how Robert had kept his back to the wall that night, gripping his shirt tightly in his hand. He must have been covered in blood.

'It was so fast afterward. Slow as it was when it happened, the rest was so fast.'

'What happened?'

'Jessie shot at me.'

'She missed,' Sara said, remembering the bullet hole in the wall.

'I grabbed my backup out of the armoire. The safe wasn't even locked. After we lost the baby . . .' He shook his head, obviously not wanting to talk about that. 'I wasn't even really thinking, other than maybe wishing the bullet hadn't missed when she fired.' Robert paused. 'She stopped, like she couldn't shoot me, even though she'd seen what I was. I just stood there for maybe a second, and I could suddenly see it all – everyone finding out what had happened, finding out who I am, and I put the gun to my belly and pulled the trigger.'

'You were lucky it didn't do more damage.'

'It was so fast,' he repeated. 'I couldn't even think. It was like . . .' He snapped his fingers.

Sara was quiet, hearing the snap echo like gunfire.

'It didn't hurt much,' he added. 'I thought it would hurt, but it wasn't until later that I felt the pain.'

'Was it Jessie's idea to say you'd done it?'

'Hell no,' he said, and she wondered if he was telling the truth. 'She went over and grabbed a handful of pills. Spilled most of them on the floor. I just looked around, thinking, "Fuck, what can I do?"'

'What did you do?'

'I guess I must've known what I was going to do when I pulled the trigger, but it took a while before my brain kicked in. I picked up the gun and the casings and wiped them off. A couple'a three seconds later, I heard somebody kick open the back door. I tossed everything on the floor, put the gun by his hand. Jeffrey came in, screaming, "What the hell happened?" He went out to get you and I told Jessie to open the window and push out the screen. First time in her life she ever did something I told her to do without asking why.'

'What about the bullet?' Sara asked. Robert had given the bullet to Reggie when he had confessed.

'Jessie got it out later. I don't know when, but she gave it to me. She told me exactly where she had found it in his head. Said it was my souvenir.'

Sara knew there was only one time Jessie was alone with the body, and that was when Jeffrey and Sara were on the porch outside, waiting for Hoss. She must have sneaked in while they were arguing.

'Jessie's a lot smarter than folks think,' Robert continued. 'When y'all got there, she just played along, acted like she was too high to follow what was going on. Me, I was freaking out. I saw all the words coming out of my mouth, making up the story, not even thinking about the parts that didn't make sense. She let me do it, just stood there, letting me feed out enough rope to hang myself.'

'Why?' Sara asked, still not understanding. 'Why did you lie?'

'Because I'd rather be a cold-blooded murderer than a faggot.'

The finality of his words hung heavy in the air, and Sara had never felt more sorry for anyone in her life.

'I'm just not right, Sara.' He paused, as if he needed time to collect himself. 'If I could get a knife and cut it out of me, I would. I'd cut out my fucking heart to be normal.'

'You *are* normal,' she insisted. 'There's nothing wrong with you.'

'It's too late.'

'You can stop this,' she said. 'You can stop this right now. You don't have to leave. You're innocent,

Robert. You didn't do any of this. None of it's your fault.'

'All of it's my fault,' he insisted. 'I've sinned, Sara. I've sinned against God. I've broken my vows. I've been with another man. I wished him dead so many times. Jessie pulled the trigger, but I put him there. I brought him into our house. There's no going back now.'

'You are who you are,' she told him, even as she saw there was no reasoning with him. 'You have no reason to be ashamed.'

'Yes,' he said, picking up the gun. 'I do.'

'Oh, God –'

He pointed the gun directly at her head, his hand steady. Sara closed her eyes, thinking of all the things she had never done in her life, wondering how her parents would get through this. Tessa still needed her, and Jeffrey . . . there was so much that Sara had left unsaid. She would give anything right now to be with him, feel his arms around her.

'You're not a murderer,' she told him, her throat straining from the effort.

'I'm so sorry,' Robert said, standing close enough for her to smell the sweat on him. Sara felt the cold metal of the gun press into her forehead, and she cried in earnest now, her eyes shut against everything else in the room. She heard the safety disengage, and another murmured apology.

'Please,' she whispered. 'Please don't. Please.' She said the only thing that she thought might get through to him. 'I'm pregnant.'

The gun stayed where it was a few long seconds before it dropped, and Robert cursed under his breath.

She opened her eyes to find his back to her. His

shoulders shook, and she thought he was crying until he turned around. Terror struck through her as she realized that he was laughing.

'Pregnant?' he repeated, as if she had just told the punch line to a really good joke.

'Robert –'

'Everything comes so goddamn easy to him.'

Instantly, Sara realized her mistake. 'I didn't –'

'Jesus,' he hissed, pointing the gun back at her head. His hand shook this time, and he faltered, cursing again. 'Fuck.'

'Jeffrey doesn't know,' she said, desperate to find the right thing to say. 'He doesn't know!'

Robert kept the gun steady. 'He never will.'

'He will!' she screamed. 'At the autopsy!' Robert's jaw set, and she kept talking as fast as she could. 'Is that how you want him to find out? Do you want him to find out when I'm dead? He'll find out, Robert. That's how he'll find out.'

'Stop,' he ordered, pressing the gun to her skull. 'Just shut up.'

'It's a boy!' she screamed, almost hysterical with fear. 'It's a boy, Robert. His son. Jeffrey's son.'

He dropped the gun to his side again, not laughing this time.

'You know what it's like to lose a child,' she told him, her body shaking so badly the chair began to rock. 'You know what it's like.'

He ignored her, nodding his head slowly, as if he was having some sort of conversation with himself. Sara saw his lips moving, but no words came out. He engaged the safety before tucking the gun back into his pants, then picked up the roll of tape again.

Sara watched him work the tape, knowing that he

was going to tape her mouth shut so he could shoot her.

'He loves me,' Sara gripped the arms of the chair with her hands, trying to break free.

Robert tore off a strip of tape.

'You're going to take that away from him,' she said, the words rushing out of her mouth. 'You're going to take away his child, Robert. His unborn child.' Sara's voice caught on the words, mostly because she knew that there was no other time in the world when she would be able to say them. '*Our* child,' she said, loving the way the words felt in her mouth. '*Our* baby.'

Robert obviously heard the passion in her voice, because he stopped what he was doing.

'I'm carrying his child,' Sara repeated, feeling herself letting go. She was at peace with this and whatever happened next. There was no explaining the logic behind her calm; it was simply the way she felt. 'Our baby.'

'He's gonna hurt you,' Robert said. 'Anybody who loves him always ends up getting hurt.'

'When you love somebody,' Sara told him, 'that's the risk you take.'

He put his fingers to her bottom lip, tracing the broken skin. Before she knew what was happening, Robert leaned down and brushed his lips across hers. It was the softest kiss Sara had ever received, and she was too shocked to pull away.

He said, 'I'm sorry,' then taped her mouth shut before she could answer. He stood in front of her, arms crossed over his chest. 'I'm sorry for hurting you,' he said. 'I've hurt enough people in my life already.' A sour look crossed his face, as if he'd had a thought that did not agree with him. 'Jeffrey's gonna think I was into him,' he said. 'You tell him that's not true, all right? I never thought about him that way – not ever.'

Sara nodded because that was all she could do.

'Tell him he's gonna be a great father, and that I would never take that from him.' Robert's voice caught. 'Tell him he was the best friend I ever had, and that there was nothing else to it.'

Sara nodded her head again, trying to understand what had changed.

'I'm sorry about taping up your mouth. I know I promised.'

Sara watched him go, helpless to do anything. Seconds later, she heard a car door slam and an engine start. She recognized the shoddy muffler of Robert's truck as he backed out of the driveway.

He was gone.

Sara began to cry again, this time from relief. She could not remember shedding so many tears in her life. Her nose began to run, and she sniffed, choking because of the tape. Her elation was quickly replaced by panic as she labored to get air into her lungs. Several seconds passed before the claustrophobia that threatened to overwhelm her started to recede. She had to get out of this chair. She could not just sit there waiting for Nell or Possum or Jeffrey to rush in and rescue her. She could not let any of them – especially Jeffrey – find her like this; helpless, afraid. No one was ever going to see her that way again.

Sara scanned the room, trying to find something that would help her get out of the chair. Rocking forward would land her face-first on the floor, so she rocked the chair side to side until she managed to tip it over. Her head whacked into the hardwood floor with a firm thud and she felt the same dizziness from before as her eardrum vibrated from the impact. A sharp pain ran up her shoulder where she had landed on it, but the arm of the chair had loosened from the fall, too. She jerked the wood back and forth several times, trying to dislodge the dowels, but the arm held firm. The chair was probably older than all of them, something Nell's ancestors had built to last a lifetime.

Sara took a breath, trying to think what to do next. The rockers on the bottom of the chair kept her from uprighting it and crawling to the door. Robert had taped her wrists, but not her fingers. Even if she could not manage to get free of the chair, she could try to take the tape off her mouth. If she could get the tape off her mouth, she could scream. If she could scream – even if no one could hear her – she would be okay.

Using all her strength, Sara pulled her arm up toward her mouth. After several minutes, perspiration on her arm helped the tape fold into a tight line that cut into her flesh, but she still forced up her arm, stretching the tape to its limit. When the tape had given as much as it would, Sara slid her arm back and forth, rubbing a nasty burn from the friction. The adhesive balled up in black dots, and Sara managed to force her arm a few inches forward. She tried to move it back, but the tape pinched up her skin, blood seeping out from underneath.

She considered the situation like a math problem, calculating the variables, adding in her pain threshold before attempting anything else. She arched her back as much as the tape around her chest and upper arms allowed, contorting her body until her shoulder screamed from the pain. Still, she kept pushing herself, stretching the tape around her chest until her mouth was inches from her hand. Her fingers had turned almost completely white from the lack of circulation, but Sara managed to touch the edge of the tape with her middle finger.

She gave herself a break, counting to sixty, letting the minute pass as the throbbing in her arm and shoulder leveled off to a dull ache. Her fingers had touched the tape. That was enough to keep her trying. Sara stretched again, trying to reach the tape covering her mouth. Sweat from her skin and blood and saliva from her mouth had worked on the adhesive, so that when she gave one final effort, she managed to grab the edge of the tape between her thumb and index finger and pull.

Though not enough to pull off the tape.

Sara's breathing was labored and she felt the room closing in on her again, but she coached herself not to quit, knowing she could not give up this close to the goal. Her body ached from the effort, but still, she managed to contract her muscles enough to make another grab. This time, the tape came off, and she opened her mouth, panting like a dog with its head out the window.

'Ha!' she screamed to the empty room, feeling as if she had vanquished some great foe. Maybe she had. Maybe she had vanquished her fear. Still, she was taped to the chair, lying pretty much facedown on the floor with few options and nothing but time.

'Well,' Sara told herself. 'No reason to give up now.' This same kind of thinking had gotten her through medical school, and she was not about to abandon it now.

She focused on her arm, wondering if she could reach the tape with her teeth. The tape around her chest was already cutting into her breasts. She could not imagine what the bruises would look like, but Sara knew that bruises eventually faded.

Suddenly, she heard a noise in the front of the house. She opened her mouth to call for help but stopped herself. Had Robert changed his mind? Had he returned to finish the job?

Footsteps crunched across the glass from the broken coffee table, but no one called out. Whoever had entered the house was taking their time, going from room to room. She heard movement in the kitchen, and waited to see where they would go next. Had Robert forgotten something? When Sara surprised him, had he been looking for something other than Possum's gun? If it was someone who belonged in the house, they would have surely called out by now.

Sara clenched her teeth, fighting the pain as she tried to stretch toward her hand. She twisted and turned as much as she could in the chair, scratching Nell's good wood floors, pushing her mouth toward the tape.

'Sara?' Jeffrey stood in the doorway, Nell's ax in his hands. 'Jesus Christ,' he said, looking around the room, obviously searching for the person who had ransacked the house.

'He's gone,' Sara told him, still straining toward her hand.

Jeffrey dropped the ax on the floor as he rushed toward her. 'Are you okay?' He put his hand to her eye. 'You're bleeding.' He looked around the room. 'Who did this? Who would –'

'Get me loose,' Sara told him, thinking if she spent one more second in the chair, she would start screaming and not ever be able to stop.

Jeffrey must have understood, because he took out

his pocketknife and sliced through the tape without asking any more questions.

'Oh, God,' Sara groaned as she rolled out of the chair, unable to do anything but lie on her back. Her shoulder was killing her and her body felt bruised and battered.

'You're okay,' Jeffrey told her, rubbing the circulation back into her hands.

'Robert –'

Jeffrey did not seem surprised to learn his friend had done this. 'Did he hurt you?' His expression darkened. 'He didn't –'

Sara thought about everything that had happened, what had brought Robert to this point, and said, 'He just scared me.'

Jeffrey put his hand to her face, checking the cut over her eye and her split lip. He kissed her forehead, her eyelids, her neck, as if his kiss could make everything better. Somehow, it did, and without thinking, Sara felt herself giving in to him, holding on to him as tightly as she could.

'You're okay,' he told her, rubbing her back. 'You're okay,' he kept saying.

'I'm okay,' she told him, and with a calming clarity, she knew he was right.

TWENTY-THREE

Smith kept smiling at her, waiting to see her reaction. 'He raped my mother,' he repeated. 'Then he killed her to shut her up.'

Lena felt neither shocked nor appalled. 'No, he didn't,' she said, never more sure of anything in her life. 'I know the type of man who can do that sort of thing, and Jeffrey's not like that.'

'What do you know about it?' Smith asked.

'I know enough,' was all she said.

Smith clicked his tongue once. 'You don't know shit,' he said, petulant. He told Sara, 'Let's get this started.'

'I can't do a block,' she said. 'The brachial plexus is too complicated.'

'You don't need to do a block,' Smith told her. 'He's passed out.'

'Don't be stupid.'

'Watch it, lady,' he warned. He rummaged through the case Lena had brought from the ambulance. 'Use this,' he said, holding up a vial of lidocaine. He took out a flashlight and shone it in his face with a smile. 'Now you can see.'

Sara did not move.

'Do it,' he ordered, his face made more horrific by the flashlight.

397

Sara seemed about to refuse, but something made her give in. Maybe Jeffrey's condition was too serious to let it go on for much longer. Maybe she was trying to buy some time. Either way, she did not look confident that what she was about to do would work.

She took a pair of gloves out of the box and snapped them on. Even Lena could see that she was scared, and she wondered how in the hell Sara thought she could remove a bullet from Jeffrey's arm with her confidence so shaken.

Sara's hands steadied as she used a pair of scissors to cut away Jeffrey's shirt. If he was awake, he wasn't moving, and Lena was glad he could not see what was going on.

'Lena,' Sara said. 'I need to know if this is really lidocaine.'

Lena felt the weight of her question. 'I have no idea,' she said.

'Why did Molly make such a big deal about it?'

'I don't know,' Lena answered, wishing there was some way to tell Sara the truth. 'Maybe she thought she could knock him out,' she said, meaning Smith.

Sara took the bottle of medicine and snapped off the protective cap. She picked up a syringe and drew back the plunger.

To Smith, she said, 'Pour all the Betadine on the wound.'

Smith did not protest the order, and he even used a swab to wipe down Jeffrey's arm. With the blood washed away, Lena saw what looked like a small puncture wound in the front part of Jeffrey's armpit.

Sara took the syringe, holding it above the site. She said to Lena, 'You're sure?'

'I don't know,' Lena repeated, trying to convey with her eyes that it was all right. Smith was staring a hole into her, though, and Lena looked down at Jeffrey, hoping Smith did not see her certainty.

Sara put the needle right into the wound, and Lena sucked air through her teeth without even thinking about it. She forced herself to look away, feeling a phantom pain in her own arm. She saw Brad had moved closer to Sonny. He licked his lips, looking somewhere over her head. She guessed he was looking at the station clock, and a current of panic went up her spine as she realized that it might be fast.

Smith held up the flashlight so that Sara could see, giving Lena a perfect view of his Navy SEAL watch. There were all sorts of buttons and dials on it, and she remembered from the ad that the time was synchronized with the atomic clock in Colorado, which was accurate to within a millisecond or something impossible like that. The watch was huge, like a chunk of metal on his wrist. In the middle of the round black face was a digital readout showing the time to the seconds.

3:19:12.

Twelve minutes. But did his watch have the same time as hers? As Molly's and Nick's? Lena did not dare check her own watch or look at the clock behind her. Smith would know immediately what was going on and they would all be dead.

'Scalpel,' Sara said, holding out her hand.

Smith slapped the scalpel into her palm, and Sara cut the skin, dissecting the flesh as she followed the path of the bullet. She used the remaining medicine in the syringe as she went, finally squirting the bulk of it into the open wound. Lena tried not to watch, but she found herself mesmerized by the inner workings of Jeffrey's arm. Sara obviously knew what she was doing, but Lena had no idea how she managed to remain calm. It was like she had become a different person.

'I need more light,' Sara told Smith, and he leaned closer with the flashlight as she probed the arm. 'Closer,' she said, but Smith did not move. Sara cursed under her breath, using the back of her arm to wipe the sweat off her forehead. She leaned closer to better see what she was doing, her body an awkward arch.

Jeffrey gave a low moan, though he did not appear to be awake.

Sara told Lena, 'Watch his breathing.'

She put her fingers to Jeffrey's chest, feeling the gentle up and down as he took in air. Slowly, she turned her wrist, trying to check her watch. The room was hot, and sweat dripped down her arm. The metal band had slipped around to the inside of her wrist and there was no way to see the time.

Sara jerked back as blood squirted straight up into her face. She wiped it off with the back of her hand and kept going, telling Smith, 'Forceps.'

He rooted around for the instrument with one hand, holding the light with the other. Sara used some gauze to wipe away blood, saying, 'I can't see it.'

'Hate that for you,' Smith said, sounding as if he was enjoying the drama.

'I can't get it if I can't see it.'

'Calm down,' Smith said, handing her the forceps, which looked like giant tweezers. 'Here,' he said, shaking them in the air.

Sara took the forceps, but she did nothing.

'You're taking all the fun out of this,' Smith said, patting gauze around the incision. 'You can find it,' he coaxed. 'I have faith in you.'

'I could kill him.'

'Now you know how I feel,' he said, flashing a nasty grin. 'Go on.'

For a second, Sara looked as if she was going to refuse, but she put her thumb and fingers through the handle of the forceps and inserted them into the wound. More blood squirted up, and she said, 'Clamp.' When Smith did not move fast enough, she said, 'Now! Give me the clamp!'

Smith held out the instrument and Sara dropped the forceps on the floor. They clattered, a crushed bullet pinging against the tiles. She reached in with the clamp even as blood pumped all around her. Then suddenly, the blood stopped.

Lena looked at Smith's watch again.

3:30:58.

'That wasn't so bad,' Smith said, obviously pleased. He used the flashlight to see inside the wound, a big smile plastered on his face, as if he was a child who had won a game against an adult.

'He has about twenty minutes,' Sara said, packing gauze into the open incision. 'If he doesn't get to a hospital, he'll lose his arm.'

'He's got more problems to worry about than that,' Smith said. He put the flashlight on the floor, but kept his hand on his leg, affording Lena a clear view of his watch.

3:31:01.

3:31:02.

'Like what?' Sara asked, and out of the corner of her eye, Lena saw Brad moving closer to the second gunman. He looked at the clock again, and she knew that he was thinking the same thing: they couldn't coordinate if they weren't looking at synchronized clocks. What if she moved too soon? What if she signaled Brad at the wrong moment, and they both ended up dead before the SWAT team arrived?

'No,' Lena whispered, too late realizing she had said the word aloud.

Smith gave her a toothy smile. 'She's figured it out,' he said. 'Ain't that right, darlin'?'

Lena gave a quick shake of her head, her hand moving behind her, feeling the outline of the knife in her pocket. She was overthinking this. What mattered was working in tandem with Brad. What mattered was the element of surprise.

Smith told Sara, 'See, some folks here don't think I'm as stupid as you do.'

'I don't think you're stupid,' Sara said.

Lena glanced down at Smith's watch again. Thirty seconds left. Brad had moved closer to Sonny, started pacing back and forth across the front of the room like the stress was getting to him. Maybe it was. Maybe he couldn't do this.

'I know what you think about me,' Smith told Sara.

Lena moved as slowly as possible, her fingers dipping into her back pocket. Her heart shook in her chest. Brad's footsteps echoed against the tile as he paced back and forth at the front of the room.

'I think you're a very troubled young man,' Sara told him. 'I think you need help.'

'You thought I was trash from the moment you laid eyes on me.'

'That's not true.'

'You did everything you could to try to destroy my life.'

'I wanted to help you,' Sara said. 'I really did.'

'You could've taken me in,' Smith said. 'I wrote you letters. I wrote him letters.'

He had indicated Jeffrey, but Sara seemed not to notice. 'We never got them,' she replied, but Lena could barely hear her past the sound of blood rushing through her ears. Smith had indicated Jeffrey. He knew who Jeffrey was.

Lena gripped the knife, using her thumb to pry up the blade. She pressed the edge of the metal into her heel and heard the click as the blade popped into place.

She held her breath, waiting for Smith to notice, but he was too focused on Sara. How long had he known about Jeffrey? When had he figured out that it wasn't Matt lying on the floor in front of him, but the man he had sworn to kill?

Smith said, 'I kept waiting for y'all to come. I kept waiting for y'all to take me away from her.' His voice was like a child's. 'Do you know the kinds of things she did to me? Do you know how she hurt me?'

In her head, Lena was screaming, 'He knows it's Jeffrey,' but she kept the words from coming out of her mouth. Whatever sick game Smith was playing had to go on just a little while longer. Just a few more seconds and it would be over.

Lena trained her eyes on his watch.

3:31:43.

'We couldn't help you,' Sara told him. 'Eric, Jeffrey is not your father.'

Lena looked at Brad. He raised his eyebrows, as if to say, 'Ready when you are.'

Smith said, 'You're a fucking liar.'

'I'm not lying,' Sara said, a certainty to her voice. 'I'll tell you who your father is, but you have to let them go.'

'Let them go?' Smith asked, taking the Sig Sauer

out of his belt, still keeping his other hand resting on his thigh.

3:31:51.

Lena swallowed, though she had no spit left in her mouth. In her peripheral vision, she saw Brad nearing Sonny.

'Let who go?' Smith asked, taking his time, obviously enjoying the drama. He smiled down at Jeffrey. 'You mean him? Matt?' He hit the *t*'s hard, spit coming out of his mouth.

Sara hesitated a beat too long. 'Yes.'

'That's not Matt,' Smith said, cocking the hammer. 'That's Jeffrey.'

'Now!' Lena screamed, lunging for Smith. She slammed the knife into his throat, feeling her fingers slide down the blade, sharp metal slicing open her skin.

Sara had jumped seconds after Lena, and she wrested the Sig away from Smith even as a gun went off at the front of the room. The three little girls started screaming as the glass entrance door exploded.

GBI agents swarmed into the station. Brad stood over Sonny, pointing the rifle at the young man's face as he pressed his foot into his chest.

'Get up,' Sara told Lena, pushing her off Smith. Lena slipped in the blood as Sara turned him over onto his back.

'Get an ambulance,' Sara said, putting both her hands to Smith's neck, trying to stop the blood. She was fighting a losing battle. Blood was everywhere, flooding out of Smith's carotid like a broken dam. Lena had never seen so much bleeding in her life. It was as if nothing could stop it.

'Help me,' Smith said, an improbable request considering all he had done.

'You'll be okay,' Sara soothed. 'Just hold on.'

'He killed people,' Lena told her, thinking she must be crazy. 'He tried to kill Jeffrey.'

'Get an ambulance,' Sara repeated. 'Please,' she begged, her fingers pressing into the gaping wound. 'Please. He just needs somebody to help him.'

TWENTY-FOUR

Tuesday

Jeffrey slumped into the row of chairs opposite Hoss's office at the sheriff's station. After the last few days, he understood what people meant when they said they felt as if they had the weight of the world on their shoulders. Jeffrey felt like he had two worlds, and neither one of them was a particularly civilized.

Sara sat down beside him, saying, 'It'll be good to get back home after this.'

'Yeah.'

He had wanted to leave this town from the moment he got here, but now Jeffrey thought that everything he needed was right here with him. As always, Sara knew what he was thinking, and when she put her hand on his leg, he laced his fingers through hers, wondering how his life could be so fucked up yet feel so good as long as she was holding his hand.

'Did he say how long he would be?' Sara asked, meaning Hoss.

'I think part of him is still waiting for me to say this is some kind of joke.'

'It'll be fine,' she said, squeezing his hand.

Jeffrey glanced down the unlit corridor toward the jail, hoping that his emotions did not get the best of him. Sara was so good at being logical that it scared him sometimes. He had never met anyone so completely capable of taking care of anything that came along, and he wondered what kind of place he could have in her life.

Sara interrupted his thoughts, asking a question he had not yet let himself consider. 'You think it changes anything because he's gay?'

He shrugged.

'Jeff?'

Jeffrey kissed her fingers, trying to change the subject. 'You can't imagine how I felt when I saw you in that chair. The things that went through my mind.'

She waited for his answer.

'I don't know how I feel about that,' he said. 'I want to kick his ass for what he did to you,' he said, feeling livid all over again. 'That kind of thing . . .' He shook his head, trying not to let it get to him. 'I swear to God, if I ever see him again, there's going to be a reckoning for that.'

'He was desperate,' she said, though Jeffrey did not understand how she could make excuses for him. 'Which is worse,' she asked, 'what he did to me or the fact that he's gay?'

He did not know how to answer the question. 'All I know is that he lied to me all these years.'

'Would you have wanted to have anything to do with him otherwise?'

'We'll never have a chance to find out, will we?'

Sara let his words hang in the air.

'When I saw Robert's jacket in Swan's closet . . .' He sat back in the chair, letting go of her hand as he crossed his arms over his chest. Jeffrey kept his own jacket in the back of his closet at home, and though he never wore it, he could not bring himself to donate it to charity or throw it away. He was worse than the

Monday-morning quarterbacks at the hardware store, holding on to that jacket like he could hold on to his youth.

He told Sara, 'I don't know. I saw his jacket, and it popped into my head that maybe there was a connection between him and Swan. Just a split second, and then I thought, "No way. No way Robert's a . . ." ' Jeffrey gave a heavy sigh, thinking he'd never be able to use the word again. He probably should not have been using it in the first place. 'I came here to the station looking for Hoss, but he was out.'

Jeffrey did not tell her that the first thing he'd wanted to do after leaving Swan's was to find Sara, but he had taken the detour to the station to prove to himself that he did not need her. Had he not been so stubborn, Jeffrey could have stopped Robert before things escalated. He could have protected her.

Oblivious to this, she kept pressing, 'Does it bother you that he's gay?'

'I can't separate it out, Sara, and that's the truth. I'm mad at him for what he did to you. I'm mad at him for not turning Jessie in, for letting all this shit stir up and not doing anything about it. I'm mad at him for jumping bail and leaving Possum to sweat it out.'

'He said he'd send money.'

'Yeah, well, I'm calling the state as soon as we get back to see how much I can pull out of retirement.' He thought of Possum's bruised jaw, and the way the other man had waved off Jeffrey's apology for hitting him. Jeffrey would not make Possum take all of the financial burden for this. It just wasn't right.

'What else?' she asked. 'What else are you mad at him about?'

He stood, needing to pace. 'For not telling me.' He

glanced down the hallway as an inmate in the jail yelled an obscenity. 'If you hadn't been in that house, the last thing we'd know is that he jumped bail for killing a man and was on the run. We wouldn't know about Jessie or his relationship, or whatever you want to call it, with Swan. All we'd know is that he was a fugitive.' Jeffrey stopped pacing and turned to Sara. 'He should have trusted me.'

She had a circumspect look on her face, like she wanted to make sure she said the right thing. 'My cousin Hare had a hard time at college,' she began. 'One minute, he was the most popular guy on campus, the next, he was getting death threats.'

He had forgotten about her cousin in all this, and now Jeffrey wondered if she was taking up for Robert because she wanted to take up for Hare. 'What happened?'

'People just figured it out,' she said. 'He had this friend, his dorm mate. They were inseparable. When people started to talk, Hare didn't try to hide anything. He was surprised that anyone cared.'

'That's pretty naive.'

'That's Hare,' she told him. 'I guess we both grew up in a fairly insulated world. Our parents never let us think that anything was wrong with being gay or straight or black or anything else under the sun. Hare was shocked when his so-called friends turned on him.'

Jeffrey could imagine what happened, but still, he wanted to hear it. 'What did they do?'

'This was at the end of his junior year at UGA, so there was summer in between for everyone to cool off.' She paused, and he could tell she was still upset by the memory. Above anything else, Sara cherished her family, and for one of them to be hurt was just about the only thing in the world she did not seem able to tolerate.

She continued, 'We all hoped it would die down during the break, but of course it didn't. His first day back, they tried to beat him up, but he was always a good fighter and he broke a few noses. I heard him tell you he quit football because he hurt his knee, but that wasn't it. He was told to leave.'

Jeffrey sat down again. 'I can't say I wouldn't have done the same thing to Robert if I had found out back then.'

'What about now?'

'Now . . .' He shook his head. 'Hell, I just want him to be safe. I can't imagine living like that, people thinking I was something I wasn't.'

'Sounds like how you lived the first part of your life.'

He laughed, because he had never looked at it that way. 'Yeah.'

'What did Hoss say when you told him all this on the phone?'

'Nothing,' he told her, then added, 'He didn't sound surprised.'

'Do you think he knew?'

'Maybe he suspected. There's no telling.' He gave her a meaningful look. 'Trust me, you don't see that kind of thing unless you're looking.'

'What's going to happen now?'

'Jessie will be arrested.' He hissed air out between his teeth. 'That's gonna be fun. I'm sure Reggie Ray will get a big kick out of all this.'

'You can't worry about that.'

'If he walked through that door right now, I'd have him leaving on a stretcher.'

'What about Julia Kendall?'

'What about her?'

'I need to tell you something,' she began, taking his hand again. 'I need to talk to you about what Lane Kendall said.'

'She's a –'

'No,' Sara interrupted. 'Not that. I need to tell you why I reacted the way I did when she accused you of . . . of raping Julia.'

'I didn't,' he told her, feeling defensive. 'I swear to you, Sara, that kid isn't mine.'

'I know that,' she responded, but her expression was so peculiar that he did not believe her.

He stood again. 'I'm telling you I didn't do it. I didn't have anything to do with it.'

'I know you didn't,' she repeated.

'You don't look like you believe me.'

'I'm sorry you feel that way,' she said, and he could see her shutting him out.

He paced again, feeling cornered and guilty even though he knew he had done nothing. All he could think was that they had finally gotten to her. Sara had finally started doubting him the way everyone else did. There was no going back from here.

'Jeff,' Sara said, angry. 'Stop pacing.'

He did, even though his body felt like a live current was going through it. 'We can't get past this point,' he told her. 'Either you trust me or you don't, but I'm not going to –'

'Stop,' she interrupted him.

'You think I'm capable of doing that?' he asked. 'You think I'd actually . . .' He could not find the words to finish. 'Jesus, Sara, if you think I'm capable of raping somebody, what the hell are you doing here with me?'

'I *don't* think you did it, Jeffrey. That's what I'm

trying to tell you.' She seemed exasperated, and her tone took on an even sharper edge. 'Even if I thought you did it – which I don't – medically, there's no way that Eric Kendall is your child.'

He stood silent, waiting for her to spell it out.

'You don't have a bleeding disorder in your family?' she asked, like she was talking to a three-year-old.

'I don't even know what you're talking about.'

'A bleeding disorder,' she said, as if repeating the words would make him understand. 'Lane Kendall said that Eric had a bleeding disorder.'

Jeffrey wondered where she was going with this. He had tried his best to block out the episode with Lane Kendall and did not relish going back over it.

She said, 'I haven't examined him, but from what Nell told me, it sounds more like von Willebrand's disease.'

He waited for her to continue.

'Blood won't clot.'

'Like hemophilia?'

'Sort of,' she answered. 'It can be pretty mild. Some people have it and don't even know it. They just think they're easy bleeders. Eric's bruises were raised, like bumps. That's also a sign.'

Jeffrey felt all the hairs on the back of his neck stand up.

His expression must have given him away, because Sara asked, 'What?'

He shook his head, thinking that this whole ordeal with Robert had made him too suspicious. 'It couldn't have come from Lane's family? Or Julia's father?'

'It could,' she answered, though her tone said she

did not think it was likely. 'Generally, women know when they have it. Their menstrual cycles are extremely heavy. A lot of women end up getting hysterectomies when they don't really need them. It's not an easy diagnosis, not many doctors think to look for it.' She added, 'As many children as Lane has had, she would know if she had it. Pregnancies can be very high risk for anyone with a bleeding disorder.'

Jeffrey could only stare at her, his mind making conclusions that turned a knife in his gut. 'What if someone gets nosebleeds a lot?'

She wrinkled her brow. 'Who are you thinking about?'

'Just answer, Sara. Please just answer.'

'It could be,' she said. 'Nosebleeds, bleeding gums. Cuts that won't stop bleeding.'

'You're sure it's genetic?'

'Yes.'

'Shit,' he whispered, thinking that as bad as everything seemed a few minutes before, it had just gotten worse than he could have ever imagined.

'What are you –'

They both looked up as the door opened.

'I'm sorry it took me so long to get here,' Hoss told them, taking his keys out of his pocket as he walked toward his office.

Jeffrey could not move.

Hoss looked at Sara, obviously taking in her cuts and bruises. 'I would've never thought Robert was capable of hurting a woman,' he told her. 'But I guess he wasn't nearly the man I thought he was.'

'I'm fine,' Sara answered, a tight smile on her face.

'That's good,' Hoss said, unlocking his office door. He went in, turning on the lights as he walked to his desk and rummaged through some papers. 'Come on in so we can get this over with.'

Sara gave Jeffrey an inquisitive look, and he returned the question with an affirmative nod.

Hoss noticed Jeffrey still standing in the doorway. 'Slick? There a problem?'

Sara put her hand on Jeffrey's shoulder. She asked him, 'Do you want me to wait outside?'

'That's okay,' Hoss said, obviously thinking she was talking to him.

'I'll wait outside.' She squeezed Jeffrey's shoulder again, and somehow, her confidence that he would do the right thing gave him the strength to walk into the office.

The door clicked shut behind him as he sat in the chair opposite Hoss.

'Guess she's had a hard time of it,' Hoss said, obviously thinking Sara was in a delicate state. He picked up a report and scanned it as he talked. 'I sent Reggie out to pick up Jessie. Jesus, what a mess. I'm sure she'll fight him hammer and claw.'

'We still don't know about Julia.'

'Robert confessed.'

'He confessed to a lot of things he didn't do.'

'Don't know that I can trust his word after what we know about him.'

'You're saying because he's gay, that makes him capable of murder?'

'Makes him capable of anything in my book,' Hoss said, turning the page over to read the back. 'Might open a few of his cases and see what he was really up to.'

This more than anything else sparked Jeffrey's anger. 'Robert was a good cop.'

'He was a fucking queer,' Hoss said, still staring at

the report. He picked up his pen and signed the bottom. 'No telling what else he was doing. We had a missing boy here a few years back. Robert worked the case like it was his own son.'

Jeffrey managed to speak through clenched teeth. 'You're saying he's a pedophile now?'

He picked up another report. 'Goes hand in hand.'

Jeffrey could only stare at him.

'He coached the Little League,' Hoss said. 'I've already called some parents.'

'That's bullshit,' Jeffrey spat. 'Robert loved kids.'

'Yeah,' Hoss agreed. 'They all *love* kids.'

Jeffrey tried to sum it up for him, to show Hoss how wrong his thinking was. 'So, he's a pedophile, has a thing for boys, but he killed Julia when they were both teenagers?'

'No telling what a sick mind like that will do,' Hoss said. 'Choke an innocent girl, kill a man for banging his wife . . .'

Hoss's words echoed in Jeffrey's head, and finally he saw it all laid out like a puzzle. 'I don't remember telling you she was strangled,' he said quietly.

Hoss shot him a startled look. 'Your lady told me.'

'Did she?' Jeffrey asked, making to get up out of the chair. 'You want me to go ask her when?'

Hoss faltered. 'Maybe I heard it in town.'

Jeffrey couldn't believe how silent the room suddenly was. Everything fell into place. 'You know he didn't do it.'

Hoss looked at Jeffrey over the report. 'I do?'

'Eric Kendall has a bleeding disorder.'

He looked back down, eyes moving as he scanned the page. 'That right?'

'He's your kid, isn't he?'

Hoss did not answer, but Jeffrey saw a slight tremor in the report he held.

'You told me once how you tried to join the Army after your brother died, but they wouldn't take you on medical grounds.'

'So?'

'Why wouldn't they take you?'

Hoss shrugged. 'Flat feet. Everybody knows that.'

'You sure it wasn't something else? Something that would keep you off the force if it got out?'

'You're just talking crazy now, boy,' he said in a tone that ordered this conversation to be ended.

Jeffrey did not obey. 'You get nosebleeds all the time. Your gums bleed for no reason. I saw you get a paper cut once and it bled for two days.'

He gave a weak smile. 'That don't mean –'

'Don't lie to me,' Jeffrey demanded, anger boiling to the surface. 'You can say anything you want right now and it stays in this room, but don't you *dare* lie to me.'

Hoss shrugged, like it was nothing. 'She was loose. You know that.'

'She was only sixteen years old.'

'Seventeen,' Hoss corrected. 'I wasn't breaking any laws.'

Jeffrey felt disgusted, and it must have read in his face, because Hoss tried a different tack.

'Look,' he said. 'Times were different. That girl needed someone to look after her.'

Jeffrey felt sickened by his words. As a cop, he had heard that same excuse a thousand times from dirty old men, and to hear it now from Hoss was like a slap in the face. 'Looking after her doesn't mean screwing her.'

'Watch your tone,' Hoss warned, as if he still

deserved Jeffrey's respect. 'Come on, Slick. I took care of her.'

'How?'

'Kept her daddy off her, for one,' Hoss answered. 'Plus, you think her mama paid for her to go off and have that baby?'

'*Your* baby.'

He shrugged. 'Who knew? Coulda been mine, coulda been yours.'

'The hell you say.'

'Coulda been anybody's, is what I'm getting at. She went with half the damn town.' He took a wad of tissue out of his pocket and blotted at his nose. 'Coulda been her daddy's, for all I know.'

Jeffrey could only stare at the telltale trickle of blood coming from Hoss's nose. He had always seemed so tough, but thinking back on it, every time the old man got stressed, his nose bled.

Jeffrey said, 'You gave her that locket, didn't you?'

Hoss looked at the tissue before putting it back to his nose. 'It was my mama's. I guess I was feeling generous that day.'

Jeffrey wondered how Hoss had really felt about the girl. If you were using someone to get laid, you didn't give the woman gifts, especially something that had belonged to your mother. He pressed, 'Why didn't you marry her?'

Hoss laughed at the suggestion, a tiny spray of blood escaping around the tissue. 'Wake up, Slick. You don't marry something like that.' He pointed toward the door, toward Sara. 'That's the kind of woman you marry.' He dropped his hand. 'Somebody like Julia, that's the kind of woman you fuck and hope to God she don't give you something you need a shot of penicillin to get rid of.'

'How can you talk about her that way? She's the mother of your child.'

'Pretty ballsy coming from you.'

'What do you mean by that?'

'Nothing,' he answered, though Jeffrey was certain he was holding back. 'Look, we just had a good time.'

'She was too young to know what a good time was.' Jeffrey stood up, thinking he had sat idly by long enough. 'Did you kill her?'

'I can't believe you're asking me that.'

Jeffrey kept silent. He had seen the answer in Hoss's eyes. Everything was turning upside down. The man he thought was good and decent was actually the kind of punk that made Jeffrey glad he was a cop who could put them away. If he had Hoss back in Grant County, shut in the interrogation room, he would be doing everything he could not to haul off and hit the fucker.

'You don't know how it was,' Hoss tried. 'I've done good by this town for over thirty years.'

'You murdered a seventeen-year-old girl,' Jeffrey said, fighting the emotions the words brought. 'Or are you going to tell me it was okay because she was eighteen by then?'

Hoss threw down the tissue as he stood. 'I was trying to protect Robert.'

'Robert?' Jeffrey demanded, incredulous. 'What did Robert have to do with any of that?'

He put his hands on the desk, leaning over toward Jeffrey. 'She said he raped her. I couldn't let that tramp ruin his life.'

'That blew over in a week,' Jeffrey countered. 'Less than a week.'

Hoss looked down at his desk. 'People still talk.

That's all this town is made up of, people talking, telling lies on each other, thinking they know what's right, when the fact is, they don't know shit.' He wiped his nose with the back of his hand, a thin streak of blood smearing across the skin. 'I've got a reputation to uphold. People in this town need me. They need to know who's in charge. I was doing it for their sake.'

'You fool,' Jeffrey said. 'You selfish old fool.'

His head snapped back up. 'You've got no right –'

'What'd she do?' Jeffrey asked. 'You sent her away to have that baby, but she came back. Did you think she wouldn't come back?'

Hoss waved him off, walking over to the window so that his back was to Jeffrey.

'You think you're untouchable. You think hiding behind that badge is going to protect you.'

Hoss did not respond.

'She came back and what, Hoss? What'd she want? Money?'

Hoss rested his hand on top of his brother's flag case. 'She thought I'd marry her. Some piece of work, huh? Thought I'd marry her.' He laughed. 'Shit.'

'So you killed her?'

'It wasn't like that.' Hoss finally looked contrite, though Jeffrey knew it was because he had been caught, not because he felt any remorse. 'It was an accident.'

'Yeah, people get strangled by accident all the time.'

Hoss's voice took on a high, unnatural pitch. 'She was threatening to tell,' he said. 'Came back from having that baby like she was the damn Virgin Mary. Said she wanted me to make an honest woman of her. Can you beat that? Me marrying her, buying a pie every man in town's done stuck his finger in for a taste? I'd be a laughingstock if I married a whore like that.'

'Don't call her that,' Jeffrey warned. 'You've got no right.'

'I got plenty of right,' Hoss shot back. 'She was nothing but trouble. She accused you of raping her. How did you like that?'

'So,' Jeffrey said, seeing where this was going. 'Let me get this right, you killed her for me?'

'And for Robert,' he added.

Jeffrey tried to quell his astonishment long enough to get the story out of him. 'What happened?'

'She came to the office.' He indicated the room, indignant at the memory. 'Here, to my office.'

'And?'

Hoss turned back to the flag, tracing the wooden case with his fingers. 'It was late, kind of like now. Not many people here.' He paused. 'She got kind of frisky with me like she does, and then just stopped. Little prick tease is what she was.'

Jeffrey waited for him to continue.

'So,' Hoss continued, 'we had a conversation about that.'

'Did you rape her?'

'She was willing,' Hoss said. 'She was always willing.'

Jeffrey felt sick, but still, he asked, 'So, then what?'

'She said she wanted me to marry her. She didn't want her mama raising Eric.'

Jeffrey looked at the flag case. He had seen the brass plaque screwed to the top a thousand times, but never made the connection. JOHN ERIC HOLLISTER. Julia had been pushing him, but she had no idea that she had pushed too hard.

'You got into a fight?' Jeffrey prompted.

'Yeah,' Hoss nodded. 'I offered her some money. She threw it back in my face. Said she would have it all when we were married, anyway.' He gave a harsh laugh. 'Can you believe how stupid she was, thinking I'd do that? Thinking she was good for anything other than a fuck and suck?'

Jeffrey felt his jaw start to ache from clenching his teeth together. Every time Hoss opened his mouth, he had to fight the urge not to throttle him.

'She kept goading me. Kept threatening me. Nobody threatens me.'

'So you killed her?'

'It wasn't like that,' Hoss said. 'I was trying to reason with her. Trying to get her to see logic.' Hoss turned around, an awkward smile on his face, as if he expected Jeffrey's approval. 'I tried to get her out of the office. Kind of roughed her toward the door. Next thing I know, she jumped on my back. How do you like that? Jumped right on my back, kicking and screaming and clawing. I knew somebody would hear. I knew somebody would come and want to know what the hell was going on.'

Jeffrey nodded, like he understood.

'Next thing I know, my hands are around her neck,' Hoss said, holding his hands out in front of him. Robert had done the same thing when he confessed to killing Julia, but Hoss reenacted the scene with the passion of a man who had been there. He was facing his demons head-on, trying to strangle the life out of the memory. A steady trickle of blood came from his nose, but he did not seem to care.

Hoss said, 'I was just trying to get her to shut up. I didn't want to hurt her, just make her stop screaming. And she finally did.' He stared at a point over Jeffrey's shoulder. 'I tried to help her. Gave her mouth-to-mouth. Pushed on her chest. She was gone. Her head just kind of . . . lolled . . . I guess I broke her neck or something.'

Jeffrey let his words hang in the air for a few seconds, trying to understand what had really happened. A few years ago, he would have taken Hoss's words at face value. He probably would have even helped cover his tracks. Now he saw the story for what it was: a lie bent around the truth so that the old man could still get to sleep at night.

Jeffrey narrowed the space between them. 'You strangled her.'

'I didn't mean to.'

'How long did it take?' Jeffrey asked, taking another step closer. He knew from a case last year that manual strangulation was not as easy as it seemed, especially when someone was fighting tooth and nail, as Julia must have done. 'How long before she passed out?'

'I don't know. It wasn't long.'

'Why'd you take her to the cave?'

'Wasn't thinking,' he said, but there was a flash of unmistakable guilt in his eyes.

'Everybody knew that's where we went,' Jeffrey told him. 'If she was ever found, people would make the connection that it was me or Robert. Or both of us.'

'That's not what –'

'She said we raped her,' Jeffrey interrupted. 'She said it less than a year before. It'd make sense, wouldn't it? We were just getting her back for telling.'

'Hold on,' Hoss said, finally looking him in the

eye. It took effort, that much was obvious. 'You think I was trying to frame you and Robert?'

Jeffrey did not hesitate. 'Yes.'

He finally lost control. 'I said it was an accident!'

'You tell that to the town,' Jeffrey countered, and Hoss's face went pale. 'You tell that to Deacon White and Thelma down at the bank and Reggie Ray when he gets back with Jessie.'

Panic flashed in the old man's eyes. 'You wouldn't.'

'I wouldn't?' Jeffrey asked. 'I don't know about you, but that badge I wear means more to me than free breakfasts down at the diner.'

'I taught you to respect that badge.'

'You didn't teach me a damn thing.'

Hoss jammed his finger in Jeffrey's face. 'You'd be down at the prison right now mopping floors with your daddy if it wasn't for me, boy!'

'Makes no difference,' Jeffrey said. 'I'm still standing in the same room with a murderer.'

'Somebody had to protect you,' Hoss said, his voice shaky. 'That's all I was doing was looking after you and that pansy friend of yours.'

Jeffrey recoiled at the word and Hoss picked up on this.

'That's right,' Hoss said. 'How'd you like it if I let it out that you and Robert were more than friends?'

Jeffrey snorted a laugh.

'For all I know,' Hoss continued, 'maybe you were.'

'Right.'

'You two fuckbuddies?' Hoss goaded, desperation pouring off him. 'You want everybody in town to hear that? You want your mama to find out?

Maybe somebody'll tell your daddy down at the prison?'

'You can tell my daddy yourself when you see him, you pathetic old fuck.'

'You watch that mouth.'

'Or what?'

'I protected you!' Hoss yelled. 'You think your father would have done that? You think that worthless bastard would've helped you?'

Jeffrey slammed his fist into the desk. 'I didn't want your help!'

'You sure as shit needed it!' Hoss screamed back. Blood dripped from his nose, but he kept screaming, his face turning red with anger. 'I raised you, boy! I made you the man you are today!'

Jeffrey jabbed his thumb at his chest. '*I* made me the man I am today. I made myself despite you.' He felt dirty being this close to him. 'I thought you were a god. You were everything I wanted to be.'

Hoss's lip quivered, as if he wanted to take Jeffrey's words as a compliment.

Jeffrey made himself clear. 'You molested a teenage girl. You took a mother from her child.'

'I didn't –'

'You make me sick,' Jeffrey said, walking toward the door.

Hoss put his hand on his desk as if he needed the support. 'Don't leave like this, Slick. Come on.' His tone took an edge of desperation. 'What are you gonna say? What are you gonna tell people?'

'The truth,' Jeffrey said, feeling his calm return. What he saw before him was no longer his mentor, his surrogate father, but a criminal, a lying old man who had destroyed the people he was meant to protect.

'Come on, now,' Hoss said, begging. 'You can't do this. You'll ruin me. You know what'll happen if you go out there and . . . please, Slick. Don't do this.' He took a step forward as if to stop Jeffrey. 'You might as well put a gun to my head.' He tried a weak smile. 'Come on, son. Don't look at me that way.'

'Look at you?' Jeffrey asked, putting his hand on the doorknob. 'I can't even stand to see your face.'

He did not slam the door behind him, but in his mind, Jeffrey heard a resounding crash. Sara stood up, wringing her hands.

He did not know what to tell her. There would never be the right words to describe how he felt. Rudderless, that was a good one to start with. He had lost the thing that gave him direction.

'Are you okay?' she asked, and the concern in her voice was better than anything she had ever done for him.

'He came to see me after Dad was arrested,' Jeffrey told her.

'Hoss?'

'I was at Auburn, just about to graduate. I remember everything about it,' he paused, picturing the multicolored leaves on the trees that beautiful fall day. Jeffrey was sitting in his dorm room, trying to figure out how he would pay for his doctorate if Auburn accepted him into the program. He wanted to be a teacher, something respectable with a steady paycheck. He wanted to give something back.

'He knocked on the door,' Jeffrey continued. 'Nobody knocked. They usually just came in. I thought somebody was playing a joke.' He leaned against the wall. 'He kept knocking, and I finally opened the door and there he was with this look on his face. Told me Dad had taken a plea. Turned on his friends so he wouldn't get the death penalty. You know what he said?'

Sara shook her head.

' "Some kind of coward," ' Jeffrey finished. 'He told me I had to be a man now, that playtime was over. Playtime, like that's all I had been doing in college, just having fun. He handed me this application. It was already filled out.'

'The police academy?'

'Yeah,' he nodded. 'I just took it and signed it and that was it.' For the first time in his life, Jeffrey found himself wondering what would have become of his life if he had told Hoss no. He would not have met Sara, for one. He would probably still be living here in Sylacauga, dealing with the same snide remarks and secretive looks that had chased Robert away.

He said, 'I don't know how I'm going to do this.'

'I'll be here as long as you need me.'

'I can't even think about it,' he told her, and that was the truth. How could he do this? How could he repeat what Hoss had told him?

'It'll be fine,' she said, just as a gun exploded in Hoss's office.

Sara must have opened the door. Jeffrey did not feel like he could move. Yet, somehow, he managed to turn around. Somehow, he was facing Hoss's office.

The old man sat in his chair, one hand on the flag from his brother's coffin, the other holding his revolver. He had put the muzzle of the gun flat to his head and pulled the trigger. There was no question in

Jeffrey's mind that Hoss was dead, but still, when Sara went around the desk and pressed her fingers to his neck, he managed to form the question with his eyes.

'I'm sorry,' she told him. 'He's dead.'

TWENTY-FIVE

Shit,' Lena hissed, trying not to jerk her hand back as Molly stuck a needle into the cut.

'I'm sorry,' Molly apologized, but she was looking over her shoulder at Sara and Jeffrey, not Lena.

Lena watched as Jeffrey was loaded into the ambulance. 'Will he be okay?'

Molly nodded, though she said, 'I hope so.'

'What about Marla?'

'They've got her in surgery. She's old, but she's strong.' She looked back at Lena's hand. 'This is going to sting.'

'No shit,' Lena answered. The knife slicing open her skin had not hurt as much as the freaking needle.

'It'll block the pain so I can suture you.'

'Just hurry,' Lena said, biting her lip. She tasted blood and remembered her split lip. Molly jabbed in the needle again. 'Christ, that hurts.'

'Just a little more.'

'Christ,' she repeated, looking away from the needle. She saw Wagner talking to Nick, both of them staring at Lena and Molly as they sat in the back room of the cleaners.

'There,' Molly said. 'It should start numbing up in a few minutes.'

'It'd better,' Lena told her, feeling phantom pains

428

from the needle. She looked through the front windows again, seeing the mess in the street. There were at least fifty GBI agents swarming around, none of them knowing what the hell they were doing. Smith was dead and Sonny was locked in the back of a squad car on his way to Macon, where he would probably have the shit beaten out of him. There was a special place in hell for cop-killers.

Lena watched Molly open the suture kit she had taken from the ambulance. 'Where are the kids?'

'Back with their parents,' Molly said, laying out the kit. 'I can't imagine what it was like for them. The parents, I mean. My God, when I think about it, my blood runs cold.'

Lena realized she had been clenching every muscle in her body, and she relaxed as her hand started to numb.

'Better?' Molly asked.

'Yeah,' Lena allowed. 'Thanks for doing this here. I hate going to the hospital.'

'That's understandable,' Molly said, using a syringe to wash out the gash. 'You only need three or four sutures. Sara's a lot better at this than I am.'

'She's tougher than I thought.'

'I think we all are,' Molly pointed out. 'You had me fooled when we went into the station.'

'Yeah,' Lena said, though the compliment rang false. She had been terrified.

Molly used a pair of long tweezers to pick up a curved needle. She dug it into Lena's skin, and Lena watched, thinking how odd it was to see her flesh being pierced and feel nothing but a dull tugging as the thread went through.

'How long have you been dating Nick?'

'Not long,' Molly said, tying off the thread. 'He

kept asking Sara out. I guess I was the door prize.'

Lena laughed as she tried to imagine Nick and Sara together. 'Sara's about ten feet taller than he is.'

'She's also in love with Jeffrey,' Molly reminded her, as if that was not obvious. 'Oh, God, I remember the first time I saw them together.' She tied the suture. Lena felt the same dull tug as she punctured the skin again. 'I've never seen her so giddy.'

'Giddy?' Lena echoed, thinking she had heard wrong. Sara was one of the most serious people she had ever met.

'Giddy,' Molly confirmed. 'Like a schoolgirl.' She tied off the second thread, making a neat knot. 'One more, I think.'

'I've never thought about him that way.'

'Jeffrey?' Molly asked, as if it surprised her. 'He's gorgeous.'

'I guess,' Lena shrugged. 'That'd be kind of like dating your father, though.'

'Maybe for you,' Molly said in a suggestive tone. She dug into the skin one more time and tied off the third suture. 'There you go,' she said, cutting the thread just above the knot. 'All set.'

'Thank you.'

'The scar shouldn't be bad.'

'I'm not worried about that,' Lena said, flexing her hand. The fingers moved, but she could not feel them.

'Take some Tylenol when it starts to hurt. I can have Sara call in something for you if you like.'

'That's okay,' Lena said. 'She's got more important things to worry about.'

'She wouldn't mind,' Molly offered.

'No,' Lena assured her. 'Thanks.'

'All right,' Molly said, wrapping the suturing kit. She gave a groan as she stood. 'Now, I think I am going home to a large glass of wine and my children.'

'That sounds nice,' Lena said.

'My mother has kept them away from the news. I don't know how I'm going to tell them about this.'

'You'll think of something,' Lena told her.

Molly smiled. 'Take care.'

'Thanks,' Lena answered, sliding off the table.

Nick passed her as she walked toward the front of the cleaners. He said, 'We'll need to debrief you tomorrow.'

'You know how to find me.'

Wagner was leaning against the front counter, her cell phone plastered to her ear. When she saw Lena, she said, 'Wait a minute,' into the phone, then told Lena, 'Good work, Detective.'

'Thanks,' Lena said.

'You ever want to run with the big dogs,' Wagner offered, 'give me a call.'

Lena looked out into the street, watching the local agents strutting around like they had saved the day. She thought about Jeffrey, and how he had given her a second chance. Being honest, it was more like a fifth or sixth chance.

She gave Wagner a smile. 'No thanks. I think I'll stay where I am.'

Wagner shrugged, like it was no skin off her back. She went back to her call, saying, 'We'll obviously need to interrogate him tonight. I don't want him talking to the other inmates and figuring out he needs a lawyer.'

Lena pushed open the door with her good hand, nodding to some of the men in the street. She belonged here. She was a part of them. She was Frank's partner again. She was a cop. Hell, maybe she was more than that.

She walked toward the college. Now that the standoff was over, the rent-a-cop from campus security was standing sentry at his car. He tipped his hat to her as she walked by, and Lena, feeling generous, nodded back.

There was a welcome breeze in the air as she walked up the main drive to the student dorms. Lena touched her fingers to her belly. She wondered what was in there, what kind of parent she could be. After today, she was beginning to think that not everything was impossible.

The campus was pretty empty, most of the kids probably glued to their televisions or sacked out on their beds, thankful for a day without classes. Downtown was still blocked off, but Lena figured in a few hours they would start to file out, rubbernecking, trying to absorb some of the drama that had unfolded today. They would call their parents and cry about how horrible it was. The dean would be handling more calls from angry parents, like this kind of thing could be controlled by anybody.

Ethan's dorm this year was quieter than the one he had lived in when Lena had first met him. All-night parties and weekend binges were not exactly his style, and he had managed to befriend the professor in charge of assigning dorm space and gotten placed in a quieter hall.

She climbed the three steps up to the concrete porch, passing a few students as they left the dorm. Ethan's room had been a closet at some point, and even though the university had no qualms about stacking students in dorms like sides of beef, they had not had the gall to make him share. He had measured the space once while Lena watched, surprised that at eight feet by eleven it was bigger than they both had thought.

She knocked on the door before opening it. Ethan was sitting in bed with a book on his lap. The little television on the bookcase showed the news, the sound turned off.

He asked, 'What are you doing here?'

'You wanted me to come by after work.'

'Wanted,' he said. 'Past tense. Not anymore.'

Lena leaned against the door. 'Do you know what kind of day I've had?'

'Do you know what kind of day *I've* had?' he shot back, slamming the book closed.

'Ethan –'

'"I'll take care of it,"' he interrupted. 'That's what you said. "I'll take care of it."'

'I didn't mean –'

'Are you pregnant?'

She stared at him, feeling an ache in the pit of her stomach. For the first time since she had met him, Lena did not want to be alone, even if it meant being here on Ethan's terms.

'Are you going to answer me?'

She finally said, 'No.'

'You're lying.'

'I'm not,' she insisted, making things up as she went along. 'I started my period after we talked. It must have been the stress.'

'You said you were going to take care of it if you were.'

'But I'm not.'

He got off the bed and walked toward her. She felt herself relax until she saw his clenched fist coming up and slamming into her stomach. Lena doubled over from the pain, and he put his hand on her back, keeping her down, whispering, 'If you ever "take care of" anything that's mine, I'll kill you.'

'Oh,' she cried, trying to breathe.

'Get out of here,' he said, shoving her back into the hall. He slammed the door so hard that the bulletin board he kept outside crashed to the ground.

Lena reached out for the wall, trying to straighten herself. Pain shot through her gut, and she felt tears well into her eyes.

Two students were at the front of the hall by the doorway, and she walked past them, trying to keep her spine as straight as possible. She maintained her composure until she was behind the dorm, hidden in the woods where no one could see her.

She leaned against a tree, letting herself sink to the ground. The dirt was wet underneath her, but she did not care.

Her cell phone chirped as it powered up. She waited for the signal, then dialed in a number. Tears streamed down her face as she listened to the ringing on the other end.

'Hello?'

Lena opened her mouth to speak, but she could only cry.

'Hello?' Hank said, then because probably no one else called her uncle in the middle of the afternoon balling like a child, he said, 'Lee? Honey, is that you?'

Lena choked back a sob. 'Hank,' she finally managed. 'I need you.'

EPILOGUE

Sara sat on the hood of her car, looking out at the cemetery. Nothing had changed about Deacon White's funeral home in the last decade, despite the fact that a large conglomerate had bought them out. Even the rolling green hills looked the same, the white gravestones sticking up like broken teeth.

Still, Sara thought if she never saw another grave again it would be too soon. She had attended funerals all week, mourning the men and women who had been victimized by Sonny and Eric Kendall's rampage. Marilyn Edwards had somehow survived being shot in the bathroom of the station, and it looked like she would pull through. She was strong, but she was a minority. Most of the other victims had died.

'The town looks different,' Jeffrey said, and maybe to him it did. He was such a different person from the man who had brought her here the last time.

'You sure you don't want to call Possum and Nell?'

He shook his head. 'I don't think I'm ready for that.' He paused, probably thinking about his son, wondering yet again what he could do about Jared. 'I wonder if Robert knew.'

'I figured it out,' she reminded him.

'Robert wasn't sleeping with me,' he pointed out. 'Man, I wonder what he's up to.'

'You could try to find out.'

'If he wanted me to know where he is, he'd tell me,' Jeffrey said. 'I hope wherever he ended up, he's found some peace.'

Sara tried to comfort him. 'You did everything you could.'

'I wonder if he ever talks to Jessie?'

'She's probably been out of prison a while now,' Sara said. Much as she had predicted, Jessie had served only a handful of years in jail for killing a defenseless man. Her addiction to drugs and alcohol had been a mitigating factor, but Nell's opinion had been that Robert's sexuality was the evidence that most swayed the jury. Sara hoped that things would be different if the same crime happened today, but you could never tell with small towns.

'She's back at Herd's Gap,' he provided. 'I got a Christmas card from her the year she got out.'

'Why didn't you tell me?'

'We weren't exactly speaking then,' he explained, and she guessed this had happened sometime around their divorce.

He said, 'Lane Kendall died three days before they came after me.'

'How did you find out?' Sara asked. Sonny Kendall had refused to talk about anything to do with his family.

'The sheriff told me.'

'Since when did Reggie Ray start volunteering information to you?'

He turned around, giving her a half-smile. 'You didn't hear about his oldest son, Rick?'

'What?'

'He's the drama teacher over at Comer High School.'

Sara laughed so hard that she had to put her hand over her mouth. Even if Rick had a wife and twelve kids, Reggie would embrace the stereotype the same as if his son was a cross-dressing hairdresser.

'Just goes to show . . .' Jeffrey said, giving a half-shrug that she could tell hurt his shoulder. He was not used to wearing a sling and she practically had to force him into it every morning.

He said, 'I wonder what happened to the letters Eric said he sent me?'

'Maybe she didn't mail them,' Sara suggested.

'Sounds like something she'd do.'

'Sonny won't even talk about that?'

'No,' Jeffrey said. 'The military wants him when the courts are through. He was AWOL since Lane died. They probably would have overlooked it if he hadn't . . .'

Sara stared at the cemetery. 'I forgot all about them,' she confessed. 'As upset as I was when we left town, I haven't given them a thought in all these years.'

'Maybe I should have told Lane the truth,' he said. 'God, she hated me.'

'She wouldn't have believed you,' Sara pointed out, the same conclusion they had come to all those years ago.

Lane Kendall's life was fueled by hatred and mistrust. Nothing Jeffrey said would have changed that. Still, at the time, Sara had not completely agreed that Hoss should be allowed to take his secrets to his grave. Jeffrey's arguments had been persuasive. Sitting down with Reggie Ray and talking through Hoss's confession would have been like rolling a boulder up the mountain. Absent any hard evidence, no one would take Jeffrey at his word, especially since Robert was not there to back him up.

Sara had always believed that the real reason Jeffrey kept silent was because he could not bring himself to speak against Hoss when the other man was not around to defend himself. In the end, it was easier for him to continue to take the blame than to stir up more trouble with the truth. Jeffrey did not live in Sylacauga anymore, and there was no need to fight that battle. The people who mattered to him knew what had really happened, and the people who didn't went about living their lives much the same as before. Reggie Ray's report said that the sheriff had been cleaning his gun when it went off, and no one had questioned him. Julia Kendall's murder was still listed as unsolved.

Jeffrey tugged at the sling. 'Damn, I hate this thing.'

'You need to wear it,' she said, making her voice stern.

'It doesn't hurt.'

She brushed her fingers along the nape of his neck. 'I need you to be able to use that arm.'

'That right?' he said, giving her a shadow of his usual sly smile.

She wanted him okay so much that she tried to keep up the teasing. 'That hand.'

'You like that hand?'

'I like them both,' she said.

'Do you remember,' he began, 'the first time you told me you loved me?'

'Umm . . .' She pretended to think, but she knew.

'When we got back to Grant after being here,' he said. 'Remember?'

'I was unpacking all my beach stuff,' she said, 'and I looked around and you weren't there.'

'Right.'

'And when you came back I asked you what you were doing, and you said –'

'Your trash smelled like something died in it.'

'And I told you I loved you.'

'I guess you hadn't had that many men take out the trash before.'

'No,' she admitted. 'And you're the only one I've wanted to take out my trash ever since.' He gave her a real smile, and she felt her heart lift. 'I want to love you so much.'

His smile faltered. 'What's stopping you?'

'No,' she told him, trying to clarify herself. 'I've been fighting it for so long. From the moment I met you, I didn't want to be in love with you. I didn't want to feel so desperate for you.'

'What's changed?'

Her answer was simple. 'You.'

'You haven't,' he told her. 'Changed, I mean.'

'Is that so?' she asked, wondering how he managed to make it sound like a compliment.

'You didn't need to,' he said. 'You were perfect already.'

She laughed out loud. 'Tell that to my mother.'

He waited for her to stop laughing. 'Thank you.'

'For what?'

'Waiting for me to grow up.'

She put her fingers to his cheek. 'Patience has always been my strong suit.'

'No kidding.'

'You were worth the wait.'

'Tell me that in another ten years.'

'I will,' she promised him. 'I will.'

He looked down at his injured arm, and she tried to stop him, thinking he was going to take off the sling. What he did instead was take her hand and look at his Auburn class ring on her finger. When all hell had broken loose at the station, she had taken the ring, knowing it would help identify Jeffrey to the shooters. At the hospital, while Jeffrey was in surgery, she had nearly worn a blister on her finger, rubbing the blue stone in the ring like a talisman, as if she could somehow make everything okay.

She asked, 'Do you want it back?'

He kept his expression neutral. 'Do you want to give it back?'

Sara looked at the ring, and thought about everything that had brought them to this place. As silly as it was, she knew what her wearing the ring would mean to Jeffrey, and to everyone else in Grant County.

She said, 'I'll never take it off.'

He smiled, and for the first time in what seemed like forever, Sara felt like things might eventually be okay.

Jeffrey must have felt this, too, because he tried to tease, 'Maybe you should take it off if you're working in the yard.'

'Hm,' she answered. 'Good point.'

He rubbed her finger with his thumb. 'Or helping out your dad.'

'I could wrap some masking tape around the band so it fits better.'

He smiled, tugging the ring, pointing out that it was hardly in danger of falling off. 'You know what they say about big hands . . .' he began. When she did not answer, he finished, 'Big feet.'

'Ha-ha,' she said, cupping his face in her hand. Before she knew what was happening, Sara had her arms around his neck, holding on to him as if her life depended on it. Whenever she let herself think about how close she had come to losing him, Sara felt a sort of desperation that made her chest ache.

'It's okay,' he told her, though he seemed to be saying this more to himself. She could tell he was thinking about the thing that had brought them here in the first place.

She forced herself to let go of him, asking, 'Are you ready?'

He glanced back at the cemetery, squaring his shoulders as best as he could.

Sara slid off the hood of the car, but he told her, 'No, I need to do this alone.'

'You sure?'

He nodded again, heading off toward the cemetery.

Sara got into the car, leaving the door open so she would not suffocate in the heat. She looked at the ring, turning her hand so she could see the football on the side. Like all class rings, it was huge and hideous, yet right now she thought it was one of the most beautiful things she had ever seen.

She looked up, watching Jeffrey make his way up the hill. He picked at the sling around his neck before taking it off and shoving it into his pocket.

'Jeffrey,' she admonished, though of course he could not hear her. He did not hate the sling so much as the appearance of infirmity.

He stopped at the corner of the cemetery where a small marble marker stood. She knew Jeffrey well enough to know he was thinking about Sylacauga marble and underground streams, cotton mills and sinkholes. She also knew that the thing he took from his pocket was a small gold locket.

As she watched, Jeffrey used his bad hand to open the heart, taking one last look at the picture of Eric inside before leaving the keepsake on top of Julia's gravestone and walking back down the hill to Sara.

ACKNOWLEDGMENTS

Sylacauga is a lovely small town located in central Alabama near the Cheaha Mountains. They have a full-time sheriff and police force and a population of around 12,000 folks who will probably read this book and wonder if I've ever been to the place. I assure you that I have, but please keep in mind that this is a work of fiction and I have taken great license with streets, buildings, and local landmarks just to make it easier on myself. Like many small towns, Sylacauga is a peculiar blend of friendly, good folks and a smattering of bad. You can find out more at Sylacauga.net. While you're on the web, you can also look up the name Billy Jack Gaither to see the darker side of small town life.

This book has been a long time coming for me. When I first wrote *Blindsighted*, I knew that one day I would delve into Jeffrey and Sara's past, so in subsequent books, I left some clues for folks as a little reward for those who were paying attention. My sincere thanks to y'all for being there from the start and making it possible for me to keep doing what I love most: being a writer. I hear from a lot of readers through my website, KarinSlaughter.com, and try to answer all the mail I get as quickly as possible. Thank you all for your patience and support.

There is a long list of people to thank this time

around, but I have to narrow it down because sixty pages of acknowledgments would be a little too indulgent even for me. My agent Victoria Sanders, is a great friend and champion of my work. Meaghan Dowling and Kate Elton are the best editors a girl could ask for. Ron Beard, Richard Cable, Michael Dugdale, Jane Friedman, Brian Grogan, Cathy Hemming, Gail Rebuck, and Susan Sandon are my heroes. Faye Brewster, Elspeth Dougall, Rina Gill, Georgina Hawtrey-Woore, Vanessa Kerr, Mark 'Wolfie' McCallum, Richard Ogle, Tiffany Stansfield, Rob Waddington and Kate Watkins have my thanks for their generous support. Marilyn Edwards is one of my favorite writers and a certain CR has my undying gratitude for you know what. Speaking of initials, thanks to CF, LM, AL and KB. There are plenty more people to name, from the ladies in Scranton to the guys who drive the trucks, but space being what it is, please know you all have my sincere gratitude for the wonderful job you do.

Dan Holod reviewed gun stuff so hopefully I won't get any letters this time. Yet again David Harper, MD came to the rescue, making Sara really sound like a doctor. Patricia Hawkins, Amy Place, and Debbie Hartsfield provided some interesting facts about Sylacauga, where they grew up, and I hope I managed to at least capture the flavor of the town through them. I toured a lot while writing this book, from London to Holland to France and back again. Thanks to my publishers The Busy Bee, Century and Grasset. Actually, thanks to all my foreign publishers. I had the great pleasure of meeting most of them during the London Bookfair, and I can honestly say I have some of the nicest publishers in the world.

Fellow authors helped me keep my chin up. I

won't name them here, but you can find most of them in *Like a Charm,* the serial novel I worked on while writing *Indelible*. Markus Wilhelm deserves special thanks, as does Harlan Coben, who is the only person on earth allowed to call me number two.

Lastly, I've had Sara drive a BMW in every one of these books in the hopes that the nice folks over in Munich will thank me with a shiny new 330ci. No luck yet, but I'll keep trying. Likewise, Tom Jones and Shelby Lynne. Y'all don't call . . . y'all don't write . . .

Read on for an exclusive interview with Karin Slaughter by bestselling author Mo Hayder . . .

MO HAYDER is the author of *Birdman* and *The Treatment*, both of which feature Detective Inspector Jack Caffery. Her most recent novel *Tokyo* is set in 1990s Tokyo and Nanking in the 1930s, and features Grey who works as a hostess in a Japanese nightclub. All three books were *Sunday Times* bestsellers; *The Treatment* won the 2001 WH Smith Thumping Good Read Award; and *Tokyo* was shortlisted for the CWA Gold and Silver Daggers for Best Crime Novel, and the Ian Fleming Steel Dagger for Best Thriller in 2004.

After leaving school at fifteen, Mo Hayder worked as a barmaid, security guard, film-maker, hostess in a Tokyo club, educational administrator and teacher of English as a foreign language in Asia. She has an MA in creative writing from Bath Spa University, where she now teaches.

Birdman, *The Treatment* and *Tokyo* are all available as Bantam paperbacks.

MH: Why did you decide to go back to the past with Indelible, *your fourth book?*

KS: The moment I finished *Blindsighted*, I knew that I'd want to go back and explore how Jeffrey and Sara got together and what made their relationship tick. I had pretty much planned out the first four books in my head, and I hid little clues in the first three novels so that readers who paid attention from the beginning would be rewarded when they got to *Indelible*. I like how we start to see different layers of Sara in the fourth book, because that is what's so great about getting to know someone over a period of time. There are always secrets about characters that only the author knows, and this story was a great way for me to reveal some of them. It's sort of like the way you talk about Grey in the first part of *Tokyo*. On the surface, she seems like this very weak, changeable being, but underneath, she's a very strong woman. Even if your plots weren't as driven as they are, I think the tension you create with the mystery of character would keep me reading.

MH: Your planning shows. And you deal with series characters so successfully – they never seem stale. This is something I was sure I couldn't do because I was afraid I'd find it restricting, so I planned two books for my detective Jack Caffery then moved on to a stand-alone with Tokyo. *You clearly don't feel the same restriction?*

KS: I wish I could take credit for the planning, but it's one of those times when your brain manages to pull off something really tricky without you really being aware of it happening. I just feel like I really know

Lena, Jeffrey and Sara, so it's a very natural thing for me to write about them. That being said, my next book after *Faithless* is a stand-alone called *Triptych*, and it's been good for me to have a break out of Grant County. The setting is urban and gritty – downtown Atlanta – and I'm having a lot of fun being in a new place with new characters, some of whom will eventually end up in the Grant County series.

I have to say, though, that I think you're selling yourself short with Jack. There's no way that the last chapter of *The Treatment* ends his story. There are scenes from that book that have stuck with me even after all these years. Don't you get a lot of letters and emails from fans asking when you'll go back to him?

MH: Um – yes. Alarmingly so. Some people get quite angry that I've left Caffery on what they think is meant to be a cliff-hanger. No Misery scenarios yet, but a lot of readers find it hard to accept that the ending wasn't designed to usher in a sequel. However, I left him exactly where I wanted to leave him – maybe I'm crazy but I thought it was a much more poignant and telling point in his life. And like you with Triptych *(great title BTW), I found moving to a new setting in Tokyo very liberating. I knew I wanted to do something different, so it wasn't just the setting I changed but the structure: particularly the switch to two first person narratives, which was a huge challenge. I remember saying to you after reading* Indelible *that we'd both written novels with very similar structures in that there were two narratives in two timescales, the earlier one not seeming initially to have much to do with the latter, until the two come together in the closing scenes. As I was reading* Indelible *it didn't even dawn on me that what was happening to Jeffery and Sara in Sylacauga would have any impact on the hostage situation, so you obviously did the juggling act to perfection. How did you pull it off?*

KS: Okay, first, I wouldn't characterize all those letters I wrote to you as 'angry'. I was just curious about Jack. That kind of talk makes me understand why Kathy Bates's character snapped.

Anyway . . . thanks for saying I pulled it off in *Indelible*. This was another case of my brain being smart without me knowing how. Originally, I assumed I'd write the Sylacauga part first then go back and do the present-day narration, then blend them together afterwards. It didn't work out that way – I ended up writing the book in a very straight-forward manner, juggling both plots in my head as I moved from chapter to chapter. That I could manage to juggle all of this in my head at the same time is surprising considering I often forget the punch lines to jokes as I'm telling them. Do you find that you have better focus where your books are concerned than you do in your real life? Because I have to say that the thing you pulled off best in *Tokyo* is what I like to think of as a writer's contract with the reader: you have the ability to make me trust you implicitly. I know when I read one of your books that no matter which direction the story takes, it's for a reason that will be made clear by the end. As I know that you got lost in Atlanta traffic the one time you came here, your ability to suspend my disbelief about direction says a lot.

MH: *Yeah, and thanks for the gallant offer to come out and help. Actually, far from being lost I was simply bogged down in your APPALLING beltway system. I knew where I was going. But as I had time (lots of it) to sit and admire your beautiful city from the parking lot a.k.a. I-285, it crossed my mind that there's a tendency to set crime novels in big, very cosmopolitan cities: it's certainly the backdrop I've used in the past (South London, Tokyo). But you've chosen a very small town setting. I wonder if that's what makes the series so powerful, what makes the menace really hit you between the eyes, the juxta-position of the horror with sleepy little Heartsdale? Is it like the world you grew up in, or where you live now? Because if the answer is yes, then statistically it's all over for you. If not now then next week, next month, next year . . .*

KS: I grew up in a small town, but I did what most folks do as soon as I was old enough – moved to the big city. In my case, that was Atlanta. It seems to me that in America, all the 'interesting' crimes happen in towns of 30,000 people or less. Atlanta, which is statistically one of the most violent cities in America, has its share of shootings, but usually it's for your average stupid reasons: drugs, gangs, robberies gone wrong. Kids killing parents, paedophiles hiding in the woodshed, pregnant women hacked to death in their sleep . . . this sort of thing is happening in small town America. If I were a serial killer, I'd certainly look for a place to hide where people don't lock their doors. And you're right about a small town setting being an unexpected place for violence. It makes what happens that much more horrifying. Walking through Atlanta, I'm much more alert to my surroundings than I am when I'm taking a stroll in downtown Blue Ridge, which is a very small community in the North Georgia mountains. That feeling of safety is something we all want – unfortunately, it *is* just a feeling. Bad things happen everywhere. For instance, you'll see about six churches per person up in Blue Ridge, and folks have signs with the Ten Commandments posted in their yards, but then you read the local paper and find out that one of the largest methamphetamine labs in the state was busted that weekend and Hazmat was called in and sixteen people were arrested. I love that dichotomy.

On the other hand, what I've found with *Triptych* is that it's very freeing to have Atlanta as a backdrop and all the resources that entails. Was it conscious on your part to write about crime in an urban setting? I made up Grant County in my head, so I'm the only person who knows where everything is. Are you ever worried you'll have Jack take a left on a one-way street and bring down the wrath of all of London? I've been very nervous about writing about Atlanta, even though I've lived here for almost fifteen years. I *know* I'm going to make a mistake, it's just a matter of how many people notice.

MH: I know what you mean: I'd lived in Tokyo for two years and made copious notes before I wrote a book about it, but I was still insecure enough to put in the acknowledgements an apology to the city for the liberties I'd taken with its geography. For Birdman *and* The Treatment *I knew that corner of London pretty well so I wasn't too worried – although I did get one very miffed reader complaining that the plot in* Birdman *was completely implausible because there were no houses big enough in that part of Greenwich to accommodate Hartveld's unseemly behaviour with corpses. The fact that said reader went on to enumerate* six points in the narrative where I *was* sending him coded love messages did nothing to assuage my mortification at getting a detail wrong.

But I think the larger point you're making is that in this genre details have to be really authentic – so you surprise me when you say you made it all up. I'd always had you down as someone who did exhaustive research. What about all the police procedural passages – you didn't make those up, did you?

KS: I do a ton of research, but I'm sure you've found that for every book or article you read, maybe .01% actually ends up in your finished story. I do make a great deal up, mostly because following every rule in the book is pretty boring. For instance, in any police-involved shooting, the officer is immediately taken off duty until there is a full investigation, but *A Faint Cold Fear* would've been pretty boring if Jeffrey's parts showed him sitting around in his underwear all week watching the Discovery Channel. I will say that I think it's very important to know the rules, because then you can break them in such a way that keeps it realistic for the reader. A good case in point is Sara's medical knowledge. I have a lovely doctor who helps me with those things, but if I followed every step for, say, intubating someone, that would take about three pages to show properly and it would seriously slow down the story.

I don't know if you've found this, but thriller readers tend to be a very savvy bunch, and if you try to trick them too much, they'll just close the book (or load their guns, as the case may be). I understand getting upset when a detail is wrong. I love Eric Garcia's books – he writes about dinosaurs living among us, only they wear human disguises. His main character is a crime-solving Raptor name Vincent. So, in one of the books, Vincent was talking about how he passed out from a basil overdose (don't ask) on the Emory University football field in Atlanta. Emory is an egghead school (Sara's alma mater) and does not have a football team. So, this really stopped me in the book until I thought, 'Wait, you'll buy that he's a dinosaur in a human suit, going around solving crimes and standing up to the dino mafia, but not the football field thing?' I guess it's all a matter of suspension of disbelief. No author can get everything right, but I understand when something in your own back yard is misrepresented. What puzzles me is why folks get so angry.

When you lived in Tokyo, was it specifically to research the book? Or did you just take notes because you knew one day this was a story you'd have to write? I think the whole idea of escorts is fascinating and very foreign to Americans. The whole idea of 'renting' someone for non-sexual companionship is not a part of our culture. Maybe it goes to our growing sense of entitlement. I have a friend who used to be a stripper as well as a prostitute, and she hates men because of the ones she came into contact with during that part of her life. I write a little bit about that in *Faithless* when Lena and Jeffrey go to a strip club looking for information. Did you find yourself feeling that sort of hate, or did taking the sex out of it make a difference?

MH: Well, first off I'm not saying there aren't places in Japan where sex is for sale: at one end of the spectrum of hostess clubs in Tokyo are the 'Snack Bars', down at heel places that employ yakuza-trafficked Thai and Filipina girls and in these places the customers really can get a hand-job under the table. (Then there are 'Soaplands' – but let's not get into that.) But sex most definitely was not on the menu in the club I worked and I certainly didn't leave my experience in Japan hating men. Nor did I feel degraded or abused because all I was doing was being paid unfeasible amounts for sitting around drinking and smoking. The only hardship was talking to people whom I wouldn't normally have talked to (though there were some I definitely wanted to talk to – I dated one of the customers for two months). I don't believe there's a soul in the world who can say that in their job they don't sometimes have to make small talk with people they don't like.

So really, it was nowhere near as seedy as the sound of the words hostess club imply. The girls I worked with tended to be part of that traveller community Alex Garland portrayed so well in The Beach. That community is a movable entity because they gravitate to the same places in whatever city, so you very often meet someone in Bangkok, say, and run into them months later in Kathmandu. In a strange way – considering it extended across several countries – it was quite a cosy group.

On the subject of men hating (!) it sometimes occurs to me that for those sex workers who, like your friend, hate men it is often the cause as much as the effect of being in the industry. Which came first, the hatred or the behaviour? It's the Aileen Wuornos syndrome, isn't it? When I think about her I'm amazed what she did doesn't happen more often – hatred stepping over into violence. A lot of the questions I'm asked by readers and the press circle around these issues: women and violence, and particularly about what it means to be a woman who *writes about violent crime (often inflicted on women). When I think about some of your toe curlers (especially the crime in* Blindsighted – *I mean, ahem) I feel sure it's something you've been asked about over and over again. How do you answer this question? Is it a male prerogative to write about violence? And do we write differently from men?*

KS: Every interview I've ever done has had some variation on that question – usually with an accusation behind it. Not that interviewers have been aggressive, but the way the question is phrased generally implies that what I'm doing is taboo and that perhaps I'd be better off in the more lady-like territory of knitting mysteries or stories where cats narrate half the book. I actually had a man come up to me after a signing and ask, 'What's a pretty little thing like you doing writing about such nasty subjects?'

I've talked about this issue with some of my male friends who are thriller writers, and they very seldom get the same questions about violence in their novels put to them. It's much more acceptable for a guy to write about nasty things than it is for a woman to do the same. For years, this was boys-only territory, and especially in the late eighties and nineties you had this myth of the broken woman emerge, where a female character who had been raped or abused had two choices: either be a catatonic or be a martyr, and always, always some brave, sensitive man would rescue her from herself in the end. I understand that this response had a lot to do with what was going on in society at large (writers could no longer rape and pillage in a vacuum) but I found it irksome if not slightly insulting that these women could not save themselves. Obviously, a lot of men did as well because you have great stories like *In A Dry Season* from Peter Robinson, where he narrates from a woman's point of view in an incredibly believable way, and Mark Billingham is making an enviable career out of having equal-opportunity murderers.

My own feeling is that it's about damn time women started talking and writing about violence against women. We are generally the victims of these crimes. We are the ones who have to live through it – if we're lucky. I think women authors look at sex crimes in a different way, and with Lena, the character in my series who was brutally raped, you see a different side of recovery than what is normally in fiction. Statistically, her reaction is more common than the martyr/catatonic one. Like many women, she subverts her anger and turns it on herself. She looks for situations and relationships where the abuse is repeated. She self-medicates. These are all stupid things that women can do in response to violence, and I want to talk about that because it's not something I've seen in many books. This is why I love Denise Mina's Maureen O'Donnell trilogy. My God, what a character. She's so raw and out there, and as a reader I keyed into her in a very emotional way that I'd never experienced before.

It's the same way with your stuff. *The Treatment*, for example, is a story that has a definite female perspective, just not the sort of female perspective we're used to hearing. It cuts straight through to the heart of violence – visceral, gut-wrenching. The people who said that Aileen Wuornos was the first female serial killer (when there have been hundreds throughout history) aren't comfortable with the thought of women committing violence, let alone understanding writing about it. Yet, if you look at really horrible crimes against children, you see that women are often much more sadistic than men. I also wonder if you get a different reaction to your work because you're British and not held to the standards dictated by America's Puritanical roots. When you wrote about child abuse, for instance, were you trying to make a statement, or were you just telling a story?

MH: *I'm always, primarily, writing a story. I agree with everything you say (a special groan of recognition for the cat narrated novel), however, it has taken me years to be confident enough to say out loud:* I'm just telling a story . . . *It's the sort of comment that guarantees you'll end up mired in Tolstoyist debates about what defines art, about responsibilities and the writerly remit to educate, elucidate, illuminate. Of course, if I feel moved by a subject (as I did by child abuse for* The Treatment *and the Nanking massacre for* Tokyo) *obviously I'm going to write more passionately about it, but I never, ever set out to write a book with an agenda. I'd be stymied if I asked myself what I was trying to say before I put pen to paper, even if I might look back on a novel in retrospect and recognize my themes and passions. As an extension of this I think that writers are too often encouraged to become pundits for every issue under the sun. For example, would you ask, in a professional capacity, a dentist/checkout clerk/ decorator for his/her opinion on the war in Iraq, and take the answers more seriously than your own opinions? Yet it's the sort of question I've been asked countless times, and I'm fairly sure people took what I felt more seriously because I'm a writer. Just because I've got some knowledge of how to arrange words in a relatively pleasing order doesn't make my moral compass any more finely tuned than anyone else's. In fact, probably less so, since most of my job is about lying convincingly.*

Or maybe I'm just subverting my anger . . .

KS: I think that any writer who sets out with an agenda is going to have a very forced narrative, and the reader will know it. Like you, it's only after I've written something that I see what issues I've raised, and generally it's about a problem that I've seen happening in the world that has troubled me. If that's subverting your anger, then I'm guilty of it as well. I hope I never get to the point where I'm being didactic or preaching to the choir. At the end of the day, I'm writing for entertainment, not education. I don't think there's anything to be ashamed of in being a good storyteller.

MH: *What you said about* The Treatment *having a female perspective is interesting, because I was very definitely shying away from writing from a woman's perspective. You've always written both male and female characters with equal believability – for example Jeffery and Sara really come alive in equal measure. Do you find it difficult to get into Jeffrey's head?*

KS: When I write from Jeffrey's point of view, I have to turn off the female alarm all women have – the one that says to always be on the lookout, to know my surroundings and who is occupying my space. The last thing a man is thinking about when he walks into a strange situation is that he could possibly be assaulted. To remove that threat is incredibly freeing, and that's the place where I can really get into Jeffrey's head. I know it's extremely reductive to talk about such a complex issue in terms of sex, but for me when I see things through Jeffrey's eyes, I feel all the freedoms he has from being a man. He went to college right out of high school while his pregnant ex-girlfriend stayed at home to raise their child. He was a prolific womanizer prior to Sara and was celebrated rather than denigrated for this fact. His mother thinks he's perfect and no woman is good enough for him. You don't often find women enjoying these same freedoms.

For instance, I sometimes get letters from folks taking me to task for Lena's cursing, but no one ever says anything about Jeffrey's potty mouth. No one cares when he's violent or insensitive, or when Sara puts aside her own emotional needs to take care of him. These sacrifices are completely acceptable because that's the way it's always been. To bring it all back to sex, I think it really makes some people uncomfortable that Jeffrey and Sara have such a good sex life. Sara is not the kind of woman who sees sex as a chore. She enjoys it and she loves Jeffrey and they are moving towards a somewhat stable relationship. The reader knows that they love each other and with their history you should also know that they're not going to end their relationship because of a fight over who was supposed to take out the trash. Like you, I often have my head in a book, and I can't think of many novels I've read lately where you see two adults in a stable, healthy relationship. Not to say I'm breaking new ground here. Lindsey Davis's Falco series does the same thing – only in ancient Rome.

But sex is still a tricky thing to write about in detail. I think you really pulled this off well in *Birdman*. Jack actually gets laid and you read about it. It seems like we crime writers are more than happy to talk about bludgeoning, child abuse and sexual assault, but when it comes to sex between two 'good' characters, it freaks us out.

MH: This is EXACTLY the point I've been making for years – except not so eloquently, so nobody understood what the hell I was talking about. There's no doubt about it, writing about sex from the perspective of two characters who want 'it' is extremely difficult for a woman – probably for some of the issues you identify earlier – it can be so easily confused and feel like a surrender, a loss of power – so how do you keep a strong female character 'on top' while still letting her have sex. (Or have I answered the question: keep her on top?)

KS: A friend of mine has said the test about whether or not to show the sex is if you can take out the scene and the story still works. If that's the case, then you probably don't need it there.

In *Indelible* and later in *Faithless*, I think the sexual intercourse (pun intended) adds a lot to the story. I see Sara as multi-faceted. There's the trusted paediatrician, upstanding citizen of Grant and then there's the other side of her, the side that really enjoys sex and wants to be with Jeffrey. I've alluded several times to her gutter mouth during intercourse, but people seem to gloss that over when they're thinking about Sara because of course good girls don't say 'fuck me'.

There's this really (I hope) great scene between

Sara and Jeffrey in *Faithless* that I worked on for quite a while – sex scenes always take much longer than the other stuff – and I really like how it turned out because it tells you everything you need to know about their relationship at that point. Sara is always going to surprise Jeffrey. I, for one, find that very sexy about her, but then I spend *way* too much time thinking about my characters.

MH: *The big problem in writing about sex is that it all feels too personal. Maybe that's because a character is easy to portray if they're just eating breakfast, having an argument, selling an ice cream, whatever, because we can be witness to these things: but we don't on the whole (and speak for yourself on this) witness other people having sex, so we have nothing to mimic. It could be the reason death scenes are so difficult – because as a society we avoid looking at death. Of course, all of these problems go up a notch on the difficult gauge when you're trying to write in the first person – then you become utterly exposed, utterly out on display. I've been very squeamish about sex and the first person, but maybe I'm getting over it now, because my next book is all about sex and all in first.*

KS: When's the book out?

MH: *Feb 2006 – I'm just finishing it at the moment.*

KS: And it's all about sex, huh? Sounds interesting. Makes me wonder what on earth you were into as a child . . .

MH: *As a child some very soft porn literature found its*

way into my house. Henry Miller, plus my favourite –
Portnoy's Complaint (although I wish Roth would
drop the sex thing now – it's all getting far too Woody
Allen). I don't know what was going on in my
mother's mind, because although my memory is of a
constant Jane Austen/Charlotte Brontë diet, some cool
things did creep onto my bedside cabinet. Probably the
most memorable was Metamorphosis. *That blew me*
away – age twelve. What did it for me was that much
analysed opening sentence: As Gregor Samsa woke
one morning from uneasy dreams . . . *I think I can*
trace a lot of my literary tastes back to the moment I
read that sentence.

But how about you – do you ever sit and unpick
your influences? What were you reading as a mini-
KS?

KS: God, I had forgotten about *Metamorphosis*. I
must have been around the same age as you when I
read it. (Hm . . . some secret international plot to
spawn thriller writers . . .?) I'd never read anything
like it and that book is probably one of the few
stories that I started reading again as soon as I
finished. Like all children, I guess I keyed into
Gregor's isolation. He's such a tragic hero, and
despite the plus of having more arms, who wouldn't
be sad to be a cockroach?

Another book that I feel marked me was *The
Painted Bird*. There has been a lot of scandal about
whether or not it's a true account, but I was a kid
when I read it and all I knew was that it was a
shocking and amazing story. *Bird* is the first book I
remember reading that had graphic violence, but in
the context where it actually said something about
the characters and moved the story. Up until that

point, it'd been John Jakes (soft porn!) and V.C. Andrews (incest!) that occupied my mind, but after reading Kosinski, I think I turned into a more serious reader, which leads me to . . . Flannery O'Connor . . .

Growing up in the deep South, I had never been exposed to a woman writing about violence in such a matter-of-fact way. I didn't think it was allowed. O'Connor was so masterful at blending everyday characters with horrific events, and she had a wicked sense of humour. I loved the way she used humour to balance the violence. There's this great line at the end of *A Good Man is Hard to Find* where the Misfit, who has just killed an entire family, says about a nagging grandmother lying dead at his feet, 'She would have been a good woman if . . . somebody had been there to shoot her every minute of her life.'

How can that not inspire you?

MH: Well, exactly . . .
It's been great talking to you Karin. I can't wait to read Faithless.

KS: I'm really looking forward to your next one too.

Blindsighted

Karin Slaughter

The sleepy town of Heartsdale, Georgia, is jolted into panic when Sara Linton, paediatrician and medical examiner, finds Sibyl Adams dead in the local diner. As well as being viciously raped, Sibyl has been cut: two deep knife wounds form a lethal cross over her stomach. But it's only once Sara starts to perform the post-mortem that the full extent of the killer's brutality becomes clear.

Police chief Jeffrey Tolliver – Sara's ex-husband – is in charge of the investigation, and when a second victim is found, crucified, only a few days later, both Jeffrey and Sara have to face the fact that Sibyl's brutal murder wasn't a one-off attack. What they are dealing with is a seasoned sexual predator. A violent serial killer . . .

'Don't read this alone. Don't read this after dark.
But do read it'
Mirror

arrow books

Kisscut

Karin Slaughter

When a teenage quarrel in the small town of Heartsdale explodes into a deadly shoot-out, Sara Linton – paediatrician and medical examiner – finds herself entangled in a horrific tragedy. And what seems at first to be a terrible but individual catastrophe proves to have wider implications when the autopsy reveals evidence of long-term abuse and ritualistic self-mutilation.

Sara and police chief Jeffrey Tolliver start to investigate, but the children surrounding the victim close ranks. The families turn their backs. Then a young girl is abducted, and it becomes clear that the first death is linked to an even more brutal crime. And unless Sara and Jeffrey can uncover the deadly secrets the children hide, it's going to happen again . . .

'This is crime fiction at its finest'
Michael Connelly

arrow books

A Faint Cold Fear

Karin Slaughter

Sara Linton, medical examiner in the small town of Heartsdale, is called out to an apparent suicide on the local college campus. The mutilated body provides little in the way of clues – and the college authorities are keen to avoid a scandal – but for Sara and police chief Jeffrey Tolliver, things don't add up.

Two more suspicious suicides follow, and a young woman is brutally attacked. For Sara, the violence strikes far too close to home. And as Jeffrey pursues the sadistic killer, he discovers that ex-police detective Lena Adams, now a security guard on campus, may be in possession of crucial information. But, bruised and angered by her expulsion from the force, Lena seems barely capable of protecting herself, let alone saving the next victim . . .

'Brilliantly chilling' *Heat*

arrow books

Faithless

Karin Slaughter

**There are many ways to die. But some are more terrifying
than others . . .**

A walk in the woods takes a sinister turn for police chief Jeffrey
Tolliver and medical examiner Sara Linton when they stumble
across the body of a young girl. Incarcerated in the ground, all
the initial evidence indicates that she has, quite literally, been
scared to death.

But as Sara embarks on the autopsy, something even more
horrifying comes to light. Something which shocks even Sara.
Detective Lena Adams, talented but increasingly troubled, is
called in from vacation to help with the investigation – and the
trail soon leads to the neighbouring county, an isolated
community, and a terrible secret . . .

Century · London

Order further books by *Karin Slaughter* and *Mo Hayder* from your local bookshop, or have them delivered direct to your door by Bookpost

☐	**Blindsighted**	0 09 942177 1	£6.99
☐	**Kisscut**	0 09 942178 X	£6.99
☐	**A Faint Cold Fear**	0 09 944532 8	£6.99
☐	**Faithless** (Hardback)	1 8441 3372 9	£14.99
☐	**Like a Charm** (ed.)	0 09 946225 7	£6.99
☐	**Birdman**	0 553 81698 5	£6.99
☐	**The Treatment**	0 553 81699 3	£6.99
☐	**Tokyo**	0 553 81462 1	£6.99

Free post and packing

Overseas customers allow £2 per paperback

Phone: 01624 677237

Post: Random House Books
c/o Bookpost, PO Box 29, Douglas, Isle of Man IM99 1BQ

Fax: 01624 670923

email: bookshop@enterprise.net

Cheques (payable to Bookpost) and credit cards accepted

Prices and availability subject to change without notice.
Allow 28 days for delivery.
When placing your order, please state if you do not wish to receive any
additional information.

www.randomhouse.co.uk/arrowbooks

www.booksattransworld.com

arrow books